Finding Father Rabbit

Finding Father Rabbit

This is a work of fiction. All events, locations, themes, persons, institutions, characters, and plot are completely fictional. Any resemblance to places or person, living or deceased, are the invention of the author.

Published by Inkblot Books
Dayton, Ohio
www.inkblotbooks.com

ISBN 1-932461-04-3

Printed in the United States of America

For those who have been there, and survived.

Also by K.A. Thompson

Charybdis
As Simple As That

Finding Father Rabbit

K.A. Thompson

1

Chip

Kevin rang the doorbell at midnight, just a few days before Nick's birthday in June; when I opened the door he was standing there with a small duffel bag hanging limply from one hand and had his other hand stuffed into his pocket. He hadn't shaved for days, his eyes were red and bleary and lined with fatigue; he looked like a lost little boy grown too tall.

"I came home for Nick's birthday," he explained before I could say anything, "and I don't know what I did with my keys."

He greeted me with a hug, went upstairs to let his mother know he was home, and then went to bed for three days.

Kevin came home for his brother's birthday and never went back.

Fatigue surrounded him in wisps of despair he was unable to hide but refused to acknowledge. Most mornings I found him sitting at the kitchen table with the newspaper spread out in front of him, his eyes unfocused, or his head in his hands, oblivious to the sounds of my footsteps coming in behind him. I only asked once if he was returning to the seminary, which he answered with a shrug, and once if he was all right, to which he replied, "It was a long year, and I'm tired."

I let it go at that.

I also kept my eye on him, afraid that whatever bubble that was overwhelming him would burst in a bloody mess against his bedroom wall. I did what I swore I would never do to any of my kids; when he wasn't home, I snooped in his room, looking for drugs, a gun, a rope. I stopped short of opening his journal, though the longer he swam in his misery the more reasons I had to give myself permission to violate his privacy.

The summer wore on and he didn't change. He'd sit out by the pool to watch his niece play in the water, and took her to movies and the park, but it was as if he operated by remote control, guided by vague memories of what his life was supposed to be like and what he was supposed to do.

My son reminded me of my father during those first few years after my mother's death, the sadness that seemed nearly unbearable.

When he first came home, I think Terry and I both assumed he would fall back into old routines. We'd gotten used to falling asleep almost every night to the sound of him playing his guitar, the music filtering through the air vents; he had no idea that we listened, wrapped around each other in the dark, quiet, marveling at his growing talent, breathing in heavy doses of parental pride at his steady improvement.

He was too shy to sing in front of us and feigned disinterest in playing for anyone other than Eileen, so we settled for those strains of music at night, and missed it when he left for the seminary. It took a long time to get used to the silence, the only sound coming through the vents the hiss of air.

Three weeks after he came home, after he'd shrugged when asked if he was planning on going back to the seminary, he had a date. That gave us hope; if he was feeling social, then he obviously felt better. If he felt better, there was a chance he could re-focus and at least begin to explain what was running through his head, why he was home and seemed intent on staying.

He had another date the next night. And another the night after that. Then another. By the time August rolled around I'd lost count of the parade of women, though I was fairly certain he never went out with someone more than twice. He was invariably home before eleven at night, so I was also fairly sure he wasn't sleeping with any of them.

I missed the 15 year old Kevin, the kid who had to be practically threatened before he would cut the grass or do the dishes. This Kevin did everything without so much as a hint. Saturday mornings he fired up the lawn mower; if he was home for dinner he started washing the dishes as soon as we were all done; the nights his brother had to work late he tended to his niece, making sure she took her bath and brushed her teeth, and he read her bedtime stories and sat with her while she said her prayers.

He oversaw her prayers, yet refused to go to church.

Terry tried once to pull him out of bed on a Sunday morning. He barely opened his eyes, rolling away from her, grunting, "God knows where I am if He wants me."

In August, when he failed to show up to celebrate his twenty first birthday with his twin sister, I promised myself – and his mother – that I would either tie him down and get answers, or I would read his journal and hope to get some hint of the hell that was tormenting him.

"There's no light in his eyes anymore, Chip," Terry whispered in the dark, both of us fighting sleep, hoping to hear him come home. "He's going through the motions. And to not be here for Eileen…"

"I'm worried, too."

"Enough to go look for him?"

I sat up, reaching for my jeans at the foot of the bed. "Enough to go look for him. He's probably at the restaurant or the park."

She sat up and tossed a t-shirt at me, quietly watching me get dressed. I had my shoes in hand and was reaching for the doorknob when I heard the squeak of the front door hinges, and then the dull thud of feet slapping against the stairs.

Terry sighed loudly; I set the shoes on the floor and got undressed, climbed back into bed, and reached for her.

"He'll be all right," I whispered against her hair.

2

Kevin

The clock above the bar blinked relentlessly. 12:00. 12:00. 12:00. For three years it screamed noon or midnight, depending on your point of view; no one could figure out how to set the time, though every one of us tried a dozen times or more. My brother tried at least twice a week, grumbling that if not for the stereo system it was attached to, he would drag it out to the parking lot and run it over with his minivan.

When Ted the Bartender decided to retire, my father closed the restaurant down for the evening and hosted a party for all his family and his friends; Ted's ten year old grandson slipped behind the bar, and in less than a minute, our wayward clock was set to the correct time.

My father and brother were thrilled.

Their customers grumbled in protest.

After a week of complaints, Paul unplugged the stereo, plugged it back in, and the clock again blinked 12:00.

"Well, there you go," one happy barfly told him. "If I don't know the time, I have my excuse for not going home early."

They wanted time to stand still, to be able to sit there and nurse their drinks, nibble on popcorn or pretzels, forget about their jobs and long days of dealing with bosses and colleagues, forget about going home to screaming kids and broken appliances, grass that needed to be cut, relationships in need of mending. Just for an hour or three, they wanted time to stand still.

I was staring at the clock, the bright red 12:00 popping on and off with military precision, trying to ignore the people around me, wanting to forget about what day it was, wishing time could stand still for just a minute, long enough for the pounding in my head to stop and long enough for me to remember what it felt like to take a long, deep breath without jagged edges of pain ripping through me. I watched the clock and flattened popcorn between my fingers, wishing for just a single minute of something that resembled happiness, when I heard my name over the din of voices, a squeal of feminine delight that instantly made me sit up straighter and smile.

If pressed, I'd admit that the first thing I always noticed about Lydia Freeman was her breasts. I'm not a total pig, it was simply unavoidable. Lydia's monumental companions undoubtedly piqued the curiosity of every male she encountered, no matter what his sexual orientation happened to be. There was more than just a little smug self satisfaction in knowing that at least up until high school graduation, I was one of few who could attest that they were 100% her.

At the sound of my name I turned and found myself staring at those unbelievable wonders and realized my fingers were itching, not to mention the creeping sensation along my lips, an almost unbearable ache to reach out and kiss her, breath in her perfume.

She tossed herself onto the stool next to me, reaching

out for a quick hug in one fluid motion. "God, am I glad to see you! If I ever needed a knight in shining armor, it's now."

"Hello to you, too."

She laughed and smiled at me, leaning in to kiss my cheek, sufficiently – albeit affectionately – chastised; after all it, wasn't as if we had seen each other just the week before. It had been three years. Three very long years. "Hi, Kevin. I need a savior tonight."

"I'm out of the soul saving business," I said. "But if you need me to kick someone's ass, I will."

"Just get me out of the date from hell," she pleaded.

A date.

I had been sure she'd be married.

"At least you had a date tonight," I sighed. "I think I give up. I haven't gone out with anyone who has more than two brain cells in the last six weeks."

"You're dating? But—"

The Date From Hell snuck up behind her, tweaking her ear, laughing. "Come on, babe, let's get out of here." His hand fell to her shoulder, fingers trailing over her neck. "I can think of better things to do than hang around a bar."

She started to open her mouth, looking at me pleadingly.

"Dude, if you don't mind, I think she'd rather stay here with me. Nothing personal, we're just old friends and we haven't seen each other in a couple of years. I'd like to catch up with her."

"You're freaking kidding me, right?"

I slid off the barstool and stood, leaning in close. A menace I've never been, but he barely came up to my chin, and his eyes went wide as he quickly calculated his odds.

"I'm not kidding," I said. "The lady would like you to leave."

His hand fell away from her. "All right," he sputtered. "I'll call you later, Lydia."

She grinned. "Second Tuesday of next week, okay?"

"Where," I asked, sitting back down, "did you find him?"

"Blind date. God, he was creepy. He's been trying to get me to go home with him since we got here. He spent the entire evening talking to my boobs and not me."

"Can't blame a guy for liking them," I mumbled, embarrassed because I was just as guilty. I had to fight the urge to let my eyes roam and concentrate instead on her face.

Emerald green eyes.

I'd known her since second grade, and finally got around to noticing the color of her eyes.

Even potential priests are human.

Green eyes, long dark wavy hair, a splash of freckles across her nose, spilling onto her cheeks, the subtle shade of her skin—I sniffed potential trouble for myself. Lydia at twenty one was as warm and inviting as she had been at fourteen, only this time there was no vocation to protect, no fear of what I might wind up confessing.

No Father Parker to confess to.

"So, come on, how's life going?" she asked.

Life.

She didn't really want to know, did she?

"Let's see … Eileen is engaged and getting married in a couple months."

"Spider?"

"Who else? I swear, she was goofy before, but it's gross now. Being around them can get awfully uncomfortable."

"I thought you two were close."

"We are. It's just that being around them is like being around people who are only half there. You know what they really want to be doing, and if it wasn't for family being around, they'd be ripping each others' clothing off."

"True love," she laughed.

"Hormones. They've been in love forever, only been sleeping together a few months."

"Okay, what about Paul? And Nick?"

"Paul's separated from his wife and thinking about divorcing her," I sighed. "Nick is still married and is cramming for the Bar Exam. No little Nicks or Katies yet, though."

She touched my arm gently. "And what about Kevin?"

"Kevin is getting along just fine. And to the question you have too much class to ask, I left the seminary two months ago. Too horny for my own good."

"And to think of all the times we jumped out of the backseat of your car because we were protecting your vocation."

"Hey, that wasn't just me," I protested. "I seem to recall a few rules being set down early on, and a soggy shoulder over the guys who tried to push you too far."

"Touché." She reached for my hand. "Come on, you can drive me home. You do have a car, right?"

My fall from grace began when I was seven years old, the day she entered our second grade classroom.

I hated girls; I accepted the fact that they were there and there was nothing I could do about it, but I couldn't have cared less for that particular half of the human race. They were noisy and giggled over the dumbest things, and if provoked they kicked *hard.* I learned to avoid random acts of provocation by the time I was five or six, thanks mostly to my twin sister, Eileen.

So I didn't like them. That doesn't mean I didn't notice them.

When Lydia showed up two months into the school year, I certainly noticed her. I couldn't figure her out. She was much more quiet than any girl I had ever met, shy to the point of staying away from most of the kids in our class, and she was pretty, even for a skinny second grader years away from the ego that thrusts adolescents in front of a mirror for an hour every morning. Seated one row over and a seat forward, I had plenty of opportunity to watch her, and I did, never quite able to figure her out. Why was she so different? Why didn't she bury herself in the gaggle of girls on the playground at recess, picking on the boys and tomboys? Why was she so tan, all the time?

"Zebra," Tyler Reed sneered.

I didn't get it, I didn't know what he meant, but I knew it was an insult, and it made my skin crawl.

I sucker punched him in the gut when the teacher wasn't looking.

I still didn't have the nerve to talk to her. Until junior high I doubt I grunted more than two or three words in her direction; an occasional "hi," when she walked past in the hall and smiled, a "thanks" here and there when she'd hand me papers in class. When we played dodge ball in gym class I never threw a ball at her; when we played softball I deliberately dropped the fly ball she'd sent my way. But I didn't have the guts to talk to her.

The manufactured hatred for girls slowly vanished and in junior high it occurred to me that they weren't all noisy, contemptible creatures. A few of them were actually kind of nice, and I was more curious about them every day. I wanted at least a friendship with one, and sometime in 7th grade I realized that it wasn't such a crime to be seen in the company of a girl—and if I selected the right girl, I could be somewhat of a transient locker room hero.

Sometime when I wasn't looking, Lydia became the "right girl."

I still couldn't talk to her.

Everyone else was talking to her; every time I dared look in her direction she had at least two guys hanging around, drooling like the pathetic hornballs that they were. She was an ongoing topic of discussion during lunch, after lunch, and in the locker room. The ultimate question: is she for real, or does she stuff her bra?

Hell, I wanted to know too, but I never joined in on the disgusting banter. Not until our freshman year when the stunning Slice Of News filtered through my ears and poked at my brain.

"If anyone can find out," someone said loudly, "Davis can. Girls like him."

They do? Since when, and why was I never given a copy of the memo making this important announcement?

I looked up in time to see a wet towel coming towards my face.

"Yeah, dumb shit. Ask her out and report back."

The problem with the task assigned, as I saw it, was that getting her to go on an actual date with me would require talking to her. Getting into her bra meant doing that more than once.

Taking her out was a problem. How? Have my dad chauffeur us around, where his never voiced but very loud opinions on How To Treat Women would echo in my brain every time I blinked? Ask my mom? Holy crap, she'd cry the whole time. Nick? College Boy was too busy between school and Katie to count on him for much of anything.

That only left Paul.

"Lunch," he told me. "Lunch is harmless. You buy her a

burger and then head back to your own classes afterwards, and if she's a total waste you're not stuck for an entire evening."

Lunch.

Where, the cafeteria, with 800 other teenagers, green blobs of petrified Jello flying through the air?

No thanks.

"I'll tell you what, squirt," he said, with what I now realize was a mixture of amusement and curiosity, "ask her tomorrow, and you guys can tag along with Monica and me at lunch. We'll go off campus. Hell, knock her socks off. We'll go to the restaurant."

"Tomorrow? To the Charybdis?"

"Grow a pair and ask her, squirt. The worst thing she can do is say no."

Easy for him to say. Hearing 'no' would be the worst thing *ever*. If the first coherent thing I ever asked her was for a date and she turned me down, there was no way I could ever go to school again.

I'd have to drop out in my freshman year of high school.

If I didn't ask her, I'd never hear the end of it. And one way or another my dad would find out what a gutless wonder he'd fathered. Paul would make a special trip to Dad's apartment to deliver the news himself.

'Yeah, well, Dad, you see, Kevin likes this girl, but damn, he doesn't have the balls to even say hi to her. I was going to be nice and drive them on their first date, but nooooo, he wouldn't ask her.'

'What a waste of my DNA,' Dad would say, sucking on the pretzel that kept him from smoking. 'He's such a little pansy. I knew that the first day I took him to karate class and he cried when he was kicked in the nuts.'

There was no choice.

I caught up with her just before first period started; she was halfway down the hall and headed for her locker. I managed to squeak out a hello, and hands that operated without my cooperation reached out and took her books.

"Hi, Kevin." She smiled, and seemed more than a little surprised that I wanted to carry her English and Math books a total of about one hundred feet.

"How's it going?" Ah, smooth. Knock her dead with your eloquence.

"It's going. You?"

"Okay I guess." We were already at her locker and I think I'd said more to her than I had in five years. Reluctantly, I handed the books back. "Uh, look, I was wondering… my brother has a car and would drive us … I was wondering if you'd, um, like to go out to lunch with me? My brother has a car…"

Dipshit, you already said that.

"Lunch?" She grabbed another book from her locker. "Sure."

"Yeah?" I couldn't believe she was smiling at me. Most likely trying to not laugh at my embarrassment. "I can meet you here."

"Okay, but we have the same class just before lunch, you know."

"We do?"

She closed the locker door, laughing now. "You sit right behind me in the next row, Kevin."

"I knew that."

I did know that. I just didn't think *she* knew that.

I watched her walk away, heart pounding wildly as if it were about to crawl into my throat. When she turned into a classroom I closed my eyes and exhaled in one long, slow breath, slumping against the cold locker. There had to be an easier way to get a date. Assign numbers or something. Anything to avoid terminal embarrassment.

"Kev. Wake up."

I opened my eyes; Debby Forrester was standing there, squinting at me. Debby was Nick's girlfriend's sister, and had wormed her way into more than one of my fantasies. She was short and blonde, and one of the few girls I had no trouble saying more than three words at a time to.

"Are you coming to history today or are you just going to stand there and hold up the wall?"

"I'd like to stay here," I admitted, pushing myself off the locker. "We have a quiz today, don't we?"

"Oh, hell."

She walked with me towards our first period history class, one hand fumbling with a backpack, the other trying to force a comb through her hair.

"Say, did you know my brother is screwing your sister?"

She groaned and flicked the comb at me, popping it against my arm, but I was too numb to feel it.

It took half a dozen more lunch dates, three movies, and a football game before I had the nerve to so much as think about pursuing the task assigned. I discovered along the way that Lydia had lips much softer than I imagined – she kissed me first, no surprise there – and when I got right down to it, I wasn't a half bad kisser myself.

The rear seat of Paul's VW Bug, left in the theater parking lot for my convenience when he and Spider took off with their dates, was an ideal place for being taught to smooch.

They went in to see a movie and we stayed in the car, ostensibly to talk. Paul knew better. I knew better. Lydia definitely knew better.

She obviously had practice and was a willing teacher.

One of the benefits of making out is that you don't have to actually talk. We were dating fairly regularly, but I still had no idea what constituted reasonable and acceptable date conversation. I didn't think she'd want to hear about my parents being split up and the pansy my mother occasionally dated, or about the stuff I'd blown up in chemistry, and especially not what the guys were saying about her behind her back.

We talked about school, classes we hated, why Paul was being so nice – I had no clue why – and what I was going to do if the school refused to accommodate me not wanting to leave and head for the community college.

After the movie that we didn't see, Paul drove her home, waiting in the car while I walked her up to the door. I managed to ask her to go to the football game with me the next afternoon, and then kissed her goodnight. She made sure it was a kiss Paul wouldn't tease me about; we both knew he was watching every move we made.

The idea that I could probably find out what lurked in Lydia's sweater kept me awake most of the night, and mostly out of guilt. The more often we went out, and the more we did talk, the more I resolved to not use her to advance my status in the locker room.

She didn't deserve that kind of treatment any more than she did the cruel barbs of the sort that Tyler Reed was willing to spit her way in second grade.

The threads of restraint, though, unraveled easier than I thought they would. We watched the first quarter of the football game, cheered when we were supposed to, stole kisses when we wanted, and headed for the snack bar when I decided I needed food before I snatched popcorn away from the kid sitting in front of us.

Lydia grabbed my hand as we stepped off the bleachers, and pulled me under them.

My protest was only half hearted. “This isn’t exactly where I was headed.”

“Necking is better on an empty stomach,” she laughed. “Makes you desperate.”

“Me or you?”

“I’m not desperate,” she murmured against my lips. “Not yet, anyway.”

Maybe not, but those kisses sure were. Any hotter and our lips would have melted together. Fusion. Screw the snack bar. Screw the game.

One by one the threads gave way.

I slipped one hand, and then the other, under the thick fabric of her sweatshirt, carefully weighing her reaction, my hands gliding smoothly over the skin on her back. Fingers that had to belong to someone else slipped under the elastic of her bra – I wondered for just a moment why the hell there was no hook to pop open – and she shivered.

Definitely all her.

And she wasn’t protesting.

I will not, I told myself, tell anyone else about this. It’s no one business. And damn, she felt good.

Somewhere in the back of my brain was a whiny little voice crying “touch me back, touch me back!”

My lips slid to her neck and I could feel her hand on my hip, hesitating.

“You,” I sighed, “are a direct threat to my vocation.”

She pulled her hand back. "Vocation?"

"It's a possibility."

Her hands were on my head, lifting it from her neck. "You're serious."

With a heavy sigh, I pulled my hands out from under her shirt. "Does it make a difference?"

"I wouldn't want to be the one who deprived the Catholic Church of a priest. You should have said something."

"Said what?" I was still distracted my the lingering taste of her skin on my lips. "That I didn't want to do this? That'd be lying now, wouldn't it?"

"Don't make fun of me, Kevin."

"I'm not. I just didn't think it mattered. That's a long way away. Okay, yeah, I plan on entering the priesthood and I seriously doubt I'll make some girl miserable by stringing her along for four years and then dumping her. But in the meantime … I'm human, too, you know."

"I wish you had told me, Kevin. I don't want you to get the wrong idea."

"What's that?"

"I don't make a habit of this. Not every guy I go out with gets this far."

"I didn't think they did. You don't have a reputation, Lydia. I'd have heard if you did."

"And will I, after this?"

My face flushed, partly from a guilty conscience, partly from embarrassment. "No. Will I?"

For just that brief moment, she thought I was serious.

"Look, I'll be honest with you," I said. "I really like you—"

"I like you, too."

"—but I probably shouldn't even think about going

steady with anyone. It'd hardly be fair, considering. But I *really* like you."

"My loss." She smiled sadly.

"Does this mean you won't go out with me again?"

She reached for my hand, holding it between both of hers, absently fumbling with my fingers. "I'd hate to think that we'd never go out again, Kevin."

I had to ask. "Could this have gone somewhere?"

"I wanted it to."

"So did I," I said, swallowing hard. "I think I've wanted it since the very first day I saw you, all the way back in second grade."

Her smiled brightened, and she laughed again. "Oh come on, you wouldn't even talk to me!"

"I was terrified of talking to you," I admitted. "And if I had, I never would have lived it down. I would have broken the big unwritten rule."

She tugged my hand, and started walking towards the open field. "And what's that?"

"Thou shalt never say anything nice to a girl. Speaketh only unto those for whom you have utter contempt and wish to make cry with thy terrible insults and really mean names."

"Well, that explains why the boys treated me the way they did. How do you explain the girls?"

"Bitches in training."

"I hated elementary school." She led me to the snack bar line; somewhere safe, I suppose. Feed me, don't grope me. "Seven and eight is too young to have to put up with all that racist crap."

"I'm sorry."

"You don't need to apologize. I don't remember you ever saying anything mean to me."

"That's because I never said anything to you, period."

"Even if you had, you never would have ripped into me for the color of my skin."

I shook my head. "No, I don't think I would have. It's one the of things that made me notice you, though. I don't think I had you really figured out until junior high."

"My dad is black," she explained. "My mom is white."

"I figured it was one or the other."

"It doesn't bother you?"

"Does it bother you that I'm Irish and Catholic?"

"No," she snickered, "but my mom is Scottish, and it might really bother her."

"Well, hell, then we need to get married so we can piss everyone off."

She leaned in and kissed me again, this time just a warm brush of lips, feather soft. "I won't ruin your vocation, I swear. Just promise me a occasional date."

I could feel the knot in my gut start to burn. "Anytime you want. When you're in between boyfriends, I'm your man."

"No jealousy, either. We both date other people and we don't hide it or deny it. I don't want any hurt feelings."

"I don't plan on asking too many girls out, but all right."

"You'll date," she sighed. "More than you think and more than I'd like."

"I could be the toy you keep up on the shelf, you know. Just take me down and dust me off when you want to play."

Another soft kiss. "No. You have to have a social life, and I can think of at least thirty girls who want to go out with you."

"No way."

"Yes way. I'm willing to bet more than half the freshman girls want a crack at you. Some of the boys, too."

So there was a memo.

I decided then, standing in a long line at the stadium snack bar, that I was going to draw a firm line that I'd never cross over, no matter what it would do to my reputation. No broken hearts. I'd be honest with every date I had, and I'd never push for anything more than a short kiss goodnight.

It was a promise that admittedly made me popular with the girls fed up with Friday Night Backseat Wrestling and girls too shy to date the boys they feared would push too hard.

The line was violated only occasionally, only with Lydia, and seldom any further than our explorations under the bleachers had taken us. And only – I made sure first – when she was in between boyfriends, something that happened at least four times a year, until our senior year, when I was positive she was deeply and permanently in love with the varsity star running back.

I breathed a sigh of relief – she'd found someone and was happy – and regret – because it wasn't me – and prepared to enter the seminary.

Home for Lydia was no longer her parents' duplex three blocks away from the school. Her father had accepted a teaching position overseas, sold the duplex, and she moved into her own apartment just half a mile from my parents' house.

"You're three doors down from Spider," I told her while I waited as she unlocked the door. "I've been that close a dozen times and never knew it. Hell, I jog by all the time."

"You're kidding. I've been here six months and I've never seen him. Or you."

"Well, once he and Eileen know you're here you can count on seeing them a lot. I hope you remember sign language."

"I doubt I can even finger spell anymore." She grabbed one of my hands and pulled me inside. "You'll have to teach me."

Her apartment was a clone of Spider's. There were no bedrooms, just one giant living room with a loft. Unlike Spider's, hers was tastefully decorated and there were no dirty jeans hanging from the loft banisters, and she had pictures on the walls, not posters plastered all over, hung sloppily with thumbtacks.

"When was the last time you and I went out?" I asked absently as I sat on the sofa. "It's been a long time, hasn't it?"

"Four years, I think."

"Whatever happened to what's-his-name? Gopher?"

"Topher," she laughed. "I think we just outgrew each other. He left to play college ball and I went to work. We just drifted apart."

"Should I say I'm sorry that it didn't work out?"

"No. I really cared about him and we stayed friends, but there was something missing."

I knew the feeling well.

"I kind of figured you'd be married to him."

"We were kids, Kevin. Even if I'd been that much in love with him we'd have been too young."

"Nick got married when he was eighteen," I pointed out. "Paul was only sixteen, though I suppose he's not the greatest example of marital success."

"I suppose there are exceptions to everything, but Topher and I weren't one of them."

"Are you seeing anyone now?"

She went into the kitchen, and either didn't hear me, or was ignoring the question. I supposed the dork she was running from at the Charybdis bar didn't count for anything, but

I wasn't about to discount the possibility that she might be chasing after someone else.

"Junior prom," she said when she came out, two soft drink cans in hand. She handed one to me and sat down, making sure we were close. "I think that was our last date."

"I swear, it wasn't my fault the prom sucked."

"We didn't stay very long, did we?"

I hated the prom, hated the tux I was stuffed into, hated the music, and realized after two hours that I was not alone in my misery. We did the requisite mingling, danced some, and then left when she swore she was going to bitch slap the next girl to come up to her and sneer gleefully about some poor misfit who hadn't found a date for the night and was likely sitting home alone, watching TV with her parents. We spent the rest of the night sitting in the back seat of my car at the park, the top down, staring out at the stars and the pond, and talked until dawn. We drew animated maps of the lives we foresaw for ourselves, and confided the dreams that seemed right at our fingertips.

It nearly killed me the next year to be stuffed into another tux, watching her on the dance floor with someone else, seeing her laugh and smile, her arms looped possessively around his neck. My date that night only had half of my attention, though she never seemed to notice. Or perhaps she didn't care; she was there, after all. She'd made it to the senior prom and had a reasonably respectable date, and for some girls not much else mattered then.

But Lydia was happy. Topher Tedeski treated her well, made her laugh, and that was enough to keep me from hating the fact that within a couple of months I would be heading off for a seminary, dedicating the next seven years of my life to that. In his hands, I thought she'd be safe.

"I missed you," I whispered, half hoping she'd hear me and half hoping she'd think I was just sighing.

She snuggled closer, setting her head on my shoulder. "I missed you, too, Kevie."

Kevie?

I allowed myself a surprised little smile. My brothers and sister called me Kev or squirt, my grandparents occasionally called me K-Joe, but Kevie?

Coming from those lips, I didn't mind.

"Can I pry?" she asked after a silence that seemed to go on forever.

"About what?"

"Why did you leave the seminary? You waited so long for that."

I tried to come up with a list of smart assed comments, everything ranging from my hormones to the butt ugly clothing required to be a priest, but in the end just said, "I suppose part of the reason is that I finally realized that some people are so religious that they stop being Christian, and I didn't want to be one of those people."

"That was only part of it?"

I shrugged. "I guess."

She lifted her head and looked at me. "You're just not ready to tell anyone."

"Not yet," I said quietly.

"That's okay. I can tell by the look in your eyes that it hurts. But just remember, you can cry on my shoulder any time you want. God knows I've cried on yours enough."

I could only nod my head.

"Can I ask you something else?"

"Sure."

"Are you going to kiss me, or not?"

"Are you seeing anyone, or not?"

"If I had been, it'd be over after tonight."

I pretended to consider it. "All right, but you have to respect the boundaries. I'm not that kind of boy, you know."

"Not yet," she snickered.

I caught a glimpse of the clock across the room, just before she leaned in to kiss me, before my eyes closed and my breath seemed to catch in my chest.

12:01.

3

Kevin

The thing about having a twin is that the normal boundaries most people have, even between other siblings, don't exist. There's a higher level of comfort twins share, at least it always seemed that way to me. The only thing separating my bedroom from Eileen's was a bathroom, and neither one of us thought twice about the other one barging in. If we needed privacy, we locked the doors, but the door itself being closed never meant Do Not Enter.

If the creature in the other room had been Nick or Paul, the rules would have been much different. I didn't care if Eileen walked in while I was taking a shower; I would have thrown a hissy fit if Paul had. I could talk to any of them about anything in the world, but it was to Eileen I could confess most of my deepest, darkest, dirtiest secrets.

Most of them.

So I wasn't surprised that she was sitting on my bed when I came home, flipping through a magazine, the TV buzzing quietly in the background. I didn't feel some immediate need to ask her what the hell she was doing there, or to get out. I just plopped down on the bed next to her and leaned against the headboard, trying to get a peek at the page she was looking at.

"Two in the morning, Kev," she grunted. "Where were you when the lights went out?"

"I was being led straight down the path into Temptation. Why are you home? I figured you'd spend the night with Spider."

She closed the magazine and tossed it to the floor. "I had this odd impulse to come home and share a birthday cake with my brother, maybe even give him a present. Only he had other plans that I didn't know about."

Our birthday. Damn.

"He's very sorry, I'm sure. And normally he'd be telling you that if you'd only told him you were staying home he would have, too, but he's really glad now that he decided to try to ignore his birthday by watching other people get drunk at his father's restaurant."

Eileen leaned in close and sniffed. "Perfume. Kevin, did you get laid tonight?"

"What? Jesus, you've got screwing on the brain."

"I take it that means no."

"It means no. But I think if I had begged and reminded her it was my birthday, I probably could have."

"This sounds good." She scooted up on the bed and sat against the headboard with me. "Ok, so if you could have reminded her it was your birthday, that means you already know her. She wasn't one of the airheads you've been dating lately?"

"No, not hardly."

"And you're trying damned hard not to smile, so it has to be someone good."

"Yep."

"And in your book, someone good has to be someone you seriously care about."

"You're on a roll."

Eileen looked up at me, grinning. "So you spent the last hours of your birthday playing tonsil hockey with Lydia Freeman."

"Damn, you're good."

"So I've been told. Kevin, this is great! If you were smooching her lips off she must not be attached to anyone else. Please tell me you're not going to let her get away this time."

"This time? There was never a last time, Eileen. We've never been together, so to speak."

"Bullshit. The only thing that ever kept you two apart was your stupid promise to remain so virginal you could take communion without choking to death."

"Depends on how you define virginal."

"Give me a break. Your idea of fooling around was licking your finger and sticking it in a girl's ear to make her scream. God forbid you actually let someone see your nipples."

"Don't be so sure about that, Eileen. I'll admit, Lydia and I came way too close more than once."

"Close, if your idea is dry humping through seventy two layers of clothing. Don't deny it. I think I have pictures somewhere."

"Now that," I laughed, thumping her leg playfully, "wouldn't surprise me. But you obviously weren't spying at the right time. There was one time when we came so damn close it's not funny. The only thing that stopped us was lacking protection, but even then we almost said to hell with it."

"And …?"

"And nothing. We didn't do it."

"I want details, mister. Well, details if you can give them without popping a boner."

"God, you're nosey."

She waited.

I took a deep breath and sighed. "All right. Spring of our junior year. We went up to Lake Berryessa to have a picnic and to see if it was warm enough to swim, which it wasn't, but that's beside the point. All the sane people stayed at home, so it was just us, a blanket on the sand, some greedy birds trying to snatch our food, and nothing on but swimsuits. I discovered the water was too cold by diving in, and she decided to warm me up. It went way past warm and got very, very hot."

"What, you got naked on the beach?"

"No. But her swimsuit and my thin little jogging shorts didn't hide a whole lot, you know."

"I hope you at least copped a feel."

"I managed to feel quite a bit, thank you very much. But most of it was through swimsuits, and we managed to stop before we went too far."

"Bummer. I at least hope the groping was mutual."

"It was."

"You must have learned a whole new meaning to the term 'feeling blue,'" she snickered.

"You have a gift for understatement."

"Ever think about how different your life might have been if you'd said to hell with it and just had sex with her?

"Too often."

"And did you think about the fact that if you had, the fire would have burned out and you would have drifted apart because you were too young for that much of a relationship?"

I had to turn and look at her; her expression was dead serious.

"No," I said after a while, "I never thought of it quite that way."

She settled back again, leaning her head against my shoulder, and stared at the almost-muted TV in the corner, quiet for a long time.

"I use to get really pissed off at Spider because he kept telling me he wouldn't sleep with me until I was old enough to promise him it would be for life," she finally said, softly. "When we finally did, I realized he'd been right all along. If we'd given in before that moment, before I knew that I wanted to live my life with him forever, with or without sex, I think we might have ruined everything."

"Yeah, but look at Nick and Katie…"

"Nick and Katie don't have the perfect marriage they try to make the world believe in, Kevin. They got married out of desperation, and that's not a good thing to build forever on."

"But I really did love her, Eileen, and it killed me every time she started dating someone else."

"She's available now?"

"Yes."

"Then you can admit to her now that you love her, which I suspect you still do, and you can do the cave man chest-pummeling thing and grunt 'my woman, hands off' to the rest of the world, but this time you don't have to worry about how old you are, or whether or not your virtue should be intact when you leave home, or even if anyone else approves. It's between you and her and God—and God approves, Kevin. He's been sticking her in your face for the better part of your life."

"Then why did I feel like I was meant to be a priest?"

She shrugged. "I suppose we're given the choice of more than one path that we can take. You chose one, and for whatever reason, you realized it wasn't the best choice you could have made. Besides," she grunted, climbing over my legs to get off the bed, "you've always been pretty passionate about religion, and it's highly possible that we all mistook your dedication as a vocation, and pushed you into it."

"It really is what I wanted, Eileen."

"Maybe so, and maybe someday you'll tell me why you changed your mind, but now you're here, and the first path you set out on is still waiting for you."

She stopped at the bathroom door, and turned.

"It's a good thing you're not asthmatic, Kevin," she said. "I have a feeling Lydia is going to take your breath away."

Chip

He was sitting at the table when Terry and I came down at nine the next morning; Nicole was in his lap, listening as he read the comics with her.

Terry darted past the table and went into the kitchen; she stood there with her back to them, hand pressed to her mouth, eyes filling with tears. "Look at him," she murmured, swallowing against the lump in her throat. "He's smiling."

I leaned against the breakfast bar and watched him; he was definitely smiling, and though he still looked like he needed to sleep for a week, his eyes were bright. He was making fun of the comics, trying to get Nicole to squeal, pretending to not be able to read the small print, forcing her to read out loud.

"Uncle Kevin," she finally said, "Grandpa is staring at you."

He looked up and I motioned for him to come into the kitchen. "Talk to your mother," I signed.

Nicole slid off his lap and he got up, unsure.

"Mom?"

She wrapped her arms around him, sniffing hard.

"What'd I do?"

"You're smiling."

"I'm sorry. I'll stop."

Paul shuffled in before she could say anything. He grunted when he saw Kevin hugging their mother, reached into the refrigerator for juice and then asked, "So what'd he do this time?"

"Apparently I smiled," Kevin said, letting her go.

"Ah." He pursed his lips thoughtfully, reaching for a glass. "What's her name?"

The smile snapped back onto Kevin's face, and he turned red.

"There's a girl?" Terry asked.

"Uncle Kevin has a girlfriend?" Nicole asked loudly. "Why?"

Paul looked over at his little girl. "Do you mean, why does he have a girlfriend, or why would some girl want to date him?"

"The potential is there," Kevin said, sighing hard. "You know her already. Lydia."

This time Terry smiled. "Really? You're seeing Lydia again?"

Before Kevin could answer I asked, "Is she why you didn't come home until after two in the morning, son?"

"Really now," Paul chuckled. "Little goody two shoes stays out past the witching hour."

Kevin ignored him. "I already apologized to Eileen for

blowing off our birthday," he said. "And I'm sorry if you were worried, but I ran into Lydia, and lost track of the time."

"You don't have a curfew," I pointed out.

"Yeah, but I would have called if I'd known I was going to be out so late. I know you were probably worried—"

"Forget that. I want to know about Lydia!"

"Your mother has her own priorities," I said. Paul and I went into the dining room to sit with Nicole; Terry kept Kevin pinned against the counter.

"Mom, we just talked, that's all. I have a date with her today and we'll see how that goes, okay?"

"Out of all those millions of girls you went out with in high school she was my favorite," Terry told him.

"Mine, too." He kissed her on the top of her head and managed to squirm away, sitting back at the table with Nicole, who was clearly more interested in watching the adults around her poke fun at her favorite uncle than she was in finishing the comics.

"You have a date," Paul grunted. "I suppose that means I can't count on you to babysit tonight."

Before he could turn to Terry I said, "And your mother and I have plans, Paul. And no"—I looked at her—"we're not changing them. We promised your parents we'd drive up this afternoon."

Paul didn't wait for her half-hearted protest. "I can ask Eileen, and if she's busy, Aunt Kris and Uncle Doug."

"Or," Kevin said, "you can still ask me. We don't have any real plans, Paul. We were just going to hang around. Nicole can hang around with us."

Nicole looked at her father, hopeful.

Paul looked doubtful.

"Dude, Lydia hasn't seen Nicole since she was a baby.

She'd be thrilled to spend some time with her now."

"Yeah," Nicole finally piped up. "Everybody loves me."

"No self esteem problems there," Terry snickered.

"We'll make it a really fun day." Kevin told Nicole. "What do girls like to do?"

"Go shopping."

"Okay, what do girls like to do that boys might like to do, too?"

Nicole thought for a moment. "Chuck E. Cheese."

"Girls like Chuck E. Cheese?"

"Well, I do," she said.

"How about miniature golf," Terry suggested. "You'll all have fun, and they have good pizza there, too. And video games."

"Is that okay with you, Nicole?" Kevin asked.

She nodded happily.

"You owe your brother," Terry said to Paul.

"No shit," he laughed. "You *know* they're gonna wind up at the mall."

"My brother's biggest problem is that he still loves his wife," I told Lydia. We were sitting at a table in the snack bar, close to the arcade, where we could keep an eye on Nicole as she played Skeeball. "He keeps saying that he wants a divorce, but I think that's just hurt feelings talking."

"And he got sole custody of Nicole?"

"It's not a legal separation. Monica never asked to have custody and she's only seen Nicole two or three times since they split."

"God, poor Nicole."

"I know, but Monica needs to get her crap together before she can be anyone's mom. She was so busy trying to prove to herself that Paul wouldn't stick around for the long haul by screwing everything in sight that she didn't stop to think what it might do to her daughter."

"She was trying to prove she wasn't good enough for him?"

"Something like that, I guess. He wants her back anyway, he just won't admit it to himself."

"He can forgive that?"

"Paul was no angel. She cheated first, but I know he used it as an excuse a couple of times."

Lydia was watching Nicole. "And she bears the brunt of it."

"I think she did, until Paul moved her in with our folks. He's worked damned hard at being a good father. He helps her with homework and takes her to the park every weekend. Most nights he leaves work for a while to come home and be there when she has her night time snack and to tuck her into bed … that way it's like being any other kid, she goes to sleep with Daddy there and he's home when she gets up. He schedules his life around her. If he's not working, he's with her."

"And when he is working, you're there."

"I know how she must feel, Lydia, only she has to be ten times as confused as I was when my parents split up."

"I remember how happy you were when they got back together."

"That was a miserable two years. Right when I needed him the most, Dad was gone. He tried hard, but having him live somewhere else just wasn't the same. I keep thinking that it might be even more difficult for Nicole. Don't little girls really need their mothers?"

"They need a lot of love, Kev. It sounds like she gets that."

"She makes me realize that I want kids someday. Now I know why my dad wanted a little girl so badly."

Nicole pulled a long string of tickets out of the Skeeball machine, and bounced over towards us. "Look," she said, holding them up. "I think I have about a hundred."

"What are they for?" Lydia asked her.

"You keep them and when you have enough you can trade them for a prize," Nicole said, handing them to me. "These aren't enough for anything."

"Are you collecting them?" I asked.

"Yep. And when I get enough, I'm getting a big stuffed animal. Or a radio."

"I like stuffed animals," Lydia said, winking at me.

I was jamming the tickets into my pocket when Nicole said, "Uncle Kevin, I think I lost my shoe."

I looked down at her feet. She had on socks, and one red tennis shoe.

"I was in the balls over there"—she pointed to a web-caged bin full of brightly colored plastic balls—"and I left my shoes in the cubby, but only one was there when I got out."

I spent the next fifteen minutes wading through the balls. I found several shoes, none of them hers. I also found half eaten candy bars, someone's underwear, and a balled up disposable diaper.

"You're never playing in there again," I grumbled. "After I go wash my hands – you stay here with Lydia – we'll go get you some shoes."

Paul was right.

We were heading for the mall.

We left the mall with two pairs of shoes, a couple of t-shirts, and other assorted odds and ends that I hadn't intended on buying, but seemed to make her happy. I buckled Nicole into the back seat of the car and was getting in, when Lydia laughed, "You're a soft touch, Uncle Kevin."

I had no doubt about that.

I also suspected I'd be in trouble when Paul saw how much I'd bought her, including the shoes Nicole said he wouldn't let her buy for school.

"Uncle Kevin, how come I always have to sit in the middle?" she asked.

I turned in my seat to look at her. "Because it's the safest place in the car."

"Then how come Lydia doesn't have to sit back here?"

"Because she's big enough for the front seatbelt to fit right, and that helps keep her safe."

She seemed pacified. I started to turn back around to start the engine when she asked, "How come you haven't kissed her?"

"What?"

"Daddy says that boys kiss girls they love. And if I saw you kiss her I wasn't supposed to say it was gross."

Lydia was trying hard not to laugh.

"Do you think kissing is gross?"

"No, but I never met a boy who wants to try it."

I leaned over and kissed Lydia. "Now, was that gross?" I asked.

"Not to me," Lydia chuckled.

"What about you, Nicole? Was that gross?"

"No, but it wasn't me you kissed."

"Someday," I told her, starting the car, "you'll find a boy who will want to kiss you. And Daddy will want to kill him."

~

Lydia waited downstairs while I got Nicole ready for bed. And Nicole, in her own six year old wise sort of way, knew better than to try to delay her bedtime any; she talked me out of a bath—"do *you* take a bath every night?"—and said she could fall asleep without a story, just this once.

"You're a good uncle," Lydia told me when I finally made it back downstairs. "Everyone should be spoiled like that once in a while."

I sat next to her on the sofa. "I'll remember that. I hope this was all okay. Paul was in a bind and Nicole really did want to meet you."

"Nicole is hysterical. I'll even babysit for her when you can't."

"Be warned, she normally talks a mile a minute and you can only get a reply in when she stops to take a breath."

"She has a lot to say."

"No kidding. I meant it earlier, though, when she said boys kiss the girls they love. I do love you, you know. I always have."

She turned to look at me. "Would you think it was totally classless for me to admit that I'm glad you left the seminary? I saw you sitting there last night and wanted to do cartwheels through the bar."

"I wish you had," I laughed, trying to picture her flipping end over end down the aisle between the barstools and the booths.

"I wondered which one of us would get the nerve to say it first. I love you, too, Kevin. I have for a long, long time."

"Even if I won't tell you why I came home?"

She leaned in and kissed me. "You'll tell me when you're ready."

I wasn't so sure about that.

I didn't think I'd ever be ready.

4

Kevin

"I cut Spider off," Eileen said, explaining why she was home before ten o'clock five nights running. "He can survive until the wedding."

"As my daughter would say," Paul grunted, shifting uncomfortably, "you're a meaniehead."

Paul was lying on the floor, his legs bent over the sofa, bare feet pressed against the back rest. Eileen was on the opposite end of the sofa, her legs curled up under her body, and she looked damned pleased with herself.

I sat on the fireplace hearth, not willing to sit next to his feet.

"You assume it was Eileen's idea," I said. "Maybe Spider just needed some well deserved rest."

Paul lifted his head up and looked at her. "Yeah, I would imagine she'd be the one to run a poor guy ragged. If she can't nag him to death she'll—"

"Don't go there," she warned.

He set his head back down. We both knew she could nag him to death if she set her mind to it, but her arms would get very tired while she was at it, and all Spider had to do to avoid it was close his eyes or turn away.

"Are you sure about this, Eileen?" I asked. "The rest of your life is going to be very, very quiet."

She shrugged it off. "He's not mute, Kevin, he just can't hear or talk. And I assume that once we have kids, I'll appreciate any quiet I can get."

Unless, and none of us said so, their kids were also deaf.

"I've never heard Spider make a sound, I don't think," Paul mused out loud.

"He can when it matters."

"See?" He craned his neck to look back at me. "She always comes back to sex."

"Does it ever bother you, Ei? That you can't even hear him say he loves you late at night when the lights are out?'

"Thanks, I hadn't thought of that before," she sighed.

"Sorry, I was just wondering."

"It bothers me for about two seconds once in a great while, Kevin. And he has his ways of making me hear it."

Paul sat up and turned, leaning his back against the sofa. "Let's leave Eileen's sex life alone."

"Thank you."

"Let's talk about Kevin's instead."

I didn't appreciate the laughter.

"Have you ever?" he asked.

Eileen just rolled her eyes.

"None of your business, Paul," I said.

"According to all the gossip in high school," Eileen said, "Kevin was nothing but the consummate gentleman, kept his hands to himself, and only offered a goodnight kiss on the second date."

"So there." I stuck my tongue out at Paul.

"And after high school?" he prompted.

"I went into a fricking seminary."

"Yeah, but it wasn't a prison, little brother. I know you guys got time off for good behavior and I'm sure you had opportunities. You're twenty one years old and you've never had sex?"

I got up.

"Go to hell, Paul."

After he'd tucked Nicole in for the night – I could hear him across the hall, standing in her doorway, telling her he loved her, and to get to sleep because tomorrow was a big day – Paul knocked on my door, pushing it open with his fist.

I was lying on my bed, reading. I looked up over the top of the magazine and grunted at him.

"Can I come in?"

I grunted again.

He took the chair from my desk, spinning it around so he could sit with his arms on the back, resting his chin there. "I just wanted to apologize, squirt. I didn't realize you took the virtue thing so seriously and if I had I wouldn't have said anything."

"I don't."

"Don't what?"

"I don't take it so seriously. And don't ask me anything about the seminary. And no, I know we've been dating for a month already, but I haven't had sex with Lydia yet, so don't ask that, either."

"Yet."

I put the magazine down and sat up. "Why's tomorrow a big day for Nicole?"

"Monica's taking her for the day. They're doing all that girly stuff that I have no clue about."

"Shopping."

"Probably."

"With your credit card."

"No doubt."

"And you don't mind?"

"It's worth anything for Nicole to have some time alone with her mother. Remember when Mom used to push us out the door to spend time with Dad even when we had other plans, and how much I used to bitch about it? I understand it now. We needed that as much as Dad did."

"I understood it then, moron."

"Yeah, well, you complained the loudest."

"Because that was my job as the youngest. What about you? Are you spending any time with Monica?"

"Some," he admitted. "She comes to the restaurant and has dinner with me. We're talking."

"And?"

"I miss her," he said quietly.

"You haven't told her that, have you?"

He shook his head.

"Moron."

"I don't know if she's ready for family yet. I'm afraid if I tell her I want her back she'll be so overwhelmed that she runs."

"Just tell her that you still love her, wonderdork."

~

Chip

The world imploded.

I banged around the kitchen half asleep, trying to find the various parts of the coffee maker, grumbling under my breath about the noise Nicole and Kevin made when thundering down the stairs at Way Too Early in the morning. Nicole plopped herself down in front of the TV to watch cartoons before getting ready for school while Kevin took the newspaper hostage and sat at the dining room table, pouring over the comics. I just wanted to be in bed, still curled around Terry, sound asleep or at least getting away with whatever she would let me get away with.

I was losing a battle with the coffee filters when Nicole ran into the kitchen. "Grandpa, you better come look at the TV," she said, her voice thick with both annoyance and worry. "They're showing the same thing on every channel and it looks bad."

I tossed the box of filters onto the counter and followed her in; I was several steps behind Kevin and stopped dead in my tracks when I saw the look on his face, the pale mixture of surprise and horror.

"Go wake up Grandma," I told Nicole, "and tell her I need her to come downstairs right now. Then wake up your dad and Eileen and tell them to come, too. Tell them it's important."

She started out the room.

"Nic," I added, "you stay upstairs and play in your room, but don't turn on a TV, all right?"

"I was right, this is really bad isn't it?"

"Sweetheart, I don't know, but I promise, as soon as I figure out what's going on I'll tell you."

Kevin watched with numb curiosity, and barely noticed when his mother shuffled in. I reached for her, pulling her close as we sat on the sofa, hoping we weren't seeing what I knew we were. Paul and Eileen scrambled down the stairs, half dressed, and stopped beside Kevin, who stood there barely blinking, looking at the TV just in time to see video replay of an airliner slam nose first into the south tower of the World Trade Center.

"Those buildings have at least fifty thousand people in them on any given day, I think," I muttered.

No one had a reply.

And the magnitude of horror grew steadily worse as we learned of a plane plunging into the Pentagon, and one into a field in Pennsylvania.

"Chip," Terry asked in a half whisper, "do you know anyone working out of the Pentagon?"

I shook my head. "The agency didn't have any offices near there."

The Agency. The Issue. The thing that nearly blew our marriage apart. The thing I swore I'd stay away from until the end of forever was just a memory.

Eileen was crying, silent tears running in thin streaks down her cheeks. "All those people…"

I hadn't noticed Paul moving, but heard the click when he set the phone back into its cradle. "School's still open today. Should I make Nicole go or keep her home?"

"Keep her home," Kevin said, his first noticeable movement in half an hour.

Terry shook her head. "We have to tell her what's happening, make sure she knows she's safe here, and then let her decide."

"Safe? *Is* she safe?" Paul asked.

Are any of us safe? It was a collective thought to which no one dared give voice.

Taking a deep breath, I looked away from the TV. "The potential is there for the Air Force base to be some kind of target, but I doubt that. This area doesn't have the demographics for a major attack."

"Demographics? Dad, you think anyone of those people in those buildings or airplanes woke up today and thought 'hmmm, I'm not a demographic, so I'm safe'?"

"No, but I think whomever is responsible picked those targets carefully, going for the biggest impact possible. Aside from Travis Air Force Base, this area has nothing to offer. I'd worry more about San Francisco. The Golden Gate Bridge. Or L.A. Nicole will be safe in school."

Paul looked doubtful.

"Just stay away from the mall," I added. "Anywhere a large population would congregate."

"Should Paul close the restaurant for today?" Terry asked.

"No." I got up from sofa, but not before kissing her. "But Paul's not working today, I am. Paul's going to keep himself available to pick Nicole up at a moment's notice, if she decides to go to school. If she stays home, he works at keeping her away from the television."

"Dad—"

"I'm going to go talk to her first, Paul. While I'm doing that I want you on the phone calling everyone scheduled to work today. If they don't want to come in, that's fine, there won't be any repercussions for the rest of the week, but tell those who are willing that they'll get time and a half. Like it or not, businesses are going to be open today and our regulars will need a place to come and catch the news on their lunch breaks."

Nicole stayed home.

She wanted to go to school; she got dressed and was in the kitchen getting her lunchbox when Paul hung up the phone after speaking with his last employee. "Grandpa is right," he told her, "you'll be safe in school, but I don't want you to go."

"Why not?"

"Sweetheart, right now Daddy just needs his little girl home with him, okay?"

She rolled her eyes, but put the lunchbox back on the counter, and let Paul hug her.

"You know what else Daddy needs?" he asked her when he let go, reaching for the phone again. "Daddy needs Mommy."

Kevin

I went to the restaurant with Dad; there wasn't much I could do at home, but at the Charybdis I could make an effort to take up some slack and bus tables or expedite food for the servers. I could keep drink glasses full and baskets of popcorn out for the people who, for the most part, were only there to watch the television in the bar.

More than half the staff showed up; Paul said they would have all come in if he'd said they had to. Most of those absent wanted to stay home with small children who needed to be kept occupied and away from the news.

"The youngest kids who see it don't understand that they're seeing the same footage over and over," Dad explained.

He was standing behind the bar, half listening to the news. Lydia was sitting there with me, trying to make what little sense of what was happening that she could.

"They think it keeps happening again and again?" she asked.

"Imagine yourself as a three year old. You keep seeing these big airplanes crash, and your parents tell you not to worry, it's only a replay. How does a three year old conceptualize video tape and playbacks?"

"I can't conceptualize any of it," she said.

"I'm glad," I told her, covering her hand with mine, "that you had today off. I can't imagine being stuck behind a teller's window trying to make small talk today."

One of the waitresses came up, reaching over the bar for clean glasses. "It's not small talk today, hon," she said. "It doesn't get any bigger than this. You should see the madhouse outside the front gate at Travis. It's going to take me three hours to get back on this afternoon."

"You live on the Air Force base?"

"Yes, and normally I love it. But when I go home today, I'll have to wait for about two and a half hours to get through the line of cars, I'll be stopped by guards carrying really big guns, and if they decide that living on the base is a good enough reason for me to enter, I get to drive the rest of the way, all alone, with two Humvees mounted with machine guns pointed right at me. I'm afraid to sneeze once I get past that first guard."

"A three hour line?" Lydia asked.

Dad nodded. "No one's getting on that base who doesn't belong there, and a lot of people are going to want on it today."

"I think the hospital is even shut down," the waitress sighed, grabbing the glasses. "I feel sorry for anyone who gets really sick."

"How could we not see this coming?" Lydia wondered out loud.

"We saw it coming," Dad said. "We just didn't believe it could happen."

Chip

Everyone else was heading out the door, Terry was reaching in the closet for her purse and I was tugging at my tie, trying to straighten it, but Kevin sat on the sofa, leaning forward with his elbows on his knees, washed in the dim glow of the television.

"We're going to a prayer service at the church, Kevin," I reminded him. "Are you coming?"

He didn't look up. "Nope."

"You sure?"

"Have a good time, Dad. Say hello to Uncle Doug and Aunt Kris for me."

Dismissed. My youngest son stared at the TV and dismissed me, without so much as lifting his head to see where I was standing.

Kevin

I sat there thinking about lives lost, about the hope that went crashing to earth with every soul ripped from the last breath of life. Did they feel fear? Did they know that they were surely facing their last moments, and did it bring them peace or fill them with terror? Did they cry out someone's name, voices filled with love, a tinge of regret?

Did they think of God?

I wasn't even watching the television anymore. It was just background static, echoes of the directional sirens of hundreds of firefighters pinging around in my head. I tried to imagine being enveloped in a cloud of thick black ash, pieces of stone and paper shooting through the air like microscopic missiles. The blinding darkness. The taste and smell of it.

I understood fear.

Did they call out to God?

I could hear in the distance of my reality for the moment, a woman's voice, filtered through speakers, saying she had been in the second building hit, but she'd had time to get out and away from the buildings before they collapsed. She was all right. God was looking out for her.

So, God wasn't looking out for the people who were stuck with no way out? God took one look at her said, hey, I like you, let's let the other fuckers jump out windows or get crushed in a million tons of crumbling waste. Did God hover over them, pointing a mighty finger, saying 'I'll keep you and you and you, but you up there, you can stay, I'm done with you for now. Get back in line, maybe we can find another life for you in fifty or sixty years'?

Was God even there?

Is He ever?

5

Chip

Kevin looked more like the father of the bride than he did her brother; his expression crossed between giddy happiness and hope for Eileen's future, and a sadness that he was losing the little girl who had grown up right beside him.

They hadn't always been so close; for the first seven years of their lives they fought like little wild men, constantly at odds with each other and forever causing eruptions of one sort or another that ended in someone crying, someone in trouble, and two older brothers who had egged them on scrambling for cover when a parent came stomping in.

At around four years old Eileen discovered she could win most fights with Kevin by driving a knee or whipping a foot into his groin, and Kevin spent the next two years running from her. When he was five I found him screaming in terror, dangling from the outside of the stairway banister, his arms wrapped around a wood post. He had been running down the hallway and tried to jump down some of the stairs, trying to get away from her, and had overshot the top stair.

Eileen swore her innocence, and Kevin knew better than to lay the blame squarely at her feet.

We punished them both.

He never grasped the idea that if he stopped picking on her, he wouldn't have to run from the wrath of Hurricane Eileen. He'd just do it, and then run like hell; most of the time she caught him and he'd end up in a painful heap on the floor, writhing and in tears.

When they were six we let Kevin join a peewee football team. He had all the talent of a fruit fly and the grace of an elephant, but he loved the idea of being on the team, and he especially loved the bright red and blue game uniform. He played right tackle; when a team is made up of five and six year old runts that's not a terribly important position, but to him it was gold. They played a game of tag with a pint sized football thrown in for good measure, their shrill little voices echoing on the field as they battled for possession of the ball and tried hard to not let a single person on the field touch them.

They all quickly learned that getting tackled hurts.

What Kevin came to realize was that his uniform came with a jock strap. And with the jock came a cup. A nice, hard plastic cup, and the best thing was that it wasn't actually attached to his uniform. It was a completely independent entity, and when he realized this, he was elated.

He waited for the perfect time to pick on Eileen. When one of her front teeth came out, he seized upon her self consciousness about it and let her know that the entire first grade thought it made her look uglier than a donkey's butt.

She plunged her knee into his groin as hard as she could.

Kevin didn't budge.

Eileen had no idea what to do. Every other time Kevin's eyes had rolled back, he grabbed himself, and slumped to the floor in hysterical tears. This time he grinned. She didn't even duck when he cocked his arm back and slugged her straight in the mouth.

Two more teeth came out.

She screamed, and we came running. Blood trickled from her mouth and she wailed that Kevin had just walked up to her and socked her in the face. Paul and Nick had seen the entire thing, and both turned on their little sister.

"She kicked him in the nads again," Nick said.

I grabbed Kevin and dragged him upstairs – noting that my daughter had this keen look of satisfaction in her eyes, positive that he was about to get the first spanking of his young life – while Terry took her hand and led her into the kitchen.

"Are you hurt?" I asked him, depositing him onto the bed in his mother's and my room.

"Nope." He made a fist and knocked on the protective cup. "Plastic."

I didn't know whether to laugh or yell at him.

"I know I'm not supposed to hit her," he added. "But she's not supposed to kick my nuts. She does it all the time, Dad. I never hit her before now."

"And you never will again, you got it? She's your sister. You don't have to like each other but you have to start treating each other better."

Terry had Eileen sitting on the kitchen counter, holding ice wrapped in a dishrag to her lip. She glanced at Kevin behind me with a smug look of 'I know you got it *so* good.' I sighed, and said to Terry, "Well, he was wearing a cup"—she tried not to laugh—"so there's no damage." Then I turned to my daughter and said, "If you *ever* kick any of your brothers like that again, I *will* spank you, do you understand that?"

None of the kids had ever been spanked. They'd been forced to sit in corners or banished to their rooms for what to them was an eternity, and they were forced to apologize in front of the entire family to whichever sibling they had wronged, but we never laid a hand on any of them.

Eileen didn't want to be the first.

It didn't stop the fighting, it only leveled the playing field. The longer Kevin played football, the tougher he got. If she hit him, he hit back, but she never again slammed her knee into his groin.

In second grade came the arrival of Tyler Reed. He was nine years old, half a foot taller than anyone else in the second grade, and he had the disposition of a dog left tied in the yard too long. Tyler hated everyone, but he took a special dislike to Eileen. He tripped her in the cafeteria, chased her on the playground, pushed her off the swings, and made going to school pure hell.

Eileen began throwing up most mornings and begged to not have to go. She wanted to be home schooled, or go to a private school; she wanted anything except to get on that bus and face second grade.

We talked to her teacher, and to the principal; "It's just a crush," was the common excuse. "He picks on her because he likes her. That's what little boys do."

In a moment of providence, one afternoon Kevin's class was let out for recess early and they spilled onto the playground at the same time as Eileen's class. It was crowded and noisy; 40 second graders and just 2 adults to watch them. Tyler followed Eileen around; all she wanted to do was survive the twenty minutes of supposed freedom and then retreat into the safety of the classroom.

Too late, she realized that she was behind a wall of screaming kids, there was no adult who could see her, and Tyler was right there. He grabbed her by her hair and began detailing how he intended to torture her, starting with slamming her face into the ground by whipping her hair around.

Frantic, in tears, Eileen was too scared to scream for help and it wasn't likely either of the playground attendants would have heard.

Tyler hadn't counted on Kevin.

Kevin saw him follow Eileen behind the group on the blacktop and abandoned his place in line at the slide. When Tyler got his hand around Eileen's hair and began to jerk her head around, Kevin came flying at him.

It was his first clean tackle. He took Tyler to the ground, sat on his chest, and pummeled his fists into Tyler's face.

This the attendants heard. A roar of kids chanting "fight, fight, fight!" erupted and they came running.

Eileen was lying on the ground, crying; Kevin was straddling Tyler – whose fist was full of Eileen's hair – and he was still slamming his clenched fists into Tyler's bloody face.

Tyler was wailing; he never made a move to fight back, he just laid there while Kevin beat the holy crap out of him, all the while screaming for his mother.

Within half an hour Terry and I were sitting in the principal's office; Tyler's nose was broken and several of his teeth were missing or cracked in half, and Kevin was being suspended.

"Let me get this straight," I said. "You're kicking my kid out because he defended his sister?"

"We have a zero tolerance policy for fighting, Mr. Davis," the principal explained. "By our rules, Kevin must be suspended for a week."

I leaned forward. "And the kid who's been torturing my daughter since school started? You never did a damn thing about that. What was Kevin supposed to do, let this kid kill Eileen before *you* did anything?"

"Until today there was never proof."

"Well, let me tell you this much: you can suspend Kevin as long as you want. If anything, I'll reward him for this fight. My daughter won't be back at school, either, not until this bully is removed from the school permanently."

"We have no reason to expel..."

"You find a reason. If Tyler Reed is still in this school one week from today, I'll slap you, the school, and the district with the mother of all lawsuits. And don't misunderstand, I can afford to let it go on for years—I can bankrupt the district before I'll go broke or you can goad me into giving up. And as part of that lawsuit I'll demand an internal investigation of how you, personally, handle parental complaints about student misconduct, and we'll find out if there are any other bullies torturing other students."

My diatribe went on for another ten minutes. We left without giving the man a chance to reply.

Two days later they were both back in school. No one saw Tyler Reed again.

The climate of their relationship changed with that fight. If Eileen had any doubts before, she knew after that no matter what was going on between them, Kevin would risk anything for her. By the time they graduated junior high they had that connection twins typically seem to share.

Kevin was the first to warn Spider that if he ever broke Eileen's heart, he was a dead man. He was the one she turned to when she was uncertain about feeling so attached to one person before she was old enough to drive. He was the one Spider wrote to, asking if his timing in proposing to her was a good idea or better left until after she graduated college.

Eileen didn't want a maid of honor. Spider had his best man and Eileen had hers; I gave Eileen away but Kevin stood there beside her, giving her tacit approval of the direction she'd chosen, and the person with whom she intended to spend the rest of her life.

He missed her when she was suddenly no longer there, as much as she had missed him when he left for the seminary.

He raised his voice in mock protest over being anointed Most Deserving Dishwasher after Thanksgiving dinner. "Hey, this is Eileen's job, not mine. Mine is to go into the living room to watch football, and wait for pie."

"Don't be a baby," Nicole teased.

"Yeah, well, just for that you get to help me clear the table."

Nicole looked to Paul for help, but he only smiled and nodded his approval.

"See, ya little sucker? That's what you get for being mean to me."

"Daddy, he called me a sucker."

"He's called me worse," Paul assured her.

Before Lydia could offer to help them both, I stood up and announced that the rest of us were going into the living room, Lydia included so that we could grill the poor girl, and when they were done clearing the table and had at least one load of dishes going in the dishwasher, Kevin and Nicole could join us.

"But that's not fair!" Nicole sputtered.

"Welcome to life, kiddo," he told her. "It's never going to be fair."

At some point, I think it was soon after we reconciled following a two year split, we started talking in the bathtub. It became a ritual; at least three times a week, usually four, Terry would light a dozen or more candles in the bathroom and fill the tub with water as hot as we could both stand, and we'd spend a hour or longer soaking, wrapped around each other, and we talked.

Yes, sure, once in a while we stopped talking and sent waves over the edge of the tub, but for the most part we only talked. It was the one sure place we had away from kids and our granddaughter, though it was not safe from the prying eyes of Max, the psychotic cat Eileen had given me for my thirty-ninth birthday.

Max often sat on the toilet lid, watching, his head cocked to one side and eyes wide, as if thinking we were either the most stupid or the bravest creatures to grace his little world. It was water, and we got in it. Voluntarily. And often. Whether it disgusted or amazed him, he had to be there; if we locked him out he stood outside the bathroom door, howling, and every minute or so he would slam himself against the door.

The inconvenience of letting him in was better than the vet bills we'd incur if we let him abuse himself like that.

Thanksgiving night Max stretched himself out on the cool tile floor, watching from the floor, safe from both water and fire.

Nosy little shit.

"He hasn't told Lydia a thing," I told Terry, flicking water droplets at Max. "The only thing she knows for sure is that he doesn't feel like he has a vocation anymore. I didn't think I should press for anything else."

"Did he ever?"

"Have a vocation? I don't know. But I think that if it were that simple he'd just say so. If it were that simple he wouldn't have spent so much time after he came home looking like he wanted to die."

"He's happy now," she ventured.

"When he's with Lydia he is," I agreed. "Or when he's talking about her. And he seems more even tempered with everyone else."

"But?"

"But whatever the underlying problem was, I think it's still there."

"Should we get nosy?"

Terry and I had a long standing policy with our kids, one that grew stronger as they grew older; we had, hopefully, taught them to deal with their problems; if they needed to talk to us about them, we would listen, and offer advice if that seemed to be what they were after, but we made it a point to let them come to us rather than risk becoming nosy, interfering parents.

I occasionally prompted them by asking if anything was wrong, but if they declined, I let it go, and hoped they knew they could come to us.

Whatever Kevin was dealing with, he refused to acknowledge it as a significant problem. We knew better.

"Not yet," I said after a while. "Give him a chance to talk to Lydia about it first. My gut tells me she's the one he'll go to."

"The older they get, the lower we are on their list of preferred confidants," she sighed, her tone suggesting she wasn't at all bothered by the idea.

"They keep finding people who suit them better hormonally. We'll just have to settle for being our grandkids' confidants."

"Well … tell those kids to get on the stick and give me more grandkids."

"On the stick?"

"Oh hush. I really thought Nick and Katie would have one or two by now."

I looked over at the cat. "Max, go get me the phone. I need to call Nick and tell him to bonk his wife."

Max yawned and stretched, rolling onto his back, his head under the sink.

"Thanks. I really wanted the view of all your kitty junk."

"Typical male," Terry mused.

"Hey, none of the rest of us lounge around naked, shoving our goodies in your face."

"Well…"

"Hush."

"Did you *ever* talk to Kevin about sex?"

"I think he knows where all the parts go, Terry."

"You know what I mean."

"I don't think I ever did more than have a cursory talk with him. I probably should have, considering the sheer volume of girls he dated in high school."

"You should make him sit down and have that talk with him now," she snickered. "'Son, now that you're dating…'"

"You're assuming he's not long past needing advice on women and what to do with them. Or at least what to do with Lydia."

"He's not sleeping with her yet," she said, sounding a bit surprised. "He made that pretty clear tonight."

"What, you asked?"

She looked up at me. "Yes, I asked him. I'm nosy, sue me."

I was surprised; given how often Lydia was in and out of his life and how happy he was when she was in it, I expected that by the time we knew they were dating again it was a fact already accomplished.

What the hell was he waiting for?

"It could be," Terry said, getting out of the tub, "that we

managed to raise one child who isn't fueled by pure hormones."

It could be, I thought, watching her dry off, but I didn't think so.

Kevin

"My dad," Lydia said, putting the phone down, "is drunk. But he's a happy drunk right now, and wanted to know how your 'bitching-assed beautiful blonde bombshell babe of a mother' is doing."

"That's a mouthful of B-words."

"He can be pretty alliterative when he's had a few," she laughed. "No, my parents are happy to hear that I haven't gotten rid of you, and happier still that I spent Thanksgiving with your family."

"I'm glad you did, too," I said, reaching for her. "But I'm sorry your folks aren't coming home for the holidays."

"My mother is terrified of flying right now. It's all right, I understand."

"Yeah, but I know you wanted to see them."

She nodded. "Next year. She'll be okay to fly by then, I'm sure. And this year they can spend Christmas in Scotland with her family. My poor dad."

"They don't get along?"

"No, they do. You just have to picture it. This sea of red hair and white-white skin, and then there's my dad. Half of them still don't know what to make of my mother marrying him, and the other half don't grasp the idea that he probably is a little uncomfortable being the only black guy there. None of them stop to think how they'd feel if they were suddenly plopped into the middle of his family's reunion."

"What about your grandparents?"

"My grandfather," she snickered, "says that as long as she didn't bring home some squirrelly Irish boy, it's okay. Black American, fine. Black Irishman, well, he'd have to shoot them both."

"Oh, great. Does he know you're dating a mostly Irish punk?"

"No, we're sparing him that small detail."

"What about your other grandparents?"

"They don't care if you're Irish."

"Very funny. Will they care that I'm white?"

"Only in the sense that they'll worry how the rest of the world will treat us when we're together, Kevin. But my grandmother"—she pulled back and pretended to eye me carefully—"she's going to take one look at you and swear your mother must never feed you. And I warn you, once she says that, you're going to get fed."

Paul was in the kitchen when I got home, standing in front of the open refrigerator. "It's not even midnight," he said when he realized I was there. He shook his head and chuckled, "and here you are."

"Eh, fuck off. Where's Monica?"

He grabbed two sodas and then pushed the door closed with his foot. "She went home after tucking Nicole in."

"And here you are, standing in the kitchen in your underwear when you could be… heh, elsewhere?" I took the soda he held out to me. "Who's the loser now?"

"I know what I'm waiting for, Kev. Do you?"

I knew. But Lydia didn't, and until she did, it wouldn't be fair.

6

Kevin

Whatever Paul was waiting for, it only took a month.

Monica, Eileen dutifully reported to me, was there for midnight Mass on Christmas Eve; she sat with Paul and Nicole, Paul's arm around her shoulders most of the time, looking both terrified of what other people must think, and thrilled that they were there as a family.

I bet her that Monica would be at the breakfast table Christmas morning; she laughed and refused the bet, saying the odds were stacked against her, then hung up with a reminder that she and Spider would be over early and to not forget she wanted a really big present.

"Well, squirt?"

I turned away from the bathroom mirror; Paul was standing there, leaning against the door jamb.

"Well what?"

"I've been waiting all day for the inevitable comments."

I turned back to the mirror; I was losing a fight with a neck tie, and decided to yank it off and look for a clip on. "Comments about what?"

"Monica." He turned and went into my room, flopping down onto the bed.

"I'm supposed to say something about her?" I shrugged. "Okay. Paul, your wife looked scared as hell to be seen in this house this morning, but she looked good and I was glad to see her. Where is she?"

"She went home."

I was digging through a drawer, looking for a better tie. "You let her leave?"

"Was I supposed to duct tape her to the Christmas tree? Of course I let her leave. Nicole's playing with all her new stuff and I think Monica was getting a little stressed out."

"I just thought…" I closed the drawer and sat next to him on the bed. "I mean, with the way Dad swept her up this morning and as happy as you two looked, I thought…"

"Don't rush it, squirt," he said. "We're still kind of feeling our way through. She's not ready for me to move back home with her."

The rest of the family was more than ready to welcome Monica back into the fold. Looking up from his coffee, Dad beamed and jumped up from his chair when she crept into the kitchen behind Paul, and scooped her into a bear hug, kissing her cheek affectionately.

She loved it, and hugged him back just as hard.

"God, I missed you, girl," he murmured.

Paul rescued her quickly and slipped his own arms around her. The attention both delighted and embarrassed her.

"What's the suit for?" Paul pressed. "Heading to church?"

"Nope. I'm going over to Lydia's, and we're going to pretend we're grown ups and celebrate a nice, quiet Christmas."

"Ah. So she's sitting there, pining away for her knight in shining armor. Tell me, is the armor plating difficult to take off in the clinch? Or does the lady have one hell of a can opener?"

I glared at him.

"Still? Kevin, come on. Male virgins over the age of sixteen are a disgrace in this family."

"You'll all get over it."

"Probably so." He got up and headed for the door. "Mom said to tell you that dinner is at six, she expects both of you, and to pick up the mail you left by the phone, or she's going to open up every single letter and read them all."

On the off chance that she would, I scooped everything up on my way out the front door. Not that I expected a surprise in one of the letters. But you never know.

"We've been writing back and forth for about six years, I guess," I told Lydia, ripping open one of the perfume scented envelopes. I had forgotten about them until Lydia squirmed out of my arms and told me I smelled like a cheap imitation of a cheap cologne. "She writes me a couple times a week, moaning about her Man of the Day, and I write her once a month to tell her if she'd quit sleeping with every guy she meets she might actually find a relationship there somewhere."

Lydia snuggled next to me on her over-stuffed sofa, and peered over my arm. "She really gives you all the gory details?"

"Sadly. We were barely even friends before she moved. Don't ask me why she decided I'd be her ideal confessor."

"Katie's sister, right?"

I nodded. "Debby. She left midway through our freshman year. She never has been happy in Washington. Every once in a while she mentions leaving and coming back here."

"Oh joy for you," she sighed.

"Like this one," I showed her the letter. "She's bitching about some lieutenant she's been seeing. I guarantee in the next letter she'll have dumped him and she'll be screwing someone else."

"Kevin!"

"Well, it's true. I don't think she understands that she's not going to land someone by lying flat on her back. The most that girl is going to catch is a disease."

She snatched the letter from me, folded it in half, and tossed it to the end table. "That was crude, and I don't want to spend what time we have before we go back to your parents' house discussing someone else's love life."

"It's not a love life," I said dryly. "She wouldn't know love if it reared up and bit her on the ass."

"Well I would!" She leaned forward to give me a kiss, but pulled back before my lips could make contact. "How much do you tell her?"

"Nothing. I sermonize. Hell, I haven't written her since I came home."

"You must have let her know you were here."

"It must have been Katie."

"She must have been surprised."

I resisted the urge to sigh just as hard as I could. "If she was," I growled, "she hasn't said so, and it's none of her business, so shut up and kiss me."

"Impatient this afternoon?"

"First you say you don't want to talk about her, then you keep asking questions. Woman, you are infuriating sometimes."

"Keeps you guessing."

"Fine, keep me guessing, just don't leave my lips itching."

"Says the king of leave them guessing."

I knew what she meant, but I wasn't going to take the opening, not on Christmas. Sometimes a kiss is just a kiss, but sometimes it's a good way to distract a woman.

"Awfully early." Dad looked over the top of his newspaper when I came into the living room. "Did you take Lydia home already?"

"She has to work in the morning," I told him.

Paul, stretched out on the floor in front of the television, lifted his head and laughed. "You're a disgrace, Kevin."

"Maybe I am," I grunted, tossing my jacket aside with a shrug, "but it's none of your business."

Besides, once Lydia knew, she might not want to take it that far. As long as I didn't tell her, I could at least keep the illusion that life was normal. I could feel almost human.

Almost.

~

Kevin's Journal
January 1, 2002

I feel like such a freak. I don't even know whether to feel like a guilty freak or just an ordinary freak. I know Paul is joking about me being the family disgrace (well, most of the time I think he's just joking) but there's that *question* behind every joke. What's a supposedly normal adult male doing with a woman like Lydia and *not* trying to take her to bed?

I never said I didn't want to. I just don't think it would be fair right now.

Cripes, I'm not sure it's ever going to be fair.

And I'm still not totally sure what the family thinks about me bowing out of the seminary and coming home. They're obviously not buying the line about realizing I didn't have a true vocation. I mean, it is true, in a way. I think I would have been happy as a priest and I would have been damn good at it. But real life has a way of kicking you in the nuts and making you change your mind. God obviously didn't want me there. Why should I stay where I'm not wanted?

Eileen thinks I came home out of some sense of destiny, because God finally had it with me and wanted me to find my true purpose, and that purpose being Lydia. Maybe so, but what a fucked up way to get back to her.

And if she is the reason I'm here now, what do I do when she finds out the truth and is so disgusted that she wants nothing to do with me?

What then?

7

Paul

"I've got to get going."

I waited, hoping for at least a half-hearted plea to stay. Slipping out from the warm bed and going out into the cold January morning, long before sunrise, was not my idea of fun.

I wasn't disappointed. But guilt, the kind of guilt I never understood until I realized that promises made to young children had to be kept no matter what, forced me to steal just a few kisses and get up.

"Nicole will be up in a little while," I said. "If I'm not there she'll wake the whole house up."

"You know this from experience?" Monica's sleepy voice drifted out from under the blankets.

I came back to the side of the bed, laughing under my breath. "Maybe."

She tossed a pillow at me.

"I've fallen asleep in the office a few times," I said carefully, sitting on the edge of the mattress. "Nicole bounces from room to room looking for me before she goes downstairs."

"I miss her," Monica whispered, struggling to sit up against the pillows and still keep blankets wrapped around her. "I even miss all the whining."

"Dad cured her of the whining real fast."

"I've been such a lousy mother…"

"Stop that." I pulled the t-shirt over my head and then stretched out on top of the satin comforter. Hair wild from sleep, eyes tired but dancing, she looked better to me than she had the entire time we'd been married. "You're a damn good mother. You always have been."

"Good mothers don't let their babies go—"

"They do when it's necessary."

"—and they don't go weeks without seeing them."

"Monica." I tried to think of an argument for that but couldn't. Her reluctance to spend time with our daughter was the one thing that pissed me off all along, and she knew it.

"Are you sure about this, Paul? Do you really think we can just pick up the pieces?"

"I don't see why not."

She forgot about the chilly air and tossed the blankets aside to pull me into a tight hug. "How can we?" she cried. "You'll never be able to trust me again."

"We have to learn to trust each other." I pulled back, keeping my hands firmly on her arms and stared straight into her eyes. When she squirmed and tried to look away, I took her chin and forced her to look at me. "Monica, you hurt me. I hurt you. We have to get past it."

"Paul."

"Jesus Christ, you're my wife. Maybe I didn't know what that meant when we got married, but I'm not about to give up on it, not now. You have no idea how much I missed you. I was more miserable without you than I was with you."

Unable to look at me anymore, she squeezed her eyes shut, trying not to cry. "I swear, it won't happen again."

"You can't promise me that. Come on, look at me."

She took a deep, shivering breath, and opened her eyes.

"Don't ever say flat out you'll never let it happen again, just promise me that I'll be the first one you come to when you feel that vulnerable. You can talk to me, I swear. I won't turn you away or make fun of you—and you know I'd never hit you."

Unlike some of the other men in her life. Her father used her as a punching bag from the time she was in kindergarten until she defiantly packed her bags and left home to marry me. The strength she found to walk out and claim her life as her own waned after Nicole was born, and was gone by the time our daughter was two.

Monica was sure that at some point I'd leave. Instead of waiting for me to get fed up and walk out the door, she began to push, first by staying out late with her friends, then by staying out drinking, and finally by sleeping with the first guy to make an offer.

She tried to hide it, but so sloppily she was sure to get caught.

It didn't occur to me until Kevin pointed it out—she wanted to get caught. She wanted to give me a reason to leave.

The first time, I stayed.

The second time, I used her infidelities as an excuse for my own.

The last time, I left. I packed up our daughter and took her to the only other home I'd ever known, hoping that my parents were willing to let us stay for a while, and that I'd never have to admit to them that they were right; we'd both been far too young to plunge heart first into marriage.

My father welcomed us with hugs and kisses; my mother with tears. The first night there Nicole slept in the bed in my old room and I slept on the floor, wanting to be close by. The next night she had her own room, completely furnished with little girl decorations and toys; while I was at work my sister watched Nicole and my parents went shopping.

They saw what I didn't; that we were going to be there for a long time, that I needed time to nurse the hurt, and Monica and I both needed time to grow up.

"You *will* come to terms with it," Dad told me with complete certainty. "Then at some point you'll figure out whether or not you want to put it behind you and get on with your own life, or if you want to forgive her and get on with your lives together."

Staying together for Nicole's sake wasn't an option; we were her only examples of married love, and the lesson she was learning was that it was all right to scream at each other. It was all right to walk away and to slam doors. All right to ignore a genuine plea to just listen.

When the anger faded and I was missing Monica more than I hated her, it occurred to me that trying to work it out might be in Nicole's best interests. She needed to know that her parents weren't going to give up on each other so easily. She needed to know I loved her mother, that it was all right for her to still love her mother.

"I'll tell you what," I told her, sitting up. "I'll cut back on the number of nights that I work. I'll hire an assistant. Maybe my dad would even take up some of the slack."

She brightened considerably. "Are you sure?"

"Dad would rather work a few hours than see us go completely down the tubes."

"Paul, since you left…" she hesitated, not sure she should

say what was running through her mind. "I swear, I've been alone."

"I believe you."

"And I'm sorry. I know I've said it before."

Without any warning, she began to cry uncontrollably, clutching at me as if I were the last life preserver on a sinking boat. She snared my shirt between her fingers, buried her face against my chest, and cried harder than I had ever seen her cry before.

I held her close and waited, rocking gently like I did when Nicole woke up screaming from a nightmare, certain that there was nothing else I could do.

When I thought she was done crying, I sighed and said, "Later this month we should go away and take the honeymoon we never really had. Just you and me, someplace fun … no kid and no work to hang over us. We can stick Nicole with my parents."

"Parents!" She sat up sharply. "Nicole! Paul, you've got to go. She'll be waiting for you."

"Me and my Coco Puffs."

A fresh start, I thought on my way out the door. We should all be so lucky as to be able to start over.

Kevin

"Heh. Look what the cat dragged in." I was sprawled out on the sofa with the newspaper, propped up on a pillow, keeping an eye out for Dad. He was starting to feel possessive about the morning paper, grumbling that in his old age he deserved to get to it first. "Rough night?"

Paul pushed my feet off the end of the sofa and dropped, setting his head wearily against the back cushion. "I wouldn't say rough," he sighed.

"You smell like a whorehouse."

He turned and stared at me through tired, half-open eyes. "What would a perennial cherry like you know what a whorehouse smells like?"

"Caught a whiff of Dad once when he was running from Mom after being locked up with her for a couple hours. Come on, you know what I mean. You reek sex."

"And you reek frustration. Why are you up so bloody early?"

"Up late," I corrected. "I gave up trying to sleep a couple hours ago. Too many things on my mind."

"And these things, measurements on the astronomical scale?"

"Some," I admitted. "But I think about more than just that."

"No doubt. Can I offer you some unsolicited advice before I drop into bed?"

I nodded.

"Don't wait too long. If Lydia is one of the things you're so worried about, don't wait so long that it's too late. You have your hooks into someone who obviously adores you and you'll hate yourself forever if you let her slip away because of some warped sense of virtue and honor. Whatever is eating you up, talk to her. Get it out in the open and deal with it before you lose her."

"You think she adores me?"

He sighed, and shoved his hands against his thighs to help push himself up. "Squirt, the first time I drove you two on a date I could see it. You both oozed hormones."

"Horniness."

"When you're fourteen, it's the same thing. And the fact that you held onto each other for so long without letting it go too far says a whole lot. Now I'm worried you don't even know what you've got."

I knew.

But in the grand scheme of things, I didn't know which scared me more: telling her the whole truth and having her back away, or telling her and having her reach out to hold me even tighter.

Honestly, I had a gut feeling Lydia could make my mom look like a rank amateur. I wasn't sure I had the endurance.

Chip

"Eight perfectly good bedrooms in this house, and he sleeps on the sofa," I grumbled, carefully prying the newspaper out of Kevin's hands. "Explain it to me, Terry. These boys have always slept everywhere except where they're supposed to."

I followed her to the dining room, where I spread the paper out on the table.

"I would guess they take after their father. But it's not fair to lump Kevin in with that."

"Not yet, anyway."

Terry leaned over and kissed me, setting a cup of coffee on the table for me. "Paul wandered in about an hour ago."

"Great. Nicole will be waking him up in about fifteen minutes, which means in twenty we'll have a whiny little brat and a grumpy son of a bitch stomping down the stairs."

"Chip…"

"All right. Nicole doesn't whine and you're not a bitch."

She pushed the paper out of the way and dropped onto my lap. "For a doting Grandpa you sure do whine an awful lot."

"I have my reasons."

"Ah, and the main one being—?"

"They're going to move out, Terry. It's just a matter of time before Paul comes in here and announces he's going home. And when he goes, he takes Nicole with him."

"We'll get reasonable visitation, I'm sure."

"And Kevin will probably move out within a year."

"That's a good thing, Irish."

"It'll be awfully damned quiet around here."

"You're just afraid to be left alone with me for too long."

I tightened my arms around her. "Yes, woman, you terrify me. I need the kids here to protect me."

"Poor baby." She placed a kiss on my forehead. "I promise, I'll be good to you."

"That's what I'm afraid of!"

I was -this- close to getting another kiss when Nicole bounded in and without so much as a good morning said, "Daddy is a big grouch!"

Grandchildren are not conducive to cuddling, no matter how wonderful they are.

"Grandpa?" Nicole crawled up onto her knees on a chair and peered at me curiously. "Did you know that when you have hairs all over your face you look like Uncle Kevin? You're cuter, though."

Still, I already missed her.

8

Kevin

Sooner or later the question was bound to come up. I was surprised my parents waited as long as they did; I'd expected it a good four or five months earlier. As summer faded and Eileen's wedding approached, the surer I became that Dad would call me on the carpet.

He believes in waiting. The biggest punishments we faced growing up were always given after we'd been sent to our rooms for long periods of time while he "mulled it over." I think he'd been mulling this one over since August.

He cornered me in the garage while we finished cleaning it out; I was suckered in there under the pretense that he needed help hauling boxes into the attic and my input in weeding out what was trash and what were keepable memories. We kept up with mostly meaningless chatter until he finally asked.

What Was I Planning To Do?

"The way I see it," he said, "you have a couple of obvious choices. You could go back to school or get a job."

I waited for The Lecture.

I had hoped than when it came, I'd have a few answers for him.

"I never wanted to rush you, Kevin, but you've been home for over six months and still don't seem any closer to finding something."

Just what the hell was it I was supposed to do? I had no skills. I'd have been spinning my wheels in school, not knowing what I wanted to study; all I'd be doing there is sucking up someone else's air and taking up someone else's space.

"If you want to try school, we'll understand if you take your time with it," he went on. "And even if you choose to work, this is your home, you won't be kicked out. Ever."

So I had a home, and wasn't about to be launched out the front door onto my ass, a suitcase flying through the air behind me.

He carefully refrained from mentioning my trust fund. We both knew I could float on that for the rest of my life; I only had to work because it would be the Right Thing To Do. Find a career, a work ethic.

"Maybe," Dad suggested, "you could talk it over with your girlfriend."

Now there's a new idea; job prospects were the least of the things I needed to talk to her about.

Nick settled into law school. Katie and Spider were both teaching. Paul ran Dad's restaurant so well that Dad was able to focus on his investment properties. Eileen was in school, a semester away from earning a degree in music education.

I took the only real commitment I'd ever made, and ran like hell from it.

"I'm sorry I'm such a disappointment," I told him, shoving a box into the corner and heading for the door. "I didn't mean to be."

Chip

I tried to catch up to Kevin, but found myself standing

in front of the locked bathroom door, listening to water rush through the pipes.

A damned amphibian. If he wasn't in the shower he was in the pool or lying in the bathtub with his head under water.

You got the wrong message, son.

"I blew it," I told Terry later, while she was cooking dinner and I was setting the table. "I tried to broach the subject of future plans and he took it to mean I want him to find something to do right now."

"Don't you?"

"Jesus, Ter, I only want him to start thinking about living beyond today. I didn't mean…" I left the silverware in a pile and went into the kitchen, leaning against the counter next to her. "Kevin thinks we're disappointed in him."

"No. Chip, you told him that's not true, didn't you?"

"I didn't have a chance. He tore out of the garage before I could get another word out and by the time I caught up he'd locked himself in the bathroom."

She set the spatula down and gave me a hug. "Talk to him again at dinner. We've got to make him understand that the only thing we want is for him to consider all the possibilities, since he's obviously not going back to the seminary."

"Does that bother you at all?"

"Me?" She pulled away, shaking her head. "No. I think he'll be happier, eventually. Does it bother you?"

"No," I said. "But when he said he was becoming a priest, for sure, we acted like we'd gotten this incredible gift. Like typical Catholic parents from the fifties—one of our boys had a vocation. Either God favored us, or we just did something terribly right."

"And you think how we reacted makes him believe that we would consider him changing his mind to be disappointing."

"I don't know what else to think."

"Chip, I was proud of him, but I'm glad he realized it wasn't the right thing before it was too late. I'll be proud of him no matter what he chooses to do."

"I just wish we hadn't made such a big deal out of it when he said he was going into the seminary."

I wanted to take it back; I wanted to tell the seventeen year old who stood there in the living room by the fireplace, his hands stuffed into his pockets, that he needed to rethink his decision. To wait a year, make sure that what he felt was a need to serve God and not a way to appease his conscience. I wanted to go back and be the father who casually casts an uncertain glance, that wary eye that tells his kids they're idiots, and they don't have a clue about life or what they want from it. Just for that moment.

Kevin wanted to be a priest; I was sure of that then.

Terry turned off the burner and moved the skillet to the back of the stove. "You are worrying far too much. Kevin had adjustments to make when he came home, because he'd never thought about what he'd do if he couldn't be a priest. It's going to take him some time to figure it out."

"What if he can't, Terry? What then?"

"Then he'll marry Lydia, have a bunch of kids, and he'll be a stay at home dad. And that's not such a bad thing."

"It was a bad thing when I tried it."

"Only" – she crept up on her toes to kiss me – "because you were always underfoot, and it was really annoying."

"I love you, too."

"Quit worrying so much, Chip. Just apologize to him, and then let it go."

~

Dear Kevin,

I think I'm in trouble. Real trouble this time, not like all the other times I've screamed for help when I really didn't need it. Remember my lieutenant? Well, I know you do, you lectured me enough about him. He's on my father's staff of all things. He's got a wife and two kids (and I swear, I didn't know anything about them). She found out, don't ask me how, and she's out for blood.

And my father knows. God, Kevin, this doesn't look good for him at all. The lieutenant is being brought up on adultery charges and everyone knows it was with me. People used to look at my dad and say, shit, Colonel Forrester, keep out of his way. Now it's like, oh yeah, that little slut's old man. He's losing respect at work because I was so stupid.

Why didn't I listen to you?

I don't even like this guy. He's cute and he's good in bed, but that's about it. He's no one I want to stick around for.

He's already talking about when he's kicked out (which is inevitable) and when he gets his divorce (which promises to be messy). I don't want to be here to pick up the pieces for him.

He's just as guilty as I am, right?

You know what bugs me more than anything? All the shit about Katie this and Katie that. I know Nicky is your brother, but I'm tired of hearing about how fucking perfect those two are. Nick and law school, Katie teaching those moronic five year olds and those pretty little picture she paints when she's bored.

She's bored a lot, isn't she?

You know, Christmas and New Years were a dud for me out here. All the snow and ice is depressing as hell. Does anyone even give a shit about it anymore? I let them drag me to church on Christmas Eve to listen to some fat bastard who wouldn't know his balls from belly button lint stand up there and preach about family love and all that crap, and he doesn't know a damn thing about the realities of it. He's written himself some kind of fantasy world with the tall, handsome man and his gorgeous wife and their 2.3 perfect babies. He'd drop dead if he ever had to face the real thing.

It's no wonder you were tempted to become a priest. That's got to be easier than facing the same person day after day and listening to a houseful of screaming brats.

How in hell did your mom survive four of you?

Oh, I talk a lot about how bad it is but I know I'll wind up doing it. Amazing what true love will talk you into. I think I'm even willing to put up with baby snot and food fights for the right guy.

Believe me, he's not here in Washington.

Are you ever going to tell me what you're up to? Somehow your letters always manage to evade telling much about yourself. Anything important, anyway. You know, I wasn't surprised you left the seminary. It must have been awfully dreary, all those old men pounding the Bible into your head day and night.

Got to have some fun, right?

I bounced another job. It was dull, dull, dull. Nothing but these stuffed shirts coming in through the slush and dirt to hassle me with too many drink orders and food demands that are only going to clog up their already sludge filled arteries. You wonder why the government works so lousy? It's because these jokers take three hour lunches, slugging down Jack Daniels like it was water, groping the little airheads they drag along with them.

But, I don't think they're getting laid. Too dried up. This place sucks it right out of you. The younger airmen, the ones who haven't been here too long, they do all right, but climb into bed with anyone who's been in government more than a couple years and it's like trying to raise a toothpick stuck in glue.

Anyway, I chucked that job and got another working in the file room of an insurance agency. I'm tired of running into the military jockeys. I'm tired of men, period. I would like nothing more than to find a good friend.

You know what I mean? Someone who won't care if I kick off my shoes but leave my clothes on. I'm tired of screwing around and not enjoying it.

I miss you, Kevin. I know you could be that friend if we didn't have 3,000 miles between us.

Love, Debby

~

The rain beating down on the windshield suited my mood perfectly. Rain drops splattered to the beat pounding inside my head, running in thin rivulets around and under the wipers, beading on the hood of the car. Damp and dark and cold.

Of course it rained. I'd washed and waxed the car, cleaned out the garage, my parents thought I was a bum, and I was beginning to agree. Rain was inevitable.

So was the conversation I was contemplating.

I drove my father's blue Mercedes convertible into the parking lot – my own car locked up in the garage with a dead alternator – and cut off the engine. I searched out her window on the face of the building, and stared at it, willing the light inside to flicker off. Hoping for a reason to turn around and go home.

I stood in the rain until my sweatshirt was soaked through, trying to work up the nerve to knock on her door. I could feel water between my toes, my wet jeans sticking to my legs. I stood there in front of her door, my hand raised to knock, waiting for something.

What that something was, who knows. When I finally knocked, it was so quiet I was sure she wouldn't hear.

Hoped she wouldn't hear.

A moment later the door was open, and she was smiling.

"I didn't want to leave the seminary," I said, barely above a whisper. "Not really."

Her smile faded as easily as it had come; she reached for my hand and pulled me in. "God, you've got to be freezing." She motioned for me to wait, then ran up the loft stairs and came back a minute later with a blanket, and wrapped it around me.

My small amount of courage was rapidly waning.

"All right," she said, pointing me towards her sofa. "You didn't want to leave? Did they ask you to?"

Turn around, run out the door, go home...

"No." I pulled the blanket around me tighter, wishing she would look anywhere but at me. "I didn't tell anyone I was leaving. I just packed a few things and left. After I got home I sent a message that I wasn't coming back, but I never gave them a reason."

"No one ever asked?"

"The only one who ever came straight out and asked," I said, "was you."

I could feel her fingers on the back of my neck, brushing away water that dripped from the ends of my hair. Very soft. Waiting.

"I was talking to Paul earlier. He made the point that I needed to tell you why I came home before I let it eat me up so much that I drive you away. The thing is, I'm afraid that if I tell you, you'll never look at me the same way."

Gently, I heard, "Why wouldn't I?"

I shrugged, still not able to make myself look at her. I looked at my feet, my wet shoelaces slimy and dirty, dripping onto her carpet. My white socks were a murky gray, and my legs were beginning to itch from the denim stuck to them.

"Have you ever thought of me as weak?" I asked.

"Never. Wonderfully sensitive, but never weak."

"Sensitive in what way? Like I was effeminate or something?"

"In that you're considerate of other people, Kevin. What would ever make you think of yourself as weak?"

Did she want the whole list, or just the main reason?

"I'm getting your sofa wet," I mumbled, and started to get up.

She clamped her hand on my shoulder. "It'll dry."

Every word I rehearsed on the way over, every coherent thought I'd had was stuck somewhere on the back on my mind's tongue. "I'm not sure I can do this now. I thought I could and I need to tell you, but I don't know if I can."

"All right." She kissed me on the cheek, and then the sofa sank with the weight of her pushing off of it. "Wait here a minute."

She disappeared into the kitchen, and I closed my eyes, willing my heart to stop beating so hard that it felt like it was about to rip through my chest. I could hear her walking back and forth, noises in the kitchen, and then the soft hiss of a lighter being flicked on.

"Okay," she finally said. "Come on."

I opened my eyes; the apartment was dark, except for three candles lit under the loft. She had piled pillows and blankets on the floor, and had a thick comforter to wrap around me.

"Just take your shoes and socks off," she said when I followed her in there. "Your shirt too. And your jeans, unless that would make you too uncomfortable, but I can toss your clothes in the dryer. I swear, I won't look."

I suspected she would, but she went back into the kitchen, and I stripped down to my underwear; after a few moments of heavy consideration, I tossed those into the pile of wet clothes and hid under the comforter.

Getting her into bed was the last thing on my mind.

After my clothes were in the dryer, she came back with two mugs of hot chocolate, and settled beside me on the floor, snuggled up against pillows, but she never made a move to get under the comforter with me.

"You can talk when you feel like it," she said.

"I'll never feel like it, Lydia. But I have a feeling that if I don't tell you, it'll just hang over us until I either explode or you get fed up and walk away."

"I won't walk away. You're entitled to your secrets, Kevin. I may have a few of my own, you know."

I slid down into the pillows, pulling the comforter up to my shoulders, my feet sticking out the other end. "Your secrets are probably fun ones," I speculated. "But I really don't want to hear about Gopher right now."

"Topher."

"Whatever."

"I might surprise you. Remember the senior class trip to Disneyland?"

"Vaguely."

"Did you hear any rumors about the group who got kicked out and wound up waiting in the security office until their parents could drive down and get them?"

"That was you?"

"That was me," she sighed. "A few of us got caught with beer."

"I heard it was grass. And some nudity thrown in for good measure."

"Well, that too."

"You're kidding me. You were one of the Topless Six?"

"I wasn't topless," she said. "But I was stoned out of my little mind and egged on the couple of people who decided to strip on It's A Small World."

"Topher was stoned? Wasn't he like the perfect, healthy little jock?"

"No, he wasn't stoned. And that was probably the first step in us breaking up. He was so disappointed in me. You'd be surprised how much alike you two were back then."

"But you smoked grass."

"Some, once in a while," she admitted. "And I won't lie, I liked it. I don't see the difference between an occasional joint and an occasional drink. I have my own secrets. Does that make you want to turn and run from me?"

"No, but that's gonna be funny as hell when I don't still feel like holding my own royal pity party. I don't think there's anything funny in what happened to me, Lydia. The only good thing to come out of it is that I'm here with you now and I wouldn't trade this for anything."

"That's enough for me, you know. That you're here with me."

"But you want to know why."

"I'm curious."

"You're also extremely patient."

"I am." She set her mug aside and snuggled next to me, setting her head on my shoulder. "Don't even look at me, Kevin. Just talk into the dark."

"Bad things can happen in the dark," I whispered.

She pressed a kiss into my neck, but didn't say anything.

I groped for where to begin, or if the beginning even mattered.

One long gush, I decided. Just spit it out right there and see if she flinches, or if she doesn't think twice about cleaning it up.

Technically, I wasn't in the seminary. Without a bachelor's degree in hand, I was a "pre-theological studies" student—as were most of the men in the dorm—and would have to spend three or four years getting through that before becoming an official seminarian. Like Pinocchio, I had to wait to become a Real Boy. A Real Seminary Student.

"A good many of you," we were told on the first day as we sat hunched over in cold metal chairs in the cafeteria, waiting to be pointed in the direction of where we'd be sleeping for the next year, "won't stay long enough to enter the seminary. Some of you will decide early on that you don't honestly have a true vocation, and some of you will come to realize that there are other equally compelling lives to be led."

The room swelled with a disbelieving hum; none of us thought we'd leave without having said that first homily.

The speaker paused, smiled knowingly, and went on. "Even if you don't stay, the time spent here will make you a better Catholic, and a better man."

We could believe that. But none of us were willing to allow for the idea that we might not be there for the reasons we thought, or that we'd turn around at some point and walk away.

The speaker turned out to be our resident advisor; after speaking to a general mass of nervous students, he marched us along the path that wound around the cafeteria and headed for the dormitories, up two flights of stairs, and pointed us – fifteen in our group – towards a common room. We dropped into comfortable chairs and surveyed the amenities: a TV, ping pong table, vending machines, and old, worn sofas and chairs that were just floppy enough to be comfortable.

"I know none of you believe that you won't still be here in a year or two," he said, easing into one of the overstuffed armchairs, "but statistically only two or three of you will go into the priesthood."

"But we'll be better men," someone snickered.

He nodded. "You will be. You'll have a better understanding of your religion, and of human nature."

"Or else," another muttered.

"There's no 'or else.' The horror stories you may have heard from uncles who survived seminaries in the past won't come to life here. We believe in fostering faith, not competitiveness. You're not going to have some ancient priest following you around, making horrific threats against your soul or your career. One of the things you'll be encouraged to do is help each other. There's no political posturing at Saint John's. You're here to learn, period."

And to grow and develop and all the other clichés that went along with the thought. When the RA left, having dropped a clipboard with room assignments onto the coffee table, no one moved. We looked at each other, seeing one another for the first time, some surely taken aback by the sheer diversity in the room.

I was close to being the youngest; still weeks away from turning eighteen, I was there by the grace of strong recommendations and a personal friendship between our parish pastor and the dean. The oldest was at least fifty years old, coming to the priesthood after the death of his wife of twenty five years.

He reached for the clipboard, and looking at me, chuckled, "Just for the irony, you and I will wind up as roommates."

We lucked out; no one was made to suffer having a roommate. There were fifteen of us, and seventeen rooms on the floor. We could, it was declared with a laugh, survive sharing the common bathroom at the end of the hall. Especially those of us who had ever had to share one with a sister.

After putting bags in our respective rooms, most of us wandered back out to the common room, plopping back down into the chairs we'd occupied before. Introductions seemed were finally made, and started with the eldest.

"Thomas Stagger," he said. "I'm old enough to be father to some of you, and uncle to the rest. And as trite as it sounds, I agree with our esteemed resident advisor—we need to foster faith here, not compete against each other. I know I don't intend to be someone who leaves after a year or two … if we help each other, maybe we can all make it."

It was a lofty ideal that everyone agreed with. As a group, we became close, spending most of our free time together studying or praying, and occasionally wandering off campus in one giant Seminary Boy mass. It was a running joke in the places we frequented: lock up your daughters for the next eight years, these boys are horny as hell and looking for a way out.

There were a few of the guys who stayed on the fringe and in any other place would have been outsiders, but they were dragged along most of the time. No cliques, Thomas declared. You can be shy as hell, but at least make the effort.

So we all made the effort. We got through the first two years unscathed, and intact. Our summer breaks were spent pounding nails for Habitat For Humanity, and when we returned we expected life to go on as we knew it—the same dorm rooms, the same common room, and the same level of privacy.

No one could have predicted that the heating and air conditioning would blow out on the first floor of the building, and that at the start of our third year we would wind up with ten first year students being dropped onto our floor.

Ten of our group would wind up with roommates.

I lucked out and wasn't one of them.

We stood in the back of the common room and listened as Greg, the RA, gave his speech, nearly word for word, to the newbies; our intention was to repeat to them what we had decided two years before: leave no one behind.

As Greg spoke, most of us noticed the scrawny, greasy haired teenager who would not sit down; he was a rail thin, twitchy kid who fidgeted mindlessly, rolling rosary beads between his fingers as he shuffled his feet back and forth.

"He's just nervous," Thomas whispered. "Probably threw up in the parking lot. He'll be all right once he gets to know a few people."

The twitchy kid's name was Jake Catero. He was an annoyingly hyper person, one of those people you put up with because you have to, and because it's polite. He was a font of nonstop chatter, endless mumblings under his breath, and hygiene that was questionable at best and intolerable at its worst.

"The talking never stops," his first roommate complained. "Not even when he's asleep."

Thomas volunteered to be Jake's next roommate. "I raised a couple of hyper boys," he reasoned, "and they're almost normal now."

Thomas lasted two weeks before asking the RA to reassign either Jake or himself to another room.

"He's not hyper. He's demented." Thomas left it at that, and Jake was moved to another room.

And then another.

And yet another.

And then mine.

Jake Catero's particular brand of neurosis had him standing in the middle of the room, usually in his underwear, for hours on end. Sometimes he would pray the rosary, other times he would simply rock back and forth on his feet, whispering to himself. I could talk to him yet never know if he was ignoring me, didn't hear me past the voices in his head, or what.

On rare occasions he would sit in the middle of the floor instead, legs crossed, as he rocked to the rhythm only he could hear, and he would stay there all night long.

It was strange, and it was distracting, but it wasn't anything I couldn't live with. Most of my time outside of class was spent studying or hanging out in the common room where others were a reasonable buffer between us, and I just learned to sleep with his constant night time chatter.

Partway through the year I got the bright idea that I might be able to cut through his fog if I made the effort to understand him. If he was standing there praying the rosary, I sat on the edge of my bed and prayed with him. If he was on the floor I sat there with him, and joined in on whatever prayer he seemed to be whispering, until my legs went numb or I could no longer stay awake.

After a while the marathon praying of the rosary stopped, and he spent more nights in his bed then he did on the floor.

Somewhere along the line he decided I was his best friend. It was like having a parasite—I couldn't go anywhere without him tagging along. If we went out for pizza, he was right there, scrambling to get the chair next to mine. If I was in the chapel for prayer, most of the time I'd open my eyes and find him either next to me or behind me.

I drew the line at having his company in the common bathroom; I at least wanted to shower without an audience, and had to enlist the cooperation of Thomas and several others to manage it.

"You know what's really funny?" Thomas chuckled as I came out of the bathroom, fully dressed instead of wrapped in a towel as I normally would have. "That little shit will be one of the ones who hangs on until ordination."

"And I'll be his freaking roommate until the end, with my luck."

"Ask Greg to give Jake his own room. Hell, if you think you can stand rooming with an old man, you can move into mine."

It was tempting. "The year is more than half over," I told Thomas. "If he's still latched onto me like a leech at the end of the year, I'll ask Greg to make sure I don't get stuck with him next year."

"He's decided he's one of the guys now, Kevin. As much as I hate to admit it, I can't stand him and neither can anyone else, and as long as you tolerate him, he's going to insinuate himself into everything we do."

"I know."

"I'm all for the fostering faith line Greg gives everyone, but we all have our limits."

Jake was pushing the envelope, for sure. His ramblings now included his joy over having friends, and his discovery of salvation in having a true best friend. He stuffed his musings right in between a series of Hail Mary and Our Father, and while everyone was used to his oddities, it took great restraint to not laugh at him.

His night time ramblings, while fewer than they had been, had begun to include me, his inept efforts at conversation.

"I'd never make it through this without you."

"Yes, you would."

"No, I wouldn't."

"Everyone can get through it if they're supposed to, Jake."

"Not me. I'm lucky you're here."

Jake rejoiced in his luck; I was beginning to think it was a cosmic joke, retribution for all the wrong things I'd ever done. I tolerated him right up until the end of the year, a week before most of us would pack up and head to a Habitat For Humanity site in Texas. I tolerated him, knowing that I was close to a respite, and knowing that I could easily get Greg to move Jake elsewhere for his second year.

I saw the light at the end of the tunnel, and couldn't wait to bask in the warmth of it.

I was beginning to feel pretty good about it; I would never be an ace carpenter, but I liked the work we'd chosen for our summer community contribution, and this year it would be peaceful and quiet.

The first year students were working in county homeless shelters.

If I could get by one more week with Jake, I'd be free.

I was so caught up in anticipating that moment when I could walk out with my bag packed that I didn't notice every person in the common room turn towards me when I returned from jogging. Jake was in his usual spot near the corner, rosary beads in hand, but he was smiling brightly, something he rarely did.

Thomas cleared his throat. “Before you wander off, Kevin … Jake just had some news for us you’ll be interested in.”

I stopped in mid-stride. A shower could wait.

“He’s not working the county shelters this summer.”

My stomach began to twist.

“He’s going with us, to Texas.”

“No fucking way.”

Jake bounced in place, up and down on his toes. “Yep, I’m going with you! That’ll be more fun than serving soup all day.”

“The idea isn’t to have fun,” Thomas pointed out. “The idea is to serve.”

“You’re not going with us,” I said flatly.

“Greg said I could.”

“Yeah, well, Greg should have asked the rest of us what we thought about it. Go with your own class, Jake.”

He shook his head. “But Greg said—”

I finally exploded. “I don’t *care* what Greg said. No one wants you to tag along, Jake. We’ve had enough of you as it is, give us a fucking break! Goddamn, give *me* a fucking break!”

“But…”

“But nothing. You’re a little freak, Jake. A weird little *freak* who never shuts up and *pretends* to pray so that you look good, only God doesn’t give a shit. Shut the fuck up for just ten goddamned minutes. Give God a break, give me a break, just *shut up* already!”

Jake's face suddenly went blank, he went rigid, and began rocking even harder. Everyone was staring, and no one knew what to do.

"Fuck," was about the best comment I could come up with.

"Can hardly blame you," Thomas whispered, his face turned away from Jake. "Most of us would have blown up months ago."

"A lot of good it did."

"Feel better?"

I shook my head. "Not in the least. What the hell do I do now?"

"Apologize. He wants to be one of the guys, well he has to learn to suck it up and take it when someone else gets pissed. Treat him like one of the guys, and apologize the same way you would if you'd blown up at one of us."

The consensus seemed to be that an apology would be best completed with a huge bottle of vodka and a couple of six packs of soda. We got Jake to sit down, and when there was a little bit of light in his eyes, I apologized. It took an hour and a dozen more apologies to get him to relax enough to accept the drink I offered; between us we polished off the entire bottle.

I don't remember why we decided to go outside, or whose idea it was. We wandered down the path that wound around behind the cafeteria, the jogging trailing that faded from smooth pavement to gravel near a small pond. We talked about salvation; he grumbled about needing it, I pontificated that he'd never find it in anyone else.

We stumbled down the wood and gravel stairs that spilled from the side of the path down to a prayer garden carved neatly next to the pond's edge. We sat there, quiet, until the last of the vodka was gone; I don't remember what happened after that, not until I woke up.

I woke, groggy, to the sharp pain of my hands tied over my head, bound to the cement bench with strips of cut sweatsocks, my mouth filled with the crumpled end of a t-shirt; my legs were tied at the knees with thick strips of torn denim and fleece, drawn so sharply to my chest that I could barely draw a breath in through my nose. In the bath of dim moonlight I could see, in violent flashes of bared teeth and clenched fists, the other side of the otherwise unassuming Jake Catero.

The smell of alcohol was stuck in the air; Jake's breath came out in rapid pulses of stale vodka, his nostrils flares and eyes struck wide in anger, as he tore into me so many times that I lost count, tore into me while I struggled to get my arms free, to spit out the t-shirt I was choking on. I struggled until he shuddered, his face contorted in grim satisfaction, my entire body engulfed in searing pain.

I struggled until I couldn't feel my hands; hot tears rolled from my eyes, pooling in my ears. My jaw ached from trying to push the t-shirt out with my tongue, but at some point, long after Jake had passed out, I gave up, and started praying that I would die right there.

I wanted to die.

"Kevin. My God." She was sitting up, crying, her fingers wound through mine tightly, possessively.

"I either passed out myself, or fell asleep, I'm not sure which. When I woke up again it was still dark, but he had cut me loose from the bench. There was blood all over … I used the strips of denim and what was left of his sweatshirt to clean myself off in the pond, and kicked the dirt around to cover the blood.

"I shoved everything deep into a trashcan outside the cafeteria and headed back for the dorm. I wasn't thinking. I was just numb and headed that way. Jake wasn't there. I looked around the room and had this overwhelming feeling that I shouldn't be there, so I threw a few things into a bag and left."

"And you never told anyone?"

"No. I didn't think anyone would believe me."

"Kevin, why?"

"Lydia, look at me. I'm six five and over two hundred pounds. I've got a third degree black belt. Jake was this little stick figure of a kid, if you blew on him too hard he'd break in two. No one was going to believe it."

"You couldn't have stopped him—"

"I never should have gotten him drunk. Son of a bitch, I never should have ripped him apart in front of everyone!"

Those green eyes flashed, sudden fury aimed right at me. "Don't you dare blame yourself!"

"Then who do I blame?"

"You blame *him*, that's who you blame." She was crying hard, but did nothing to wipe the tears away. "How could anyone do this to you? Why you?"

"I humiliated him."

"That's no excuse for raping someone! Goddammit, you were in a seminary!"

"I wasn't…"

"There's nothing else to call it, Kevin. He raped you."

Nothing else to call it. I never wanted to call it anything. I just wanted to forget.

She fell asleep on the floor next to me, one hand clenching the corner of the comforter and the other on my shoulder. When I was sure she was deep enough asleep that I could move without waking her, I slipped out from under the blankets and got my clothes out of the dryer, dressing in the dark.

So she knew.

I wanted to swallow it whole, pretend it never happened. I wanted to be numb again.

After closing the front door as quietly as I could, I walked past Spider and Eileen's apartment, got into my dad's car, and headed for the Charybdis. It would be quiet there, only a few persistent drinkers taking up space at the bar. Paul would have left, Will would either be on his way out or distracted by cleaning up. I could grab a bottle from behind the counter, hide in the office, and drink it all away.

Chip

"Will found him in the office," Paul grunted, dragging a barely cooperative Kevin through the front door. "He was sprawled out on the sofa cuddling an empty bottle of vodka."

I grabbed Kevin's arm and helped Paul pull him into a standing position, holding tight to keep him from toppling over. "What the hell?"

"He is totally soused, Dad," Paul laughed. "The entire drive home he sat with his head hanging out the window, howling and giggling his ass off."

I was not amused. "He drank the entire bottle?"

"Probably not. He grabbed something from behind the bar. I doubt any of them were full."

Nothing I could say to Kevin was going to get through. "Get him upstairs and into bed," I told Paul. "He can deal with it himself in the morning"

"Oh, Paulie…." Kevin moaned and struggled to stand on his own. "I don't have the guts to try. Cherry's gonna be hanging on the fricking tree until I die."

I frowned and looked at Paul. "What?"

Paul just laughed and headed his brother up the stairs. "Nothing, Dad. He's just talking out his ass."

Paul

"Know what I hate, Paulie?"

I maneuvered Kevin onto the mussed up queen bed in his room, and was trying to tug his shoes off his feet. "What's that, squirt?"

"Jerking off. It's so goddamned lonely. You start out alone and you do it alone and when you're done you're alone. Lonely, lonely, lonely."

I tossed his shoes onto the floor. "So don't do it alone anymore."

"Always alone," he sighed. "I told her the truth, Paulie. I told her why I came home. All it did was make her cry."

"You want to tell me why?"

"I blew it. Just like I blow everything. Poof! All gone. She'll never want to see me again."

"I doubt that, Kev."

"I am so stupid," he moaned. "So stupid, stupid, stupid…" He slowly drifted off, mumbling under his breath, the liturgy of self-deprecation unfinished, tears dripping from the corners of his eyes.

Kevin

Morning brought light bright enough to cut through the fog, a raging headache, and a sour taste in my mouth that had weight to it. It had that heavy, acrid taste that reminded me of the smell of the boys' locker room after a track meet. A hundred sweaty adolescent hornballs sitting around in jockstraps, boasting of their athletic prowess on the field and the girls they planned on nailing in the back seats of family Buicks all over town.

I started out the day under a cold shower, hoping to shock myself back into total sobriety, then followed that by snapping at Nicole when she crept into my room to see if I was awake. I felt lousy about making her cry, but not enough to chase after her and apologize.

Avoiding the parents seemed to be the best bet for the morning; I could vaguely remember seeing Dad's disappointment when Paul dragged me home and wasn't up for another round of it, coupled with what would surely be his demand for an explanation. I threw on clothes I picked up from the floor, ran a comb through my wet hair, and headed for the door.

"Early plans," I muttered when I passed Mom in the hallway.

I spent part of the day wandering around the mall, ignoring the few help wanted signs that I noticed, letting my pool of self pity fill to the brim. I didn't want to be a clerk or a salesman or a box boy. I didn't know what I wanted.

Except Lydia.

And I doubted she wanted me, not after having time to think about how pathetic I must really be.

I found a bench outside the bookstore and watched the people wandering in and out. Young women with their babies tucked safely into brightly colored strollers, older harried housewives brandishing armloads of paperback books, old men sucking in stale air like a cheap cigar, discreetly folding their magazines under their arms as they slinked away. I watched them all come and go, the same bored look on their faces, the same dull, pretentiously polite smile when they realized they were being watched.

Somewhere in that misery there was a spot for me.

I didn't want it.

Chip

"I left him snoozing in the office this time," Paul said wearily, tugging at his tie. "He was so far gone that bringing him home would have been a waste of time."

I felt like someone had plunged a white-hot needle into my chest. "What gives with him?"

The same old song, Paul surmised. Women and pride. Kevin had both but didn't understand either. He didn't even know where to begin.

"If he's expecting to ever understand women, he's in it for the long haul," I said.

"Yeah, but he'll never know that until he tries."

"Keep him out of the bar, Paul. I don't mind an occasional drink, but I'll be damned if I'll let him fuel whatever this is in our restaurant."

The image of quiet, thoughtful Kevin in the grip of an alcoholic binge frightened me. We managed to escape the worst of teenage boozing with his brothers, but Kevin rarely bothered with even a small drink. He was the last one of the kids I expected it from.

Terry had her sensitive son, all right. So sensitive he was looking for comfort in the bottom of a cocktail glass and he had no idea how to handle the consequences.

Too sensitive altogether.

Trying hard to be the disappointment he was sure he already was.

9

Kevin

I stayed drunk for three days. When Paul cut me off from the restaurant's bar, I marched into the nearest liquor store, picked up a small bottle of cheap but effectively strong whiskey, found a comfortable spot under a tree towards the back side of the park, and sip by sip worked to numb every nerve in my body. When the first bottle was empty I lingered around just long enough to sober up, found another store, and plunked down ten dollars for another bottle.

The rain continued in fits and starts, drizzle that occasionally gave way to pounding bursts. I moved to a dry spot under the playground playhouse, confident that I could avoid human contact until the weather improved and the kids came out to play.

I drank until my money ran out, and I was so nauseous that it felt like my stomach was going to turn inside out.

At some point, halfway through the second bottle, I decided I had made a total ass of myself. I was so busy staring inward at all the nicks and cuts and bruises on my soul that I didn't stop to take a look outside myself. I had everything that I really needed, and more than I had a right to want.

No, they weren't disappointed in me. Not before.

Lydia wanted me. Or she did before I dropped a bomb in her lap and then left without so much as a thanks for listening.

Calling her and apologizing might have worked if I'd done it the next day.

Going home was pointless.

I considered staying there, sitting cross-legged under the playhouse, eyes closed, until everything just slipped away. Let the whole world just disappear.

It might have worked, too, but my temporary peace of mind was interrupted by a hand on my shoulder, shaking vigorously.

Perturbed, I opened my eyes.

"Damn." I slumped back against one of the playhouse support pylons. "Nick."

"Mom is past frantic, Dad is pissed off, and your girlfriend hasn't stopped crying since she found out you were missing."

I settled back onto my bed, warmed by the hot shower Nick had – almost literally – thrown me into, and by the clean sweats he'd pulled out of a dresser drawer and then tossed at me. "Wasn't missing," I said. "I knew right where I was."

Nick, older brother and stand-in father for the times our dad wasn't around, was standing next to the bed, angry and trying hard to control it. "We've been looking for you for two days, you little ass munch. For some reason they're all blaming themselves but not you."

"I'm sorry." I didn't want anyone to blame themselves for my dark mood. "I wasn't thinking. I really didn't mean for anyone to worry."

"Well guess what, Einstein." He softened, and sat on the edge of the bed. "Dad says that whatever the problem is, he started it. Lydia is crying her eyes out because she thinks she let you down. I think they're all full of it. You've been a moody prick off and on for months and no one is holding you accountable. You've got to get over yourself."

"Ah, sage advice coming from Mr. Perfect. Mr.-I'm-Gonna-Graduate-At-The-Top-Of-My-Law-Class. Perfect wife, perfect car, perfect house. Only thing missing is the two point five kids and the dog."

"Shut up, Kevin."

"Sorry, Nick. But from where I sit you've got it pretty good."

Shaking his head, Nick pulled himself all the way onto the bed, sitting up against the wall. "You need to move your chair, little brother."

"Trouble in paradise?" I asked, trying to remember something Eileen had said. Nick and Katie didn't have the perfect marriage they wanted the world to think. Too much too young.

When Katie's father moved the family to Washington, D.C. during her senior year of high school, Nick's sophomore year of college, he was inconsolable. He invented the model for being the Family Prick. From the time she left in January until Nicole was born in March, Nick was an insufferable son of a bitch. He didn't completely snap out of it until Katie came back in June, just before his eighteenth birthday; they married just a couple of weeks later.

If anyone should understand, it should be him.

I didn't stop to think he had real problems of his own.

"I'll probably graduate near the top of my class," he admitted. "And I have job offers pouring in."

"But?"

"But I don't think this is what I want. I *hate* law. I don't mean I dislike it, I mean I detest it."

I didn't see the problem. "So don't be a lawyer."

"It should be that simple. Do you have any idea how disappointed Mom and Dad will be? Katie's pissed off like you wouldn't believe, I can't even imagine how upset they'll be."

"No more upset than they are that I'm not going to be a priest."

"They're not upset about that."

"That's my point, Nick. It's your life. It was your money spent on law school. If you don't want to be a lawyer, then don't be a lawyer. Why would you waste your life being something you hate just because it might make other people happy? And why would Katie be so bent over it? She wanted to lose you to all the hours you'd be gone working as a scut slave in someone else's firm until you could make partner?"

He almost smiled. "I don't think she's thought of it that way."

"It can't be the money."

"I'm not really sure what it is."

"Maybe she just wants you to finish school?"

He nodded. "That's probably part of it. I don't know what the hell to do. Sometimes I think she just hates all the time it takes for me to study, and I don't think she knows that it'll just get worse later. Other times I think she's just generally unhappy and this is what she's latched onto."

"Quit thinking and ask her what she wants."

"Says the bachelor."

"Give me time."

"Is Lydia why you went off on a drunk?"

"No. But she knows why, and I'll talk to her about it.

And I'll stick around and face whatever I've got coming from Dad, Nick. Just swear that when he's done stringing me up you'll cut me down when he's not looking."

"I think," he sighed wearily, tired more from relief than fatigue, "that he's is the least of your problems. Lydia is going to rip your nipples off."

Dad left me alone. As much as he wanted to scream at me, as hurt as he was, he decided the best thing to do was leave me alone to stew in my own misery. Time to let go.

Letting go for him was hard. I knew what he wanted to do from the moment Nick told him I was upstairs and in bed asleep, was rush up the stairs two at a time to see for himself. He wanted me to be five years old again, the terrified kid hanging off the side of the stairs, so he would have an excuse to grab me and hold on as long as he could.

And then ground me for life.

I suspected the only thing that held him back was a short blonde with twinkling blue eyes and a good understanding of what I needed. She realized that my gray funk had nothing to do with them, and that I would turn to someone else when the time was right.

And Lydia – I was terrified beyond reason to even call her – wasn't going to wait for me to do anything.

"I decided that one, you're not a saint and you have the right to be thoughtless once in a while. Two, telling me was harder than anything I've ever had to do, even when I had to face my father at Disneyland. And three, I wasn't going to wait for you to call me."

She came into the kitchen late in the afternoon, when I was losing a battle with the electric can opener.

"And four, in spite of the fact that you scared the bejeebers out of me, I still love you."

"Bejeebers?" I looked up from the can opener, confused at first, and feeling awkward.

She ignored the brightening in my cheeks – or maybe it just amused her – and came around the counter to take the can out of my hands. "You would say 'scared the fuck out of,' but then I'm tired of the language you use."

She popped the can under the blade and pushed down hard. It opened easily.

"Cooking? I suppose you owe it to your mother for the hell you put her through the last few days."

"You're really pissed," I managed.

"I'm upset," she insisted, allowing just enough anger to flare in her voice to put me in place. "Silly me, I thought you'd be there in the morning, and when you weren't, I thought you would call."

I was pinned against the counter, not by Lydia's proximity, which was close enough I could have leaned forward to kiss her, but by my own guilt. "I was embarrassed."

Softly, "Why?"

I shrugged.

"You didn't do anything wrong, Kevin. It wasn't your fault. It was never your fault."

"I didn't know what else to do," I said quietly, so that no one else would hear. "I came home because I was scared, Lydia."

"And that's okay."

"But it's not. I wasn't just afraid they wouldn't believe me. I was afraid I'd kill him. I mean it literally. If not him, myself."

Her arms were around me in an instant, holding tight.

"God, please tell me you don't still feel that way."

"I don't want to die. I don't think I really ever wanted to, but I don't know."

She let go, but reached for my hands. "Kevin, have you had an HIV test?"

I shook my head. The thought had crossed my mind, once or twice or a few thousand times, that I should, but taking that step meant admitting to someone what had happened, and I wasn't ready for that, not even anonymously.

"You have to, you know that, right?"

There were a million things I wanted to say right then, but all I could do was nod.

"I'll go with you," she offered. "There's a clinic—"

"I should go to Uncle Doug," I said, hating it the moment it was out of my mouth, hating the hot sting of tears that welled up in my eyes. "I don't know, I just … I don't want to tell him."

"He'll keep your secret. So will I."

Paul wandered into the kitchen and headed straight for the refrigerator. "Secrets? Cool, let me in on it." He pulled a beer out and turned to look at us when he shut the door. "Or maybe not. I'll just back out slowly and pretend I didn't hear a damn thing. I'm sorry."

"He probably thinks we had a fight," Lydia said when he was gone. "It's okay."

"But now he's in the living room telling my parents something's wrong, which will worry them even more. I'm not allowed to lose you, you know. My mom thinks we're perfect together and my dad is half in love with you himself."

"You won't lose me."

"Stay for dinner and make them believe that, too."

"I will if you promise me something. Talk to someone, Kevin. Someone who can really help you sort through what happened and everything you're feeling."

"A shrink?"

"Will Parker, maybe? He's not your priest anymore, but he probably knows a thing or two about helping people get through a crisis."

"Will's a shrink," I told her. "Or he used to be. I think he gave that up when he gave up the priesthood."

"And you'll talk to him?"

"Only if you stay for dinner. That'll make my parents happy, and me happy, too."

"Are you ever going to explain things to your parents?"

I turned to the stove, scraping the tomato paste out of the can and into the sauce, stirring. "I don't know if I can. My mom tends to mutate into this Catholic-Jewish kind of mother when she thinks one of her babies is hurting. I'm not sure I can stand to be smothered at this point."

"You'd eat it up and you know it."

"For a little while," I admitted. "My mom hugs great, you know. Nick always says that when he's sixty he'll still want hugs from her. I think I will, too."

"Ah, Mama's boy."

I pointed the goopy spoon at her. "You're treading dangerous waters, woman. I may be my mother's boy, but I am not a mama's boy."

"All right." She grabbed my wrist and pushed the spoon away. "What about your father? Or did you give up hugging him with puberty?"

"Are you kidding?" I rolled my eyes and groaned. "I couldn't even if I wanted to. He's a huge believer in hugs and kisses, and even when we hated it, he insisted on it."

"So you oblige him."

"I don't hate it as much as I used to want him to think."

"You don't hate it at all," she laughed.

"Don't tell him that."

"I envy you. I haven't really touched either of my parents in years."

"They seem like okay people to me."

"They are. We're just not close the way your family is."

"Close can be a pain in the butt, Lydia. There are days when it feels like they don't want me to grow up. Mom doesn't want the last one to leave."

"She has Nicole."

"For now. But that won't last. Paul is taking Monica on a vacation for a couple weeks, and then they're buying a house. After that, my mom is going to drive me up a wall."

"Poor baby. I think I'm going to help her."

She threw her arms around me again, just in time for my dad to come in, the look on his face suggesting going into the kitchen to referee was the last thing he wanted to do. He stopped, raised an eyebrow and then smiled, and turned around to go back into the living room.

"You busy Friday night?" I asked, holding her even tighter.

"I keep my Fridays reserved for this really cute guy I met in a bar." She leaned back, but kept her arms around my neck. "Did you have something in mind?"

"Well, there's this really hot chick I met in a bar, and I'd like to take her someplace really nice for dinner. Or fun, if she'd prefer fun."

"A girl dating you has to have a sense of humor. I'd guess she'd like to have fun."

"All right. Fun it is. Let's go to a club, watch a couple of comedians, and have a really great dinner after. And not at my dad's place."

"You're paying for a meal? Wow, I'm impressed."

"I'll even wear a suit."

"This hot chick better be worth it," she said, stretching up on her toes to kiss me. "The cute guy definitely is."

"It's negative," Uncle Doug said as he breezed through his office door. I recognized the change in him in the three steps he took to his desk; coming in he was Doctor Stone, but by the time he sat down he was the guy who had played with me when I was little, someone who had changed my diapers and never forgot a birthday, the guy who was my uncle because my parents chose for him to be, not because we were related.

I wanted to ask him about Lydia, but knew better. Doctor Doug might not have been sitting at that desk, but he still wasn't going to violate someone's confidence.

And he wasn't asking. I could see it there on his face, but he wasn't asking why I needed to know, and why I wanted to know as soon as possible.

"I appreciate it, Uncle Doug," I said, trying to figure out a graceful way to get out of his office before he pressed for more.

"My door is always open, you know that."

I did know that. I'd gone through it many times, asking him questions I didn't think my parents were comfortable with, or things I wasn't sure Nick would know. He only broke my trust once, telling Aunt Kris what I'd asked; I'd been angry for about two minutes, until I understood that he told her knowing she'd run to my parents, because he was terrified I was going to kill myself.

Curiosity had been my only objective; I asked him about autoerotic strangulation, but didn't tell him why I wanted to know. He was afraid I was heading home to tie a rope around my neck and hang from the closet bar while I jerked off. His fear made him forget that I asked questions about everything when I was a kid, and that turning fourteen hadn't changed that.

A classmate had died and the rumors suggested that was how; I only wanted to know why.

"So," he went on, "how was the hangover?"

"No hangover," I said, grinning. "You know better."

"Damn Irish genes. Any fallout from your girlfriend?"

"Not really. She wasn't happy about it but she understood."

"At least someone does," he sighed. "You can't make a habit of that, Kevin. We're too old to be that anxious for so long. If you're going to drink, do it at home."

"Yes, sir."

"All right, can I pry?"

Not that I wanted him to, but I nodded.

"This sudden desire to get HIV tested—I presume it's mostly because of that beautiful young woman sitting in my waiting room?"

"Pretty much."

"Tell me to mind my own business if I step over any lines, but are you getting this test because you two think one of you infected the other, or is it a preventative type of thing?"

Neither, I was thinking, but said, "We haven't slept together, Uncle Doug."

"Well, you have my respect for getting the test first, kiddo. You wouldn't believe how often it's an afterthought."

I could believe it. I was just relieved that I got out of his office without having to tell him the truth. And I didn't even have to lie.

Eileen's mission, whether she wanted to accept it or not,

was to help me find a suitable sports coat and matching slacks; her taste, I reasoned, was a hell of a lot better than mine. I leaned toward wild colors that caught my eye; Eileen could pick out something classy.

"Borrow one from Dad," she snapped when I showed up at her door on Thursday afternoon.

"Dad's a size smaller than I am," I told her, grabbing her jacket and shoving her out the door. "His arms are shorter. And I need your help because you have better taste than I have."

"At least that's true."

She sulked in the car, punishing me with her silence; she stared out the window, refusing to answer my occasional questions with more than a grunt. If she'd been five years old, she would have crossed her arms in front of herself and stuck her bottom lip out to make sure I got the point: she was pissed.

Out of habit I started to open her door for her after I parked the car; she stormed out and slammed it, practically tearing my fingers off the handle.

"Well, come on."

"Christ, you say that a lot," she snapped. "Come on. You moan it, groan it, laugh it, sigh it … you're a veritable walking dictionary."

I stopped in mid-stride, just outside the mall entrance. "What's with you?"

"Me?" She spun at me, savagely poking at my chest with her index finger. "You spend three days drunk out of your frigging head, God knows where, leaving me worried half out of my mind. Nick says he doesn't know what the problem is but that you were just fine after he got you home. He can't tell anyone what happened and you sure as hell won't even try. Now you're all Howdy-Doody on me, and you want me to help you buy a suit? You used to talk to me, Kevin."

Howdy-Doody? I mouthed the words but didn't say them.

Eileen jerked the door open and walked into the mall. "You used to trust me."

"I still do." I ran the few steps I needed to catch up to her. "Hey, you're really hurt, aren't you?"

"How astute of you to notice."

"Eileen, whatever I did, I'm sorry."

"Damn, you are one dense sucker." She was walking as fast as she could, past the pizza place and the candy store. As hard as she tried, though, her legs were no match for my long stride.

I reached for her arm and stopped her just outside of Taco Bell. "Do you really want to know? It's a long story."

"I have time."

I sighed and led her into the Taco Bell. We took a table near the back, and she waited while I bought sodas and nachos.

I started with the conversation with Dad, how I felt more like a parasite than a son, and the inexplicable need to square things with Lydia before I could even begin to consider what my options for the future might be. If she had chosen to not be a part of it, it could dramatically impact my decisions.

There were, I told her simply, other seminaries.

And then, not quite able to look up the from congealing mass of tortilla chips and microwaved cheese sauce, I told her about Jake, and the overwhelming feelings of guilt and inadequacy that plagued me from the minute I set foot back home. It surprised me that I was able to tell her with less emotion than I had Lydia. It was a fact, something that had happened. Something she would deal with knowing.

Eileen's love was a given, I realized later. Her only vested interest was in being my twin, the other half of who I was until I left for the seminary.

Being honest with Eileen was easy.

Seeing her cry was not.

"I'm all right now," I promised. "That's what the whole drinking thing was. I told Lydia and didn't know what else to do, so I went out and got drunk. The funny thing is, when I was so drunk I could barely see straight, I realized that everything would be okay. I don't have a fricking clue what I want to do with my life now, but at least I know who I want to be clueless with."

With a hard sniff, blinking away a tear or two, she let it go. "So what's the suit for?"

"I want to look stunningly good tomorrow night. I promised her a real night out, not a freebie at the Charybdis."

"God, one of the men in this family finally gets it right."

"We're cheap at heart, darlin'. I figured we'd go into San Francisco, hit up one of the comedy clubs and then have dinner someplace nice."

"And then?"

"And then what?"

She took a sip of her soda, laughing into the straw. "Moron."

"I'm not a moron, you're just awfully damned nosey."

"Yes, I am. So tell the nosey sister, are you ready to move on?"

"Can you keep something to yourself?"

"You're blushing like crazy so I probably know the answer, but sure, I can keep a secret."

"Just in case," I told her, "and I mean just in case, I reserved a room at the Marriot."

~

"I'll give you credit," Eileen said, coming out of the Men's Wearhouse, helping me sling the suit bag over my shoulder, "you're not a cheap date."

"I'm looking for perfection here, Eileen."

"I think you could accomplish as much without the drain on your bank account." She poked at me playfully. "At least until you can find a job."

"I was thinking of bumming off Dad for the next couple of years. You know, with Paul taking Nicole home where she belongs, Mom will need someone to coddle."

"And you'll make the supreme sacrifice?"

"Unless you're planning on moving back, I think I have to."

"No way," she said emphatically. "I'm having a pretty good time where I am. It's quiet and the bed is usually warm."

"Only usually? Do I need to give the Spider man a little pep talk?"

"You keep your nose out of my sex life, little brother. I'm not complaining at all."

I steered her into the pizza place, whining about sudden hunger and deadly thirst. She rolled her eyes, but took the suit from me and found a booth towards the back; I bought her a slice and a drink, neither of which she said she wanted.

"You knew I'd say I wasn't hungry," she protested.

I shrugged, "Yeah, but this way I won't feel like a pig when I eat yours. I'll feel like I'm not throwing away good food."

"Hollow legs," she mumbled.

"Growing boy," I countered.

She rolled her eyes at me again, and reached for her drink.

"What was it like?" I asked, taking a bite out of the pizza.

"The first time you slept with Spider."

"Kevin."

"Come on, Eileen. I never planned on doing this with any woman, much less Lydia. If I'm going overboard—"

"Minor detail."

"I want this to be perfect. Not just because its my first time, but mostly because I doubt it's hers. If I turn out to totally suck, maybe I can dazzle her enough she won't notice."

The smart remark I expected didn't come. "Somehow I think you'll do just fine," she assured me. "It's not like you have to do everything yourself. Someone else *is* going to be there, you know."

"I just don't want anything to be out of place. You know, sweep her off her feet."

"Don't turn it into a job, Kev. You only have to remember two things … be playful, and be tender. That's all that really matters."

I could handle playful. I could even handle tender.

Rejection, now that was another matter entirely.

10

Dear Kevin,

Well, I really did it this time. Remember the karate classes I took a couple of years ago—the ones *you* told me I should take? They worked. I managed to get myself arrested for a swift sidekick to the midsection. My victim just happened to be a security police specialist. I swear, I didn't know he was a cop, not that it would have made any difference. I don't give out free gropes anymore. He didn't take the news very well and tried to help himself anyway.

Three broken ribs convinced him I was serious. I wound up being taken in for assault and battery. My father was *so* mad.

It's my own fault, I suppose. I've come onto this guy dozens of times, but he picked the time when I decided to cool it with men to take me up on it.

Don't go gagging, either. I mean it. I'm tired of playing all the silly games. I think you're right, if I ever want to meet someone worthwhile I should keep my clothes on.

Or I could move back to California. At least I know you're nice.

Anyway, I don't have much to say this time. I just wanted

to write and let you know you were right. I'm trying, even though it isn't as easy as you make it sound.

How the hell are you surviving celibacy?

All my love,
Debby

Terry

"Why do I get the feeling you're tired of hearing from her?" I slipped Kevin's dress slacks over the end of the ironing board, watching him fold the letter and toss it onto the table. "Every time you get something from her you groan and then wait two or three days before you open it."

"I don't mind. She's just predictable. And increasingly obvious."

"Oh?" I wanted to pry but knew better. Kevin's lips could stick together tighter than a stale Oreo cookie. Stubborn Irish male pride.

"About me, Mom," he groaned. "She totally flashes these neon hints that she wouldn't mind in the least if I asked her to come out here for a visit. If I cooperated, she'd be more than happy to stay."

I had no doubt that it wasn't his vanity talking. At least he never seemed to notice before when girls were panting after him.

I turned the slacks inside out and began pressing them. "Have you explained to her that you're taken?"

"Who I'm dating really isn't any of her business. Besides, if she really wanted to know what I was up to, all she'd have to do is ask Katie."

"Who wouldn't volunteer a thing without asking you first."

"Maybe." He began toying with a crumb floating in his glass, dabbing at it with his finger. "You haven't said much."

"About what?"

He gestured to the slacks. "About tonight. You keep looking at me funny, though."

"Do I?" I feigned surprise. Of course I was looking at him funny. He was putting more effort into a dinner date than he had in planning for his Senior Prom. He was taking a girl to a restaurant I refused to set foot in simply because of its exorbitant prices. He was out to impress Lydia, and the part of me that understood why was feeling fairly blue.

Kevin was my baby. It was a position he earned by less than three minutes, but my baby nonetheless. He was heading into romantic assignation with more grace and good intentions than either of his brothers ever had, combined. I was looking at him funny, as he put it, because I knew I had lost him.

"Lydia deserves a really good night out," he said, not looking up from his floating crumb.

"So do you. I just hope she knows what a good thing she has in you."

"God, Mom. I'm lucky she puts up with me."

"Who's putting up with whom?" Chip came into the kitchen, dressed in his usual jeans and sweatshirt. He had developed a theory that if he refused to open the closet that contained his business suits, then he would never have to actually work again. The suits I dragged out for him every Sunday didn't count. Mass is not work, he'd said. Mass is just, well, an obligation.

He was covering for Paul some nights dressed in black slacks and t-shirts, but he stayed in the bar, lounged comfortably at a booth, doing the payroll or ordering inventory, refusing to admit it was work.

"We have a gross inequity," he protested. "She never pressed *my* suits."

"She loves me," Kevin boasted.

"You never had a hot date like this," I told Chip. "Or at least I never cared what you were wearing."

"Or not wearing," Chip said, grinning.

Kevin groaned and got up from the table. "At least wait until I'm out of the room to start mauling each other."

Kevin

"I think they were gonna do it right there in the kitchen," I told Eileen, rolling my eyes. "I swear, Dad looks at her like she's a buffet."

"Good for them," she said. "I hope they're still munching away when they're ninety."

"God, Eileen. Just … God!"

All right, sure, my parents were always affectionate people, but picturing them naked and doing it was the last thing I needed in my head. I wondered if they suspected the extent of my plans for the night.

"If it were Nick or Paul," Eileen said, "yes. Mom would be rolling her eyes and Dad would be shoving condoms into every pocket of your jacket. But you? Dad suspects and Mom wouldn't admit it if she did. She thinks you're a goddamned little angel."

Eileen and Spider were sitting together on my bed, cuddled up near the headboard, watching me pace.

"You have to quit worrying," she went on. "I swear, it'll be all right."

"You're assuming I'll survive dinner. My stomach is churning so hard I might puke all over her."

Spider was shaking his head. "Relax. Dinner's the easy part. If you lose your nerve after, so what? You haven't begged her for anything else, right?"

"Right," I sighed.

Sure, there would be nothing lost with Lydia. I only had to face *them* after.

"Kevin, sit down." She reached for my hand and pulled me onto the mattress with them. "You're going to wear a hole out in the carpet."

"I'll blow it," I insisted. "I'll either throw up on her, or step on her toes, or I'll spill something on her. God, I bet I say something asinine."

"She expects that," Spider signed.

"Kev, she's probably going to be nervous, too, once you take her into that restaurant. It's not everyday she gets taken to a place like that."

Spider looked at her suddenly. "Jealous?"

"No, but I'd like to be a fly on the wall tonight."

"Eileen!" I leaned back against the wall and closed my eyes. "That'd be all I need, coming back to your play by play."

"Play by play, hell. I'd take pictures."

My eyes flicked open. "You would, too. Eight by ten glossies pasted in the family photo album."

"Just for posterity," she said. "Something to remember forty years from now when you're all dried up and doing it in the same position month after month. Hell, year after year if you're lucky."

"I can't worry about forty years from now. I'm just going to worry about tonight."

"You're a weenie," Eileen laughed. "It's a good thing she loves you."

~

I quit worrying when Lydia answered her door. She looked like she had stepped out of the pages of a magazine, a bronze beauty wrapped in white and light blue, spirit dancing like fire in her eyes. I could imagine the popping of hundreds of flash bulbs going off around her, the fans straining to catch a glimpse of this perfection, but she didn't notice. She was completely oblivious to the effect she was having on the people around her, the men who had to turn and take a second and third look. The only thing she noticed was me.

That should have terrified me even more, but as we headed for San Francisco, the possibility of tossing my dinner onto her shoes seemed more remote. The two hours we spent at the comedy club I didn't think once about making an ass of myself. It only briefly crossed my mind on the way to dinner.

I had her in my arms on the dance floor at the restaurant, and it felt right. Every other time I had danced, all the high school dances, the proms, the parties, it was all practice for this one moment, for that instant when she melted into me and sighed happily, for that instant when I felt completely safe.

"Would I be considered too much of a chauvinist if I said you look incredible tonight?"

She sighed happily and looked up. "I think I'd be disappointed if you didn't. And you"—she ran her fingers over the front of my jacket—"you look great."

"I look like I'm headed for a job interview."

"Ah, then you get the position," she laughed. "When you said dress nice I didn't expect semi-formal."

The music faded away, and we wound our way through the crowd of people back to our table. "What did you expect?"

"Honestly, Kevin, I learned a long time ago to not try to figure out what you have spinning through that head of yours."

I leaned back, slipping an arm around her shoulders and watched thoughtfully as she took a delicate sip of wine, deciding it was a good thing she had no idea what was going through my mind at the moment. "How long? Days, weeks, months? You've been confusing me for almost fifteen years."

"Seven," she said flatly. "And don't try to snow me. You hardly noticed me before then."

"I noticed you. I kept you filed away for future reference. You scared me then, I've told you that before."

"You were curious," she countered. "The difference between you and the rest of the knotheads on the playground was that you kept all the snotty comments to yourself."

"We were seven years old, Lydia. Kids teased you because they were stupid and didn't know any better. And I don't like being grouped with them. I never made any snotty comments because I didn't have any. I ignored you because you were a girl and I knew even back then that girls are nothing but pretty little bundles of trouble."

The sudden bite softened and she smiled. "Still think so?"

"Don't hit me if I say yes. But now I think they're worth the trouble."

"For someone with a twin sister, I think you doth protest too much."

"She's not a girl. She's just Eileen," I mused. "But you know, I miss her being there. It's a little strange having the room on the other side of the bathroom empty all the time."

"How do you think she felt when you left for the seminary?"

"She was so wound around Spider she probably didn't notice I was gone."

"Kevin." She reached out and touched my cheek, feather soft, electric. "Even I noticed you were gone. I woke up one morning and just knew. All the way to work I kept thinking that was it, you'd really done it. I doubted I'd ever see you again."

"Someone had to be here to rescue you from the blind date from hell," I managed to say, distracted by the sensation of her fingers against my cheek.

"Ever the knight in shining armor. A perpetual Sir Galahad."

"I don't think I want to be Sir Galahad," I said through clenched teeth, not trusting my reflexes. "I'll be your knight any time you want, but I'd rather not feel forced into being so frigging courteous all the time."

She slowly moved her hand away. "You can't help it. That's just the way you are."

"Maybe it's just the way you see me."

"You are unfailingly kind to women and children. Probably puppy dogs, too."

I took the wine glass from her hand. "And you are slightly tipsy. Too much to drink and not enough to eat."

"Don't judge me by your appetite. I swear I've never known anyone who could eat so much and stay so skinny."

"Slim," I corrected.

"I can't imagine what your poor mother went through when you and your brothers and your dad hit the table at the same time."

"She cried a lot."

"Poor woman will go catatonic when you all start having kids. Holidays will kill her."

"She's not thinking about the downside to more grandkids yet," I said. "She's deluded into thinking she wants tons. Poor Nick can't get by her without her asking when he and Katie are going to start a family. My dad is just as bad, only he wants nothing but granddaughters."

She looked at me curiously. "And what about you? What do you want?"

"I want kids someday."

Lydia smiled, fingers toying with the glass I'd set on the linen tablecloth. "You like kids."

"Sure. Other people's kids."

"For now. I can see you with three or four of your own. Little blond haired, blue eyed imps running around in your front yard."

"Okay." I scooted a little closer. "What about their mother?"

"She'll be a lucky woman," she said with a light laugh, and turned to kiss me. "Don't let me drink anymore, Kevin. I have a buzz already and I don't want to get drunk."

She wasn't too drunk, I decided later, standing against the car with her arms looped around my neck and lips probing mine. She tasted faintly of fish and white wine; it was sweet and slow, and I didn't want it to end.

"Lydia," I breathed, slowly peeling my lips off hers, drawing back just far enough to look into her eyes. "God, I love you."

She smiled and kissed me again. "I love you, too."

I was suddenly nervous again.

And she was waiting for me to say something else.

"You've been very patient with me over the last few months," I said. "I know I've been frustrating … going back to your place at the end of a date and then leaving at totally the wrong time."

"It's okay. I understand now."

"But you didn't, and you never once tried to make me feel like a freak about it."

"I thought you were still caught up in old rules. Just because you were home never meant you were ready to go any farther than we had before."

"That wasn't it. Not entirely, anyway. At first, you're right, I wasn't ready, but later I just didn't think it was fair for me to push for anything until you knew where all my demons were hiding. And I didn't want to use you to prove a point to myself."

"You've never used me, Kevin."

I fought the shiver working its way up my spine and reached a finger to her cheek to brush away a stray hair. "And I never will, I swear." I pulled her close, my chin touching the top of her head. "When I hold you like this I can feel your heart beat against mine. It's like mine beats left, yours beats right. Mine beats right, yours beats left. Perfect timing. You're the other half of my heart, Lydia. I do love you. And I want to make love with you."

She caught my hand against her cheek and held it tight, the barest hint of a smile tugging at the corners of her mouth. "Tonight?"

I managed to nod. "I swear, I won't run off and drink myself into oblivion if you say no."

Lydia slipped her arms around my waist and tilted her head back to be kissed, amused, I think, at my sudden nervousness. "No one needs to run away. But it's an awfully long drive back home, and I frankly don't want to give you time to change your mind."

I started fumbling with the keys to the car. "I had something a little closer in mind," I said, trying to get the door open for her. "If you don't mind."

She smiled and when I was finally behind the wheel, reached over and set her hand on the back of my neck. Cool fingers massaged me, playing with the hair prickling at my collar.

I tried to stick the key in the ignition and missed, distracted by my own pounding heart.

"You planned this," she said, not accusingly.

"I had high hopes."

She took the key from me and slid it into the ignition. "I'm flattered," she said, "and you're blushing."

As preoccupied as I was, had she not been drinking, I would have asked her to drive. Either way our odds of plowing into a lamp post were about the same.

We wound up in the hotel elevator with an older couple; on one hand it irritated me – I had my arms around Lydia but wanted more – and on the other it amused me. This woman who was older than my grandmother kept staring at me with this knowing look, but there wasn't a hint of disapproval.

Her husband probably thought I was a young lech.

He was probably right.

"Relax, Rabbit," she murmured against my chest.

"Rabbit?"

"Jumpy as a bunny rabbit," she explained, planting a quick kiss on my chin. "Kind of like one of those cute little furballs half crazed parents give their six year old munchkins at Easter. The ones that know as soon as those sticky fingers get hold of them they've had it."

"Is that a warning?"

She laughed and leaned into me, arms around my waist. "Maybe. But don't feel bad, you're not the only one whose stomach is doing a few carefully orchestrated flip flops."

"You? We don't have to—"

"You're not getting out of it that easy, mister."

"I just didn't expect … you're nervous?"

She poked at my stomach. "I'm allowed. Nervous doesn't mean reluctant."

I hoped not; I hated to think that the few thousand butterflies bouncing off my stomach walls were screaming in aversion.

The last time I'd been this nervous was the first day of kindergarten.

I think I wet myself then.

"Do you want something to drink?" I asked once we were in the room. "Champagne? I could call—"

She shook her head before I could finish. "No more drinking. You've gone to too much trouble to get me drunk for this, and I want to remember it in the morning."

"No trouble," I muttered, surprised when she threw her arms around me, and the ferocity behind her kiss.

Fine, all right, I told myself when she pushed my jacket off and onto the floor. Let her lead. Relax.

Fat chance of that, my fingers were starting to tremble; I wondered what she was thinking but I was afraid that if I tried to speak my voice would come out in a mouse-like squeak. A high pitched squeal wasn't on my personal list of Things I Find Romantic, and hearing her burst out laughing wasn't on my agenda for the moment, either.

Be playful. Be tender.

Eileen.

Crap. The last person I wanted to be thinking about. But I could hear her voice rattling around inside my head, something I needed to consider but hadn't. What?

Dad.

I reached down and picked up the jacket, fumbling in the pockets, trying not to grin foolishly as I tossed the half roll of condoms onto the night stand.

Lydia was kneeling on the edge of the bed, toying with the buttons on my shirt, deliberately slow as she undid each one. "You don't need those, you know," she said quietly."

"No?"

She slid off the bed and into my arms; the dress seemed to float away. "Let's just say I anticipated the possibilities one night when my Rabbit told his little niece that he loved me. I took care of it, Kevin."

"That long ago?"

I shrugged out of my shirt and tossed it onto the floor with her dress. The silkiness of her slip was cool against my chest, and I let my fingers linger at the straps, hesitating, wanting to prolong the moment and yet at the same time rush ahead.

"If you'd given me any hint it was what you wanted, I would have slept with you the night we found each other in the bar," she said, her slip falling to the floor. "You seemed content to just make out."

"That was my birthday," I mused. "Turning twenty one could have been a real trip."

She stepped back, her hand against my chest. "Are you serious? Why didn't you tell me it was your birthday?"

"I was so happy to see you, I forgot," I said, pulling her back. "But it's better this way. Isn't it?"

"I think you might be right."

I was standing there in nothing but red briefs and black dress socks, and suddenly felt incredibly self conscious. She had on less than I did, and I didn't know where to look.

"You're awfully shy now," she snickered, thumbs hooked

onto the waistband of my underwear. "I can remember when you weren't afraid to touch."

"I knew where I was supposed to stop then."

"You're not supposed to stop at all now."

Nothing but black dress socks. How in the hell does someone take off their socks when they have this wonderfully naked woman in front of them, and they don't have on anything else, either?

We fell to the bed together, joined at the lips.

Tender. I remembered tender, my fingers exploring familiar territory, gently, wanting this to last as long as possible.

Your first time should count for something.

It should mean something.

This meant everything.

Cuddling her in my arms afterward, I wondered what it was I had been so afraid of.

"Kevin," she giggled later, propping herself up on one arm. "Black socks?"

Paul would be so proud.

"You know," Lydia sighed, stretching next to me, her foot sliding down my leg, "you're pretty romantic for having been such an awkward seven year old. You could have just said 'hey, wanna do it?' and I would have said yes."

"I'll save being crude for later. If I totally sucked at this, I'm sorry … but I'm a happy boy."

She lifted herself up and leaned against my chest, long wavy hair tenting around my face. "Tonight has been wonderful, Kevin. All of it. You're the polar opposite of suck. You weren't in a hurry and you made me feel completely loved."

"That's because you are."

"I know. I just hope I make you feel the same way."

"You make me feel like I'm the only person who really matters, Lydia. Like the world exists for just us, and everyone else is here to take up space."

"You know what?" she asked, kissing me. "I love that you're not afraid to say totally dorky, drippy, romantic things."

"Well … I love that you don't laugh at me when I say them. At least not yet. When the hormones have settled a little, feel free to giggle if I say something really over the top."

She stretched out on top of me, burying her face against my neck, and was quiet for a long time. I could feel her breath against my skin, and thought that she had drifted off until she whispered, "I can feel it."

"What?"

"One heartbeat," she said. "When we're this close it really is like there's only one heartbeat, and it's ours."

"I walked in on my parents when I was about four or five," I said sleepily, face half buried in a pillow. Lydia was lying on her side, head propped up on the other pillow, her hand on my hip. "I ran out of their room crying like a little freak. My dad had to get up and throw some pants on and then had to try to find me. I was hiding in my closet—I really thought he was trying to hurt her."

"What'd he do?"

"Crawled into the closet with me and about a hundred stuffed animals. He pulled me onto his lap and leaned back into the pile of fake fur and just held me. Sometimes when I think about it I can even still smell the aftershave he used to wear. He sat there in the middle of all those toys and tried to explain that it was just grown up play, that he wasn't hurting her, and I didn't need to be so afraid of what I'd seen. I must have sat in his lap and cried for about an hour."

"They weren't mad?"

"I think they were more worried that they'd scarred me for life. I'll give my dad some credit; he was never afraid to hold any of us. Still isn't. Feeling like I wasn't loved was never a problem."

"You know, I've never even seen my parents touch? Not even to hold hands."

"They love you, Lydia. Your dad has that look, it's that 'this is my baby girl and she's my life and if you hurt her I will break your knees' look. They might be a little reserved, but they love you and they love each other."

"I know. I just wish they'd been a little more affectionate."

I rolled onto my back and pulled her with me, holding her close. "If it helps, I'll always be affectionate."

"You always have been," she said. "Except our senior year, when you started to ignore me again."

"I wasn't ignoring you."

"It felt like it, Kevin. You started pulling away, and it hurt."

"I'm sorry. I didn't mean for you to be hurt."

"But you know you were pulling away?"

I nodded. "I had to. You were getting tight with Topher and I didn't want to get in your way. And I didn't want to hate him just because you were dating him. Maybe that should have been a clue. Your other boyfriends were only mild irritating, but when I felt like I wanted to beat the snot out of him, I knew I had to leave you alone."

"You wanted to hurt Topher?"

"Not really. But he had you, and I thought you had fallen hard for him. That hurt, too, Lydia. I know it's not fair, but damn. Every day there you were, holding his hand or he had his arm around you. I'd walk into the cafeteria and you two would be in line and he'd be kissing you. You'd look at him and smile that completely beautiful smile—"

She sat up, handing me her pillow, gesturing for me to sit up against the headboard.

"Rabbit, did it ever occur to you that I started getting serious with Topher to make it easier on myself, knowing you were going to leave at the end of the school year?"

"You at least cared about him."

"I know, I cared. And I probably convinced myself that I loved him, but it wasn't the real thing. God, he was so much like you, but when it came right down to it, he *wasn't* you. Like everything you did tonight—he never would have thought of any of it. Instead of all the romantic things he really would have just asked 'wanna do it?'"

"I don't want to know about your previous love life," I said dully.

"But I can't pretend it never happened."

"You shouldn't. That doesn't mean I want the details."

She sat there and looked at me, biting her bottom lip, considering. "You want some of the details, don't you? I get the feeling that you've wanted to ask but don't think it's any of your business."

"I want to know if he made you happy," I said. "And I want to know if he hurt you when you broke up."

"And you want to know if I slept with him."

Without thinking, I nodded. I wanted to know, yet I didn't.

"Topher was fun, Kevin. And I meant it before when I

said we mostly drifted apart. After graduation we both got busy with other things and there was more and more time between when we'd call each other. I stopped thinking about him every day. By the time he left for college, it was like having a casual friend. That was a good thing. Because in the end, I was using him to avoid facing how much losing you hurt."

"Okay."

"And yes."

"Okay."

"I'd give anything if I could go back to that moment. I would give anything if you had been first. Anything."

"I didn't expect to be," I said quietly.

"Oh, Rabbit..." She slid closer, her hands on my cheeks; tears pooled in her eyes but didn't fall. "Maybe you didn't expect it, but it's what we both wanted."

I nodded.

"If it means anything" – she reached for my hand and held it tightly to her chest – "you were in here first. And you never left."

"Did he treat you right?"

"He treated me just fine."

"If something happened and this was it, we'd never be able to make love again, would you still want to be with me?"

"It's not about sex, Kevin."

"But if we could never have it again—?"

"I don't think I'd be thrilled about losing this part of us, but I don't love you for the sex. I love you because you're you."

"I'm keeping count, you know."

"Oh God," she laughed, throwing her arms around me and pulling me back to the mattress. "Why am I not surprised? How many?"

"Five so far."

"And you think it would be a shame to see sunrise on an odd number?"

"I think that's a requirement for the first time people have sex together."

"We wouldn't want to break any rules, would we?"

"Not this particular one," I said.

"We are going to be so sore tomorrow."

Lydia dozed on the way home, her head resting against the back of the seat, fingers clenched around the seatbelt. I slept sometime between five and nine in the morning, deeply, the most sleep I'd had in a single stretch in months. When I woke up she was sitting up in bed, wrapped in a hotel robe, watching me.

"It occurred to me about a half hour ago that we'll have to put on the same dirty clothes, and that completely grosses me out," she said. "But I don't want to let you go home right off. I want you to come home with me."

I mumbled something unintelligible and started to go back to sleep, but she leaned over and kissed me.

"Come on, sleepy head. I'm starving."

After breakfast I headed up the Interstate and towards home while she slept, and pulled off at the mall; no, I didn't really want to go home, either, I told her. She could dress me for the day, pick out anything she wanted me to wear, right down to my underwear.

When I woke her up, I demanded veto rights, just in case her idea of dressing me turned out to be oversized jeans slung down around my hips and t-shirts five sizes too big.

"Old Navy," she said as she climbed out of the car, stretching. "It's cheap and you'll look good."

"I always look good."

"You're also modest."

Within five minutes of walking into the store she picked out khakis, a sweatshirt, and underwear, stacking them in my outstretched arms as we walked the aisles.

"I don't wear boxers," I said when she set them on top of the sweatshirt.

"You do today."

"The pants are probably a size too small."

"I know."

"Perv."

She smiled. "Indulge me. What about shoes?"

I looked down at my feet; the black dress shoes would have to go. "Okay. Do I get to dress you today, too?"

She laughed and walked towards the cash register.

"All right then," I said as we headed towards a shoe store, "can't we just be nekkid today?"

"Maybe later."

"Okay, what are we doing before we get nekkid?"

"Kevin, you've got a one track mind."

"Yes, I do."

"I was thinking," she said, laughing, "that we'd go to my place, shower up, and maybe go do something outside. Fresh air and all that."

I stopped outside the Athlete's Foot. "You're not making me mow someone's yard, are you?"

"We could pack a picnic lunch and spend some time in the park. It's a little chilly, but it's still nice out."

"And we could warm each other up later."

"One track, Kevin. It's all one track now, isn't it?"

"It's always been one track," I assured her. "But going to the park sounds fun. We can play on the swings and pretend we're second graders again."

She headed into the shoe store. "Great. That means you'll be ignoring me all afternoon."

All right, the innocent in me did not grasp the phrase "we'd go to my place and shower up" when she said it. She started peeling off clothes the minute the door was shut and she headed straight for the bathroom, grumbling about feeling grimy and sweaty. I heard the water go on, and sat down on the couch to wait my turn.

A few minutes later she stuck her head out the door and asked, "Well? Are you coming in or not?"

I managed to rip off all my clothes in the 1.67 seconds it took me to get from the living room to the bathroom.

"Since I don't think you'll fit in my tiny little tub," she said, pulling me under the spray, "a shower will have to do."

I wasn't complaining.

Not until I got dressed and discovered the khakis really were a size too small.

"That's why I made you buy the boxers," she said with a sly grin. "Tight khakis do things to me."

I looked down.

"Hell, darlin' I think I'm doing things to myself."

We drove to the park – abandoning the idea of a picnic after opening her fridge and discovering only two cans of diet soda and a bag of salad turning brown; "I'll buy you lunch," I promised – and decided to walk around the pond. She huddled close for warmth, holding my hand tightly, her other hand hidden inside the sleeve of her jacket.

"My parents used to come here all the time," I told her. "My dad says when they were dating they'd walk over here and routinely get molested by some horny white and black spotted duck."

"My parents brought me here a lot in grade school," she said. "My dad used me as an excuse to play in the sand."

"Same here. We had a sandbox in our back yard, and even a swing set, but they still used to bring us over here at least once a week to play. I think my mom was still looking for her duck."

"Do they still come?"

"I think so. Sometimes they bring Nicole, but most of the time I think they come here to just talk. They're really big on having time alone. After they got back together they started making rules about when we could interrupt and when we couldn't ... if they were here we could call them on the cell phone if it was an emergency, and from ten to eleven at night they lock themselves in the bathroom and you'd better be bleeding to death if you knock on the door."

"Your parents are cute together."

"They're also not afraid to smooch in front of other people, so don't get embarrassed or anything if you're in the kitchen and Dad walks up and plants a big one on her."

"And if they're both there and I feel like planting big one on you, will anyone get embarrassed?"

"Only if you stick your hand down my pants when you do it."

"Kevin!"

"Well, that would do it, you know."

Still holding my hand, she pulled away a little bit. "I really miss my parents, Rabbit. I never thought I'd admit it, but I do."

I stopped and turned to her. "Are they still coming home this summer?"

She shook her head. "My mother is still terrified of flying. I'd go see them but I can't take that much time off work. Now they're saying by next Christmas."

"I'm sorry."

"The nice thing about you," she said, stretching up on her toes to kiss me, "is that you really mean that."

"Maybe at Thanksgiving, if she still doesn't want to fly, you can go see them. And if you're willing to take a side trip to Ireland, I'd go with you."

"If I didn't want to see Ireland?"

"I'd be very disappointed, of course. But I'd still go with you, if you wanted me to."

"Then we'd better start saving now, Rabbit. No more McDonald's for you."

I frowned. "Now that's just mean. I'm only two Happy Meals away from a complete Teeny Beanie Baby collection."

"Do they still have those?"

I shrugged. "I dunno, but it sounded good. The few times I buy Happy Meals Nicole steals the toys. Like she thinks I buy them for her."

"You do," she snickered. "But I bet you tease her and tell her they're yours."

"They are," I insisted. "But I share my toys."

She laughed and skipped a few steps ahead of me, walking backwards. "I've noticed. You've got nice toys."

"Quit looking. You might embarrass me."

"Listen."

I lifted my head from the pillow and strained to hear over the sound of the wind whipping against the windows. The steady pelting sound became more obvious, drops of rain pinging off the glass in a steady stream.

"Raining," I muttered, lying back down. "We need it."

"I like lying in bed, listening to the rain. Open the curtain, Rabbit. I like watching it, too."

The warm part of me wanted to tell her to get up and open the curtain herself, but I crawled out of bed and pulled it back, draping the end of it over the loft railing so that it would stay open. Moonlight flooded across the bed, the streaks of rain dancing in shimmering patterns on the bedspread.

"That okay?" I leaned against the wall by the window, watching her. She had the sheet tucked up under her arms, covering everything but her shoulders, her hair spread out wildly across both pillows. It only occurred to me after standing there a while that I was completely naked and no longer self conscious about it. I didn't mind the way she was looking at me, not at all.

"Come back to bed, Kevin. It's cold."

"In a minute." I wanted to stay there and look at her, watch the way her eyes sparkled in the moonlight. Downstairs the stereo was playing, quiet strains of the Moody Blues singing *Nights In White Satin.* I watched as one song ended and another began, late night radio sifting through decades of old rock. Songs from the sixties. The decade my father lost his mother, the decade he left home, thinking his own father hated him and blamed him for her being gone. The decade he felt his most pain.

How had he coped? I wondered that often, and listening to the strains of sad and slow songs, I wondered how any of us cope without someone there to hold us up.

"Can I ask you something?" she whispered, beckoning me to come back to bed again.

"Anything." I slid under the sheet with her, slipping my arm around her as she set her head on my shoulder."

"If not for me, would you have tried to get into another seminary?"

Careful, I warned myself.

"Probably," I said.

"I should feel so guilty, Kevin," she murmured. "I knew it. I think I knew from the moment you told me what had happened. Could you get into another one? Would they take you back?"

"Probably."

"God, I'm ruining your life."

She had no idea, did she? I held onto her quietly, while she struggled with guilt that she didn't need to feel, trying to say something that wouldn't sound insincere.

"Woman, you didn't ruin my life," I said softly. "You saved it."

"You were supposed to be a priest, not my bed buddy."

"I don't know. Eileen thinks God had propped you up in front of me for so long that I just didn't take the hint. I was too busy looking at everything that was wrong around me to see what was right. You know, I decided I might have a vocation at a pretty bad time. If my parents hadn't gotten back together when they did, I may have never given it a second thought."

My parents, for whatever stupidities they were working through, split up when I was twelve years old, right at the time when I needed my father around the most. They barely spoke for two years, and never once saw each other, not until he caught a nasty case of the flu and Nick brought him home, so out of it that he didn't know where he was for a week.

I sat by his bedside for as much of that time as my mother would allow; I read to him out of the Bible, I prayed, and I promised God that if they would start talking, if they could see past whatever the problem was and get back together, that I would become a priest.

I bargained my future in the hopes that my parents would

remember why they were so deeply in love; a month later when I got up at seven in the morning to get ready for school and Dad was there, in the pool, stealing kisses from her – and Paul was grumbling that she'd spent the night with 'that guy,' not realizing who was splashing around in the pool – I knew I'd gotten what I asked for.

When I left for the seminary I thought I was honoring the commitment I'd made. Holding up my end of the deal.

Lying in bed with Lydia, I was certain that I'd had it wrong all along.

"By your book this is still a sin," she whispered later, fingers tracing across my chest. "A mortal one at that."

"Mortal sins for mortal people," I whispered back. "I'm not worried about eternity, Lydia. Right now the only thing I'm worried about is making sure I never lose you again. Without you, the idea of eternity means nothing."

11

Dear Kevin

No surprises, not much of anything this time. I'm bored and I'm lonely and the only thing I could think of doing at two in the morning was to curl up in bed and write to you. I hope you don't mind. Trying to change a lifestyle is pure hell. I keep thinking of you behind me, cheering me on, and that makes it a little bit easier.

Saint Kevin. Remember when everyone used to call your brother Saint Nick? I suppose they still do. He was a real goody two-shoes, wasn't he? My poor brother, it seems like all he hears now is about how polite Nick was, how your parents must have done something right to raise four kids and not one of them any real trouble (not like *his* stupid second daughter.)

Of course, he doesn't really know anything about Paul and Monica, and I'm not going to tell him.

I'm hanging onto this job. It's dull and I go home with a bitch of a headache every day, but I'm hanging in there. No military jockeys to turn my head. Just dried up old men who understand the word 'no.'

My brother is graduating at the end of the year. I think

he's shooting for the Air Force Academy, but he won't tell me if he is. Dad is getting antsy and Brian is studying like a bear, taking stuff like calculus and physics and getting straight A's. I figure it has to be the Academy.

I hope he gets it. For once Dad would be proud (Katie doesn't count, she's too perfect for the rest of us peons) and Brian deserves it. He tries so hard at everything he does, not like Dad, who seems to turn everything he touches into gold. He should be pretty psyched about his graduation gift—Dad's getting him a motorcycle. Me, I got a Zippo lighter inscribed "Set the world on fire" when I graduated. Brian gets a Honda.

I found a bunch of old letters you've written over the years. Sure, I kept them. I keep everything. I'm glad I did, too. Rereading them made me realize what a perfect little whore I must sound like. Your message was always the same—stop, you're better than that.

Well, I wasn't. But I'm glad you thought so.

I needed to thank you, Kevin. For everything. Just for being a friend, even if it has had to be long distance. I really love you for that, you know. It helps to know someone really cares.

Love,
Debby

Kevin

"Found your mail, I see," Mom said. She pounced down the stairs, ruffling my hair as she stepped off the bottom stair where I was sitting. "Where's Lydia?"

I nodded in the general direction of the dining room, shoving the letter back into the envelope. "Eileen and Monica grabbed her and dragged her off before I could get the front door shut."

"You don't look too pleased."

"I wouldn't mind but I think I'm being dissected in there."

"Your grandmother is in there, too, you know."

"Cripes, it's a fricking conspiracy."

"She just wants to meet Lydia, sweetheart. Curious to see what kind of woman can trip you up. And your grandfather" – she pointed to the study – "is in there with your father and brothers and he wants to see you. Last I saw he was winning a game of eight ball."

She went into the living room, probably headed for the dining room, and I was sure poor Lydia was being grilled over an open pit filled with flaming Davis females.

If Lydia really wanted to know what a big family was like, she was about to find out. No such thing as complete privacy.

I steeled myself before going into the study, trying to psych myself for the ribbing that was sure to come. My father was bent over the pool table and my grandfather was standing nearby, waiting his turn. Nick and Paul were slumped in chairs, watching, and Spider was stretched out on the couch, asleep.

"Good Lord, boy," Grandpa chuckled when I came in. "Don't you ever stop growing?"

"I'm not growing, old man," I said, hugging him. "You're shrinking."

"You need to quit feeding him Chip. Any bigger and he'll be able to swat you down like a fly."

Dad shrugged. "He already can, Pop."

"Who's winning?" I asked.

"Who else?" Dad grunted. "The man is a shark. Don't ever play him for money."

"Which one of these suckers gets to play the winner?"

Nick sighed hard. "Me. Basically, we're all taking turns letting Grandpa beat us. You can have my turn if you want."

"Ah, no thanks. I can't even beat Nicole."

"She's across the street at a birthday party," Paul said, "but I can get her back over here if you want someone your skill level."

I took the soft drink he held out to me. "If I'm going to be humiliated I'd rather it be done by an adult."

"Did you bring Lydia over?"

"She's in the kitchen."

"And?"

"And what, Paul?"

"She decide to become your personal farm hand?"

Nick leaned forward, turning to look at him. "What?"

"Kev was moaning about fruit bearing trees last week. I was just wondering if he'd found someone to pick that last cherry off the tree."

"Knock it off, Paul," Dad ordered. "It's none of your business."

Grandpa was setting up for his shot, chuckling under his breath. "Like you don't want to know. What about it, K-Joe? Did you and when do I get to meet her?"

"Just go into the kitchen and there she is," I said, trying to ignore Paul. "She's the tall one with the freckles."

"Freckles, my ass," Paul laughed.

"Paul, you leave him alone, and I mean it," Dad barked.

"It's all right, Dad," I sighed. "And Grandpa, whatever you do, please don't call me K-Joe in front of her. She'll pick up on it in a heart beat and she's already got half a dozen other names I'm supposed to answer to."

"Humor her," Nick grumbled, rising from his chair. "Anyone want another beer or soda? I'm gonna restock the mini-fridge."

He left before anyone could answer.

"Where's Katie?" I asked.

"Don't ask him, Kevin," Paul said. "He says she'll be here later but I got the feeling that's just high hopes talking."

"Fighting?"

"You know Nick. He won't fight. He sulks. Whatever the rub is he's probably trying to ignore it and it's driving her up a wall."

Too much like Dad, who would rather run from a room naked and on fire than stand there and fight with Mom.

"Or," Dad said, taking the chalk from Grandpa, "Katie has work to do and couldn't make it, or she'll show up when she has a chance."

"Nah. They're pissed at each other. Nick's too grumpy for it to be anything else."

"Can't Nick be in a bad mood?"

"Sure," Paul allowed, "but he's been in a bad mood for a month or more, and I'm betting it's because of Katie."

"Maybe not," I said.

Dad turned from the pool table, leaning his cue against the wall. "Do you know something, Kevin?"

"If I do, it's between Nick and me," I said, not wanting to sound like a snot, but sure that's how it was coming out.

He looked like he was about to say something else, but after a moment he took a deep breath and just nodded.

"You worry too much," Grandpa told him.

"I'll worry until they're ninety and have great-grandkids of their own," Dad sighed. He dropped into the chair Nick had vacated; he looked tired and worn out, and I noticed for the first time that his temples were flecked with silver, tiny streaks of white that stood out against his neatly trimmed brown hair. "Kevin, I want to talk to you later."

"Grounded," Paul chuckled, popping a fist against my leg.

I wondered if they would try to ground Lydia, too.

Paul

Nick never came back into the study; instead he went out into the back yard and parked himself in a lawn chair. I leaned against the breakfast bar, blowing foam off the top of my beer, and watched him sit in the rain without a jacket on. He sat with his head thrown back and eyes closed, a condemned man waiting to be executed.

More than anything I wanted to go outside and drop into the chair next to him, to let him know I would listen. After all, Nick was the one I had cried with years before, when I wondered what kind of mess I'd gotten myself into; those first frenzied, frightening days when I realized that I would be a sixteen year old father, and aside from the terror of that certainty, I had no idea how to tell our parents.

Whatever Nick's private hell was, he wouldn't confide in me. He might talk to Kevin if he could pull his head out of his ass long enough to realize that Nick had a real problem.

Father Kevin became our confessor when he was too young to handle the responsibilities. Quirky, surprised Kevin, who was never sure exactly what he was supposed to say, who never fully realized that sometimes it was just nice to have someone to talk to, someone who would listen and then not spread what he'd heard to anyone else. The few times he dared to offer an opinion on our confessions, he generally got it right.

He would have been one hell of a priest.

I drained the glass and watched the remaining suds slowly slip to the bottom, a frothy pool that looked more like spit than beer. Nick used to win the spitting contests, held out in the backyard by the sandbox. Little Kevin was always there, trying hard to fit in, to measure up to the big guys, always a step or two behind.

He shot past all of us right about the time Nicole was born. One day I looked up from the tiny baby I was holding and saw a little brother at least four inches taller than I was, and the squirt kept right on growing.

So what does he do? He brings home a girlfriend who towers over most of us as well.

"Dude, I owe you an apology," I told him when he came into the kitchen for another soda.

"For?"

"The cherry remark. It was in bad taste and I know it."

"Didn't bother me," he said, popping the can open. "I expected you to pick on me. Who knew Dad would get so bent?"

"Mom's probably been driving him crazy. You pulled out of the driveway Friday and I thought she was going to start crying. She knew damn well what you had on your mind."

"Christ, it's not like I'm fourteen."

"No, but you're her baby," I said. I had an inkling how she felt. Nicole was only six and I was reaching panic levels some days. Those six years went by so fast, and I was sure the next six would zip by even quicker, and there was no end in sight. "She wasn't pissed off, Kev, just a little sad, that's all."

"She's going to have to get used to it."

"Eventually. I think it helps that it's Lydia and not one of the space cadets you tried dating last summer."

He was looking out the back door, staring at Nick. "If anything, she should be worrying about him. What the hell is he doing? It's freezing out there."

"I think he's planning on sitting out there until Katie comes over."

"So call her. Tell her to shag her butt over her before he catches pneumonia."

I stopped him before he could reach for the phone. "Stay out of it. Whatever it is, it's none of our business."

"Bull. If my virginity is family business, so's his problem with Katie." He shrugged my hand away and picked up the phone. "She's probably sitting at home waiting for him to call or come get her."

I lifted my hands and backed away, saying fine, I give up. Call. Make an ass of yourself.

Later, when Katie and Nick stopped staring and tumbled into each others arms, I wished it had been my idea.

Chip

When the study was finally empty – Terry's father had humiliated everyone enough for one evening – and the kids were either in the kitchen with Terry or going though old photo albums, I cornered Kevin.

He plopped down onto the sofa where Spider had been sleeping earlier and crossed his arms defiantly, expecting a lecture, waiting to be told again that he was a disappointment. I picked up a cue and chalked the end of it, hoping to entice him to the table.

"I never talked to you the way I did your brothers," I said, racking the balls. "The last time I tried you were fourteen and I swear you did all the talking."

The apprehension drained from his face and he laughed. "You mean this is about sex? Don't you think I'm a little old for this?"

"Are you?" I asked, lining up for the break.

"Dad, I've known about the particulars for a very long time."

"I'm sure you have, but I'm not sure you're so concerned about the particulars of keeping yourself safe."

"Which prompted you to stuff my pockets full of condoms. I was damn lucky they didn't fall out on the table during dinner."

"Yeah, well. I hung your suit up a while ago and you brought them all back unused."

"Was I supposed to bring them home used?"

I glanced up from the table and glared.

"She's on the Pill," he said, sighing hard. "We didn't need them."

I kept glaring.

"Do you want to see our HIV tests? I can show you. We're both perfectly fine, healthy people. No cootie swapping."

Relief.

"Dad, if it makes you feel any better, I'm head over heels in love with her. This whole weekend wasn't some drunken, stupid impulse."

So serious. Looking at him as like staring into a mirror a quarter decade in the past. Everything was the same—his hair, his eyes, even his smile. I looked at him and understood why Terry was so attached to our youngest son.

The biggest difference was that Kevin was my emotional opposite. At his age I was dead inside and was still almost a year away from realizing that were was something out there for me other than misery.

"Can I pry?" I asked him, staring down at the green felt, pretending to consider my options.

"I suppose."

"Was it your first time?" I looked up, surprised at the splash of red across his cheeks. "Are you all right?"

"I think I'm chafed."

"That's not what I mean and you know it." I tossed the cue onto the table and sat next to him on the sofa. Of course he knew what I meant, but he had no idea how to answer. All right? Sure—and scared, numb, excited, overjoyed, exhausted and exhilarated. "I asked Eileen the same thing, son. I probably should have asked Spider instead. He was the one bewildered out of his mind."

Kevin stared down at the floor and nodded as if he understood.

"I'm asking because I'm worried about you. You're like two people most of the time. Half the time you're this uncertain, scared little boy who uses booze to drown out the noise in his head, and the other half you're the young man who walked out of here Friday night, all dressed up with the intent to win his girl's heart. I can't connect the two."

He pushed himself up and picked up my cue stick, absently pushing balls around on the table.

"It was too swift a change. Last week you were drunk out of your mind—"

"Lydia knows why," he said.

"And I'm supposed to leave it at that?"

He turned and looked straight at me. "Yes. You're supposed to leave it at that. It's done, Dad. I'm not going to go hide in the park again and drink myself sick. She knows why I did it, and it won't happen again. That should be enough."

"It should be, but that was never you, Kevin. You weren't the kid who went out weekends and got plastered. You weren't the kid who stayed out all night without letting someone know where you'd be."

"Dad. I'm not a kid at all anymore."

"That's what terrifies me. Whatever is bothering you so much has got to be bigger than worrying about some playground bully. It would have to be something huge for you to go off like that."

"You'll have to take my word that I'm all right."

And that was it. Whatever it was I was not going to be among those he would confide in.

"What else is bothering you, Dad?"

"Well, if you're as all right as you say you are, then I don't have any problem issuing ultimatums," I said, getting up. I took the cue stick from him and set it aside, making sure I had his full attention. "You have one month to either get yourself enrolled in school or find a job."

"Or?"

"Or nothing. Those are your two choices. School or work, you decide."

"There has to be something else, Dad. School or work, or what? You'll throw me out? We both know I don't need a job for the sake of money. If I went back to school it'd be to appease you, because I don't have a fricking clue what I'd want to major in."

"It's not about money, Kevin. It's about finding some direction."

"I had direction. It didn't work."

"This isn't a debate. It's not even open for discussion. You either find a job or get into school. At the very least the community college has late registration for another week."

"Anything else?"

"One more thing. Either get your car fixed or buy a new one. I want mine back."

He fished in his pocket for the keys and tossed them

onto the pool table. "Fine. Thanks for letting me use it. Now if you'll excuse me, I'm going to walk Lydia home."

"You need to spend some time with your grandparents."

He stopped at the study door. "I'm sure they'll understand. There's no way in hell I'd let her walk home alone."

"Kev, you can take my car."

He was shaking his head.

"At least come home tonight."

"Unless I have a sudden and completely unenforceable curfew, no. You can't have it both ways, Dad. You can't have grown up Kevin and little boy Kevin and expect me to know which one you want to play with at any given moment. You want me to do something, fine. I'll find something to do. I'll get a new car. I'll be as little trouble to you as humanly possible."

"I blew it again," I told Terry later. "Only this time I may have seriously blown it."

We were in bed with the lights off, the house quiet except for her father's occasional deep laughter pouring through the walls. She rolled over and pushed her pillow closer to mine. "You always think you've seriously blown it. What happened this time?"

"I gave Kevin an ultimatum. Find a job or go back to school."

"That's reasonable."

"My timing was all wrong, Terry. I should have waited a day or two, not dumped it on him the day he comes home looking better than he ever has. He was pretty ticked off."

"He'll get over it, Chip."

"I also told him I wanted my car back. I didn't mean right this minute, but he stormed out saying he'd walk Lydia home."

"Well you just stepped in all kinds of doo doo tonight, didn't you?"

"Quit laughing, woman."

"Irish," she sighed, leaning her forehead against mine, "you have every right to expect him to do something with his life now. He wasn't expecting it, but he'll get over it. Trust me, if he grumbles too loud about it, you can bet Lydia will put him in his place."

I hoped she was better at it than I was.

Kevin

"Walking won't kill us," Lydia said halfway home in response to my tirade. "Getting a job won't kill you, either."

"Doing what?"

"Anything, Kevin. Get as mad as you want, but you're living in his house, he has every right to expect you to work."

"Traitor."

Later that night, lying in bed, while I pretended to watch the TV over her shoulder, she lifted her head and said, "Go to school, Kevin."

"You're blocking the news."

She moved until her face was in front of mine. "Kevin. Go to school. Don't major in anything. Just pick and choose the classes that interest you, and maybe you'll figure out what it is you really want to do."

"It's a little cold outside for underwater basketweaving one-oh-one," I grumbled.

"Give me that" – she took the remote and turned the television off – "and listen to me. As long as your parents will support you you'd be nuts not to take them up on the offer. You can take all the classes you wanted to in high school but couldn't fit in your schedule because of the academics they were stuffing down your throat. I remember how frustrated you got. You wanted to try photography and creative writing and even choir, but they had you in so many advanced classes there was no time for it all. You got to take a guitar class but that was it. Everything else was phys ed and brain busters."

Our junior year the drama department staged *South Pacific*; she was right, I had auditioned for it and landed a decent role, but then physics and organic chemistry reared their ugly heads.

Instead the role went to Byron Fink.

After high school Byron went to Julliard.

"I have one month," I reminded her. "Even if I apply now, I can't start until the summer term. Working is my only option."

"Community college," she said, sliding off me and onto her side. "You can apply tomorrow morning and register by noon. You might have to try to get teachers to let you in their classes in on the first day, but it's not too late."

Beg for entry. Please, oh please let me in your class so my daddy doesn't ground me.

"Can I take Latin?"

"No," she laughed. "Take something you know you won't get an A in."

"Anything else seems like work." I was still grumbling but warming up to the idea.

"I never understood why you didn't just leave high school when they wanted you to. You could have finished a degree before the rest of us graduated."

"Because I saw what it did to Nick," I said. "He started college when he was fifteen, and it turned him old. He got so frigging serious, never seemed to have much fun, and then there he was at eighteen—married. I wanted the chance to be a stupid kid for as long as I could."

"Rabbit."

"I know, I'm not a stupid kid anymore."

"Well."

"Phffft. If you're so hot on school, why didn't you go?"

"I did, for a while," she said. "Part time. But then my parents decided to go overseas, and I had to work full time. I'd go back if I could manage it. There's so much out there that I don't know … I blew off high school. I'd like another chance."

"I suppose I could take a few classes to appease my dad."

"He just wants you to get excited about something."

"But—"

"Something where you keep your clothes on, Kevin."

"Oh."

There's always a catch.

The next morning I woke up when Lydia's alarm went off, ignored her feigned protests and jumped into the shower with her, fished my clothes out of her dryer, and dropped her off at work before heading for the community college.

By ten thirty I had seen a counselor, filled out an application, been admitted, perused the course catalog, and registered for four classes.

By eleven I was standing in line at the bookstore, armed with textbooks for creative writing, designing web pages, and Spanish. The gym class I'd decided on at the last minute required no text books, though I could have picked up any number of books on running, weight lifting, and bowling for beginners, if I'd wanted to.

By noon I was at the mall, looking for a good notebook computer.

By one I was at home. I stacked the books on the kitchen table, slapped the receipt for my tuition and books down, and told my father, “There. I’m in school.”

He picked up my schedule and looked at it, but said nothing about my class choices. He just nodded and said, “Holler if you need help with the Spanish. It’ll be the first time since junior high that you’re doing something I can understand.”

“Lydia won’t let me take Latin.”

He laughed and tossed the schedule back onto the table, and wandered out into the living room.

There was no reason to pretend.

We both knew who was in charge.

12

Kevin

The day Paul and Monica left for Lake Tahoe, their second honeymoon more or less, Nicole stomped down the stairs, dragging her coat in one hand and a crumpled spelling assignment in the other. She dropped both near the table and climbed into her chair – loudly – and scowled at me.

Dad ignored her not-so-silent indignation and continued making her breakfast. I was sitting across from her at the table, trying to get in a few more minutes of study time before taking off for my first class.

"What's wrong, munchkin?" I finally asked, after she'd kicked the underside of the table for a fifth time.

"I wanna stay home," she grumbled.

I closed the Spanish book; with her there and babbling I wouldn't be able to remember a single thing I'd read, and if she went into full tantrum force I could wind up with orange juice and Cheerios plastered all over pictures of Señor Gomez telling us all *¡Hola! Me llamo Ricardo Gomez* and *Hasta manana.*

When Nicole realized that Mommy and Daddy were going somewhere fun without her, the whining began in earnest. She hadn't whined more than twice in the eight months I had been home, but in two days she managed to piss off the entire family and burned any bridges she might have had towards sympathy. I figured she was good for about ten more minutes of it, then Dad would lower the boom.

I wanted to be out of there when he did.

"I don't wanna go to school, but Grandpa's making me."

"I feel your pain, kiddo," I told her, getting up and grabbing my book. "I feel your pain."

In Spanish I sat between Autumn Webster, who whined about every homework assignment and who stated loudly, and often, that after 9-11, all Muslims should 'go back where they came from,' and Devyn Powter, who was 14 years old and taking classes here and there to fill in what his mother didn't feel she was able to teach him at home. He didn't whine, but his topics of conversation were still centered around Lego blocks and Nintendo games, neither of which I had touched in years. He had a crush on a girl in his computer sciences class named Britney, but she was 18 and only wanted to be his friend.

He didn't understand when I told him to get used to the concept.

The phys ed class was filled with teenagers wanting to get their 2 units of sweat equity over with, kids who dabbled on the weight machines but didn't really put much effort into it, and a couple of elderly people taking the class because it was cheaper than joining a gym. They worked hard, but slow, and were frustrating to pair up with.

Most days I wound up working out with the teacher, Lauren, a former female body builder who could match most of my weights and didn't mind taking the long way when jogging for cardiac conditioning.

"Next semester," she said while we were making the turn for our fourth lap of six, "take the advanced class. Half of them are still screwing around, but at least there are some serious students in that class."

I was trying not to think beyond this particular semester.

She wasn't surprised that I'd trained most of my life in a martial art—"you have that long, hard, lean look of someone who does a lot of cardio work," she said, without any hint of coming on to me—but she was very surprised to find out I'd spent three years in a seminary.

When she asked why I'd given it up, I shrugged and said, "there was this girl…"

She didn't need to hear any more.

Lauren was close to my mother's age, but had a harsh look about her, the years of physically beating herself up to have as little body fat and as much muscle mass as possible showing in sharp angles around her jaw and in fine lines around her eyes. Her boyfriend of 15 years had also been a body builder; I wasn't quite sure why she shared that particular detail of her life, other than to answer the unasked question most of the kids in class had: is she gay?

I couldn't have cared less. She could keep up with me, and in our long jogs and competitive runs up the bleachers, I was reminded of why I had trained with my karate teacher for so long. That absolute feeling of freedom after hitting the wall and breaking through, the second wind that rushes in after feeling like fatigue is about to overtake and consume everything in its path.

Rushing up the bleacher steps, I realized I missed it.

~

Lydia

Kevin was waiting for me when I got off work; I stepped out of the bank and into the snap of cold air, and he was sitting there on the hood of my truck, his feet planted on the rusting bumper, eyes fixated on a woman walking down the sidewalk.

I didn't know whether the red in his cheeks was from the cold or from embarrassment over being caught so flagrantly ogling someone else.

"If you're going to watch women," I said, kissing his cold lips, "you'll have to learn to blink once in a while."

"At least I wasn't drooling." He put his arms around me, pulling me close. "You're freezing. Where's your coat?"

"I didn't think I'd need it today. No one told me I'd be standing out in the parking lot after work, smooching some cute guy."

"You forgot I had your truck."

"Only for a minute."

In three minutes he had the heat inside the truck going. "Can I show you something before I take you home?"

"Here, in the parking lot?"

"Ha." He put the truck into reverse and pulled out slowly. "So, good day at work today? Crappy? Indifferent."

"Good day," I said, sliding across the bench seat to sit closer to him. He turned his head and glared—"put your seat belt back on"—but he didn't object when I set my hand in his lap. "There weren't many grouchy people at my window today, and it went by pretty quick. How was school?"

"School was good. School is why I'm dragging you off to show you something."

"Any hints?"

He grinned. "It involves a lot of sweating, and sometimes grunting."

"We could have done that back in the parking lot."

Three or four miles down the road he turned off into an empty parking lot and pulled up to an old brick building. There was a showroom window filled with trophies, and a small sign on the front door that said "Self Defense Taught Here."

"Your old karate school?" I asked.

He nodded. "Yep."

He unlocked the door and opened it, letting me in first. It was dimly lit and not especially clean, the floor littered with scraps of paper and discarded candy wrappers. He led me through a second door, into a large room that had one wall lined with mirrors than nearly ran floor to ceiling. On the far side of the room there was a heavy canvas bag suspended from the ceiling by a chain, and an assortment of equipment that I didn't recognize.

"Kevin, what's that smell? It's like old feet."

"It *is* old feet," he laughed. "The carpet needs to be cleaned."

I could picture him working out here, sparring with old friends. He seemed at ease standing there in the middle of the floor, soaking in old surroundings.

"Are you getting back into classes here?" I asked, peeking around a corner. The room had a space off to the end where the carpet ended and rubber floor mats began. "Or are you just thinking about it?"

He was quiet for a minute and then said, "I bought it. I came here after my last class to talk to my old instructor about getting back into classes, but he wants to retire. He was planning on closing it down."

I wasn't sure I heard him right. "You bought it?"

"He's got two hundred students who would have been

without a school. And three instructors who would have been out of jobs. It just felt right, so I bought it."

With what, I wondered, keeping it to myself. Your dad's platinum MasterCard? Kevin had never held a job that I knew of; he had money, yes, I was aware of that, but other than a couple of wild dates, he didn't make a show of throwing it around. He was downright frugal sometimes, going as far as rinsing out sandwich baggies, pointing out that I could easily reuse them. He had money, but I didn't think he had that much.

The look on his face, pure joy, quieted any sudden doubts I had. He stood in the middle of the room, his hands stuffed into the pockets of his khakis – something I noted he was wearing so often he either bought more or was washing the one pair five times a week – and watched me absorb everything, a slight smile tugging at the corners of his mouth.

On one wall there were pictures, rows of students in uniform, smiling brightly, some in groups and some standing with the instructor's arm around their shoulders. I found one of Kevin at ten or eleven years old, his instructor on one side and his father on the other.

His first degree black belt test, I realized. He had trained with Chip, and they had made it to that first black belt together, but I wasn't sure if his father had kept on after that.

I was looking for more signs of him there, pictures of a taller Kevin, when I heard him take a deep breath, and then say, "You should marry me."

"What?"

He had taken a few steps towards me, but stopped when I turned around. "You should marry me," he repeated. "We're good together, Lydia. As much as we love each other, we should be married."

"For that matter we could just live together."

He shook his head. "Great fringe benefits but no real commitment. I love you, and I want to marry you."

When I reached him, certain he wasn't teasing, I set my forehead against his chest, fingers tracing lines over his sweatshirt. "Rabbit … too many surprises for one afternoon. You're serious, aren't you?"

I could feel him tense. "You don't want to marry me."

"I didn't say that," I said, looking up. His eyes were filled with pain, and he squinted against it. "Kevin, I love you, you know that. You make my head spin, I love you so much."

"But?"

"But you're still too innocent to have to face marriage on a daily basis."

"Innocent?"

"It's a compliment," I said, hoping to soothe hurt feelings before it got out of hand. "Rabbit, we're still so excited to have each other again, and we're still floating on our own little cloud because we finally got the nerve to make love with each other, but I don't think either one of us is ready for that much."

He didn't try to pull away, and when I touched his face, tracing over his beard, he kissed the tips of my fingers.

"Will you let me know when you think we are?"

"I think we'll know."

He took a deep breath and then let it out slowly, deliberately, rolling his eyes. "Innocent?"

"I can't think of the right word. Innocent might not be it."

"Naïve," he suggested. "Maybe."

"Maybe."

"I reserve the right to ask you again."

"Fair enough."

"Repeatedly."

"Can I ask you something?"

"Yes," he sighed. "I'll marry you."

I laughed, but ignored it. "When are you going to talk to Will?"

"Honestly, I was hoping you'd forget about that and let it slide. I think I'm okay, Lydia. I hardly ever think about it, and when I do I'm angry but it's not like I felt before."

"Will you do it for me?"

He looked over my head, glancing at the pictures on the wall, the trophies, the fingerprint smudged mirrors and chain dangling from the ceiling. "All right. But you promised you'd go with me."

"I will."

"I've only told you and Eileen," he said on the way out the door. "I don't have a clue how to tell Will."

He couldn't tell Will.

Will Parker had been a priest before he was a bartender; he was the person Kevin turned to the most when his parents were separated, the person in whom Kevin confided his deepest spiritual concerns. When he left the priesthood to pursue his own love, he left an entire parish mourning their loss. He also left 15 year old Kevin unsure of who he could talk to, and later left Kevin wondering if his advice to wait a year or two before committing himself to seven years in a seminary was advice born out of wanting to be sure it was the direction Kevin needed to go, or if he thought Kevin shouldn't be there at all.

But he trusted Will. If anyone could help him find closure, it would be Will.

Kevin tried, in a dozen false starts, before finally turning to me with a look that begged for me to bail him out. We sat together on the sofa in Paul's office; Kevin seemed intent on staring at his shoes, and Will, who perched himself on the desk, seemed intent on trying to hear what Kevin wanted to say without forcing him to actually say it.

While Kevin picked at a loose thread in the sofa, I told Will everything I could. As I spoke I could hear Kevin's breathing quicken, and he swallowed hard several times, never looking up.

"He claims he's all right now," I said, looking first at Kevin and then at Will. "I'm not so sure."

The sympathy that tumbled in Will's gray eyes settled on us both, a thick blanket of comfort; from that look alone I knew that if he could, he would take Kevin's pain and make it his own.

It shouldn't have surprised me; he loved Kevin as much as I did.

"I am okay," Kevin protested, his voice barely above a whisper.

Will never asked him why he hadn't told anyone at the seminary or why he had never gone to the police. He did ask why Kevin had never been able to tell his parents, but the only thing Kevin could say was, "I can't do this to them."

He stood up suddenly, flustered. "I'll be right back, I need … I'm going to the bar for a minute. Just for a soda, I swear."

The door clicked shut before I could say anything to him.

"All right," Will said, sliding off the desk and sitting next to me, "from your point of view, how is he, really?"

"Lately he's been fine," I said, not sure how far back I

needed to go. All the way back to the night we'd found each other in the bar? To the nights when I had been sure he'd ask to stay, only to have him pull away and say he needed to go home before he did something we weren't ready for? Will already knew about Kevin's three day drunken spree, that in itself was completely out of character.

"He was angry when Chip gave him the choice between getting a job or going to school," I said. "It didn't seem reasonable to me. I mean, he wasn't screaming or throwing things, but he was obviously unhappy about it."

"Yet he's in school."

"He registered the next day. And then today he comes to pick me up from work and takes me to his old dojo. Will, he *bought* it. He didn't think about it, he just bought it."

Will paused to consider, and then said, "If you could go back to one of the happiest points of your childhood and own it, wouldn't you grab that while you could?"

"I would think about it first."

He shook his head. "If you didn't have to weigh the consequences, if money wasn't an issue, and time wasn't an issue ... wouldn't you jump to own that piece of yourself?"

"You don't think it has anything to do with what happened to him?"

"Of course it does. But it's not a bad thing."

Then what about his awkward marriage proposal, I asked. He stood there with his hands stuffed into pants pockets and made a declaration – I should marry him – not a request. It was a statement out of nowhere and not even related to being there in the school.

"Of course it was," Will said. "You're a part of his past, Lydia, a major part of his childhood, when he felt safe. He wants you to be a part of his future, and owning that school will be a part of his future, too. It sounds like a clunky way to propose, but I can see where he was coming from. He had two treasured things in his life right there, and he wanted to make sure they'd both be there for good."

"It felt like an impulse," I said.

"A huge part of him has thought about you becoming his wife from the moment it occurred to him that girls are here for a reason," Will told me. "It's been in the back of his mind since the first time you kissed him. Lately that thought has been pushing its way out … something recently must have given it that final kick."

I could feel myself blushing.

"Don't be embarrassed. If he's sleeping with you, that's a good thing. It means he's able to separate what happened to him from what he does with you."

"Pretty much."

"Meaning?"

While Kevin was off finding a soft drink, I was trying not to melt into the sofa cushions or die of embarrassment.

"There are some things he can't bring himself to do," I said with a heavy sigh, closing my eyes. "It's not a major thing and I can live without it, but it strikes me as being a little odd, especially for a guy."

He waited, and I felt my face burning.

Don't make me say it.

He kept waiting.

In one long breath I finally said, "Don'tmostguyswantablowjob?"

Someone, anyone, take me away.

"Do you know if the man who molested him performed oral sex on him?"

Molested. Even Will was tap dancing around it.

I didn't know, but before I could say anything, Kevin was there, his face pale, jaw set in anger. "No, he did not," Kevin spat. "And thanks a hell of a lot, Lydia."

"It matters," Will said.

"No, it fucking does not!"

"Then explain it to me," Will said, getting up, standing in front of Kevin. "Something two adults generally do as a routine part of play. She tries it and you, what…?"

"Wilt like lettuce," I muttered.

"Lydia, shut the fuck up!"

Will was in his face before I could say anything else, his hand against Kevin's chest. "I don't care how pissed off you are, or how badly you feel about what happened. You don't speak to her like that. Not ever."

Kevin took a surprised step back.

"I'll help you any way I can," Will went on, "but don't expect me to coddle you like a five year old. And don't expect me to allow you to use your pain as an excuse to abuse others. I *will* help you get through this, Kevin, but I want you to think about that little outburst first, and then come back later and tell me everything is all right with you."

I watched Will leave; Kevin didn't move, not until the door was closed.

"I'm sorry," I said. "That little tidbit was something I should have kept to myself."

"Does that really matter to you? Is it important?"

"It doesn't have to be. It just strikes me as odd, that's all. We haven't been sleeping together very long, Kevin. I'm sure we'll find things one of us doesn't like."

We suffered through strained silence on the way to my apartment; I stared out the window and Kevin fiddled with the stereo, changing the station every other minute. When he pulled into the parking lot and cut the engine, he handed me the keys.

"Will you be hurt if I don't come in?" he asked.

"You're that angry?"

"No," he said, shaking his head. "I just need some time to think. I'll walk home."

I tried to hand the keys back. "I have tomorrow off. Take the truck, just don't go off drinking."

"It's okay. I'll walk. And I'll go home, I won't detour and wind up at some bar, I swear."

He waited until I had my door unlocked before he turned and headed down the street. I watched him until he disappeared around the corner; he walked with his hands in his pockets, his head hung and shoulders hunched.

I understood why he wanted to be alone.

I just didn't share in the feeling.

"We should be passing a joint back and forth," Eileen snickered, taking a glass of wine from me. She'd seen Kevin walk away from her front window and stepped outside to see if he wanted a ride home; when she saw me watching him walk away, she wandered down the walkway to make sure everything was all right.

Spider was grading papers and would welcome her absence, she said when I asked her to come in. His idea of peace and quiet was not being distracted by seeing her move around out of the corner of his eye.

We flopped back on piles of pillows under the loft, the space lit by nearly a dozen candles.

"I can stand in the shower and howl until the people downstairs call the cops," she'd said, "but if I get up and cross the room one time too many, he gets annoyed."

Now she was contemplating the wine. "You'd never guess that my dad was one of the most straight laced survivors of the sixties and seventies. If he'd ever caught any of us smoking grass we'd have been crucified."

"Grass got me thrown out of Disneyland," I laughed.

"Spider and I tried it a few times, just to see what the big deal is. He never managed a buzz and was really pissed off that I liked it. A lot. I would have loved to have gotten Kevin stoned. He was always such a straight arrow."

"Not always. His quills were ruffled a few times."

Eileen looked at me over the rim of her wine glass. "He's ruffled like hell now, isn't he?"

I fell back on a big pillow, arching over it until my head touched the floor. "Eileen, he was so upset. His knuckles were white on the steering wheel."

"He was embarrassed," she said, waving it off. "He'll get over it. If you'd insisted he come in for a while you'd have already smoothed it over and instead of you getting me tipsy, he'd be jumping your bones."

I didn't think so. He'd been so excited when he picked me up from work, and in just a few short hours looked like he wanted to curl up in a tight little ball and disappear inside himself. That was my fault. I'd pushed him to go talk to Will instead of celebrating with him.

"Why," Eileen asked later, when the bottle of wine was nearly gone and the room was starting to spin, "did you turn down his proposal? You don't want to marry him?"

"Of course I want to. I just don't think we're ready yet."

"We?"

Shades of familiarity; lay the blame where it belongs. "All right, I don't think I'm ready. I have a job I'm starting to despise and I don't want to worry later that I used Kevin to get out of it. And I've barely gotten used to living on my own. I'd rather wait until I'm settled."

"Oh, bull poop," Eileen snipped. "Marry Kevin and you'll have all the time you need to get out of that job and find something else. He's not as lazy as he wants everyone to think, and it'll be a long time before he's broke. Crud, make the little booger happy and just get engaged."

"I smell a hard sell."

"I happen to think you two make a terrific couple, and I want him to be happy. You make him happy."

"Horny. I make him horny."

"Well, there's that, too."

"He still has a lot to sort out," I said.

"Yes, he does," she agreed. "And you'll be there to help him sort through it whether you've made these huge formal vows or not, right? Hell, you're already committed to each other. Why not make it legal?"

I emptied the rest of the bottle into my glass. "Maybe after we've gotten him stoned."

Kevin

I did as I promised; I went home without any detours, and walked straight into a poker game.

"Sonofagun, I'm never playing cards with you again," Grandpa roared, tossing the cards on the table. "Damned if you aren't the luckiest little pecker."

I swept the chips to my side of the table and grinned as he popped the top to a beer can open. "It's skill, mister," I laughed. "Luck is for losers."

"Shut up and deal the cards, boy."

Dad leaned back in his chair and watched as I shuffled the deck. "Friday night," he quipped. "I didn't expect to see your hide around here until at least tomorrow afternoon."

"I smelled money," I said. "Grandpa's wallet was screaming to be lightened up a little."

Grandpa frowned at the card in his hand. "Bull. He had a fight with his girl. Give me three cards."

"Dad?"

"Two," he muttered, tossing his down. "So, the lovebirds are going at it?"

"Not really. We just needed a night apart."

"Hmph." Grandpa threw his card to the table. "I fold. You said something stupid, I'm sure."

"Thanks for the faith, Grandpa. Dad?"

"Lousy pair of jacks."

I grinned again and spread my cards out. "Read 'em an weep, pops. Two aces, two queens. I thank you, my bank account thanks you."

"Bank account my ass," Dad sniffed.

"Women," Grandpa said. "Expensive little creatures."

"But they're worth it," I sighed. "Most of the time, anyway."

Nick came in, face red from the cold. "Who's worth what?" he asked, shrugging out of his jacket.

I pushed the deck towards Dad. "Female type people," I answered. "Expensive but worth it."

"Christ, I can tell you're not married," Nick grumbled. "The numbers on your MasterCard aren't worn down to nothing."

"Nope, but then I don't have one anyway."

"Keep it that way, squirt. Damn little pieces of plastic aren't worth it."

"As I understand it," Dad offered, "and this is straight from your mother, shopping with cash doesn't carry the same thrill as loading up a credit card. Don't ask me why, but somewhere written in stone is the rule Thou Shalt Charge To Thy Heart's Content."

"Isn't monster spending a substitute for sex?" I tossed the cards down. "Four."

Dad laughed and counted from the top of the deck. "Son, your mother couldn't spend that much if her life depended on it."

"Must be hell, Dad," Nick said.

Grandpa looked over the edges of his cards. "I would remind you three that the woman you're speaking of is my little girl."

"Well, Grandpa," I told him, "your little girl is pretty fricking loud at two in the morning. I think I'm emotionally scarred for life. That's my *mom*."

"You mean old age hasn't quieted her any?" Nick asked.

Dad just smiled.

"Squirt, you want to take a ride with me? I've got to go to San Francisco."

"What for?" I asked.

"Katie's sister. We're stuck with her for a couple weeks. I figured since you two are friends—"

"He'll go," Dad said firmly.

"I will?" I handed the cards back to my grandfather and got up. "I guess I will. But it's not like we're great friends, Nick. I had a couple of classes with her in ninth grade and she writes me strange letters three or four times a week. I'm more like her personal Ann Landers."

"You're one up on me. I don't know her at all." He shrugged back into his jacket, tugging at the sleeves. "All I know is that the Colonel has been desperate to get rid of her for months, so guess who gets stuck with her?"

"I suppose she accounts for some of the sore spots between you and Katie?" Dad pressed. "Fighting the inevitable?"

"Something like that," Nick said. "I'm not real thrilled about this. Debby is a fruitcake and has been in so much trouble it's not funny. What the hell am I supposed to do with her? She needs a shrink, not a vacation."

"Could be she needs the vacation first, sport," Dad told him. "Damien Forrester can be a hard man sometimes and I would bet she's had enough. Getting away might be what she needs."

"She hates Washington," I added. "Maybe it won't be so bad, Nick. Just from what she's told me, a few days out here and she'll be looking for a job and an apartment. I doubt she'll go back."

"Just what I needed to hear."

Speeding down the highway, cold air rushing in through windows that no longer stayed completely rolled up, Nick confided on pain of two broken knees, that Debby's presence in his house was the least of his problems. At worst, she only complicated an already sticky situation.

"So what's the rub?" I asked.

We were at the airport, fighting through the long lines of people waiting to check in, trying to worm our way closer to the passenger security gates. Under the bright terminal lights I could see the weariness in his eyes, the tired ache that consumed him. We were seated by the passenger gate before he would answer, the long drive and a fierce need to talk to someone lowering his inhibitions.

"For starters, she's still pissed about law school. Only now she's pissed off because I quit and still haven't told Mom and Dad. She thinks I'm some kind of dickless wonder."

"It's none of their business, Nick."

"I should still tell them," he said. "But now on top of everything she decides now is a good time to start a family.

It's like an obsession. She even threw out her birth control pills."

"So?"

"So," he sighed, "we're not sleeping together."

"Dude, seriously? She kicked you out of bed?"

He slumped in his chair, resting elbows on his knees. "So to speak."

"What the hell is wrong with you?"

He turned his head. "There's nothing wrong with me. It's not like she wants a new car or a different house or something I can handle. She wants a *baby,* Kevin. A person. Once its here it won't go away."

"You don't want kids?"

"Someday."

"You've been married for almost seven years, Nick. Katie waited through undergrad crap and most of law school, and you want her to wait some more. For what? You know, all she had to do was go off the pill and not say anything to you. You can't sit here and tell me that if she suddenly announced she was pregnant that you wouldn't be happy about it."

"I don't know."

"You'd be thrilled and you know it. Why fight it?"

Nick leaned back, running his fingers through his hair. "Why now? What is so important about having a kid now?"

"Maybe Katie finally feels like a grown up."

"Why," he groaned when we heard the overhead announcement that Debby's plane had pulled up to the gate and passengers were disembarking, "do I get the feeling that not one person in this family will be on my side in this one?"

"Because you're being a jerk."

"Maybe we can call a truce while Debby's here."

"Dream on," I said. "Katie's as stubborn as you are."

Nick started to reply, but was cut off by the short blond who flew past him and jumped up at me, throwing her arms around my neck.

"Kevin! God, I knew you'd be here!"

I stared over at Nick, enduring this stranger's frenzied embrace.

The perfume, I noted sourly, was the same cheap fragrance splashed on nearly every letter and birthday card she'd ever sent. It was the first thing I noticed, that smell.

It was more than that, I realized on the way home.

I smelled trouble.

13

Kevin's Journal
2 Feb 2002

Holy shit, whoever first said that life's a bitch and then you die wasn't screwing around. Just when things seem to have taken on a shade of normalcy, the carpet gets pulled right out from under your feet and you find yourself flat on your ass trying to figure out what happened.

Paul called Dad from Tahoe and asked him to drive up to Sacramento and meet him at UCD Medical Center. Monica thought she had just pulled a muscle in her back, but when the pain didn't get any better Paul took her to an ER up there. After the x-rays they did an MRI, and then shoved her into an ambulance and sent her to Sacramento.

It's so fucking unfair. Paul left here thinking they were starting over, he never had a clue that it was just the beginning of the end.

Bone cancer.

Osteosarcoma.

Monica has this creeping crud growing inside her body. It started with a tumor on her pelvis but they found cancer cells everywhere they looked. They can't operate, not without doing some really radical chemo and radiation to try to shrink the main tumor, but all that buys her is time.

Doug says without any treatment she's probably got two months left. That's it. Two lousy months.

Paul's a wreck. He looks like someone took a white-hot steel rod and slammed it into his chest. I don't even know what I can do for him. Nothing I say or do will make him feel any better or hurt any less. He's twenty three years old, for Christ's sake. He should just now be venturing out into life, not facing losing his wife.

And what about Nicole?

She turns seven in just a few weeks. And a little while after that, she'll lose her mother for good. At least when Paul and Monica were just split up, Nicole always knew her mother was there, somewhere, as close as a phone. How do you tell a seven year old about dying, especially when it's her mother?

I have no goddamn right to be wallowing in the huge pool of pity I filled up for myself. My problems are nothing compared to this.

I sucked it up and went back to talk to Will. I don't really understand why Lydia and Eileen both seem to think that I've latched onto all this pain. I don't think that's my problem. I think my problem is that I've never really had to think about what I was going to do with my future. It was just there, more or less laid out for me.

Now I have to think about it, and before I can decide what to do with it, I think I have to find myself, but frankly, I don't know where to look.

I like school, I have to admit that. I enjoy not having to worry about grades for now, and I like the classes I'm taking. Or maybe it's the positive feedback I get off on. I get a hell of a lot of support in the creative writing class, and for the most part I help teach the body conditioning class. Lauren works with the newbies, and I spend my time now helping the few who have decided they really need the workout.

Helping teach pretty much reaffirmed for me that buying the dojo was a good idea. Better yet, Dad thinks it's a good investment. I wanted him to check out the building before I committed to a long term lease with the owner; Dad thought I'd be better off to make the guy an offer to buy it outright. I was looking at it as having the school; Dad looks at it as future growth potential.

And he's right. There used to be a little bistro at the far end of the building, but the location wasn't terribly great for that kind of business. All the equipment is still there, though, and the first thing I thought of when we were looking at it was all the times after class that we got the munchies, when we wanted food but not frou-frou food. We wanted sandwiches. Big, thick, meaty sandwiches.

Dad concurred. He also peeked over the fence to the vacant lot behind the dojo and one to the right of it, and thinks there's investment potential there. So I made an offer of the building and he made offers on the land.

We got them.

I'm going to be a fricking business owner. Not just of the dojo, but a sandwich shop, too, with Dad's help.

I don't know the first thing about business.

Now if only Dad could help me with dastardly Debby. This girl is loony. I wasn't sure I was going to survive the ride back from the airport. She wouldn't keep her hands to herself and she pretty much ignored Nick. The whole way back she talked at me, pawing and groping. She never talked TO me, just at me.

I suppose I should be kind of flattered at the attention, but it's not what I'm after. Sad thing is, Debby doesn't look much different than she did when she was 14. And she acts it. About the most mature thing out of her since she got here has been an honest effort to find a job. Katie said she started looking within two days.

Nothing really matters, though, does it?

And what's really sad. Monica is in the hospital, terrified that Paul will forget her. She's lying in that bed, wracked in pain, worrying that after all this, he'll forget her.

She just doesn't understand.

Love never forgets.

~

Nicole played in her room, her murmuring just loud enough for me to hear over the buzz of the television static. I sat on my bed, watching but not really seeing it, listening to her help Barbie berate Ken for being late for a date and not shaving. While she nagged the poor guy about the evils of facial hair I scratched at my own, and for a minute contemplated shaving it off.

Another minute and I might have, until the woman who seemed to like it best wandered into my room, looking a little lost and unsure she should be there.

"Your mother told me to come up," Lydia said, standing in the doorway. "She didn't think you'd mind having your territory invaded."

"You can invade my territory anytime you want," I said, holding out my arms to her. She curled up next to me, her head on my shoulder. "Mom probably figured it'd be easier to talk up here with Debby prowling around down there."

"Poor baby. All these women drooling after you."

"She's a fruitcake."

"Come on, give her a break. She came here expecting you to fall all over her. You can't blame her for hanging on a little."

"I never said I was interested."

"You answered her letters, Rabbit. Implied interest."

"So what the hell do I do about it? Tell her to take a flying leap?"

"You don't want to hurt her feelings, do you? She can't help it if she's half in love with you and it's not her fault that I got my hands on you first."

"A rational person would accept the inevitable and just walk away, Lydia. I don't need another lunatic in my life."

"She's rational," Lydia said. "Just not patient."

If I had an answer for that, the thought was lost to the sound of Nicole's humming. We crept towards her bedroom, the music coming from her too much to resist in a house that had been grim and quiet for two days. We stood at her open doorway, watching her play with her dolls, making them dance in broad circles across the wood floor.

At the end of the dizzingly fast dance she shoved them under her bed and jumped up, spinning to the music in her head.

She giggled when she saw us there, but she kept on spinning. "Hi!"

"Hi yourself," I said. "How come you're in here playing alone?"

Nicole stopped and considered me seriously. "Uncle Nick and Aunt Katie don't wanna play because they're in bad moods, and Grandma is talking to that lady."

"That lady," I told her, "is Katie's sister. Her name is Debby."

"I *know* that," Nicole groaned. "She's *boring*."

"It's nice outside today," Lydia said. "Do you want to go out and play tag with Kevin and me?"

Nicole looked at her, brightening. "Sure!"

She scrambled around my legs and was headed for the stairs before I could blink, and Lydia was close behind her.

"You're it, Rabbit."

Tag with an almost seven year old wasn't as easy as I supposed, Nicole being as wiry and fast as only a small child can be, twisting and turning away from my hands, my height and her lack of it making it impossible to get my hands on her.

I knew better than to tag Lydia.

Nicole demonstrated an uncanny ability to scramble under the bushes, just out of my reach. After fifteen minutes of chasing her, I collapsed onto the grass, venting a pseudo-protest and surrendering.

"You're old, Uncle Kevin," she giggled from behind the bushes.

"You cheat," I shot back. "Go in my room and get my football. We can play catch instead. You can't cheat at catch."

I would let her if I could, though, Lydia reminded me. We spent the afternoon playing games with Nicole, listening to her laugh, and it was all I could to keep from scooping her up and holding her tightly.

She didn't know.

We played catch and then Simon Says; the whole time I had the thought spinning around in the back of my head was that these were the last days she would feel so happy, and there was no way any of us would ever be able to soften the blow when it finally came.

Chip

I laid awake in the dark, staring blankly at the ceiling,

my arms folded behind my head. I listened to Terry's uneven breathing; she was awake and on her side facing away from me, probably wrestling with the same monsters I was, probably pretending sleep to avoid bothering me.

Every breath I took came with the weight of pressure that I hadn't felt in over twenty years, not since Nick was a baby and Paul no bigger than a dust mote. I could feel it constricting, wrapped around me in tight coils, its heaviness pressing me deeper into the waterbed mattress.

In the next room my granddaughter was fidgeting in her sleep, feet slapping against the wall as she rolled over. I knew that if I bothered to check, there would be a light shining under the door that connected her room to her father's.

The hell I saw swimming in Paul's eyes terrified me. He looked too much like a wounded animal, too crippled to limp away from the cage rapidly descending on him. My son's eyes, brightened lately by renewed love, were now aching red, bleary and confused. His bewildered face screamed the same question that tore through my own mind like clockwork, a precise ticking swing of a pendulum.

Why?

Terry rolled over and lifted herself up on an arm. "Can't sleep either, Irish?"

I sighed in response and reached out for her. With the exception of Nicole, none of us had been able to do more than sleep in snatches. Terry and I felt consumed with the reality that we were losing Monica; Kevin felt burdened by the guilt of having ignored her for so long.

He'd disapproved of his brother's conduct during his marriage, but when push came to shove, he took Paul's side. Kevin loved Monica but rarely spoke to her; he tried to understand her, but wouldn't face her.

Terry and I had been married for over twenty five years. We'd been together longer than we'd been alive before we met. Through the worst of it, I knew that no matter what, she was safe. She was healthy. She might not want to look at me or speak to me, but she was there, and it was likely that there would be another breath to follow, another breath to be sucked in sharply in anger, or let out slowly in contentment. I wouldn't lie in bed at night, wondering if the last sound I would hear before falling asleep would be the last breath she'd ever exhale.

"I couldn't do it," I whispered. "I'm not that strong. If I knew for certain I was going to lose you and never have a chance to get you back…"

"Don't give Paul any ideas," she said.

Paul's backbone was stronger than mine. He was capable of shifting his focus to his daughter; he'd live for her if no one else.

I wasn't so sure I could do that.

"If I don't say it enough, I love you."

She lowered her lips to mine and kissed me, very slowly. "You say it every day, Irish. Sometimes twice a day and three times on Sunday."

"Just so you know."

"You don't have to say it for me to know. I can feel it, Chip."

"I feel it, too, woman. Every time you look at me."

She brushed her lips over mine again and then settled against me, her head on my shoulder. "Is it my imagination or do I still hear Kevin and Lydia downstairs?"

"Not your imagination. When I came upstairs he was trying to teach her to play pool. Think we have an over night guest?"

"I don't care," she sighed, stretching against me. "She's good for him, and I could get used to another person at the breakfast table."

"What, no tears over losing your baby boy to some trashy woman?"

"He's dating Lydia, not Debby."

"Terry!"

"All right," she snickered, "I'm sorry. That was mean. I've just always liked Lydia and if I had to choose between the two, I'd prefer it was her bed he was crawling into."

"A bed I don't think he's been in lately."

"I think they had a fight," she told me. "But I think they've kissed and made up now."

"Good. So if she's here in the morning, can I tease her about the noise?"

"No, you cannot." She lifted her head and looked at me sheepishly. "We raised a horny little brood, didn't we? It's embarrassing sometimes, you know. They all know so much and they're not even shy about talking about it."

"Neither are you."

"But I am! I just can't deny anything when the walls are made out of Kleenex and spit. They *know*, Chip. They tease me about the noise."

"You're not exactly the silent type."

Maybe not, but she was quiet for a long time, until she sat up, tears wetting her lashes.

"I want to make love with you tonight," she said softly. "I'm not sure how I feel about it, not with Paul two doors down feeling so miserable."

I sat up with her, drawing her close. "Paul would understand. I don't know about you, but right now I want to be as close to you as I possibly can be."

"Quietly," she whispered.

I nodded and puller her closer. I listened to the sounds of her breathing, the thump on the wall whenever Nicole turned in her sleep, the beating of my own heart. I heard the muffled music coming from Paul's room, something sad and sweet, and with the pressure of grief wrapped around my chest, I made love to my wife of over twenty five years.

Quietly.

Kevin

"I should go," Lydia whispered, shivering against me.

I wrapped my arms around her tighter, the cold steel of her truck biting into my back. The last time I had checked my watch it was well past one in the morning; I wasn't sure how long we had been standing there in the driveway holding on to one another, but neither one of us wanted to let go.

"It's a cold drive home. Sure you don't want me to take you?"

"It'll take me five minutes and the truck has a heater. And you"—she stretched up on her toes to kiss me—"shouldn't drive. I can still smell liquor on your breath."

"A couple drinks after dinner. I'm fine."

"Maybe, but you're not going anywhere. You can come over later, though. I get off early."

"You have to work? Why didn't you say so earlier? You should have been home hours ago."

She set her head on my chest, obviously tired, tempted to ask me to come with her anyway. "It's probably stupid, but I didn't want to leave until Debby was gone."

"I don't think it's stupid. You could stay, you know."

"With your parents right down the hall? I don't think so."

I shrugged sheepishly. "Just a thought. It's been a while, you know. Not since— "

"—since I forced you to see Will," she finished for me. "I'm not avoiding you, Rabbit, we just haven't been alone lately. Maybe tomorrow?"

"Nicole," I moaned. "Paul's bringing Monica home tomorrow and I can't do that to him."

"No, you can't."

"Would it be okay to bring her over? Paul wants everyone out of the house when they get home to give Monica a chance to rest. We could order pizza and ask Spider and Eileen to come over, too."

"That sounds perfect."

"She likes you a lot, you know," I said. "I think my feelings were hurt when she wanted you to read her a bedtime story and not me."

"Poor baby." She hugged me hard. "Now I really have to go. Make sure you bring some toys for Nicole tomorrow. And your wallet, because I'm not paying for the pizza."

I was smiling as I went back inside and up the stairs, until I heard the music coming from Paul's room. He played the same song over and over, and just as I was drifting off I realized where I had heard it before.

A Time For Us.

Romeo and Juliet.

I didn't like the idea of Nicole stuck in the restaurant office all evening and protested, admittedly mildly, when Mom showed up to take her off my hands right after lunch.

"She'll be bored out of her mind, Mom. What's she supposed to do all day?"

"Bang on the piano? Pester Will? Relax, Kevin, it's not

as if there will be customers up to the rafters after lunch and I doubt your father intends on plastering himself behind the desk and ignoring her all afternoon. He wants to spend a little time with his granddaughter. Is there anything wrong with that?"

Nicole obviously didn't think so. She ran out the door to Mom's car without so much as saying goodbye, waiting impatiently in the back seat.

"Paul's bringing Monica home in about an hour," she told me at the front door. "Can you find someplace else to be by then?"

"I'll go pick on Eileen until Lydia gets home." I bent over and kissed her. "Don't expect me home for dinner, Mom. We'd planned on eating with Spider and Eileen, and I don't suppose one missing munchkin will change things."

"Okay." She started towards the car but stopped in the middle of the sidewalk and turned back towards me. "Any chance I can count on you to be home tomorrow night?"

"I can be here."

"Lydia, too," she added. "I don't want to louse up any of your plans and you won't have to stick around, but Monica would like to have family around for a while."

"It's not a problem, Mom," I assured her. She sounded as if she was apologizing for something she had every right to ask. I grinned and leaned against the door frame. "You really do like her, don't you?"

"Kevin … she put the light back into your eyes. You know, when you came home last year I was terrified that I'd come home one day and find a dead body in your bedroom. You were that depressed. Now I just don't see that." She blinked back the tears that suddenly stung her eyes. "She gave me back my son. I love her for that."

I stepped off the porch and scooped her up into a tight hug, lifting her off the ground and swinging her around. "You are one terrific mother," I said, setting her back down. "I love you."

"Don't make me cry, Kevin," she sniffed. "Your father would never believe why."

"He'd believe that I made you cry." I kissed her again and started back into the house, only then realizing that not having Nicole meant time alone with Lydia.

Even if I did have to suffer part of that with my sister.

Until Eileen said something, I didn't realize how big a deal it was that I'd been given The Key. I thought it was for Lydia's convenience, so I could be there when she came home or occasionally have dinner waiting for her. I didn't know that her having given it to me was some kind of milestone.

"You have a key," Eileen informed me, "because she intends for you to use it one day and never leave."

"The female version of a promise ring?"

"Something like that."

"Maybe it's just a hint for me to pay part of the rent since I sleep here so often."

"Well, there's that, too. Or maybe she wants you to move in."

That idea had crossed my mind a few times. We were sharing everything except a toothbrush it seemed; why not take the next step and move in?

Because moving in, I told Eileen, didn't have the level of commitment I wanted. It said I thought she was good enough to sleep with, to have fun with, but if it got rough, leaving would be easy.

"Why didn't you live with Spider?"

"Because he's too much like you," she said.

We were waiting for them in Lydia's apartment, plastered on either end of the sofa, feet up on the coffee table. I could live in that apartment, I thought. I loved the space, the loft, and all the fluffy pillows she had piled up under the loft. It felt like a slice of life teetering between the last scraps of teen years and adulthood. Almost grown up.

"Why do you guys stay in the apartment?" I asked her. "Why not buy a house?"

"Why do you still live with Mom and Dad?" she countered. "Why not move out?"

"Because I'm spoiled and lazy."

"At least you admit it. We like the apartment, Kevin. If we ever have kids, we'll think about moving then."

"If?"

In a family that revered infants, the idea of not having them was bordering on sacrilege. I'd always pictured Eileen with two or three, all little clones of the terror she used to be.

"We want kids, just not anytime in the near future."

"Too busy swinging nekkid from the loft railings?"

"Wild monkey sex," she laughed. "I'm lucky, though, Mom and Dad are more focused on Nick having kids right now than they are me. I think I have a few years before the subtle nagging begins."

"They need to refocus. I don't think Nick wants any right now."

"Katie does," she said. "If Nick's not careful, he's going to lose her over this."

Katie, Eileen went on, married Nick thinking he wanted at least three kids, and was willing to have them as soon as he'd graduated. With no graduation in sight, he was taking steps backwards, away from everything they'd planned on, and that included a family.

"What about you?" she asked. "Have you given any thought to kids now that you're not spending the rest of your life dreaming about women you can't have?"

"I want kids," I said. And I'd dream about women no matter what, but I kept that to myself.

"Does Lydia?"

The door creaked open and then clicked shut. "Do I what?" Lydia asked, tossing her purse aside.

I craned my head over the back of the sofa to look at her. "Do you want to have sixteen kids with me?"

"Tonight?" She leaned over and kissed me. "What happened to the one we were supposed to keep entertained today?"

"My parents took possession of her."

"Really now." She grinned at Eileen. "Then we can have all kinds of fun with the boys tonight, can't we?"

Eileen jumped up and headed for the door. "I'll go see if Spider got what we needed," she said. "We'll be over around sixish."

"Should I be afraid?" I asked.

Lydia was going up the stairs, pulling her sweater off over her head. "Be very afraid, Rabbit. Now what's this about sixteen kids?"

"I want kids. Do you?"

She leaned over the rail. "Is this another marriage proposal?"

"If I say yes, will you?"

"I want kids, Kevin. A couple, at least. But if you're serious about sixteen…" She shook her head. "I think you might have to hire someone for that."

She finished changing clothes.

And she never said no, that she didn't want to marry me.

~

When I came out of the kitchen after putting the left-over pizza in the refrigerator – careful to not touch anything resembling a mushroom – Lydia and Eileen were under the loft, lighting candles. Spider had a cigar box under his arm and was turning off lights around the apartment; when he was done, it was dark except for the glow coming from under the loft.

Sure, candles are nice, soft lighting is romantic, but those two had enough fire under that loft to cook a small animal.

"Spider needs to be able to see to read lips," Eileen explained, as if I had no clue.

Lydia beckoned me under the loft, and then turned on the stereo, the air swelling with soft music.

"What gives?" I asked. "A séance?"

"Nope." Eileen glanced at Lydia and then at Spider. "We decided it was time for you to kick off that last little bit of goody two shoes."

Spider sat next to Eileen and opened the box, pulling out a plastic bag and small white cutting board. He handed it to Eileen, and then grinned at me.

"We're going to get you stoned and have an orgy."

"You're fucking kidding me."

She glanced up from the cutting board. "Well, we can skip the orgy," she said, and held up the baggy. "Nick's home grown. He swears it's excellent."

"Nick? Nicky grows this?"

"Don't make a public announcement, for Christ's sake."

"Not my idea," Spider signed. "These two cooked this up the other night. I went along with it because I thought it would be funny."

I looked over at Lydia. "Seriously?"

"We're not trying to turn you into a junkie, Rabbit. We just wanted to see you get a little high."

I watched Eileen roll the paper. "I don't know about this, Ei. You like this?"

"Only tried it a couple times, and I liked it then. Come on, Kevin, don't be such a drag. One night out of your life isn't going to kill you. And it's not like we bought this off the street. Nick gave it to Spider. It's okay."

"You don't have to," Spider said as she lit the joint.

She handed it to Spider first, and I watched, fascinated, as the tip glowed dimly when he inhaled, and when Lydia took a long, deep drag from it.

"I don't know how," I whispered when she handed it to me.

"Inhale deep and hold it as long as you can, then let it out slowly. Don't be surprised if it burns a little at first."

As I reached for it, she pulled back.

"Seriously, don't do this if you don't really want to."

I didn't want to, but I took it anyway. I shrugged and put it to my lips, inhaling as deeply as I could. Pain exploded in my throat, searing down into my chest, building until I could no longer stand it.

I exhaled with a cough, gasping for air.

The tingling in my jaw intrigued me.

"You realize this isn't like an everyday thing for us," Eileen said. "Nick's a little pothead, but Spider…" She leaned over and kissed him. "He won't admit that he likes it."

"God. Nick. Amazing. Mr. Perfect."

"Don't exhale so quick, Rabbit," Lydia said after my second drag. "Give it a chance to work."

"Does this do anything for you?" I asked her.

"It makes me horny," she laughed.

I didn't want to ask how she knew that.

Spider kicked at my foot to get my attention. "She calls you Rabbit?"

"Yes, I do," Lydia answered. "He's jumpy, just like a bunny rabbit. All that energy."

"Don't rabbits do it in like two seconds?"

"Only the first time," I said. "We're good for at least a minute the next time around. When I'm an old, old rabbit, I aspire to last at least ten."

"One can only hope," Lydia giggled.

"He's a rank amateur, Lydia," Eileen said. "Give him time."

"Am I that bad at it?"

"Rabbit, no." She set her hand on my thigh, and kissed my cheek. "You're that good. If you weren't, I wouldn't tease you."

"Yes, she would," Spider said. "You're really that bad at it. I've heard things. These two sit on the couch and talk about you. I lie in bed and eavesdrop. You suck and you have a tiny pecker."

Eileen was laughing; Lydia was not.

"She also thinks you have freaky feet," Spider went on. "That long second toe really grosses her out. That and all the hair on your toes. You could braid them all together and make your own webbed feet."

"They talk about all this, and you snoop, huh?" I asked, reaching for the joint.

Lydia sputtered and pulled it from my fingers. "I never said—"

"Give that back. Lydia – he was lying in bed *listening* to you?"

"At least we know her sign language is good, even if

she's only firing on one cylinder right now," Spider signed, laughing.

"Oh, bite me," she finally said.

I took a hard drag on the joint, sucking in until there was nothing left but paper burning. This wasn't like drinking, but that was about the only thing I was sure of. With a drink, I knew when I felt a buzz. Two or three good stiff ones and I could feel the numbness wrap around me, my eyelids go heavy, and a sweet dullness drip down my body.

With this, I wasn't sure what I felt. It burned in my throat and made my jaw tingle, just under my ears, but I didn't feel anything, at least nothing I could put my finger on. Everything was funny; I was laughing, yet I felt quiet. Calm. I could hear the dark in whisper like taps around us; the ticking of the living room clock; a drip coming from the kitchen; the soft rasp as Spider leaned back against a stereo speaker.

I could hear the sound of Lydia's smile about to break as she sneered at Spider for teasing her; he was snickering, deliberately leaning into Eileen so that their arms would touch. He made every effort he could to touch her, inventing lint to pick off her shoulder, hair to push out of her eyes. Every excuse he could find to touch her, he took.

Every time he looked at her, his eyes were burning, intense; it was passion exploding in glances that said he wanted her, but he could wait. He would wait, he'd wait forever, and a day after that if he needed to.

Spider's foot tapped to the vibration of the music coming from the speaker; Eileen rolled another joint, and Lydia set her hand on my leg, leaning over to plant a kiss on my jaw, right under my ear, where it tingled most.

This was the place I most wanted to be. In that moment of Quiet, the place where my brain didn't seem to be able to reach on its own. And I wondered, out loud, if Monica was able to find the Quiet, or if that space was occupied by nothing but terror.

And I wondered how much pain she was in.

"She's heavily medicated," Spider pointed out. "If they have to, they can give her enough drugs that someone could drop a fifty pound weight on her foot and she wouldn't care."

Eileen lit the next joint and passed it to Spider. "You'd think she would have been in pain before this. The cancer is everywhere, for Christ's sake. Dad says the biggest tumor is the size of a damned grapefruit."

How would any of us have known if she was in pain? When she and Paul split up I was gone, and when I came home I never made the effort to see her. Paul was as guilty as she was in the crimes committed against their marriage, but it was Monica I ignored. I played with her daughter, promised Nicole that her mother loved her more than anything, but I never once bothered to check to make sure that Monica was all right.

She could have been lying in the middle of the living room floor, trying to claw her eyes out through the pain, and I never would have known.

"I didn't make any grand gestures, either, Kev," Eileen said. "Mom and Dad talked to her three or four times a week and I guess I figured that was good enough."

"Paul's your brother," Lydia said. "Of course you'd be biased. Your brother's heart explodes, you comfort him, not the person who hurt him, even if you do love her. Besides, it's not too late to make amends with Monica."

"I think she understands," Spider added.

"I can't even comprehend the pain she must be in," Lydia said, taking a long drag. "If I ever complain about my back aching again, whap me one, Rabbit."

"Back aches?" Eileen asked.

"Comes with the territory," she explained. "Massive boobs cause massive backaches."

"And quarter inch grooves in your shoulders," I said. "If I'd known when we were in junior high they'd hurt you so much, I never would have gotten as excited about seeing you do jumping jacks in gym class."

"Yes you would," she snickered.

Spider made a scissors motion with his fingers, and then said, "Reduction."

"Honestly, there are some days I'd pay to have them lopped off."

"You should go see Spider's dad," Eileen said. "He can refer you to someone who can help. A couple inches might make all the difference in the world."

"Go flash Dr. Stone? I don't think so!"

"He's only moderately kinky," I told her. "Sheesh, he's probably seen every single one of us buck naked. It's not as painful as you think. He doesn't laugh."

"Much," Eileen added.

Spider was shaking his head. "I don't believe we're sitting here talking about her breasts. You need to stop before I get turned on."

"If you're turned on, then we're going home," Eileen told him.

"I don't get an orgy?" I asked. "You two said you were gonna get me stoned, then have an orgy."

Eileen was standing, reaching for Spider's hand. "Kevin, I love you, but I don't want to *do* it with you. Or near you. Or even think about you seeing me do it. Frankly, the idea kind of turns my stomach."

"You can go, just leave Spider," Lydia said, giggling.

"You are such the little hornball," I said to Eileen. "Sit down. We can stop talking about Lydia's boobs. Even though I think I'm upset I don't get an orgy."

"I'm not," Spider said. "Disappointing one woman is enough."

Eileen was still standing.

"Well?" I said. "Are you staying or going?"

"Normally I'd stay, but I'm not fèeling so hot right now."

She did look pale, made worse by the washed out glow of the candlelight. Spider shoved the cigar box towards me and stood up, nodding. "My stomach is starting to do a slow turn, too," he said. "Bad mushrooms?"

"I feel fine," I said.

"And you ate the other pizza," Eileen reminded me.

"That's because fungus doesn't belong on food."

"Pace yourself," Spider said, gesturing towards the cigar box. "There's enough there to light up a dozen people."

"I have to admit," Lydia said after they left, "I'm starting to feel a little queasy. I thought it was just the grass. It's been a while."

Ten minutes later she was running for the bathroom, her hand clenched over her mouth. Fifteen minutes later she was lying in a tight ball on the bed, and I was emptying a trash can to set beside her and looking for something to clean the trail of vomit that streaked the bathroom floor.

Later, after she'd thrown up so many times I lost count, she leaned against me and whispered, "You're a keeper, Rabbit. If I can throw up and not even make you flinch, it's got to be true love."

14

Terry

I woke to find Nicole kneeling beside the bed, waiting patiently, her little hands holding onto the padded rails of the waterbed as she rocked back and forth to the tune that seemed to spin through her head constantly.

"'Morning, sweetheart," I said as brightly as I could for first thing in the morning. "Have you been here long?"

She shook her head. "Daddy's crying."

So determined; there wasn't an ounce of fear in my granddaughter's eyes. She was simply stating a fact, something she knew I'd want to know about. "Where's Mommy?"

"Sleepin'."

I sat up and threw the blankets back, swinging my legs over the edge of the bed. "Is Grandpa downstairs?"

"He's trying to make muffins," she said, crinkling her nose. "He's not very good at it."

"Grandpa tries hard. Why don't you go downstairs and tell him I said it would be all right for you to make your own chocolate milk, and if he wants me to, I'll be down in a few minutes to make breakfast."

"Eggs?" she asked, grimacing.

"Pancakes. But tell Grandpa not to start them, okay?"

She scrambled out the room and was halfway down the stairs when I heard hear yell out, "Grandma says to stop cooking!"

With Nicole downstairs and out of sight, the room felt dark and hushed, every sound an exaggeration. I could hear Paul moving around, his occasional sniff, how quietly he tried to sift through dresser drawers in his room. I opened the curtains to let in light, ran fingers through my hair to tame the tangles, and headed through Nicole's bedroom.

The door that connected her room to Paul's was wide open, and through it I could see him standing in the middle of the floor, dressed only in faded jeans, struggling with a pair of knotted sweat socks.

The frustrated etched onto his face reminded me of the little boy who was determined to not let the world know when he was scared. Paul stood there fighting with a pair of sweat socks, and he was the six year old who lashed out in anger before he'd let anyone see him cry. His eyes were red and lashes wet, but it was the frustration that clung to him. Frustration and fear.

"Are you all right?" I asked, trying to speak quietly in case Monica was still asleep.

"Goddamn socks," he sputtered. "Mom, I wish to hell you would just roll the frigging socks instead of tying them into knots."

"I'll try to remember that."

"Did Nicole wake you up? I don't know what it is with her. If Kevin's not home she wakes you up, or Dad. Why can't she just play in her room or watch TV like a normal kid?" He threw the socks onto the floor. "Hell, at least she can get herself dressed."

"Come on." I reached for his hand and pulled him through Nicole's room, into my bedroom. "You need to take a few deep breaths." I sat with him on the bed, running my fingers through the hair on the back of his head. "Anything I can do?"

"Not unless you can turn the damned clock back and get her to a doctor six months ago. Mom, what the hell did we do to deserve this? She won't even fight it."

"Nothing," I said, pulling him into my arms. "You didn't do anything wrong. Don't be angry with her for not wanting it to drag on. She'd rather have two wonderful months with you instead of four miserable ones."

"But we could beat it, I know we could."

He let it out; I hadn't seen him cry so hard since the day he told Chip that Monica was pregnant.

"Sweetheart, do you want to see her suffer? Fighting it might mean endless hours of pain and nausea, and whole days chewed off by being too clouded mentally to even know you're there. And it would only buy her a little time."

"I know that!" He tore away from me, and went to the window by the fireplace, staring out at the back yard. "I've done nothing *but* think about that. Goddammit, Mom, it's not like we're contemplating putting Max to sleep because he's old and sick. This is my wife!"

Max looked up at the mention of his name, yawned, and went back to sleep.

"I love her, too, Paul."

He slumped against the window, pressing his forehead against the glass. "I know you do."

I sat there at the edge of the bed, not sure if I should get up and go to him again or not.

"Can you get me in to see your old boss?"

"Brad? I don't see why not."

Paul took a deep breath, turning away from the window. "I think I need a lawyer," he said. "Monica wants to make sure her father can't get his hands on anything when she dies, and she wants to make sure we have a guardian for Nicole in writing, in case something happens to me."

"You know we'd never let Jeff Russell get his hands on Nicole," I said.

"I know. I think she just needs to have a say in Nicole's godparents. Or godfather, as the case might be."

"Kevin?"

"We're leaning that way. I don't want Nick or Eileen to feel hurt, though."

"They'll understand. She's closest to Kevin and if you gave her a choice, she'd pick him."

He shoved his hands into his pockets, hesitating.

"What is it?"

"What about you and Dad?" he asked. "I know you, if something happens to me your first impulse is going to be to wrap yourselves around Nicole and not let go. How hurt are you and Dad going to be?"

"We won't be," I assured him. "You do whatever you have to do to protect Nicole's future, and to make Monica feel good about it."

"This fucking sucks, Mom."

"Yes, it does," I agreed, getting up to put my arms around him again. "And be as angry as you need to be, just don't fight Monica on this. As much as it hurts, let her have her way, and just love her through it."

Paul

"Basically, it boils down to this: if I die or become incapacitated, Nicole goes to Kevin, on the stipulation he's been married for at least a year. If he's single, unwilling, or for whatever reason unable to care for her, then Eileen gets her. If not Eileen, then Nick. If none of them can take her, and you and Mom are still in sound health, then she falls on you."

Dad was sitting at the big desk in the study, his feet propped up, watching me wander aimlessly around the pool table.

"We went with what Nicole would most likely want," I went on, trying to not look at him. "She's closest to Kevin, and I just thought…"

"Why are you apologizing? I understand why you did this. It's not like any of them would ever dream of cutting me off from my granddaughter."

"Mom said you'd understand, but I didn't think that meant you wouldn't be hurt."

"I'm not hurt. Paul, we went through this when Nicky was a baby. Your grandparents were stunned when we didn't name them as his guardians, but the simple fact was that we had to be realistic. Doug and Kris were much closer to us in age and more likely to live long enough to see him all the way through school. And they were expecting a baby of their own."

"How'd you smooth it over?"

"I sent Sheila a dozen roses every week for a year. And then had another baby. We understand, son, but you better discuss it with Kevin before it's set in stone."

I nodded and dropped into the armchair in front of the desk. "God, what a day. Nothing but talking about dying and she's making dumb jokes about it."

"She has to deal with it."

"We went to talk to a priest today. She told him that she's fairly certain she'll burn in hell, but she still wanted to know what kind of funeral she's entitled to."

"Oh, God," he tried to laugh. It sounded like Monica, so sure she was going to get the worst, but looking for a reasonable way out. "What did he say?"

"He didn't know what to say. She listed all these reasons why she should be excommunicated before she dies, and the poor guy sat there with his mouth hanging open. I'll give him credit, though, he didn't feed her any bullshit and he didn't go out of his way to make her feel guilty about any of it."

"But was he able to help her at all?"

"Not in the way she wanted."

What Monica wanted was for someone, anyone she thought might have an inside line straight to God, to tell her that she wouldn't spend the rest of eternity fighting fire in hell. She thought that if she knew for sure she could be forgiven for all her screwups, that she could die happily, and peacefully.

I could tell her everything she wanted to hear until I had nothing left to say, but it didn't count coming from me. God probably wanted to kick my ass, too.

"They're sick," Kevin told me, explaining why he'd come alone. "It's probably nothing Monica can catch, but no one wanted to take chances."

I didn't think Monica would be able to do more than make an appearance at dinner. She'd wanted the whole family over, without realizing that she didn't have the energy to face anyone yet.

Kevin and I were in the study, half-heartedly trying to play a game of nine ball. He racked the balls, watching as I chalked my cue.

"What'd you want to talk about?" he asked.

Astute for a general pain in the ass.

I took a deep breath and explained, the details of Nicole's guardianship as quickly as I could, feigning a greater interest in the game.

If I paid closer attention to what I was saying to him, I'd crack.

"It's asking a lot of you," I said. "We won't be offended if you say no."

"I love that little girl, Paul. You never even had to ask. But why do I need to be married?"

"I want Nicole to grow up as normally as possible," I said carefully. "If you were single and wound up with a young child to take care of, it would put a serious crimp in any chance you had at a love life."

"Are you kidding? Nicole is a chick magnet."

"All right, then, I don't want you using my daughter to get women. Seriously, Kevin, we just thought it would be wiser all the way around. It would be better for you, and it would be better for Nicole to have the stability of two parents, especially after losing both of us."

"Okay," he said, shrugging. "I don't intend to be single much longer anyway."

"Really now. Are you two engaged and not telling anyone?"

"I wish." He reached for the chalk, spinning it over the tip of his cue stick. "I keep asking and she keeps saying that she doesn't think we're ready."

"You were born ready."

"Tell her that!"

"Maybe I will," I said. "I'll call her up and say, 'Lydia, I know he's a pathetic loser, but he loves you and no one else is ever gonna have him.'"

"Oh yeah, that'll make me more attractive to her."

"But if it works, you'll be thanking me."

"I might."

"Why are you here, anyway?" I asked. "You should be with Lydia tonight."

"I promised Mom I'd be home for dinner. Plus Lydia has to work in the morning, and we have an understanding that if she has to get up really early, I won't stay the night before."

"Squirt, when I think of all the nights I stayed at the restaurant working late when I really didn't have to, and all the weekends I worked because I was afraid Dad would think I was shirking my responsibilities … it's all wasted time. Maybe if I'd had more time for her all along, none of the crap would have happened."

"You don't know that, Paul."

"You think she would have wanted to fool around if I'd been there when she needed me? Don't make my mistakes, Kevin. Put her first, always, or you'll regret it."

He set the cue down. "Let me ask you something. If you'd proposed and she'd said no, but wanted you to move in with her, would you?"

"Probably not, at least not knowing what I know now," I admitted. "Face it, that little piece of paper kept us from walking away more than once. Getting married when we did was a mistake, but ending it would have been a bigger one. Being married gave us chances I'm not sure we'd have taken on our own."

"I really don't think Lydia and I would ever walk away from each other. I don't think we can. But I still want to be together married and not just living together."

"Take what you can get, Kev."

He got up, and conceded the game.

"Tell Mom I'm sorry, but I had to get back over there. She is sick, after all. She shouldn't be alone."

Lydia

"Look out your window."

I pulled the curtain back just an inch or so, peering out into the parking lot, holding the phone to my ear. Kevin was standing in the parking lot behind a pickup truck, waving up at me. And he wasn't alone.

"Who are you with?" I asked over the crackle of his cell phone.

"Your stalker."

I let the curtain go and opened the door. I could barely make out Kevin; I knew it was him from his sheer height and the sound of his laughter, but I couldn't see his face, and could make out no features on the person he was standing there with. "I have a stalker?"

"Yep. I got here and he was staring up at the building, hoping the address fairy would magically appear and tell him which apartment was yours. Can we come up?"

"Well, you can," I said. "Who are you with?"

"Some football player. He says he used to have a crush on you."

I pulled the phone away from my ear and stepped out onto the walkway. "Topher?"

They were headed for the stairs before I could say anything else, Kevin leading the way.

Instant awkwardness. Kevin led Topher into the apartment and I had no idea how to greet him. He leaned forward and brushed a very light kiss on my cheek and said, "Hi," almost shyly.

"You haven't seen each other for like three years," Kevin said. "The guy's been standing in your parking lot mentally willing your door to open. He at least deserves a hug."

It was like hugging a cousin I hadn't seen since childhood. Familiar yet distant, almost obligatory.

"I admit, I was surprised to see you walk up, Davis," Topher said. "Weren't you off learning to be some kind of a monk?"

"It was a priest, and I changed my mind."

Topher smiled. "Coolness. I should have bet money on it when I had the chance. We all knew you two would wind up together one way or the other. Though a few people thought Lydia might become a nun and chase you from parish to parish."

They were sitting on opposite ends of the sofa, and Kevin was laughing.

I was stunned.

"You thought I'd wind up with him?"

He watched as I moved magazines off the coffee table and sat there, on the end closest to Kevin. "I knew I was just a place card. That was okay."

"*I* didn't know that," I muttered.

"I knew that, too."

"Still playing ball?" Kevin asked. Rescuing me again, taking me away from a conversation he knew I didn't want to have. "You went to SMU, didn't you? Football scholarship?"

Topher played football until the second game of his sophomore year, when a low tackle ripped his knee to shreds; two surgeries and months of physical therapy put the knee back together, but the speed that had made him a standout in high school was gone.

"A slow running back is pretty much useless, you know,"

he pointed out. "I never had aspirations of going pro, so it was all right. I finished my degree a little early and decided to come home."

"What'd you major in?"

"Accounting. I got on with Brickman and Associates, at least until I blow the CPA exam." He turned to me finally, his head cocked to one side. "I didn't mean to weird you out by just showing up, Lydia. I got your address from a couple of friends, but no one bothered to tell me it was an apartment building."

"That's why he was waiting for the address fairy," Kevin explained.

"I just wanted to see how you were doing. I didn't come here to … well."

"Pick up where we left off?" I asked.

He nodded. "Mostly, I just wanted to see if you were doing all right, if you were happy. I'm assuming you are," he said, gesturing to Kevin.

"Well, *I* am," Kevin said brightly.

"When's the wedding?"

Before I could say anything, Kevin shrugged and said, "When she finally says yes. I keep asking, but I think the wedding fairy went on vacation with the address fairy and they're too busy doing nasty things to each other to come back right now."

The smile on Topher's face waned as he went from truly happy for me to concerned. "You waited for him your whole life. What are you waiting for now?"

"Damn, I think I like this guy," Kevin declared.

When I dated Topher during our senior year, he only seemed dimly aware of Kevin's existence. Kevin was my friend, someone I mentioned once in a while, someone other girls squealed over and praised for his manners. Topher asked, only once, if Kevin was gay, if that was why he had the reputation of being the class Big Brother, the boy all the girls loved simply because they knew he could be trusted with their hearts, and with their virtue on the weekends. He was satisfied with the explanation that Kevin had a vocation and was becoming a priest.

He never asked me how close Kevin and I were. I never told him that when I wasn't dating someone else, Kevin and I tortured each other with games of What We Were Giving Up. I never told him that on more than one occasion we'd nearly thrown in the towel and slept with each other.

I never realized I'd made Topher feel like second best.

I never realized he knew.

But he did. We dated for the entire year, he said he loved me, that he wanted me, but he never hinted that he knew where my heart really was.

Sitting there, his and Kevin's voices a dim buzz in the background, I tried to remember if I had ever told Topher that I loved him. We slept together, but I never thought of it as making love with him. I don't think I ever considered it as anything more than having sex. It was hurried, curious, teenage sex, usually in the back of his van, usually just a way to end a date.

Topher loved me, but he never talked about the future as if he expected us to be together. He talked about going away to college, playing football, someday seeing the world. But never with me. I wasn't part of that vision.

I'd never noticed that, and it never bothered me.

More than once, I told Kevin that I loved him. He avoided mentioning the seminary, because he knew it might make me cry. When we talked about the future, it was almost always as "if things were different."

If things were different, we could jump in a car and travel the country after graduation.

If things were different, we could go to college together.

If things were different, some day we could stand on a beach at sunset, waves lapping at our bare feet, our families circled around us, and we could make these moments last forever.

If things were different.

Things *were* different.

"Lydia." Kevin's fingers were under my chin, lifting my face. "Where did you go?"

"Ask me again."

His eyes went wide, his eyebrows raised.

Topher laughed, and tossed a throw pillow onto the floor. "You might want that to cushion your knee."

Uncertain, sure he'd heard wrong or misunderstood, Kevin slowly slid off the sofa and knelt in front of me, ignoring the pillow.

"I swear, I'll do it right this time," he said, reaching for my hands. "You know I love you, I've always loved you. I'll be with you forever if you'll let me, but I'm asking you, please, be with me as my wife."

The words got stuck in my throat; when I looked at him it was through a cloud of tears, and when I blinked, they spilled over.

"Hon," Topher said, "if you don't tell him yes, I will. He's just too cute, being on one knee and all."

"I don't have a ring yet," Kevin went on. " I mean, I almost bought one a dozen times, but I thought that was something we should pick out together. Something that means as much to you as it does to me. God, I love you. Will you marry me?"

I pulled my hands away from his and reached out for him. "Yes," I said, sniffing through tears. "Yes."

When we finally parted, when I'd stopped crying and had kissed him, I turned to thank Topher for the reminders, but he was gone.

15

Kevin

I was dreaming about Christmas lights, an eight foot pine tree wrapped in layers of tiny multicolored bulbs. Standing off in the shadows, I marveled at the glow swelling across the floor and up the walls. In the darkened living room, the off white carpet and white-white walls were bathed in soft red. I looked at the tree and saw the dozens of pinpoints of blue and green and orange, but the glow that wrapped around me was red. Soft and warm; inviting.

The longer I stared at the lights, the more unfocused they became, until they were a prism of spectacular red.

I woke with a start, sunlight flooding through the window that I know I had closed.

And -boom- there she was, kneeling at the edge of my bed, completely naked, her hair framing her face, even though she had tried to tuck it behind her ears.

"Jesus Fucking Christ!"

In one awkward, bumbling, but incredibly quick move, I scrambled from the bed and jumped into sweatpants, hopping on one foot as I put them on, hopping until I was on the other side of the bedroom, away from her.

Debby Forrester naked is, well, not exactly what I would have imagined. Clothed she always managed to look about 14. Buck naked she looked, well, 14. Almost masculine in her narrowness, she was a skinny white stick with an abnormally large head.

A lollipop.

I did what any normal human male would do upon waking to find a naked and presumably willing female crawling into his bed.

I bolted out of the room and went screaming for my mother.

Lydia

I cradled the phone in my lap, the receiver in hand, listening to the click as the line went dead on the other end. My parents called every week out of an exaggerated sense of familial obligation; I didn't mind the calls and most of the time I looked forward to them, but I knew the litany of questions by heart, and the answers were always the same.

Yes, I'm doing fine. Yes, my truck is running. No, I don't need money to pay my rent/utilities/insurance/grocery bill.

Their replies were fairly constant, too.

No, angel, I don't think we'll be coming back anytime soon. It's the flying, I know, it seems unreasonable, but your mother just can't do it. The very idea of twelve hours on a plane terrifies her.

"When do you think she'll be able to manage it, Dad?" I asked this time, hoping he'd be able to tell me she was starting to feel less enveloped by fear, that she felt like less of a target.

"I wish I could tell you. I'll probably have to fly back in

July or August for a few weeks to do some paperwork with the university, but your mother will probably stay here when I do."

"It's important."

"Important?"

"A good important," I said, realizing there were a thousand terrible things that could shoot through his head in a split second. "Kevin and I are getting married."

"Baby girl, are you serious? When?"

"We haven't set a date yet, but if I know Kevin, he won't want to wait too long."

I could hear him sigh, and then his hand cover the mouthpiece as he called for my mother. "I wish we could be there right now," he said when he took his hand away. "I'd give anything to see my baby's smile."

"No warnings about rushing into this or about us being too young?"

"You don't need my permission," he chuckled.

"I know."

"But you have my blessing, sweetheart. You know you have that."

I knew I'd have his blessing, and my mother's, too. What I hadn't known was whether or not I could count on them being there. I understood that they wouldn't, and I half expected it. But I had hoped.

Kevin

The carpet did smell like feet, there was no getting around that. Twenty years of sweat was ground into the fabric, soaked clear through the rubber pad underneath. I knew that in various spots there was more than sweat: places where very young students had lost bladder control, places where very tired students had thrown up. It had been cleaned on a regular basis, but the smell was practically ground into the molecular level of the fiber that made up the carpet.

It had to go.

The years of sweat had also caused the rubber padding to stick to the cement floor underneath. I cut down through both layers with a utility knife and pulled it back, leaving thick splotches of yellowing foam on the floor.

"It was glued down?" Lydia asked.

"Nope. Just stuck there from all the sweat, I think. Once we get the carpet up we'll have to scrape the cement clean."

"This is gross, Kevin," she said, crinkling her nose.

"This is why I'm having a wood floor put in. And fans. It gets so damned hot in here."

When I was ten or eleven years old I made a list of all the things I wanted in a dream dojo. We all did; we were tired of freezing during the winter and overheating in the summer, and as a group we routinely listed all the things we wanted to see changed in the dojo. Central heat and air. A swimming pool. Racquetball court. Basketball court. A dungeon.

Basically, we wanted a country club. With a dungeon.

I don't remember exactly why we wanted the dungeon, but I suspect it was proposed after a particularly difficult class. Let's shove the instructor into the dungeon and torture him. Give him his just rewards.

Lydia picked up a knife and began slicing into the carpet. "I could be lounging on the sofa eating bonbons this afternoon, but no … I'm here, inhaling decades of other peoples' athlete's foot."

"'Cause you love me."

"I expect something major in return, mister."

"Damn, you know, if you'd said you wanted something big, I could give you that."

"Not on this stinky carpet, you wouldn't." She set the knife aside and sat down. "I talked to my parents a while ago. They're both very happy for us."

"I hear a 'but' in there."

She nodded. They were happy, they were thrilled, we had their blessings, but … her mother couldn't fathom getting on a plane. As badly as she wanted to be here, she couldn't. She could barely force herself out of the house and into public, and there was no way she could get onto a bus or train, much less an airplane.

"They don't want us to wait for them, Kevin," she said. "They want us to get married when we want to, and if we ever decide to do our vows in a church—hopefully she'll be able to fly by then."

Where we'd get married hadn't crossed my mind.

Being married was the only thing I'd given much consideration. How we got from her saying "yes" to us saying "I do" pretty much escaped me.

"Did you want a church wedding?" I asked.

"I want what we used to talk about, back when it was all just talk. I don't even know if you remember—after we left the junior prom and went to the park, sitting in your car, when we talked about all the things we would do together, if we could."

"I remember."

We did that a lot, played a cruel game of "what if," always with the thought in our heads that "what if" was more likely "never would be." We'd mapped it out: graduate, go to college, get into the same co-ed dorm, eventually cave in and have sex (because, after all, if I wasn't going to be a priest in this vision of the future, we might as well do the one thing we tortured ourselves the most over), graduate, and then get married. She wanted a wedding on the beach at sunset, surrounded by people she cared about. She wanted flowers in her hair, and she didn't want a traditional wedding dress. She wanted to be barefoot, to feel the sand between her toes, and then she wanted to dance by the ocean, under the moonlight.

"I still want that."

"If you're telling me we both have to graduate from college first, you're insane. I can't even pick a major."

"I bet my mother would be able to fly by then," she said, laughing. "I don't want to wait, Kevin. If they can't be here, then I'd rather we got married sooner rather than later."

"We should tell my parents first."

Her eyes went wide. "You haven't told them yet?"

"I wanted you to be there when I did," I explained. "When my dad finds out we're getting married he's going to want to pick you up and swing you around the room until you puke. I can't deny him that one little thing."

"Fine. But I'm not cleaning it up."

"Hey, if he makes you barf, he gets to clean it up." I leaned over and kissed her. "They'll be here in a little while to help pull the carpet up. We can tell them then. Trust me, it'll make their day. They need some good news."

"Monica," she sighed. "She's another reason we shouldn't wait. You know she'll want to see you get married."

"We'd have to do it really soon, then. Is that okay? I mean, will you feel rushed if we push to have the wedding within a month or so?"

"No. As far as I can tell, the only reason to have a long engagement is to make plans for this huge money sucking event that's mostly for other people. It won't take much planning to have a small wedding with just family. Pick a place on the beach, pick a minister, buy some food, and get married."

"My dad owns a house on the beach," I said. "Midterm break is next week. Eileen and I don't have classes, Paul can get someone to cover the restaurant for him, Nick's not doing anything right now."

"What about the dojo?"

"Classes are being held at the Community Center until I get the floor in. I don't have to be here while that's being done."

"I'm not sure I can get time off with this short notice."

"It won't hurt to ask."

She picked up the knife and stabbed at the carpet, cutting a vicious slice in one angry movement. "Actually, it could hurt to ask, Kevin. Our Gestapo-trained supervisor is liable to tell me I'm fired if I even think of taking time off."

"You hate that job," I said, inching away. "Cripes, put the knife down."

"It doesn't matter if I hate it. It pays halfway decent and the benefits—"

"The benefits aren't worth crap if you're miserable working there. There are other jobs in places a lot less stressful, Lydia. Besides, whatever happened to *you* going to school? I thought you wanted to go back when you could afford it."

"When you're done, I might," she said.

"Why wait?"

"Rabbit … Someone has to pay the rent. I don't mind it, not at all. But until you get this place going and have some clue about school, I need to keep my job."

"No, you don't."

"Kevin."

"You're cute when you're clueless," I chuckled. "You know why my dad pressured me to either go to school or get a job? Because it's the right thing to do. Have a work ethic.

Some sense of direction. Anything but sit at home all the time watching TV or drooling all over myself. Neither of us *needs* to work, sweetheart. We have enough money to float on for a long time."

"Your dad is not supporting us," she said flatly.

"Well, not directly, no." I dug my fingers into the cut she'd made in the carpet, and started to pull. "My finances are just fine. You can quit your job and go to school, if that's what you want to do. You don't need to worry about the rent or anything else. And my dad is not paying it."

"This dojo will pay enough right off the bat?"

"It might, if we lived a bit frugally. But then I'll probably have to sink anything it brings in into the sandwich shop for the next year or so."

"So what, then?" she asked, tugging on the carpet with me. "We live here, in a corner of the dojo? I think I'd rather keep my crappy job."

We kept tugging until we'd lifted a good five foot section of the carpet up.

"We live wherever you want to live. I'm not broke, Lydia, not by a long shot. We'll be fine."

She dropped her side of the carpet. "How far from the long shot, Kevin? I've more or less assumed you've been living off some savings account for the past six months but I never thought it was my business to ask."

"It's your business now," I said, cutting through the section we'd peeled up. "Remember the day we ran into each other in the bar?"

"Your birthday, which I'm still kind of ticked you didn't remind me about."

"It was also the day I got my trust fund," I told her. "My dad made sure none of us would ever hurt for money … he wants us to all work, or do some greater good for the community, but not for the money."

"Is it crass if I ask how much?"

"I don't think it's crass. I'd have to consult Miss Manners to be sure, though." I got my fingers under the edge of the carpet and tugged again. "Ten," I grunted.

"Ten?"

We were pulling hard, leaning back to get as much muscle into it as possible; the carpet was starting to come up in one long sheet, stuck only in a few odd places.

"Million."

She let go. "You've got to be kidding me."

"Well, I spent a little of it," I said, trying to keep the momentum going. "This building, the dojo … Aw, shit, I thought this thing was going to finally come up." I let go and picked up the knife. "If I'd known getting this up was going to be such a pain in the ass, I would have hired someone else to do it."

She didn't say anything.

"Well, it is a pain in the ass."

"So are you sometimes," she sputtered.

"All right," I sighed, closing the knife. "Finances. My trust fund was just a little over ten million. So was Nick's and Paul's and Spider's and Eileen's—which, when you think about it, sucks since they got married. Double dipping little weasels. When my grandfather died he left my dad a fricking huge inheritance, and he just sort of built on it. He invested a lot of it, got into real estate … so yeah, my family is rich. What I have, I haven't earned, I know that, but I think my dad's idea wasn't what we'd be worth, but what we'd be worthy of."

"Greater good for the community," she said.

I nodded. "Spider teaches in a school that barely pays minimum wage, because it's his chance to be a role model for deaf kids. To show there are no barriers to what they can do, or who they can be. He can use his money to make sure no one gets turned away who needs that school. He can offer the school endowments, which he does anonymously through his accountants.

"Nick's original plan was to get his law degree and make the bulk of his practice pro bono, but I don't know what the hell he's going to do now. Paul has set up scholarships for abused kids, unwed mothers, and young families, including some living expenses.

"Eileen wants to bring music to kids who can't afford instruments and lessons. She wants to teach, she wants to reach out to kids who will never know if they have creative talent without a step up. I think some day she wants to open some kind of high school aged conservatory. They're all doing exactly what Dad expects us to do. I don't mean there are strings attached or anything. He just taught us to give back. To invest what we can, live on less than we have, and give back."

"I'd say with ten million you could do that." She finally smiled, the surprise giving way. "You were going to be a priest, giving back a lot more than just money. What's the plan now?"

"I thought I'd train my own little army of ninja warriors, and take over the world. Or maybe just Northern California."

"That's taking *from* the community," she said, wagging a finger at me.

"But it would be so much fun."

She waited.

"All right, spoil sport. Do you know what major thing is

missing from the martial arts in huge numbers?"

"Judging from the smell in here, I'd say the routine use of soap and water."

"Besides that. Women. It's better than it was fifteen or so years ago, but women are still a big minority when it comes to the martial arts."

"And your plan is to train an army of female ninja warriors?"

"Something like that. I want to make self defense training available to any woman who wants it. Face it, women who are beaten up are usually beaten up by men. They don't know how to defend themselves against someone bigger and stronger. But if we get them early, before they've been beaten down and made to feel like they deserve it…"

"Then maybe they'll never be abused at all," she finished for me.

"Empowerment. Empower a woman, and she'll never be a victim."

"Or at least she'll have a fighting chance," Lydia said. "What about men, Kevin? Don't men deserve that chance?"

"We don't seem to have the same problem as women do in seeking out defense training. Hell, we're drawn to it. I want to increase the number of women who train, and I want to teach them practical defense. Angel, I know this isn't perfect and no matter how good you are you can become a victim. I just want to give them something, get them here to find out that there isn't testosterone dripping off the walls."

"Well," she said, gesturing to the carpet, "It kind of smells like there is."

I was trying to think of some smartass comeback when my cell phone went off.

"Your pocket is ringing," she snickered.

"Funny." I fished it out of my pocket and flipped it open.

"Kev." It was my dad, and he sounded out of breath. "I think I just set your car on fire."

"Paul and I pushed it out onto the street so that I could fit it with a new alternator," Dad explained. "I took out the old one, went back into the garage for the new … when I came back flames were shooting out from the engine."

We were standing on the sidewalk, staring at the car, which was little more than a blackened, burned out hull. Even the tires had melted.

"I'm sorry, Kevin. I don't know what the hell I did to it."

It was difficult to get angry over losing a car I hadn't driven in months. His intention was to get it running again, so I could stop bumming rides off everyone else. I didn't believe his intention was to force me into buying a new one.

"Well," I said, sighing as if I were truly upset, "it's a goner, that's for sure. You'll just have to buy me a new one."

"What?"

"Yep. A brand new Benz, I think. Convertible, of course. Silver, or maybe midnight blue. That'd be nice."

"Very nice," Lydia echoed.

"Nice, my ass."

"Really, Dad. You just destroyed my car. I *loved* that thing. I almost had sex in it *twice*."

"You are so full of shit," he laughed.

"Okay. So maybe you just buy me a new car for a wedding present."

"With whom did you almost have sex in it?" Lydia asked.

"Hush, woman, I'm working the old man, and it seems to have flown right over his head."

I waited until it sunk in.

"You're getting married?"

"Soon."

I was right. Dad whooped and then picked Lydia up to hug her, swinging her in a wide circle, until her foot hit the side mirror on my now-dead car. The mirror broke off with an awful crack, and skidded down the sidewalk.

"Now see there," I said. "Now you have to buy me a new mirror, too."

"You know the house rules, son," Dad said, popping open his can of beer. Lydia was nowhere in sight, presumably kidnapped by my mother to some nefarious female place to make wedding plans. The only thing I knew for sure was that Eileen had been called, and before she came over she intended to call Katie, and probably Uncle Doug and Aunt Kris as well. "She's hands off until your wedding night."

"Like hell."

He nodded, taking a sip from the beer. "If you're marrying her next week, you can damn well sleep here until then. I don't think your pecker will fall off before then."

"It might."

"Talk to Nick. He's surviving, you can, too."

I followed Dad from the kitchen into the study. "You know about Nick and Katie?"

"A little bit," he said, reaching for the pool rack. "You can feel the tension around them, and I don't think having Katie's sister in the house is helping."

"No shit," I muttered.

Dad was laughing under his breath, dropping balls onto the table. "Your mother had a nice talk with Debby," he said. "A very loud discussion about respecting her house and the people in it. I don't think you'll have to worry about her trying to jump into your bed this week."

My mother could snap Debby Forrester in two if she wanted.

I had no doubt she would, if she thought she had reason to.

"I don't get it, Dad. I don't think I ever led Debby on or anything like that. And she *knows* I'm in love with Lydia."

"So your mother told her. But Debby seems to think that until Lydia has a ring on her finger, or you have one through your nose, you're fair game. And she wants you."

"Son of a bitch."

"I really feel for you, son," he said, without any trace of real sympathy. "Two women who want you that badly. It must be horrible."

It was more than Debby just trying to crawl into my bed. There were phone calls, notes—at one point I turned around in the kitchen to find her right behind me. She stretched up on her toes and kissed me; I admit, the thought went through my head that she was one hell of a kisser, and it took me a second to get my head together and push her away. The old joke 'she could suck the chrome off a trailer hitch' rode on the tail end of that thought.

"Psychobitch," I muttered, reaching for a cue.

"Making a play for you doesn't make her psychotic," Dad said.

"Not accepting no as an answer doesn't make her look especially bright."

He put the cue ball down and lined up for the break; his shot sounded like the crack of a whip, and the balls exploded from the rack, but he didn't sink any.

"You two are sure in a hurry to get married all the sudden," he said, changing the subject. "Any particular reason for the rush?"

We'd explained it before, Lydia's mother's terror over flying, and wanting to be sure Monica was there; Dad wasn't satisfied with just that.

"Lydia doesn't see any reason to wait. Hell, neither do I. She's never wanted the huge church wedding with a dozen bridesmaids and five hundred people packing the pews. She thinks it's impersonal and a huge waste of money."

"You could at least give everyone time to arrange their schedules a little better."

"I didn't think it would be a problem, Dad. Midterm break—"

"I heard you the first time you said that. Kevin, I have no problems at all with you getting married and I'm thrilled with the bride. I just want to know why it has to be next week."

"It doesn't," I said, lining up my shot.

"So?"

"Next week is convenient, that's all. I figured we'd all be able to spend some time at the beach, not just drive down there for the day. Take a few days, play in the sand, just have a good time. Maybe Nick and Katie will relax a little. I know Spider and Eileen could use some down time. Maybe Grandpa will get lucky in the motorhome."

If he'd had the beer in hand, Dad would have done a spit take.

"Damned motorhome would roll down the hill, son. So that's it, just a convenient time, and you want the whole family there while you're honeymooning."

"She's not pregnant, Dad."

He was quiet for a moment, staring at the table.

"Not that it would be a bad thing if she were," I added.

"No, it's not like you're sixteen and trying to play at

being a grown up," he said, thinking about Paul. "And I would have far fewer doubts about you marrying Lydia now than I did your brother seven years ago."

"Paul always tried hard."

Dad nodded thoughtfully. "Part of the time I think we never should have let him get married. Neither one of the them was ready for that. Other times…"

"You look at Nicole and know it was the right thing."

He nodded again. "I can't stop this from hurting her, Kevin. It's like she's holding her breath, waiting to get up one morning and find her mother gone. She barely reacted when we told her … she just held her breath."

"She's too young to understand."

"Hell, son, *I'm* too young to understand." He looked up, and his eyes were filled with tears. "I can barely cope with losing my daughter-in-law, how can Nicole cope with losing her mother?"

"She'll turn her soul inside out with grief, Dad, but she'll find a way to get through it. We all will, I swear."

"Paul…"

"Paul will want to die right along with her, but he'll get through it, too. He'll do it for Nicole, if nothing else."

He tossed the cue onto the table. "I'm sorry, Kevin. This was supposed to be about you and Lydia, and it's supposed to be happy. And I am happy for you."

"I know you are."

He took a deep breath, blinking away the tears. "I want grandkids, son. After the wedding, you better get to it."

I started to tell him it didn't necessarily have to wait, but he was adamant about the house rules: I was sleeping at home until we left for Bodega Bay.

16

Kevin

"The same rules apply."

Dad sounded like he did when we were all still teenagers, that tone of 'I know I'm talking to a brick wall, but I'm saying it anyway in case one of you stupid little monsters can actually hear me.' We were acting the same way we had then, watching him with affected disinterest, eyes glazed, waiting for the lecture to be over. Eileen and Spider were on the sofa, poking at each other, Nick was stretched out on the floor, staring up at the ceiling, and Lydia and I were sitting on the hearth; she was paying attention, I was just pretending.

Katie was supposed to be there, but Nick offered no explanation for her absence.

Paul was upstairs with Monica, helping her get out of the bathtub; Nicole was still in school.

"No drunken stupidities. I don't honestly expect you won't be drinking, but I'm adamant about you respecting the limits. No rip roaring drunks. If I find out the police have been called out there, I swear, I'll find a way to ground you all for life.

"The noise level drops at ten. Any later than that and the

neighbors probably *will* call the police. Party if you want, just do it at a reasonable decibel level." He looked specifically at Eileen. "That means you, young lady.

"Fires on the beach are fine, as long as you keep them twenty five feet from the outside edge of the porch. The condition of the house when we get there better be spotless. Work it out the same way you did when you were kids, agree who does what and when, and stick to it." He pointed at me. "And that means you. Dirty dishes are not going to rear up and swallow you whole."

"They might," I offered.

"Mostly, you have to remember that Nicole is there. She doesn't swim alone, wade in the water alone, she doesn't see any of you completely drunk, naked, or fooling around. If you have a fire going, she's never near it unless one of you is with her. And someone has to keep her attention off her mother when her meds are wearing off. That means one of you has to get her involved in something in the early evening. There's about a one hour window where Monica's in too much pain to deal with her, and she doesn't want Nicole to see her like that."

"That's not a problem," Eileen said. "Spider's bringing his laptop and we can load it with games for her. We'll keep her occupied."

"I talked to Will a little while ago," I told Dad. "He went to Modesto to some little church that does Internet ordinations. He's officially a nondenominational minister now."

Nick raised his head to look at me. "Why the hell does Will need to be ordained? He gave that up."

"I asked him to," I said. "We wanted him to be the one officiating."

"At?" He sat up, interested now that the lecture was over.

"Our wedding. That's what this little trip is for, Nick. We're getting married on Tuesday."

Nick exploded up off the floor. "Are you fucking kidding me? Why the hell doesn't anyone tell me these things?" He hugged Lydia, and then me.

I decided not to tell him his own wife already knew.

Eileen wisely kept her mouth shut.

"Don't drag a suit along, it'll be casual dress. The groom is wearing khakis, the bride is wearing—" I turned to Lydia. "What are you wearing?"

"I'll let you know when I find the right thing." She kissed me and got up. "Eileen and I are going shopping this afternoon. If I don't find what I'm looking for, I suppose I'll be getting married naked."

No one said anything, but I know Nick and Spider were both thinking it.

Please don't find anything. Please.

Lydia and I left for Bodega Bay at seven the next morning; I snuck out of the house at five – leaving a note so no one would worry – and walked to her apartment. I wanted an hour or two of quiet with her there, before they all showed up in our grandfather's motor home and began the parentless-lunacy that always seemed to transpire when we were there without a chaperone or two.

The original parts of the beach house were older than my dad; his father bought it when Dad was still in grade school, hoping that having an escape from the boredom of home would curb his wife's wandering eye.

All accounts point to that not working. But it did give Dad a place to run to when he found life overwhelming; when he hit his teens he ran away from home with astonishing frequency and almost always wound up at the beach house, standing in the sand, watching the ocean stir and churn while he drowned in his own misery.

It became a whole new place after he married Mom. It was still his hideaway, but a happier place; as the family grew, so did the house. He had a second story added with four small bedrooms, and later when Nick and Paul were married he had the garage converted to two slightly bigger bedrooms.

"There will be someplace for everyone to crash," he declared.

I don't think he thought ahead to how it would be when we all had kids, if we tried to share the beach house at the same time.

I staked a claim to the smallest of the upstairs bedrooms when I was eight or nine years old. There was barely enough room for the bed; between the edge of the mattress and the door there was just enough room to get in and close the door, and the closet couldn't be opened at all if the bedroom door was open, but I didn't care.

The bed was on the wall farthest from the door, a wall that was mostly window. It was frigid in the winter and annoyingly hot in the summer, but from it I had a perfect view of the ocean. I could lie there at night and watch moonlight bounce off the waves, and if I was feeling depraved enough I could watch my parents snuggle by the fire.

By ten o'clock we were sitting on the porch, sharing the padded bench that faced the ocean, huddled together under a blanket.

"This is tradition, you know," I told her. "My parents spent their first honeymoon here, my brothers and sister did … I think the only ones who didn't were Aunt Kris and Uncle Doug, but they would have if they hadn't run off to Reno to get married. Even Will did."

"I'm glad Will is doing this for us," she said, snuggling closer, setting her head on my shoulder. "It's kind of funny, though, him having to be ordained over the Internet."

I didn't tell her that while he was more than willing to make the effort to do whatever he had to in order to be the one who married us, he had his doubts. Will was worried I was marrying Lydia to make a point, pushing her into it as some sort of proof that I was perfectly all right.

"Unresolved anger," Will said, and often. "You have deep wells of it, kiddo, and it's not going away until you acknowledge it."

All I acknowledged was that I loved Lydia – something he had no doubt about – and that lingering in some sort of wait-and-see limbo made no sense at all. "Kind of like some guy I know who married the love of his life before he was dispensed from being a priest," I told him. "Whether we do it next week or next year, we're getting married, Will. Neither of us can see a reason why we should wait."

He could think of a few, but kept them to himself.

"Why aren't your parents coming up until Monday, Rabbit?" Lydia asked.

"My dad is closing some business deal, I think. And they can only take so much of their kids under one roof these days. Before they get here there will be at least one fight, probably between Paul and Eileen over something as stupid as on which refrigerator shelf the soda goes, someone will get drunk and throw up in the kitchen sink, and at some point Nick will dig a pit in the sand and start a huge fire in it that he might not be able to control. I think they're just avoiding the things that drive them nuts."

"And your mother wanted more of you?"

"Yeah, well she was young and dumb," I laughed. "But

fair warning, my dad will probably start picking on you about giving him grandkids before the end of the week."

"All sixteen of them?"

"That would make him very happy."

"Would he settle for two or three?"

"He doesn't get to vote in this one," I said, planting a kiss on top of her head. "Is that how many you want? Two?"

"Three, I think. But not right off the bat. I'd like at least a year alone with you before we start thinking about a family." She lifted her head and looked up at me. "Or did you have other thoughts? We really should talk about this now, you know."

"I'll have as many kids as you want. Whenever you want, as long as you don't try to stack them back to back like my mom did. It damn near killed her, that's why Eileen and I were the last."

"I've always thought about three kids as being ideal."

"You have the right to change your mind at any time."

"Now, if I told you later on I don't want any kids, you'd have a problem with that. You want kids, Kevin. I know you do."

"I do," I agreed. "But I'm marrying you, not your uterus. I want you more."

"You're sweet," she said, kissing me. "Even sweeter for remembering that when I was seventeen I said I wanted to get married on the beach."

"In the middle of a circle of people you care about," I added. "I used to wonder why you never wanted the huge church wedding with five hundred of your closest friends, and the reception of the decade. I thought that's what most little girls dreamed about."

"I did when I was very little. You're the one who made me rethink that."

"Me?"

"Our sophomore year, during lunch. Remember Jessica Patterson? She was a senior and engaged to some college frat boy."

"The one who could never shut up about her summer wedding? I remember."

"Exactly. That's all she talked about. How many people would be there, the ten layer cake, how many bridesmaids she was having. We were all sitting there at lunch trying to not pay attention to the chatter, when she said something about her parents taking out a second mortgage on their house to pay for it, and you nearly flipped. I can still even hear your voice, how pissed off you were. 'It's not just their house, they're mortgaging their *future* so you can have a pretty little party for a hundred people who don't know jack shit about you and really don't care about anything other than how much booze there will be.'"

"Oh yeah. She wanted to deck me."

"But you were right. She didn't listen, but you were right. She never heard you talk about the fact that she was focused on the wedding and not everything that came afterwards. It was a real eye opener for a lot of us, Kevin. I know I wasn't the only girl at that table who changed her perspective on the perfect wedding. Whether we do it in front of your entire parish, or just our family, we're just as married."

"But I never meant to imply there was anything wrong with a big wedding, Lydia."

"I know you didn't, but after that I started to realize that when I got married, I didn't want to throw some big thing for people who would only be there for the free food. I wanted it to be with people who had a stake in it. People who give a damn whether or not we'll still be together five years from now."

"What happened to Jessica? Do you know?"

"She was divorced by the time we graduated high school. And you have to wonder just how long her parents will be paying for that wedding."

"Well, as much as we're spending, I think we can have it paid off in about eight days. Nine if you count the new underwear I bought. Boxers, just for you."

"Ten," she said. "I hope you don't mind, but I bought you new slacks. They're not your coveted khakis, but they're nice and they match my dress."

"I hope they'll match the t-shirt I brought along for the wedding."

"You wouldn't dare," she laughed. "But I bought you a shirt, too. Do you realize that you're awfully hard to buy for? When I told the salesman that you're six-five his eyes bugged out and he started muttering about having to dig through the back room to find your size, if it even existed."

"I cause problems everywhere I go."

At the sound of the motor home pulling into the driveway, we got up, going down the porch steps onto the sand, where we could see Eileen and Spider climbing out of their car. Eileen stretched and then looked over at us, shaking her head.

She didn't look happy.

Thirty seconds later I understood why, when the motor home door banged open and my stomach started to do a slow, painful turn.

Debby.

This was anger I fully intended to resolve; I dragged Nick, protesting, onto the sand, away from the house and away from Debby, who had gone inside with Katie. As soon as she'd seen Debby, Lydia turned and went inside, muttering about going upstairs to put our clothes away.

I wasn't angry at Debby for being there; I was mad as hell at Nick for bringing her along.

"You stupid son of a bitch," I seethed. "What the hell were you thinking?"

Nick took a cautious step away from me, holding up his hands as if he were warding off traffic. "Take it easy, Kevin. They'll hear you up there."

"You think I care? You knew better than to bring her."

"What was I supposed to do?"

"Leave her at home," I growled, shoving him backwards. "Whatever. Drop her off on the fucking highway. Just not bring her here!"

"Cut it out." He braced himself, grunting when my hands thundered against his chest. "Grow up already."

"Yeah?" I swung a clenched fist, knuckles landing squarely on Nick's chin. He stumbled backwards and fell, landing on his back in the sand. "Goddammit, we're getting married, and she is *not* invited. Think how Lydia felt, seeing *Debby* of all people getting out of that motor home. Son of a bitch, Lydia was counting on me."

"Yeah, well maybe Debby was counting on me. Goddamn, Kevin, I couldn't leave her home and risk losing Katie over it."

"Keep her out of our way, Nick," I warned. "I don't want to even know she's around."

"I'm not her babysitter."

I stood over him, looking down. "Understand this, big brother. If you ruined this wedding for Lydia, if she feels even remotely like her dream has been squashed, I'll make your life so much hell you'll wish it was you dying instead of Monica."

I stormed back into the house.

The thing that made me feel worse was that I meant it.

We avoided the 'D' word; Lydia and I managed to occupy the rest of the day by exploring the beach and ignoring Katie's sister. We drove into town for dinner, stayed as long as we could in the restaurant, and when we got back she headed upstairs to shower while I stayed on the porch to call my parents.

Yes, I was tattling on Nick.

By the time I went back upstairs Lydia was in bed, curled up on her side, watching Eileen and Katie on the beach below.

"Can they see us in here?" she asked as I slipped into bed beside her.

"Only if the light in the room is on. Though if you press your ass up against the glass, they might be able to figure out what it is."

She snuggled against me, letting me slip my arms around her. "I really wish you hadn't hit Nick," she said after a while.

"He'll live. I don't get him at all, he knew better. My dad warned him, he told Nick all the problems I've had with her lately. And he specifically told Nick to not bring her here."

"Your dad is angry, I take it."

"He's not happy, but I got the impression my mom wants to gouge Nick's eyes out."

She turned to look at me. "It's not that bad, Kevin. I'm not happy that she's here but I won't let that ruin anything. He had to have a reason."

"He said he couldn't leave her behind, not and hold onto what little he has left of his marriage."

"Well, there you go. I don't want the start of our marriage to be the end of his. Let it go."

~

The sleep that Lydia dropped into so easily eluded me, and after an hour of twitching and rearranging the blankets, I gave up and slipped quietly out of bed and left the room.

Nick and Paul were in the living room, plastered on the sofa, a thin cloud of smoke hovering in the air above them. They stared at the fireplace as if it were a television set, eyes glazed over, disinterested but just bored enough to sit and watch the fireplace equivalent of static.

"So when did you start smoking this crap?" I asked Nick as I dropped into the armchair. "Hell, when did you start growing it?"

"It dulls the pain, squirt," he sighed. "I suppose I should thank you for the excuse to get totally lit."

"Seriously. When did you start?"

"I dunno. Maybe three years ago. Maybe four. Katie bought some and thought it'd be a kick to try. I was the one who liked it and figured it'd be cheaper to grow my own. So I do. Right out there in the greenhouse with the beefsteak tomatoes."

"Aren't you afraid of getting caught?"

"Not especially." He held the joint out to me. "A little creativity and I'd have a get out of jail free card. No sweat. Want a hit?"

"Eileen swears you grow the best," I said, reaching for it.

"That I do." He sat up, running his fingers through his hair. "I'm not total scum, Kevin. I don't sell it. If you want any, just ask me for it. I won't sell it."

At that moment I couldn't have cared less, as long as he wasn't hanging around the junior high parking lot, waving it in front of kids too eager to prove how cool they were. I took a long hit, and passed it to Paul.

"You know," I said with a cough, "you get caught and Dad won't use his connections to get you out of it. He'll let you rot in jail for a drug rap."

"I have my ways."

"Oh, sure."

"I do."

Paul just snorted his disbelief.

"Look, weenies, I spent enough time studying law to be able to wiggle out of a whole lot of crap. I don't have that much in the greenhouse ... just enough. And you never know, I may have a connection or two of my own."

Paul snorted again.

"How's your face?" I asked Nick.

"I'll have a black eye for a couple weeks. Maybe it'll earn me some sympathy points. And I don't expect you to apologize, I know I screwed up."

"Like it or not," Paul said, "she's family, Kevin. And you said you wanted family here."

Nick reached for the joint. "Dad told me to find a polite way to leave her behind. I couldn't think of one and I didn't have the balls to tell Katie her own sister wasn't welcome in our family."

"Wait, wait, wait, wait, wait," I said. "It's not about her not being welcome in the family. She *is* welcome in the family, Nicky. She's just not welcome to calling me at all hours of the night, and sneaking up on me and shoving her hand down my pants, or trying to jump into the shower with me. I'd be fine if she wanted to be like a sister or something."

"Tell her that," Paul said.

"I can't talk to her. I don't even know why she's so interested in me."

"Because," Nick said as he rolled another joint, "she

knows you won't be like all the other jerkoffs who used her, then humiliated and dumped her. If she's physical it's because that's the only way she's ever been able to grab someone's attention. You have to admit, it works. You noticed her, all right, and if not for Lydia—"

"I don't think so," I said. "No matter what, I'd want someone a lot more self-secure. Someone I can share my secrets with and not worry that they'll be spilled."

"Just what are your secrets, Kevin?" Nick pressed.

"None of your fucking business, that's for sure."

"I know," Paul snorted, trying not to laugh. "Kevin never went into the seminary. He was off doing covert things for the good ole U.S of A."

"That would be Dad," I said. "Spying for the USDA."

"The department of agriculture?"

"Yep. His job was to leave no cow untipped."

"Dee-fence a-gen-cy," Nick drawled. "It would totally piss him off if one of us signed on with them."

Paul shrugged. "No worries. We'll never pass the drug test."

"If Dad walks through that door right now there won't be a drug test," Nick said. "We'll all be dead."

"He'd have to catch me first, and I'm quicker than he is," I pointed out. "Goddamn, I'm hungry now."

"Munchies." Paul looked at the joint he was holding as if it were a brand new thing. "Maybe Monica should try this. She's already losing an awful lot of weight. No appetite at all."

"I have enough to keep all of Bodega Bay baked for a week," Nick said as he got up and headed for the kitchen. He came back with a bag of tortilla chips and a bowl of picante sauce, dropping them onto the coffee table. "She can have all she wants."

"I don't know if she would. It might screw up her other meds."

"She looks pretty good," Nick offered.

"She sucks it up well. Most of the time she's in so much pain she can barely think straight, but she doesn't want Nicole to see it."

"Dad said you'd told her," I mumbled, not sure what else to say.

Paul nodded. He'd picked up a chip, but was crumbling it between his fingers. "She doesn't seem to grasp any of it. She knows cancer is something awful, and other people die…"

"I think Nicole might surprise you," I said, quietly. "She grasps a lot more than any of us give her credit for."

He could barely whisper. "She shouldn't have to."

"Neither should you."

Nick was sprinkling part of his stash into the picante sauce. "Happy thoughts, gentlemen," he said. "We're here to have happy thoughts, and to make sure the groom doesn't take off screaming into the night."

"Not a snowball's chance in hell of that."

"The bride might," Paul said. He pointed at me, very serious. "You have something good there, squirt. You fuck it up and I'll kick your ass." He turned to Nick. "And you, you're fucking up all over the place. Whatever the hell is wrong between you and Katie, you better fix it, and do it soon, because you have about one more 'no I have a headache' before you lose her."

"I know that, Paul."

"Then fix it already."

"I would if I had a clue how."

"Knock her up," I suggested.

"A baby shouldn't be a bandage, squirt. I have to figure out what the real problem is."

"Did you ever stop to think that maybe that *is* it? It's that simple?"

"Even if it is … I've got too much crammed into my head right now. I'm just not ready."

Paul snorted. "You think I was? I was sixteen freaking years old. I wasn't ready, and I didn't have a damned clue about what I was getting into." He stubbed out what was left of the joint and turned on the sofa, inching closer to Nick. "By all rights Monica and I never should have gotten married. It was a mistake, Nick, it was the biggest goddamn mistake I've ever made, but if I had to go back and do it over, I'd do it again."

"Nicole wasn't a mistake, Paul," Nick sighed.

"Nicole wasn't," he agreed, "but getting married—everything was so unplanned and hurried and neither one of us was ready for any of it. I was *terrified*, Nicky. I woke up every morning from the day Monica and I got married until Nicole was walking, wondering if I'd done the right thing, or if we should have done the smart thing and let Dad just get Monica a place to live and me shared custody."

"You have a point?"

"Get past the idea of a baby being so much responsibility and get to the idea where Katie gets what she wants. No matter what, your own kid will be a blessing."

"Are you fucking nuts?" Nick sat up sharply. "A kid *is* a big responsibility and I won't shortchange mine by being a loser father. I don't want kids until I've gotten myself straightened out and have a goddamn clue what it is I'm doing!"

We both stared at him, waiting for the light bulb to go off over his head.

When it did, he sighed hard and slumped back against the sofa. "No, I haven't told her that, not exactly."

"How much do you need to straighten out, Nick?" I asked.

"What do you mean?"

I reached for the stub of the joint. "Is this all you need to straighten out from?"

Dead silent. He stared at the stub between my fingers for a long time, then closed his eyes. Paul shifted uncomfortably, waving at me to put it down.

"What else is there, Nick?"

"Come on," Paul pressed when he didn't answer.

When Nick finally opened his eyes, he wasn't looking at me, or at Paul. He stared into the fireplace, taking deep breaths. "I'm drinking a hell of a lot. I don't think Katie realizes … I drink during the day, and when she comes home I wander off to another part of the house to read or surf online, long enough for her to not smell it on me. She doesn't think twice when I have two or three beers after dinner, but by then I've had so much it's not funny."

"How much?" I asked.

"Six-pack and a half a day, maybe two. If I'm drinking beer. I smoke half the day away, too. God, it's not just that. What the hell am I going to do with rest of my life? I can't sit at home all day and commiserate with Oprah."

"Why not?"

"Come on, Kevin. What the hell will I do all day?"

"I don't know, maybe raise the kids you know you're going to cave in on once you get yourself sobered up?"

"Be a stay at home dad."

"Why not? There's not a thing wrong with you staying home and being there for your kids. Dad did it for a long time. When we were little he was always there."

Paul reached for Nick's plastic baggy. "We don't need

this to have fun here, Nick. We don't need the booze, either. You get your ass out to the motor home and start talking to your wife, and Kevin and I will dump it all."

"Just like that."

"If you think you can handle going cold turkey, yes, just like that."

"Actually," I said, taking the baggy from Paul, "you'd better go out to the motor home with him and clear it out. He did say he had enough grass on him to keep the entire town stoned."

"I'm more worried about the alcohol," Paul said, his eyes locked onto Nick's.

I could almost feel Nick's pulse pounding in his head, how quickly everything was spinning, the fear tinged with relief.

"All right," Nick finally agreed. "You grab all the beer, and I'll try to get Katie to sit out on the beach with me."

"Good," Paul grunted, getting up.

"Squirt." Nick turned at the door. "I am so sorry. I never intended for this to become the Get Nicky Sober Show. I swear to God, I won't let it ruin your wedding."

As I was pouring out the last of the beer I wondered if it even mattered. Debby was already there, which thrilled me about as much as an early morning wedgy. We couldn't ignore the fact of Monica's short future. Sobering Nick up was just another thing to deal with.

I tried to slide back into bed without waking Lydia; she was still in the same position she'd been in when I left, on her side, facing the window, the sheet and blankets drawn up tightly to her chin. I slipped an arm around her and drew close; she sighed and stretched against me, pulling my arm tight across her, my hand near her face.

"You snuck out," she said, kissing my hand. "Where'd you go?"

"Just downstairs."

She took a deep breath. "Have you been smoking?"

"A little. Nick brought it."

Nick was outside, lighting another fire. Katie was sitting on one of the long logs we'd circled the pit with, huddled in a baggy sweatshirt, hugging her legs for warmth. I wondered how he'd begin to tell her, and if she'd react with anger or sadness, or even relief.

She could deal with him not wanting to be a lawyer.

She could deal with him taking time off to figure out what he wanted to do with his life.

I wasn't sure she could deal with him fighting against alcohol and drugs, or if she would even want to.

"We got rid of all the beer and most of his grass," I said, watching the flames leap out of the pit. "Nick's having some trouble with it."

She rolled onto her back to look at me. "Are you serious?"

"He says he's drinking and smoking a lot. Paul cleared everything out of the motor home and I cleared all the beer out of the fridge, but I kept the baggy he had in the living room, in case you wanted it."

"Better to remove all temptation, don't you think?"

"Yeah, maybe."

I didn't want it. At that moment I was sure I'd never want it again.

He was sitting away from Katie. He had picked up a stick and was drawing circles in the sand, but he was talking to her. Spider would be able to watch and see what he was saying; all I could do was wait for her reaction.

"You're snooping," Lydia accused lightly.

"Can't help it. Now that I know why Nick's been such an ass, I'm worried about him."

"Katie will deal with him."

"Either that or she'll shove him into the pit."

She might have wanted to, but after fifteen minutes she got up and went over to him, sitting close. Nick had his head in his hands, and Katie slipped her arm across his back, leaning her head against his.

"It's not your fight, Rabbit," Lydia whispered.

Maybe not, but it was my burden. Nick was my surrogate father, the person I'd turned to most when our parents were separated. He was the person we'd all turned to, heaping more responsibility onto him than a sixteen year old should have to bear. He was the one we turned to first, before our parents, and he was the one who disciplined in the absence of our parents' knowledge of our transgressions.

I was grounded at least three times that my parents never knew about. And it stuck; there was no question about Nick's authority.

Realizing that, it was no small wonder that he'd started drinking. School was almost over, and he knew what came next. As soon as he had that diploma in hand, Katie would want kids. It was what they'd agreed on.

But Nick had already been a father, he wasn't ready to face that again.

"He's never been a father to a newborn," Lydia pointed out. "You know the second he's holding his own baby all of that will melt away."

Nick was sitting up straight now, holding Katie's hand.

"One would hope," I agreed.

"They'll be okay, Kevin."

Katie leaned towards Nick and kissed him, her lips lingering long enough to say she'd heard him.

"Damn," I said, sighing hard. "Those two don't even get make up sex."

"Why not?"

"Debby. It'd be a little awkward to get the motor home rocking with her in there. I'd think, anyway."

She put her hand on my chest and pushed me onto my back. "Quit watching them. You have better things you could be doing."

"I'm not supposed to do those things until we're married. My Dad said so."

"I won't tell if you won't."

"You better be quiet, then," I warned. "You might not tell, but if Eileen hears anything, she will."

Chip

I found Terry sitting on the stairs, right in the middle, halfway up.

"Listen," she said when I stopped at the foot of the stairs.

I cocked my head and strained to hear, trying to figure out what I was supposed to be listening to. There was nothing, just the dull hiss of silence.

"That's the point," she said. "It's so quiet. You and I are the only people in the house. When was the last time that happened?"

"I'm sure it happened a few odd times when the kids were in school," I said, though truthfully I wasn't sure. I'd spent too many days and nights completely alone when we were separated, but while we lived together, it seemed like someone was always there, some teenager or child in need of attention, or two or more of them fighting.

"You realize this is what we have to look forward to? A year or so from now you know Paul will move out with Nicole. Kevin's leaving. This is it, Chip. This is how quiet our lives will be."

"This isn't so bad," I told her, climbing the stairs to sit with her. "Nicole will come over to play, and we'll be ready to send her home after a couple hours. And we can demand our parental rights, make the kids have dinner here a couple times a month."

"It's still depressing."

"Just think, when they're all gone, we can run around the house buck naked if we want."

"We could do that now," she sighed.

"Want to?" I asked hopefully.

She patted me on the thigh. "Why don't we give Doug and Kris a call and see if they want to go out tonight?"

"I'd rather run around the house naked."

"Tell you what," she said, getting up, "I'll give them a call, and you and Doug can run around the house naked while Kris and I go out for dinner."

"You're no fun."

"Humor me, Irish. I'm feeling very old right now, and it's your job to make me feel young again."

I thought running around the house naked would accomplish that, but she was already headed for the phone.

Kevin

"Family pow-wow," I said brightly, bouncing on the edge of the bed. "Nick is building a mega-fire on the sand even as we speak."

Lydia groaned and rolled over, pulling the pillow over her head. I pried it from her fingers and tossed it to the foot of the bed, out of her reach.

"Come on. You don't want to be the only one left out."

"Yes I do. Wake me in another hour."

Laughing, I peeled the blankets away. She was curled up in bed dressed in my heavy sweatshirt and sweatpants, thick socks, and she was still complaining about the cold. Ice water in the veins.

The chill hadn't bothered her earlier in the day, when we walked along the beach, or when we tried to play volleyball with Spider and Eileen.

It hadn't seemed to bother her at six in the morning, when she sat on the porch watching me jog up and down the beach with the neighbor's spastic terrier yapping at my heels.

It didn't bother her until she started drifting off after lunch, claiming that fresh air was foreign to her, and she needed to rest to recover from it. She burrowed under the blankets and was silent for most of the afternoon.

"Nerves," Paul declared. "She's having second thoughts."

She could have all the thoughts she wanted as long as she didn't change her mind.

I poked at her. "We're roasting weenies."

She opened one eye. "Yours, I hope."

"Funny, woman. Come on. Nick and Katie are even being civil to. They're actually touching each other—she even kissed the poor slob. We need to get down there and witness Nick's good mood first hand. It might not last."

Groaning, she finally sat up. "He's not suffering withdrawal or anything?"

"I don't think he's an alcoholic. I think it just got out of hand and he didn't want to admit it."

"And you and Paul and Spider can survive partying without the beer?"

"Trust me," I said, getting off the bed. "We don't need any help getting stupid."

Nick

The pyromaniac in me watched curiously as the flames leapt out of the pit, fed on an entire can of lighter fluid. I only dimly hoped it would die down enough for us to be able to see each other across the pit.

"Overkill, isn't it?" Katie asked. "Or are we planning a sacrifice tonight?"

I looked up at her thoughtfully. "Know any virgins we can toss into the flames?"

"Aren't they extinct?"

Paul was helping Monica into a lawn chair. "The only virgin here is my daughter, and you damn well better keep your grubby hands off her."

"There's always Kevin," Katie suggested. "He's the one closest to it. I'll grab him when he comes out."

"I'll help," Monica snickered. "But I don't think we'd be grabbing him for the reasons these two think."

Paul plopped down next to Monica. "You're both degenerates."

"I want to paint him," Katie said. "Think he'd pose for me?"

I tossed more wood into the pit. "That depends. Nude?"

"Of course."

"Figures. Paul, they're going to de-pants our little brother."

Katie jumped up and slipped her arms around me. "I bet he's not so little anymore."

"Yeah, well, if you're curious, ask Lydia, not him."

"Ask him now," Monica offered. "He's on his way down here."

"No! The little shit just might whip it out."

Kevin had closed the front door, and was walking out

onto the beach behind Spider and Eileen, his arm possessively around Lydia. Debby, reluctant to join in on anything we did as a group, straggled out of the motor home a few minutes later and walked very slowly to the beach, looking completely unsure she'd even be welcome.

I had Kevin's word he'd be nice.

Monica looked up at Kevin and asked sweetly, "Did you bring your weenie?"

"Don't do it, Monica," Paul said with a twist of a groan in his voice. "Don't ask, squirt. She and Katie are being especially crude today."

Kevin shrugged indifferently. "I like lascivious women. Makes life interesting."

"Interesting enough to pose for me?" Katie asked, pushing my hand away before I could clamp it over her mouth. "I'm talking the real thing here. No fig leaves or anything."

Before he could answer, Lydia piped up. "You paint it and I'll buy it. We'll hang it in the bathroom."

Sheepishly, Kevin looked from her to Katie and said, "I'll pose for you on one condition—she poses with me. As long as it's not sleazy or anything."

I couldn't believe it. "Are you serious? You'd really pose in the buff for her?"

"Sure, why not?"

"*Naked*, Kevin."

His offer was repeated. "As long as Lydia poses with me."

Eileen was laughing. "Mom and Dad will never believe this one. Who has the hot dogs?"

"Spider," Lydia said. "And just what makes you think I want my nude body hanging on the wall?"

"You have a great body," he said, skewering a hot dog

and handing it to her. "Though I admit, I've never pictured you hanging on the bathroom wall."

"And you might not."

Katie tossed him a bun. "How big are you, anyway, Kevin?"

He didn't miss a beat. "Six-five and a few odd inches. Why, Katie, how big are you?"

"Big enough for a few odd inches," Katie replied happily, dodging my jabbing finger.

Kevin skewered another hot dog and handed it to a surprised Debby.

"By the way," Kevin said, "Nicole is waiting for the fire to die down a little bit before she comes out. She said she thinks Uncle Nick is a weirdo, and that he wants to catch us all on fire."

Paul nodded toward the house. "She's been looking out the window and watching us. I really think she just wants some time alone."

"We're boring her," Eileen added. "Too many grown ups and not enough fun things to do with them."

"I'm fun," Kevin said.

"You're also distracted. I think she's being very good about not being the center of attention from her favorite person in the whole world."

"And she understands," Paul said before Kevin could start to feel guilty. "She's old enough to grasp that not everything is about her."

But, for a while, Lydia said to the agreement of all, it should be about her. When Nicole finally came out of the house, satisfied that the fire was a dull enough roar to not swallow us whole, we declared her to be Queen of the Barbeque and spent the better part of an hour singing kiddy songs, everything from a morbid ditty about some bunny beating the crap out of field mice to friendless losers eating worms.

On any other beach trip she would have glued herself to Kevin, but this night she shifted between sitting on Monica's lap and Paul's.

I watched Paul with his arms around her, laughing, placing absent minded kisses on the top of her head. When we stopped singing and turned a radio on, he jumped up to dance with her, swinging her in wide circles, the song on the radio drowned out by the music of her laughter.

I watched my brother do what he did every day, I watched him fall in love with his daughter.

I watched him and I knew they were right.

I wanted that.

Kevin

I made a discovery while sitting there on the beach, singing silly songs with my brothers and sister—Lydia cannot, not in any way, shape, or form, carry a tune.

Nicole, in her youthful honesty, looked at her and said, "You should stop."

The horrified look on Paul's face was priceless. His impulse was to snap at her, correct her for being rude, but he couldn't believe he'd heard her right. Before he could gather a coherent thought, Lydia laughed, "They kicked me out of choir in junior high. I was throwing off the entire alto section."

"You two should go smooch or something," Nicole suggested.

We opted for the 'or something,' and left Paul to explain the rudimentaries of manners to her. Lydia wanted to walk along the water's edge to the jetty, holding hands, looking at other peoples' houses. Imagine what they were doing. Figure out which belonged to people who lived there all year, and which belonged to weekenders.

Inside, I was jumping up and down like a five year old at Christmas. In less than 48 hours we'd be married. It took all the restraint I had to keep from emitting a high pitched, girly-like squeal. She could babble on about what other people might or might not be doing all she wanted.

I was going to get what I wanted.

"My parents will be here tomorrow," I reminded her. "Getting nervous?"

"Nope. But you need to figure out where you're sleeping tomorrow night, because you know it won't be with me. Your dad will stand guard outside the bedroom door all night to make sure you don't get in."

He would, too.

"I'd planned on sleeping in the motor home."

"Like hell."

"That was before the she-devil arrived."

"Stop. She's not that bad, Rabbit. She thinks it's a fair fight and she came out here intending to win. There's really nothing wrong with that."

"There's everything wrong with her tactics, Lydia. What could possibly make her think I'd want to be with someone who doesn't think twice about walking up and copping a feel?"

"Kevin, listen to yourself," she snickered. "You sound like one of those reruns of an old late sixties' sitcom."

"Well, I'm not that kind of girl," I sniffed pretentiously.

"Come on. If *I* walked up and copped a feel, you wouldn't mind."

She had me there.

I'd salute.

Happily.

"She's got a thing for you. She'll get over it when we're married."

I wasn't so sure. I'd read years of her letters that spoke differently. Debby never had a problem with going after married men; hell, she seemed to prefer married men. It was damn near her specialty.

I had my own theories about her behavior; she certainly hadn't bounced from one guy to the next in high school, before the Air Force uprooted her family to deposit them in Washington, D.C. If she'd stayed in California, I'm sure I would have dated her occasionally, with all the boundaries I insisted on in place.

The girl from ninth grade would have respected those boundaries.

Hell, I was sure the girl I'd been writing to all those years respected the boundaries, when she knew I intended to be a priest. Coming home changed everything, including how she viewed me.

But those years in between, starting sometime during her junior year of high school, Debby changed. She started up a dating frenzy, sleeping with anyone who asked. I was sure it was because she felt like she came in last place in her family; everything Katie did, she did well, from graduating top of her class in high school and then college, to her talent in painting. Their younger brother was no genius, but worked his ass off in school; he wasn't a natural athlete, but killed himself every day trying to be a good one, playing football and basketball. He wanted to be an Air Force pilot, and wanted to go to the USAF Academy to accomplish that.

Debby always felt like everything she did wasn't good enough. If she couldn't be good enough, then she'd do everything she could to make it an obvious point.

At least, that was my theory.

After we reached the jetty we headed back for the fire, presuming they were done singing and Lydia wouldn't be offending Nicole's sense of musical talent. Paul had already taken her back into the house – I guessed that she was in the bedroom, talking fast, trying to get out of a bath – and Nick looked like he was deep into an argument with Debby.

Spider was looking everywhere but at them.

Eileen looked amused.

Before we could get within earshot, Debby jumped up and ran into the house, slamming the door as she stormed in.

"Squirt," Nick sighed as we sat down, "once again, I am *so* sorry"

Before I could ask, Katie added, "I am, too. We were so preoccupied with pissing each other off that neither of us told Debby exactly why we were coming here this week. She thought it was just a family vacation."

Eileen was trying to not laugh, and failing miserably. "She's a wee bit ticked off."

I looked up at the house. "Just a wee bit?"

Debby was in the living room on the sofa, staring at the TV, and even from where I sat outside I could see she was angry.

"She's embarrassed, Kevin," Katie said.

"Rabbit." Lydia out her hand on my arm, squeezing gently. "You need to go talk to her. Make sure she knows it's okay that she's here. She's part of your family."

"And in two days she's part of yours," Eileen reminded her.

"Go," Lydia urged. "You two should have talked this out weeks ago."

I did as I was told.

I left Lydia sitting there by the fire and slowly, stubbornly, walked towards the house, trying to figure out what I could say to Debby.

Be nice, I kept mumbling.

Just. Be. Nice.

Really.

There are some conversations you just don't want to have; this was one for me. Writing generic letters to her every now and then was one thing; sitting down and actually talking to her was another.

I dropped onto the sofa on the end opposite Debby and watched TV for a minute or two as she surfed channels, her finger practically pounding on the remote. When she settled on CNN, the sound barely audible, I finally said the obvious: "We have to talk."

"Go away, Kevin." Stubbornly, she wouldn't look away from the TV.

"I am really sorry no one told you why we were all here."

"Like hell."

All right, I really wasn't sorry. But if she had known, chances are she wouldn't have come in the first place.

So I lied.

"Yes, I am. Nick should have told you."

"Gee. You think?"

"I also think that's just a small part of what we need to talk about. Too many things have happened lately to avoid it."

"Get over yourself, Kevin."

"Right. I just imagined you trying to crawl into my bed. You trying to shove your hand down the front of my sweatpants was just a figment of my imagination. You kissing me was just some kind of freaky afternoon kitchen fantasy."

She didn't say anything, but turned up the volume on the TV.

"Whatever I said," I grunted, grabbing the remote from her to turn the volume down, "that made you think I was interested, I'm sorry. I never meant to lead you on."

"Lead me on," she snorted.

"For lack of a better way to put it."

Then she turned on me, eyes wide with anger, voice dripping with venom. "What was I *supposed* to think? All those times you said 'if it was me you were involved with' or 'if I was dating you.' Every time you told me I'd be better off leaving D.C. and coming back to California, what was I supposed to think?"

"That I was being a friend."

"Yes, when you were in the seminary that was *fine*. But I had every reason to think that it could be more than that once you left."

Sure, I'd probably said all those things. And meant them. But I didn't see how she made the leap from "if" to "it could be me."

"Deb," I said after a while, after she'd turned away, "I didn't even write to tell you I'd gone home. Didn't that say something?"

"It said that you were tired and needed some space," she said, voice beginning to break. "I waited to fly out here until I was sure you'd had some time to rewind. I never thought there'd be *her*."

"So … all that time I was just sitting at home learning to knit?"

"Son of a bitch. No, but that short amount of time isn't enough to fall in love!"

She had no clue.

"I've loved Lydia all my life."

"Give me a freaking break. If she was this great love of your life, why did you never, not once, mention her?"

Good question.

Debby wasn't there in grade school to see me falling all over myself every time Lydia walked by. By the time she'd started school with us, Lydia had a pack of boys around her all the time, and none of them were ever me.

By the time I was dating Lydia at all, Debby was gone.

"Because," I answered carefully, "she was something I couldn't have, and it hurt like hell. And you seemed to need me to listen, not dump my crap on you."

She turned again, the anger all but a small flicker behind the sadness that fell over her face like a veil. "I thought you were my friend."

"I was. I am."

"It's a fucking two way street, Kevin. You thought I was so shallow all I wanted to talk about was myself?"

Yes, I did think that.

But I kept it to myself.

"You're making a mistake," she went on. "This is your rebound relationship. You don't marry your rebound."

"Rebound from what?"

"From *whatever.* It can't last. A year from now we won't be sitting around talking about how wonderful your life is. You'll be picking your heart up off the floor."

"And you'll be there."

"This isn't over, Kevin, not by a long shot. In the end, I'll win. I know I will."

Nick was up and on the phone at seven the next morning, asking our parents to drive up in two cars. Debby was going home one way or the other; if they didn't bring Nick's car, she'd walk if she had to. Hitch hike her way through Petaluma back to Fairfield, no matter what potential harm she might invite.

"She swears she doesn't want to ruin the wedding," he told me.

I grunted my disbelief.

"No, squirt, she meant it. She doesn't want to ruin it for Lydia. You, she thinks you're an idiot and hopes you wind up with a swarm of fire ants nibbling on your balls, and *then* she wants to hurt you, but she didn't think it would be fair to ruin it for the bride."

I didn't know whether to laugh or not. Lydia felt bad she was leaving – she didn't want Debby there but she also didn't want her feelings hurt – but no one tried to talk Debby into staying.

I'd argued with Debby for an hour; she was convinced my marriage was doomed from the first kiss, and I couldn't convince her that it was meant to be. She was positive some horrible wrath was going to ascend from hell and ruin my life; I was just as sure that she needed some sort of psychiatric help.

And yes, in the end, I did tell her that.

Jesus Christ, girl, you need a shrink.

She spent the next morning waiting in the motor home, determined to not give me a chance at any more pot shots. She told Katie to make sure I came nowhere near her, that if I did she felt fully justified in whipping a kick into my groin. "Though, actually," Katie admitted, "she said she'd kick you in the groin so hard your nuts would be hanging out your nostrils."

I stayed away.

I didn't have another apology left in me.

The rest of us were on the beach tossing a Frisbee around when Mom pulled up in Nick's old Camaro. Debby stomped out of the motor home with a small bag in hand and took the keys before Mom could even close the door.

She did, Mom later said, thank her. And she gave my grandparents time to get out of the car before she took off.

I had visions of her peeling out of the driveway, leaving in a squeal of rubber, but she backed out carefully, waving at my dad as he pulled in, Doug's car right behind him.

It was a freaking convoy.

Everyone was there except Will, who wasn't arriving until morning. Nicole squealed when she spotted them, and ran towards Dad; he climbed out of his car and scooped her up in a hug, letting her stand on the hood of his car so she could plant a kiss on the top of his head.

And then the back doors to Dad's car opened. Lydia noticed before I did; she squealed louder than Nicole had, flying past me in a blur, kicking up sand in her own wake.

"Daddy! Mom!"

Looking rather rumpled, Jim and Nan Freeman climbed out of the back seat, both reaching for their daughter, who was bouncing up and down on her toes, waiting impatiently for her father to close the door so she could hug him.

"Couldn't do it," he said when they finally ended their loud, bouncing family hug. "We couldn't miss our baby girl's wedding."

Lydia was hugging her mother again. "How, Mom? How did you make yourself fly?"

"The groom's father," she explained, "refused to take no for an answer. He reasoned that I could survive a few hours on the Concorde. And he was right."

"Valium helped," Jim added.

"Chip, you did this?" Lydia asked, her eyes filling with tears.

He smiled and shrugged.

The hugfest went on; Lydia grabbed my dad and kissed him on the cheek, and when she let go her mother reached for him. I stayed out of the fray, watching.

Nicole jumped off the hood of the car and went over to Uncle Doug, tugging at his hand. "Is that Lydia's Daddy?"

"Yep."

"Is he going to be my uncle?"

"No, you won't really be related," Doug said. "But I bet you two can figure out what you want to be for each other. I'm not really your Daddy's uncle, you know."

She rolled her eyes. "Yes you are!"

"Nope. I was your grandpa's best friend when Nick was born, and we just pretended I was his uncle. And Aunt Kris is really his cousin."

"You can do that?"

Doug nodded.

Nicole watched Lydia with her parents, considering carefully. "Well, I don't know what I want them to be, but I think Lydia is happy that they came here."

"Do you want to meet them?" he asked her, taking her hand to lead her over.

She refused to move. "No. Not yet."

"How come?"

Her gaze shifted to me. "I wanna make sure they aren't mad at Uncle Kevin. He kissed Lydia a lot, you know."

We all knew that.

But, maybe she was right.

Making sure my future in-laws didn't hate me was probably a good idea.

~

Monica was asleep, curled up in a chaise lounge on the porch, a thick quilt tucked up under her chin, and she was sound asleep. I ventured out onto the porch for the same reason she had: I needed a break from the uproar of loud talk and laughter that started at lunch and continued past dinner.

While she snoozed, I perched myself on the porch railing, staring out the ocean, watching the waves lap back and forth, looking for bubbles in the sand as the water receded.

When I was five Paul convinced me that the bubbles in the sand were filled with mini-killer crabs, and if I sat down they would wiggle out of the holes and climb up my shorts to gnaw on my skin. I was safe, he said, only if I stood on one foot, and only if I didn't stand in one spot too long.

I alternated feet, shifting across the sand so much that Mom finally decided I needed to pee and made me go inside.

Out of habit, just in case, I kept an eye on those bubbles, still.

A few minutes later Dad followed me out onto the porch and sat on the railing next to me. He turned to look at Monica – probably checking to make sure she was still breathing, though I could have told him I'd already made sure – and then sighed, looking out at the water with me.

"You have the look of someone who's dying to light up," I said after a while. "If any of us smoked you'd be bumming cigarettes right now, wouldn't you?"

"Most likely."

"I remember the look. You used to sit out on your apartment balcony sucking on pretzel sticks to keep from smoking."

"Doesn't matter how long I go without it, I still want to. I don't think I've touched one in fifteen years, but dammit…"

He'd smoke if he thought he could get away with it. But, in the grand scheme of things, he'd rather crave the tobacco than lose Mom again. More addicted to her than nicotine.

Still, if I had a pack, he'd be sneaking one.

"Dad … I wanted to thank you for getting Lydia's folks here. You couldn't have given us anything better as a wedding gift, but how did you convince Nan to fly? She was terrified."

"She wanted to be here more than she was afraid, I guess," he said. "I got Jim on the phone, told him about what you'd said, how this really was the wedding Lydia always wanted. How important having just her family around was, and I thought it would break her heart to not have them here no matter what she said. When Nan got on the phone I pointed out that even if you two said your vows in a church someday, this is really the only time you'll be getting married, and she didn't want to miss her only child's wedding."

"And then you offered tickets on the Concorde."

He nodded and chuckled, "And Jim offered her sedatives. She had to do it. She knew she'd never forgive herself if she wasn't here. I know how I would have felt if I'd missed any of you kids' weddings."

"So it's a good thing we didn't elope?"

"A very good thing. Maybe if it had been someone else … we love Lydia, Kevin. I hope you know that."

I turned to look in the window; Lydia was laughing hard, her head leaning against her father's shoulder. "She's kind of irresistible."

"So why aren't you inside with her?"

"It was getting a little too loud," I sighed. "Why aren't you inside?"

"Mostly I wanted to make sure you were all right. I'd hate to have to chase the groom down the beach to make sure he wasn't running away."

"Nope."

"You're not going to get all drippy on us and start calling each other Mr. and Mrs. Davis for the next couple of days, are you? Because if you are, we're leaving. Goofy I can take, sickly sweet, no."

If we did, it would be in private, and I wasn't going to discount the possibility that we might. I liked the sound of it, Lydia with my last name. I wanted to hear it.

Though, technically, it wasn't the family name. Dad's father had changed it along the way, after Dad was born. The world called him Chip Davis, or Jeremy if the cause required more formality, but his birth certificate claimed he was Michael Ian Brennan the third.

"Why didn't you ever change the family name back to Brennan, Dad?"

He sighed. "I toyed with it once in a while, but I thought it would be more trouble than it was worth. All you kids—it was just easier."

"Nothing says we couldn't change our names."

"I know." He sighed deeply. "It's just a name, Kevin. What people call me doesn't much matter."

"You might want to consider it. With Lydia's folks being relatives now, you might want to push the Irish thing just to tweak her mom."

"That would be a benefit," he chuckled.

We both turned at the sound of the door opening. Jim Freeman came out, shaking his head in wonder, still laughing at whatever they'd been talking about.

"They chase you out of there, Jim?" Dad asked.

"I was sent out to discuss the groom's intentions for my daughter," he chuckled. "I'm fairly sure I already understand what they are."

"They're not honorable," I told him.

"Really, they sent you out here so they could discuss *you*," Dad said. "I've been victim to that many times myself."

"I believe they're discussing the good doctor," Jim said. "Their consensus is that he looks like an actor named Sam Elliot, and that going gray has added charm to his character. As I left they were discussing whom his wife resembles."

At the same time, Dad and I said, "Kathy Bates."

"Kathy Bates," Jim repeated.

Dad nodded. "One hell of a whole lot of woman, though if you tell her that, she gets pissy as hell and starts lamenting getting older and softer. Doesn't matter that she's sexy as hell, she still gets pissy on you."

"Women ought to learn, a backside is a beautiful thing to have," Jim said.

"Well, she might partially agree with you on that. Somewhere along the way her motto became 'screw it, life's too short to not have chocolate and cake, and on as many occasions as possible, chocolate cake.' And she thinks at her age, if that means chocolate cake for breakfast, all the better."

"Oh yeah, that's funny now," I lamented. "The few times I tried logic like that I got in trouble. But it was perfectly okay to have four bowls of cereal dripping with enough sugar to light up an entire class of five year olds."

Dad shrugged it off. "At least the cereal had some kind of vitamin component to it."

"Well I could have just taken vitamins and had the cake, now, couldn't I?" I protested.

I really wanted cake for breakfast when I was six or seven.

Even argued about it once or twice, to no avail.

"Just wait," Jim said. "When you have kids of your own, you'll be hiding cartons of ice cream behind bags of broccoli in the freezer, waiting until you're sure the kid's asleep before you can have anything even resembling junk food."

"You got junk food?" Dad asked. "Terry would slap a Ding Dong out of my hand before I could blink."

"I didn't say I wasn't also hiding it from Nan."

"Ah, you're both whipped," I said. "I'll still be able to do anything I want."

I didn't appreciate the ensuing laughter.

"Son, men may rule the world, but women rule the men. They have what we want, and they know it. We're pathetic enough to do anything we can to get it."

"Dad, I've seen Mom chase you around the house. I'm pretty sure you've got what *she* wants."

Jim held his hand up to stop me from saying anything else. "I don't need to know anything you've done or might do with my little girl. As far as I'm concerned, neither of you has anything the other wants, you're going to live blissfully and platonically, and any children you might have will be delivered by Federal Express."

Dad offered to dig a hole out on the beach so that Jim could bury his head in it.

"I'm just saying, that's all."

The door opened again and Mom stuck her head out to tell Dad he had a phone call. I watched him go inside, and then turned to Jim.

"I'm glad you came for the wedding," I said to him. "It felt like something was missing before, but now that you and Nan are here, it feels right."

"She's my baby girl, Kevin. She always will be."

I nodded.

"I know teasing you about ice cream is one thing, but you honestly have to consider what things will be like when you have kids. You have to know what you're getting into."

I was fairly sure I knew, but listened quietly.

"Your children are going to be multiracial, and whether you like it or not, that carries a significant burden. They'll have an entire cultural background that you probably know little to nothing about, and as much as I hate to admit it, my daughter never truly cared much about it. But I think it's important that they know where they came from and where they may be headed—I don't want my grandchildren facing the ignorance their mother did, and I truly fear you and Lydia will be targets of the same bigotry Nan and I lived through."

"Some people are idiots," I said.

"It's more than that, Kevin. It's on both sides of the fence and you can't possibly be prepared for it. Once you marry you may find bigotry in friends you believed to be entirely supportive and enlightened, and only tolerance in others. And your children…"

"I saw how Lydia was treated," I said. "I can't change how the world sees us, Jim. If we lose friends because we get married, then they weren't people I want to associate with, anyway."

"It may not be that simple."

"It has to be. I love your daughter more than anyone in this world. I won't let what other people think get in our way. And our kids … I'm hoping that by the time we start a family you'll be living here again. Who better to learn about that part of who they are than from than their grandfather?"

Jim took in a deep breath, letting it out in a deep sigh. "We will be here. By all rights I should be huffing about how you'd better take care of my little girl—"

"I will."

"—but I trust you."

When he went inside, I couldn't help but wonder if his trust was well placed. Sooner or later I was bound to screw up and hurt her.

Monica sighed and opened her eyes, stretching against the quilt. "You guys sure talk a lot," she grumbled. "Damn, it's cold out here."

I slid off the porch railing and went over to her, gesturing for her to get up. "I'm not cold. Come on, sit on my lap, I'll warm you up."

She got up long enough for me to sit in her place, and then curled up on my lap, her head on my shoulder.

"You were listening," I accused lightly.

"Not really. You were mostly background static."

"But you weren't really asleep."

"Just drifting. Contemplating. Feeling very happy that I get to be here for your wedding."

"Contemplating what?" I pressed.

She was quiet for a while, clutching the quilt tightly. "What comes after, I suppose. Paul brushes it off any time I try to talk about it, but I think about it a lot."

"He doesn't want to admit it to himself."

"I know. But face it, I'm going to die. I want to know what comes next, and I'm terrified that for me the next step is hell."

"I doubt it," I said, truthfully. "I'm not even sure I honestly believe in hell as this fire and brimstone kind of place. Part of me suspects it's something invented by puritanical type parents to keep their offspring in line."

"Still. If it is true…"

"Know what? I don't think it matters. I don't think God

looks down and points this giant accusing finger at us the way some people want us to believe. I've always subscribed to the theory of God as our Father. Fathers forgive their kids for their screwups, they don't condemn the little shits to an eternity of damnation. And if Paul can forgive you, why wouldn't God? I know Paul, he's not saint. If he has reserves of forgiveness, God's gotta trump that."

"I hope you're right," she said quietly.

The door opened again and Dad stepped out.

"I'm just keeping her warm," I said, before he could say anything. "I'm not groping my sister in law."

He tried to smile.

"What?"

"That was Will on the phone, Kevin. Son of a bitch … I wasn't going to tell you until tomorrow, after the wedding, but your mother thought otherwise."

"Will's coming tomorrow, isn't he? Well, hell, he is, or else you wouldn't have said after—"

"The dojo burned down, Kevin," he said. "The dojo, everything in it, and the sandwich shop. It's gone."

17

Chip

Just a few minutes before sunset, we created a circle around the bride and groom, who stood there on the sand, facing the ocean, watching Will expectantly. The temperature was beginning to fall, slowly shifting from the warmth of a spring-like afternoon to the chill of winter not quite ready to retreat. Nick had the pit ready to go, filled with firewood that he intended to light as soon as the ceremony was over, and Doug had already fired up the grill, ready to throw on it the steaks and chicken and hot dogs he and Kris had brought as part of their wedding gift to Kevin and Lydia.

They had asked that gifts be minimal, reasoning that they had everything they really needed and couldn't imagine wanting anything other than each other.

I waited until Kevin's back was turned to roll my eyes, and refrained from obnoxious gagging sounds. I remembered the feeling, as sickly sweet as it was, and wasn't about to make fun of him, at least not when he could hear me.

Paul wanted to know what they considered 'minimal' to be: towels and sheets, or a whole new kitchen?

I had no idea.

Minimal or not, Terry was determined that we would replace the car I'd managed to destroy. My offer to give him mine and buy myself a new one was stubbornly ignored.

"Piss him off," Paul said. "Buy him a minivan."

Nick argued in favor of a pickup.

Eileen vetoed them both. "Paul wants the world to suffer in a minivan with him, and Lydia already has a pickup. Kevin wants another convertible. Something seriously sporty. And dark green, he likes dark green."

The bride, she swore, would want what Kevin wanted. So while everyone else made arrangements to be off for the week, Terry and I let Eileen drag us around Northern California while she searched for the perfect car for her twin brother. We ended up at an auto mall outside of Sacramento, where she spotted it before I could even get my seatbelt off.

"The little boy in him will be squealing 'vroom, vroom' every time he drives it," Terry laughed.

"And the adult in him will be swearing 'what the hell' every time he pays insurance on it," I pointed out. "Do we really want to give a twenty one year old a ticket magnet?"

Evidently we did.

Eileen drove it home, and parked it in Nick's garage.

"A Toyota?" he asked, looking it over. "Hell, I thought you'd go for the big bucks and get them a Beemer or something."

"They'll love it," Eileen assured him.

"No shit. And to think for our wedding we got a blender."

"A multi-speed blender," I reminded him. "And I didn't incinerate your car."

It wasn't until we stood there in the circle on the beach, when I glanced at Eileen leaning against her husband, that it clicked with me.

Her perfect car for her twin was a Spyder.

Will was droning on about the sanctity of marriage; I only half-listened, watching Kevin instead. It had been less than six months since I'd given his sister away in a ceremony saturated with matrimonial formality, and now he was standing on a beach at sunset, his wedding a relaxed exercise in casual.

Lydia was a stunningly beautiful bride, wrapped in almost-white linen, with tiny white flowers woven into her hair. Kevin wore slacks to match her dress, his shirt halfway unbuttoned and sleeves rolled over his forearms. They paid little attention to Will's brother, who crept outside the circle with camera in hand, quietly clicking away, capturing the brightness in every moment.

Later Terry would look at the photos and realize with light laughter, that both the bride and the groom had been barefoot. Three decades earlier and they might have been dressed in bright tie-dyed colors, or nothing at all.

As they repeated their vows, I could feel Terry's hand squeezing mine gently. I looked at her, expecting tears, expecting the mixture of joy and sadness that had seeped through at each of the other kids' weddings. She was beaming proudly, a mother watching her baby take his first real steps; if there were any tears, she hid them well.

The night before, after we'd made sure Kevin went to his room alone, and long after everyone else was asleep, we sat on the floor in front of the fireplace, immersed in the quiet, when she whispered, "It feels complete now."

"What does?" I asked, not sure where her mind had been.

"Our family. It finally feels like it's supposed to."

She was right; I'd felt it, too, when everyone was shouting to be heard at dinner, the laughter so loud it left my ears ringing. In the center of all that chaos was a calm that she and I had waited to find since the twins were learning to walk.

"Maybe this is what we were longing for all along. Not another baby, but for the kids we already had to find partners to fill in those empty spaces."

I'd had a brief moment of panic, worried that the dojo burning to the ground would ruin the wedding, but Kevin was furious only for a few minutes; he decided it would be all right, one way or the other, and he'd deal with it when he got home.

Nothing was getting in the way of this wedding.

Kevin kissed his bride, grinning like a twelve year old who finally got the ten speed mountain bike he'd been pleading for half his life. When the kiss ended he put his arms around her and lifted her up, spinning in a wide circle; the look on my son's face was pure joy. I wanted to remember that face, the happiest he had ever been.

Kevin

"Think they realize we're not down there anymore?"

We were lying sideways on the bed, looking out the window, watching my brothers toss a Frisbee back and forth over the fire pit, our parents lounging nearby in lawn chairs, talking. Eileen and Nicole were digging in the sand; Paul sat next to them with Monica in his lap.

Music was still blaring loud enough that we could hear it from the bedroom with the door closed. While everyone else seemed occupied, Lydia had grabbed my hand and pulled me into the house and up the stairs; we plopped down on the bed, still dressed, to watch them.

"I think," she snickered, "they realize it, but they're adult enough to not point up here and laugh."

"My brothers would surprise you."

"Hmm. I think my mom might, too."

I stared out at the ocean, mesmerized by the blanket of fog that hung in a bulky layer between water and sky. It appeared as a streak of light against the black of night, milky white cotton batting blocking out all but the barest fraction of moonlight. I pointed to it and said, "Check it out, Lydia."

"Pretty. It looks like you could climb on it and float away. Kevin's magic carpet."

"It's more like this long bridge stretching out across the bay, light and soft as a feather. You could step out onto it and dance to the other side. If it went high enough, you could reach up and snag yourself a star."

She leaned over and kissed me. "Your streak of romantic is growing, Rabbit. I could get used to that, you know."

"You're my muse," I whispered. "My inspiration."

"Your muse is horny," she snorted. "Now, I liked spending last night with my parents because we caught up on a lot, but I would have rather been here, with you."

"My dad stood guard last night. You couldn't have snuck up here if you wanted."

"Your dad's idea of standing guard was feeling up your mom in front of the fireplace," she said, pushing me onto my back. "I peeked once. You think when we've been married as long as they have we'll still be groping each other when no one's looking?"

"I hope so."

I also hoped that we'd make it that long without the bumps my parents had hit along the way. Or even the bumps Nick and Katie were stepping over. Especially not the bump that was tripping Paul up, giving him road rash so badly he might never again feel whole.

When our clothes were strewn all over the room and I was reaching for a blanket to protect us from the chill seeping off the window, she reached out to put her hand on my chest and asked suddenly, "Do you trust me?"

"Of course I do."

She took the blanket and tossed it to the foot of the bed. "Good. Then hold still."

"Why?"

She started kissing me, lips playing over mine, over my chin and down my chest, her fingers tracing delicate lines over my skin. When she got to my stomach, I reached for her, pulling her back up to where I could kiss her lips.

"Trust, Kevin," she whispered. "I'm not asking you to reciprocate. Just let go, and trust me."

Somewhere written between the lines of our vows, sandwiched in between 'Love, Honor, and Respect,' were the words, 'Trust, and Try New and Potentially Kinky and Nasty Things on Request.'

I let go.

And promptly yelped as if she'd bit me.

Later, when the fire on the beach had been put out and everyone else had gone to bed, and when we were both too tired to do more than curl around each other and breathe, she snuggled as close as she could and sighed, "I love you forever, mister. Don't ever doubt that."

"I don't. I won't."

She pressed a kiss onto my shoulder.

"Can I ask something, though?"

"Anything."

"Now that we're married, can I go back to my old underwear?"

18

Kevin

Monica made her deadline; she lived to see Nicole's 7th birthday, and two weeks later she was still holding on. Every single one of us kept looking for the next big thing she could hang on to be there for, and every single one of us struck out. Paul wanted her to focus on our mother's birthday, just a few weeks away, but all Monica could say was that she didn't want to die *on* Mom's birthday, and she doubted she could make it.

She was fighting to live day to day, but I didn't see how she was coping with even that much. Every day it seemed as if there were less of her there; the average ten year old probably outweighed her soaking wet. She wanted family around as much as possible, so we spent more nights there than not, fighting to share a bathroom with Eileen and Spider. We'd already gotten into a routine; I'd get home from school and wait for Lydia to get off work, we'd spend a little time together, and then head for my parents' house before dinner.

Most afternoons Eileen wandered over to wait for Lydia with me, carting her textbooks along, pestering me for help with math ("why the hell do I need math to teach music?") or

Latin ("Latinos don't speak Latin, dammit. The only people who speak Latin are dead or in the priesthood.")

This afternoon she left the textbooks in her car, and called me to come over to her apartment, where she plopped down on the sofa with exaggerated exhaustion. She leaned her head back and sighed hard before asking, "Why am I doing this? What is so all important about getting that degree?"

"So you can hold it over me," I told her.

There were other reasons, sure, but I went with the one most likely to make her feel better.

"I had to play an original composition in front of the entire department today. Almost a hundred people, and I couldn't tell which of them were other students and which were faculty. Someone in the back kept piping up 'you're flat, you're flat.' I finally got rattled and shouted out 'well I'll get a goddamn padded bra, just shut up!'"

"Heh."

"Oh, you laugh. I'm sure it didn't earn me any brownie points."

"But then you went on and played well, right?"

She shrugged.

"You worry too much," I said, putting my feet up on the coffee table. "You know what they call the guy who graduates last in his class in medical school?"

"No."

"Doctor."

She lifted her head up and smiled. "Okay, I get the message. Quit worrying about overkill."

"All you have do is graduate. Unless you're going on for a Master's."

"God, no. So … have you heard from your in-laws since they got back to England?"

I nodded. "Nan thinks she might even be able to stomach flying again. And they both think they'll skip another year there and come home when Jim's contract is up. I think they got together with Mom and Dad and decided there would be a grandchild on the way by then. It's their motivation to come home."

"Hey, maybe by then you'll even have a job," she quipped.

"Bite me. Maybe by then I'll have worked it out with the insurance company and can rebuild the dojo."

That was a dim hope; based on the fire marshal's report they were "further investigating" the possibility of arson. That I told them up front there were several different accelerants in there at the time seemed to bear no weight. The contactor who was putting the floor in admitted he'd left containers of polyurethane in the dojo; I left several gallons of paint and a few containers of paint thinner.

The students were still displaced at the rec center and the other instructors were not especially happy about it.

"They can suck it," Eileen said. "It's not like you planned this."

"Yeah, but I understand how they feel." And I also wondered if any of them thought that I was behind it, hoping to collect on the insurance.

"It's not like you need the money, Kevin."

"They don't know that."

"Maybe. What are you going to do once everything is settled? Rebuild or let it go?"

"Rebuild. I don't even know if I'll wait for the insurance. Until I saw what was left of it I didn't realize how badly I wanted it. Only this time I can have a better say in the design. At the very least it'll have a freaking air conditioner."

"You should add to it," she said. "Put in a second floor and rent it out to an aerobics studio for the moms."

"Possibility," I agreed. "Why not your future music school on the upper level? It doesn't have to be related to the dojo in any way. Just a place you can start teaching music."

Surprise brightened her eyes. "Are you serious?"

"We both want to reach out to people who can't really afford what we have to offer, and if it's tied together, maybe we can reach some of the same kids. I was already toying with the idea of having a class for deaf kids and offering it to students at Spider's school."

"Wouldn't you have to teach that yourself, all the time?"

"Dad's a black belt. I might be able to convince him to teach a class once in a while."

"There might be an ego thing there," she laughed. "He's never really been happy that you outrank him."

"Yeah, well, Dad never should have quit when he did. If he'd stayed with it he'd have his fourth degree by now."

If I hadn't left for the seminary, I'd be close to testing for it, too.

"You can push him," she said. "Complete change of subject, or else we'll start dwelling on when Mom and Dad separated. How's school for you?"

"It's all right. I'm not sure I want to go full time next semester, though. I like the gym class"—Eileen rolled her eyes and grunted—"and I'm really getting into the writing class, but I don't know … half the time I think school just isn't me."

"So what about the writing class?"

I shrugged. "I don't think I'm any good, but there's some potential there."

She seized on it. Good or bad, she wanted to read something I'd written. First effort or latest. I wasn't sure, because I'd never even let Lydia read what I was working on. Any time she asked what I was doing I dismissed it as "just homework."

Eileen wasn't giving me much choice. She grabbed my hand and pulled me up, heading for the door. Lydia was getting out of her truck, so Eileen waited until she was up the stairs before telling her emphatically, "We're reading one of Kevin's stories, whether he likes it or not."

Suddenly, I felt very, very small.

The Before Time
Kevin J. Davis

I can tell by the way he watches me in the mirror, his face slathered with shaving cream as he attempts to scrape away the whiskers and watch me dress at the same time, that he doesn't see the same person anymore. He doesn't care about the stray gray hairs, the way gravity is gradually taking its toll on me, the extra five or ten pounds. But he sees someone different. Someone who looks like me but isn't completely me. Someone else. And I know when he turns around, his hand towel sliding quickly over his chin, that what I see in his eyes will be pain and guilt, and he won't understand why.

"I have no frame of reference," he says, almost in a whisper, looking down at his clenched hands, his feet crossed at the ankles. The way he sits, with his back hunched slightly and head hung down, symbolic of his fear, is one of the few ways I can ever be certain of what emotion is surging through his veins. I know that if I could see his eyes, bright blue and liquid, they would be dark with feeling.

We have been "a couple" for fourteen years, long enough to read the signs, the almost imperceptible nuances that make up character. Ten of those years have been bonded by marriage, the four before we were high school sweethearts. Scott and Lisa. Lisa and Scott. Mr. and Ms. Perfect. The Couple Most Likely To... To what? Mutilate each other before the ten year reunion? Live in ecstatic bliss until doomsday? Shack up, have fifteen kids, grow our own vegetables and shun red meat and dairy products? No one ever said.

Ten married years, long enough to accumulate all the dust and dirt of adult baggage, memories of weddings and birthdays, a baby's first step, first word. Long enough to photograph thousands of happy moments, smiles frozen inperpetuum and plastered on page after page of plastic photo albums. Long enough to endure heartache, and changes made willingly an unwillingly. Long enough to have a sense of "before" and "after."

"God, no. No point of reference at all."

Christy is Scott's pride, one of his Reasons For Living. She squeals with delight at the sound of his car crunching gravel in the driveway, and races to the door as the front gate creaks open. It is a ritual that began as soon as she learned to walk; she hides around the corner and waits for the front door to swing open and for Daddy to step through, her little fingers creeping around the corner in search of the nearest shoelace, pulling it quickly and to her father's feigned chagrin. "Gotcha again, Daddy!" she squeals. Scott frowns pretentiously and swears to replace his well worn Reeboks with slip on deck shoes, but his day would never be complete without having at least one shoe cheerfully violated.

It is also the only ritual that remains. The others, the

games they played with abandon and at ear splitting decibels are long gone, memories from the before time. Scott is terrified of chasing her through the house, threatening to tickle her, afraid that the squeals of laughter may become screams of terror in a later memory.

I lie awake most nights to watch him sleep, wishing that I could wipe away the worried frown, praying that a gentle caress might unknot his eyebrows, ease the pain, that is seeping around the edges. I never move, I lie there frozen, knowing that the touch won't come, not yet, not until all the demons have been exorcised from my own memories.

Not until I can fully understand why a half hour in hell has touched every corner of my life and turned the bright colors of my existence into a murky, watercolor gray.

Therapy was Scott's idea. It was one of the first things out of his mouth, after the police were gone and the doctors told him he could take me home, he quietly pleaded with me to find the best therapist as soon as possible. His quiet understanding was something I should have expected; it fell neatly into character.

At first he waited at home, staring at a blaring TV set, or blindly playing games with Christy. He would be out the door at the first sign I was home, waiting by the front gate, and the same question slipped from his lips each time: "Are you okay?"

Taking him with me was an impulse, an idea that suddenly seemed right. With a willing neighbor to watch Christy and a surge of courage pumped up from some deep well I was barely aware of, I urged him into those godawful leather hightop sneakers and out the front door. He watched me as I drove, his fingers scrunched around the shoulder harness of his seat belt, his back against the car door. "Are you trying to tell me I'm going crazy?" he said lightly as I maneuvered the car into a parking slot. "My mother always suspected it, you know. If you're looking for confirmation..."

His laughter dies off uncertainly, as if he wonders.

We make love on my terms, tentatively and infrequently. Most of the time it is quiet and mournful, Something That We Have To Do. His gentleness then touches me more than his body; he is afraid to touch me, afraid to do anything that might remind me of my half hour in hell. Most of the time it is easier to simply whisper "I love you," and turn out the light, hands barely touching under the covers. And when we do, when I summon the courage to make the first move, Scott's touch is careful and practiced.

He is afraid that I will scream and lash out at him.

I hate what I am doing to him. I hate the control.

"Should she be afraid of me?" he asks the therapist, the puzzlement on his face suggesting that the idea is fresh, a sudden revelation. "Am I some kind of threat to her?"

I want to protest; no, I have never been afraid of Scott. He is my safe haven, the one steady rock I can count on in my life. But the therapist raises an eyebrow, impressed with this lanky blonde's insight.

"Stereotyping is a natural human trait. Women tend to generalize men, toss them all into the same pot, so to speak."

He laughs lightly. "Bastard stew. Deep down we're all the same."

"Do you honestly think so?"

Scott leans forward, the fear all but gone. "I don't ever want to hurt her," he says emphatically.

"Do you think that you could?"

I have never given Scott any of the gruesome details. What he knows he knows from police reports and quick, agonizing discussions with doctors after the fact. He has never pressed me for any information that I haven't volunteered. I sometimes wonder if he's afraid to know.

He tapes talk shows; Oprah Winfrey and Maury Povich, sometimes Sally Jesse Raphael. Late at night, the times he can't sleep, he wades through the piles of videotapes in search of enlightenment. Oprah, he tells me, admits that she was molested as a child.

"I'm a grown woman, Scotty," I tell him, unsure of his point. "I'm not sure it's the same."

And I'm not. In the quiet moments of the early morning, just before the alarm is set to go off, I wonder which is worse: a knife held to your throat in a deserted parking lot, or a child's trust shattered by a relative. I'm not sure there should be a comparison at all. But I do know that Scott won't find his answers on videotape.

God knows, I watch those shows live.

Work prevents Scott from going to every therapy session; it's just as well, and he admits that I need the time by myself. I'm not so sure.

"I think more about what this is doing to Scott than what it's doing to me," I admit for the first time, though she can already see that much. "He blames himself, and for the life of me I can't understand why."

"He's frustrated. He probably thinks he should have been there. He reasons that if he had been, it wouldn't have happened."

"He doesn't treat me the same way," I complain.

"You're not the same person. Neither is he."

"I didn't want to change. I never wanted to change."

Scott holds me through the nightmares, the only time he dares to touch me first. His arms envelope the pain, and I wake to the sound of his whispers saying my name over and over. When he is certain that I'm awake, that the man I see before me is him and not some stranger, he retreats to his side of the bed, lifting himself up on one arm, gentle eyes searching my face.

For the first time, his retreat bothers me. I snuggle up with my head in the crook of his neck, trying to push him onto his back. "It's not your fault," I murmur, hugging him tightly. "None of it is your fault."

Does he think I blame him? I wonder sometimes. He rushes about the house, picking up after Christy, making sure the dishes are done and the laundry put away, all as if he were trying to make up for something he did, some wrong he desperately wants to right.

There is no reasonable way to blame Scott. He couldn't have been there; he never, under the most normal of circumstances, would have been there. Seven fifteen in the evening, the same as 14 out of every 28 days, coming off a 12 hour shift at the hospital; Scott never picked me up from work, I never would have wanted him to.

And I wonder, when I finally go back to work, will he be able to let me go off by myself?

Scott finally quits taping Oprah and Maury. He throws himself back into his work, planning the upcoming baseball season for his high school team. His talk revolves around a potential wonder, a freshman first baseman worth Scott's weight in gold. His only worry for the entire season is convincing the school to let this athletic prodigy on the field; no girl has ever before played varsity.

Scott only goes to the therapist with me every sixth session. More and more I think the doctor is discouraging him from being there, and what's worse is that Scott seems to understand and agree. I find myself looking forward to those sixth sessions, sitting together on the couch, his arm resting behind my shoulders.

His openness and honesty confounds and touches me. When asked if he could have anything he wanted, he replies simply, "For things to be the way they were."

I feel selfish for admitting that all I really want now is a new car.

"You need to tell him," she says firmly, unblinking. "Scott can't be expected to get a good handle on this when you evade the little details."

"Does he really need to know?"

"Doesn't he?"

I hate that, being answered with a question. How could knowing the gruesome facts help Scott? How could him knowing help me? He had enough pain to deal with anyway, he didn't need more.

"Because," she says quietly, "he has no idea what you went through. He has no idea how it could even happen."

"So he blames me?"

"Does he?"

Scott finds it necessary, crucial, that Christy attend a

community center class on child molestation. She needs to know the difference between and good touch and a bad touch. She needs to know what to do.

You never know what to do, I think, unsure that her five year old mind is capable of digesting such heady information. I thought I knew what to do. You always think you know what to do.

Talking is easier at night. Not in bed, not in such intimate quarters, but on opposite ends of the sofa, the light off, room dark except for the soft glow of fluorescent aquarium lights. It is easier to tell him without seeing him, to explain about the feel of sharp metal poised just so, feeling the knife point with each pulse of blood surging through my carotid artery. It is easier to tell him why he can't touch my breasts, that some stranger found his perverse thrill in dogging his fingers sharply into my flesh, twisting the nipples angrily, my absolute befuddlement that this man who chose to violate me carefully—protecting himself with a condom—found it necessary to complete his debasement by urinating across my bare chest. It was easier to tell him how it felt to have my wrists tied painfully above my head, my hair caught under my right shoulder, twisting my head to one side. The sudden, searing pain of penetration.

It is always easier to talk through the dark.

"I'm afraid I'll do something to make it worse," he confesses, his hands twisted against each other. "To remind her."

I am finally brave enough to interrupt. "I'll tell you if you do, Scotty."

His head turns just a little; he hears me, though he doesn't want to look up from his hands.

"We can't go back to before," I go on. "We have to quit looking behind us."

"Can you?"

I don't know; with a life divided into sharp pieces of Before and After, I'm not sure I can keep my eyes forward to the after part and not look back. I'm not sure I can talk in the light.

I'm not sure that a half hour in hell can ever be named for what it really is.

Paul

One of the last things I noticed before I turned out the light was my daughter's amazing calm. There was no fear or anger dancing in her eyes, only a burning curiosity that seemed to well up from deep inside.

She had drawn to Monica like the proverbial moth to a flame, hovering when she could, always close enough to be there in less time than it took to blink. She missed school days at a time, doing work sent home with a friend, allowing Dad to help her learn the things she was missing in class, but always, always close enough to her mother that she could scramble to her.

Lingering in the doorway, I could still feel the bite of the floor on my knees from listening to nightly prayers with her, leaning heavy elbows into the spongy mattress, watching her tightly closed eyes as she mumbled obligatory thanks and wishes for the people in her life.

I thought my heart was going to crack in two when she opened them and turned to me, clearly and knowingly whispering, "Mommy's going to be happy with God, Daddy."

All I could do was nod, and then tuck her in, drawing the sheet and blanket up to her chin.

I didn't want to turn and go back into my own room, knowing that as soon as I did I would have to face the fear that worked to choke me day and night. Frozen, I listened to Monica's painful shuffling about the room, readying herself for bed like she did every night.

Every nerve in my body was screaming at me, reminding me that she had survived her deadline and there was nothing left she was looking forward to. There was not much left, period, save for the sparkle that floated on the surface, pinpoints of light that swirled in her eyes, much the same way that Nicole's did.

Oh, baby, I sighed to myself, *you are your mother's daughter and every time I look at you I know who it is I'll see. Dear God, will you even remember her?*

When Monica first realized she was pregnant with Nicole, she was terrified – we both were – but she never once expressed any regrets about having the little girl who spent the first three weeks of her life shrieking up a storm. For all her faults, she was a good mother and she loved our daughter as deeply as she could.

I wanted Nicole to remember that.

"Paul?"

Swimming out of my reverie, I turned from my daughter to my wife. She was sitting on the edge of the bed, and contrary to what I had assumed, was trying to slip shoes onto her feet.

"There's someplace I have to go," she said in a hushed tone. "I won't be gone long, I promise."

Reluctantly, I knocked on Kevin's bedroom door, then crossed my arms in front of myself, hoping to hold all the pieces together. I hated it, I hated the idea, but knew there was not one thing I could say to dissuade her from what she wanted to do.

She couldn't walk more than two steps, but she was going.

Kevin, clad in only blue boxers, opened the door, surprised to see me there.

"I hate to do this to you, squirt," I apologized, "but there's somewhere Monica wants to go, and she wants you to take her."

He sighed sympathetically. "Where?"

I hesitated. "Church."

He leaned against the edge of the door. 'No' was on his lips, but he nodded and said, "All right. I'll be ready to go in three minutes."

Kevin

"Why me, Monica?" I asked, lifting her from the truck, making sure she was clear before I kicked the door shut. "Paul would have brought you. He would have preferred it."

She smiled weakly, wrapping both hands around my neck, and leaned into me. "Paul doesn't need this," she replied carefully. "He's done enough praying the last couple of months to last the rest of his life."

"And I haven't?" I tightened my grip on her for just a moment, long enough to get the church door to open. "You might be surprised."

"Then again, I might not." She looked up at me. "I haven't seen you here since Eileen's wedding, and even then I felt like you were only here to placate her. I suppose you've turned into one of those Catholics who only make an appearance for midnight Mass and their annual Easter Duty."

"Regular little apostate, aren't I?" I grunted, setting her down carefully.

We picked a pew up front and close to the center; she took my hand and set her head on my shoulder, exhausted. "I don't know what made you run from the church, Kevin, and I'm not going to ask because it's none of my business, but I want you to take a good hard look at it from my point of view. Try, just for tonight, to put yourself in my shoes and see it the way I do."

"You haven't exactly been a candidate for the Perfect Attendance Award the last couple of years yourself," I pointed out.

She nodded sadly. "Because I didn't understand. I wasn't born into this church, Kevin, I married into it. That took some adjusting. It's not perfect, far from it, and that's what kept me away so much."

"Tell me about it."

"You love this church. You know what I remember from the first time I saw you?"

I shook my head; I wasn't sure I even remembered meeting her.

"You were out by the pool, lying flat on your stomach on the diving board, and you were reading. Paul and I came out of the house and were headed your way when he snickered 'Yeah, that's my little brother. I swear that Bible is welded to his hands.'" She laughed through her nose. "At first I thought he was making fun of you. It wasn't until I got to know him better that I realized he was proud of you for it. He loved calling you Father Kevin and I think he's still a little disappointed that you didn't become a priest."

"I wasn't meant to be one."

"I know that." She gave my hand a tight little squeeze. "You went into the seminary because it was expected of you, because for years you thought it was what you had to do."

I swallowed hard. "I was wrong."

"Not so wrong," she said gently. "But you don't give up your loves so easily and I can't understand why you turned your back on this one."

"Because," I said, looking down at her, "it doesn't need me."

"But it does." She slipped her hand away from mine and laid it on my cheek. "Kevin, a lot of people can go through their whole lives and never set foot in a church and they're perfectly happy. That's just the way they are, and I don't think there's anything wrong with that. Good people have different ways of coping with their faith. But you"—she took my hand again—"love God more than anyone else I've ever known, and you'll never be completely happy shutting off this part of yourself."

I sat there quietly, staring at the altar, feeling the pulse in my fingers run in tandem with hers. "You didn't ask to come here for yourself, did you?"

"But I did." She lowered her voice to a near whisper, mindful of the people scattered around us, most deep in prayer. "I'm going to die, and soon. I need every shred of hope I can grab onto."

"You've made your peace, haven't you?"

"As much as I can, I think. I don't think there is such a thing as total peace, not when you don't know what you're facing. I know fear, Kevin. I know what being spiritually uncomfortable feels like and looks like. It's like being naked in church—you're vulnerable, and you're ashamed, and you think everyone is pointing and judging and a few of them even laughing at you." She lifted her head and looked at me. "You know what? You can stand in here naked and not be afraid. Everything you have, God gave you. He's not laughing at you. He's not pointing. I'm terrified of what comes next, but I know this much."

"God loves you, Monica," I whispered.

"I know."

I decided to give her one more secret. As I set her in the truck and hooked her seatbelt I said, "Before you condemn me for running away from the church, I want to tell you why I did."

I climbed behind the wheel, and did just that.

"It doesn't change anything, Kevin, and you know it."

I cut the engine as we pulled into the driveway and popped the lights off. I didn't say anything as I went to her side and opened the door, picking her up from the seat and carefully swinging her into my arms.

"Think about it," she said against my shoulder as I went up the three stairs to the front porch. "God didn't rape you. Jake Catero did."

Lydia was already asleep by the time I crept back into the bedroom, curled in a tight ball around a pillow, her hair fanned over the side of the mattress. I undressed in the dark, tossing my clothes over the chair by the desk, and knelt by the bed.

Night prayers. I felt the hard wood floor digging into my knees, the muscles in my legs pulled taut and my feet burning from the pressure of my weight bearing down on them. My mind was blank; I wanted to say something, anything, but nothing would come out.

As a child, it had been easy. Every night I waited patiently in my room, listening to my parents in the next room with Eileen, their gentle murmuring floating on the air. I listened for the quiet "Amen" and rushed out of my clothes, knowing that as soon as they had tucked her in they would come into my room and go through the same thing with me.

I missed how that felt. That night time ritual was something my dad loved desperately and ended it reluctantly when he realized his children were better off ending the day on their own, understanding that we had begun to weave tapestries of privacy around ourselves. And then, before he could completely break it off, he was gone.

In those two years he was absent from the house I found my own way, paved my own path towards a devotion I was sure no one would ever shake me from.

Monica was right, more right than I would ever admit. I loved my church with a desperation that frightened me. The initial decision to become a priest had been made while my father lay in a haze, sick with a case of the flu that looked far worse than it actually was. It was enough. The sight of him so sick—and back home in the bed he should have been in all along—was enough to make me think I could bargain with God.

If she would take him back, I swore I would become a priest.

Gladly.

It was a certainty I never tried to escape from; it felt right. Father Kevin came to life.

Now, with my knees going numb and nothing that made any sense springing to my lips, I tried to understand why I was as frightened of that part of myself as I had been sure of it then.

I gave up and lifted myself off the floor, sliding onto the bed gently, wrapping myself around my wife. She stirred and turned in my arms, her eyes fluttering open as she sighed. I kissed, her, meaning for it to just be a kiss, for her to snuggle close and go back to sleep, but it erupted quickly into passion; it was quiet and urgent, my mind not completely on the woman making desperate love to me, but on the woman across the hall, the tears in her eyes when I handed her over to Paul, the gentle whisper as she brushed her lips against mine, saying softly, "Goodbye, Kevin."

I tired to shove the image away, my heart thundering wildly in my chest; in a sudden violet surge, the taste of a melting communion wafer filled my mouth, and as the last waves of passion left me I swore I heard someone whisper, "The body of Christ."

Paul

The sunlight peeking over the trees barely caught my attention; I stood by the window, watching but not really seeing the sky go from pitch black to blue to startling shades of red. The fact that it was dawn barely registered, my eyes open yet seeing very little.

Instead I stared deep into myself, and watched as my heart was slowly rendered into tiny pieces.

How did she know?

After Kevin went into his room we curled up on the bed together and she chattered almost nonstop, extracting promises from me, goading me into agreeing no matter how outlandish the request. Donations to help abused kids in her name. Pose for Katie. Buy Kevin a lifetime subscription to *Playboy*.

I didn't start to fill up with fear until she took off her crucifix, the one I had given her for our first anniversary, and slipped it around my neck. "Make sure Nicole gets this when she's old enough to appreciate it."

I agreed numbly.

Don't wear black to my funeral.

Keep an eye on Kevin; he's running more scared than I can tell you.

Make sure Nicole knows how much I love her. How much I love you. How that will never change.

Live your life, Paulie. Find someone.

I turned away from the window, looked over to the still form lying under the blanket. Tears flooded my eyes; I tried to swallow but the fist jammed in my mouth made that painful.

I could still feel the streak of moisture from her breath across my chest, how my arms felt wrapped around that tiny body, listening to her tired murmuring slow from the breathtaking chatter. She lifted her head once, smiled at me, and placed a gentle kiss on my lips.

"I love you, Paulie."

She settled her head back on my chest and drifted off, her breathing slow and gentle for the longest time, until it stopped.

I glanced at the clock by the bed

Six a.m. Gone two hours.

The threads unraveled, the well sprung up and I fell to my knees, the cry that erupted from my throat as full of love as it was pain. I laid my head on the edge of the bed, chest heaving, sobbing wildly, and when I felt my father's hand gently squeezing my shoulder, I straightened up and stared into the darkness.

"I never even said goodbye."

19

Kevin's Journal

4/5/02

The funeral was hard.

Paul tried to hold it together for Nicole's sake, but he could barely function enough to tie his own shoes. Dad made sure that the coffin wasn't lowered until they were both in the car and headed home; Nicole understood the concept of burial and that her mother's body was in that coffin, but she didn't need to see it dropped into a hole so deep that she couldn't even see the bottom. And Paul—I think Dad was afraid he would dive in after it.

He couldn't take the house full of people afterwards. At the first hint of laughter coming in hushed tones from the other side of the room, he grabbed Nicole by the hand and left, telling Mom they were going for a walk, to call his cell phone when everyone was gone. I think it pissed him off that so many people had shown up for the funeral and then at the house after, so many people who hadn't bothered to stick by her when she was alive. Friends who bolted when her marriage was shaky, and friends who backed away when they found out she was dying.

I feel numb. I have since the moment we knew she had died. I feel like I'm walking through this surreal fog, waiting for it to clear, and when it clears, for everything to be all right. For Monica to be there and alive and not sick, for that part of the last couple of months to have been just a really screwed up dream. I wasn't the ideal brother in law, I know that. Most of the time Monica was just a fact of life, Paul's sometimes-wife, someone I certainly cared about but didn't think about often enough.

I didn't realize until later that the last thing she said to me was goodbye, not goodnight.

Why didn't I say anything back?

One of the things that keeps poking at my brain is knowing that if Paul hadn't had the guts to suck it up and forgive her, she might have died alone.

How you find that kind of forgiveness is beyond me.

I just don't know how.

I think I used to know, or at least had some idea of how to get beyond hurt and anger to forgive someone. Now, I'm not so sure.

My head is filled with so much static most of the time as it is. It's not like I don't feel great; I come home now, and realize this really is my home, that Lydia is my family, and I'm overwhelmed by how good I feel. There's just that one place I can't get to inside, the place where all the noise comes from.

A few nights ago I started looking for it, and figured I could get to it best if I went back to the spot where I found so much quiet. With the lights dim, Lydia stretched out on the sofa reading or watching TV, I sit in the middle of the floor under the loft, my legs crossed, arms draped along my thighs, hands gripping my knees. I close my eyes and wait.

Sooner or later I'll have an idea what it is I'm waiting for.

I didn't find much of anything that first night. Impatience, maybe. Lydia was over at Eileen's, bravely letting my sister chop her hair off, and I gave it a try. I looked through the static for the quiet and failed miserably. It was a relief to hear the front door open and then slam shut.

Lydia was a little upset. Not with her haircut – which actually looks good – but with Paul. Mom called Eileen, Eileen told Lydia; Paul decided going back to work just two days after the funeral was a good idea. His head hadn't stopped swimming, but working was a good idea.

I gave it up and went over to the restaurant to talk him into going home. I walked through the office door like I owned the damn place, ready to pounce. Paul looked up when I went in and anything I had to say was just gone. His eyes were bloodshot and had lines around them that made him look ten years older than he really was. His hair looked like he'd been pulling at it, and he hadn't shaved.

I got it, then, seeing him behind the desk, looking like hell. He'd gone to work to have someplace he could grieve without worrying about what Nicole saw, or how it made Mom and Dad feel. He knew Will would keep the staff out of the office. Paul needed a place to cry, and I walked right into it.

So, I closed the door and didn't say anything. I took a couple of steps into the office and did something I never figured I'd do. I held out my arms to him the way he does to Nicole, and he didn't fight it. He got up and fell into them, and cried so hard that he couldn't stand up. We wound up sitting on the floor, and as hard as I tried not to, I wound up crying with him.

Paul sobbed uncontrollably. The only coherent thing I understood for the first five minutes was, “Oh God, Kevin. It hurts. It hurts so much.”

I couldn’t tell him how I knew, or that it would get better. I don’t know. I don’t know that it will get better. I don’t know what I was crying for; the fact that Monica is truly gone, or for Paul and his pain.

When he could draw in a straight breath without choking on it, I told him I’d drive him home when he was ready. There were a dozen things I wanted to say to him on the ride home: if you need a place to be alone, you can use our apartment; if you want to go out and have a drink, call me, I’ll go with you; it’s all right for Nicole to know how badly you’re hurting. I didn’t say any of them, though.

I wanted to tell my brother I loved him, but I didn’t.

I went home and went to bed, curled up in the dark around my wife, and thanked God for the chance to be with her.

Chip

“He just sits there like that,” Lydia explained in a hushed voice. “He barely moves a muscle. It’s almost like he swallows himself whole for an hour at a time.” She shrugged, wiping her hands on a dishtowel. “When he’s ready, he snaps right back.”

“Meditating?”

“I’m not sure what it is. As far as I can tell he’s just thinking. It makes him feel better so I leave him alone.”

He didn’t so much as twitch as I crept under the loft and sat in front of him. He was sitting with his back straight, hands on his knees, eyes closed, and his breathing was slow and shallow. The only thing missing from this picture was heavy incense and love beads.

I resisted the urge to reach out and touch my son's face. From the moment we brought him home and showed him and Eileen to an awestruck Nick, I think we sensed something special about him, though I was never able to put my finger on it.

I wondered how he would feel if he knew I hadn't wanted to see him after he was born. I waited longer than a day, too frightened that I was going to lose his mother, terrified that she had given me two more children and then would die.

After Paul was born Doug warned Terry to give her body a rest, but she was determined. She wanted the house filled with kids, and she wanted them close together. In those last few weeks before the twins were born, though, when her blood pressure shot through the roof and she was looking at life through spotty, liquid eyes, she agreed that she could live with only having four kids.

Eileen was born first, and easiest. Kevin hung in there, refusing to ease his way into this world. By the time he was finally born, Terry had lost so much blood that I was sure she wouldn't make it through the night. They took my children away to be warmed, and then bathed, and I didn't care.

The first time I saw Kevin he was almost 36 hours old, and he was eerily quiet, trying to focus on the world around him, ignoring the screaming of his sister, who kicked the sides of her bassinet so hard that Doug joked the plastic might crack. Kevin blinked and squinted, letting out little sighs; he grabbed the finger I placed in his tiny hand and held on tight enough that I thought he would never let go.

No one warned me that I was the one who had to let go. I had no idea it would be as hard on me as it would be on his mother.

"Kevin." I finally reached out and touched him, putting my hand on his arm, shaking lightly.

He sighed and his eyes fluttered open.

"Where were you?" I asked.

"Off in some far away land avoiding homework and helping with the dishes, I think."

"You're missing some prime smooching opportunities by avoiding the dishes," I told him. "You'd be amazed what you can get if you domesticate yourself."

He grinned.

"I have a favor to ask," I said.

The grin faded. "Anything."

"I need you to go to work at the restaurant." I waited for a reaction, but he simply listened patiently. "Paul insists on going back to work and he needs someone there to keep an eye on him. I can't do it, not without making the staff think I'm there as his boss."

"And they'd just think he gave his loser baby brother a job if it were me."

"You're not a loser."

"What would I be doing to cover up the fact that I'm there as his babysitter?"

"Help Will in the bar. Let him teach you to bar tend, and once in a while pester Paul to show you how to inventory and order, maybe let you keep track of the timecards."

"And keep the people out of his way if he looks like he needs to be alone," Kevin mused.

"I imagine he'll need more of that than he thinks."

Kevin sucked in a deep breath, letting it out slowly. "I should talk to Lydia first, but I don't think she'd have an objection. I'll get the canned speech about school and grades, but she'll probably be glad I'm working."

Worrying over Kevin's grades was almost laughable. He'd been class valedictorian and if not for his plans for the seminary he would have had his pick of colleges. He never applied to any of them, yet had universities offering him a full ride.

The idea of him flunking out of a community college was amusing.

"What are the job benefits, Dad?"

"Insurance for full time employees," I started before he waved me off.

"The real benefits. How much free food and beer do I get?"

"No beer on the job," I said, rolling my eyes at him the way he had at me as a teenager. "But you can have dinner there every night for free."

"I can do that anyway. I need some kind of perk. An incentive."

"You'll get a name tag that says "Hi, my name is Kevin. I got this job only because I'm the boss's worthless son.'"

He nodded. "That'll do."

"It's just for a while, Kevin. By the time you have the dojo rebuilt and running I'm sure Paul will be all right."

I wasn't sure if that was hope or prayer on my part. Paul was a classic case of the Walking Wounded. He wasn't sleeping much – he'd abandoned his bedroom and taken over Eileen's empty room – and he ate only when prodded.

He reminded me of Kevin during those first weeks after he came home.

"It's only been a few weeks," Terry said later, watching me undress before climbing into bed. "He's doing better. He and Nicole are both starting to smile some."

My granddaughter was the other walking wounded. She tried, twice, to return to school, only to call home in tears halfway through the day.

"No one will even talk to me," she complained the first day. On the drive home the second day, when she was able to stop crying, she confided to Terry that the boys were ganging up on her, telling her that because she was going to grow up without a mother, she was going to be gay. The final straw was the boy who sat in front of her, Clay, who turned around and told her that if her mother had really loved her, she wouldn't have died.

Our first impulse was to find Clay and twist his little seven year old head off. Katie intervened, arranging a meeting between Nicole's teacher and the parents of her classmates, hoping to stem the tide of cruelty before Nicole drowned in it.

Terry refused to make Nicole go back. She would, she informed Paul, home school Nicole the rest of the year if that's what it took to make her feel safe. If she wanted to go back at the end of summer, that was fine, but she intended to stand between her granddaughter and a class full of prepubescent Neanderthals.

Paul accepted it without protest and promised his daughter she never had to go back; she could go to a private school, starting second grade with her friends from church.

"We gave her the option of enrolling now," Terry went on. "She's not ready. She still needs to be able to run to her room and hide when it feels overwhelming."

"I wish," I said, leaning over the bed to plant a quick kiss on her lips, "someone like you had been there for me when my mother died."

She grabbed the shorts I was reaching for and tossed them aside. "Don't wear those. Maybe you should talk to Nicole. Tell her you honestly know how she feels. It might help her to know you lost your mother when you were young, too. She might feel less alone."

"I've thought about it. If you think she's ready for that kind of talk, I will." I climbed into bed, propping the pillows up behind me. "If I get cold tonight, it's your fault."

Terry tossed her own bedclothes to the floor and slid in beside me. "I'll keep you warm. We haven't made love in a long time, Irish."

"I know," I said quietly. "It just seemed wholly inappropriate under the circumstances."

"And now?"

"Do I have a choice?"

She snorted, a wicked little laugh that made me grin. "You always have a choice. I'm not asking for screaming wild sex. I just want to be with you."

"Can I scream just a little?"

"Only if I bite."

Later, when she was asleep, it occurred to me that for an hour or so, I hadn't thought about Paul or Nicole; I hadn't missed Monica or worried about Kevin or mused over what was bugging Nick. I hadn't thought about anyone except Terry.

20

Kevin's Journal
June 3, 2002

Oh, man, I now know why Dad always hired night managers for the restaurant. The hours are crappy. It seems like I see Lydia for this 45 minute window most days, right after she gets off work and before I leave for the restaurant. And the people in the bar—don't these people have homes to go to? I was surprised at how many regulars there are. Will says a few of them have been growing roots onto the barstools for as long as he's worked there. Eh, whatever.

I think the clashing hours is getting to Lydia. She's kind of moody lately, and gets upset a lot. I haven't said the magic words ("quit your job") in a while, but it's tempting. I know she hates it. She says at least three times a week she hates it. So why does she stick it out? Because I'm working in the bar?

It shouldn't be much longer. The dojo should be done by the middle of fall, and Paul doesn't really need me there any more. I think he likes having me there, but he doesn't need me. He hired Monica's best friend, Sherry, as a server, and they kind of keep each other company. They're not dating or anything, but they talk a lot. It's odd to see Paul in such deep conversation with a woman that's not Monica, but I suppose at some point we'll have to get used to that.

And ugh. I promised Nick I'd help him level part of his back yard today. Why? I don't know … he wants to set up a shed. I'm the sucker that volunteered. Phfft.

Chip

"Grandpa?"

Grudgingly, with my face half buried in the pillow, I opened my eyes. Nicole was kneeling beside the bed, looking at me curiously.

"What's sex?"

I groaned and forced myself to roll over. Terry pulled her pillow over her face, trying not to laugh. "Shouldn't you ask your daddy this?"

She shook her head. "Huh-uh. What is it?"

"Nicole," I yawned, "you really should ask your daddy, not me."

She cocked her head, pursed her lips thoughtfully, and then said, "You don't know, do you?"

This, I groaned inwardly, is yet another reason I didn't cave in and agree to having another child seven years ago. "Can it at least wait until I've had more time to wake up?"

She frowned. "Uncle Nicky told Daddy that it's been so long since he had sex that his pecker's gonna shrivel up and fall off."

"Christ."

"Won't that hurt?"

I reached under the blanket and swatted at my giggling wife. "I suppose it might, hon. Is Nick still here?"

"Nope."

They put her up to this, I swore under my breath. Revenge for something I probably never did. I sighed and decided to get it over with, brushing over the basics while Terry struggled with fits and starts of laughter, all the while keeping her face under the pillow.

Her eyes grew wide. "And it's gonna fall off?"

"No," I sighed. "Nick didn't really mean it. He was just joking."

"That's not very funny," she said seriously.

No, I agreed silently, it's not. "Go on and get dressed, Nicole."

"You did that just fine," Terry snickered, looking out from under the pillow. "All the practice talking to your own kids paid off."

"You were no help, woman."

"Sex is your domain. I commiserate with broken hearts and hurt feelings. You educate about hormones and protection."

I would not, I swore, have a discussion with my granddaughter about boys and condoms.

"What about a discussion with Nick about the imminent demise of his favorite body part?" she asked, throwing the blankets back. "I don't know exactly what the problem is, but I know Katie isn't happy."

I sat up in bed, watching her cross the room to the dresser, and kept watching as she changed clothes. "I think Nick dropped out of school," I said.

"I know."

"I was waiting for him to say something—I suppose it's time to just get him to admit it."

"Tread lightly, Irish. Technically it's none of our business."

"Like hell. It became my business when I had to tell my seven year old granddaughter about sex and male anatomy at eight thirty in the morning. And I'll tell you what, if Nick is doing something to hurt Katie, I just might help those gonads fall off."

I found Nick on his knees in his backyard with a can of spray paint in one hand and a tape measure in the other. He was surrounded by garden tools, his shirt hanging from the deck, a beer can on its side by his feet, foam dribbling onto a shovel.

"Most people do graffiti on walls," I said, latching the gate.

He looked up. "Dad. Perfect timing. Will you hold the tape measure down while I spray the grass?"

I held it in place while he painted lines around the area he was going to dig up.

"I keep promising Katie I'll get the shed up so we can clear out the garage. It's only taken two years."

"Is she around?"

"Last week of school," he grunted, stretching out to mark the grass by the fence. "Right now she's got twenty kids squirming around, thinking that summer should have started last week and she's holding them hostage."

"And your semester is over?"

He sighed heavily, and set the paint can down, sitting back on the grass. "More or less."

I waited.

"My semester was over a long time ago, Dad."

He was about to say more, but stopped when the gate cracked against the side of the house and Kevin came through, loudly proclaiming his presence, and that Nick had better be prepared to pay him for his labors.

He stopped when he saw me. "Nick enslaved you, too?"

"Just bad timing on my part. I don't intend to sweat."

"I'll feed you," Nick told his brother. "That'll cost enough as it is."

"Pizza." He peered through the glass patio door, squinting. "Is the Evil One here?"

"She moved out a couple of weeks ago. Got a job, got a car, and then got an apartment."

"God, please tell me she's not one of my neighbors," Kevin groaned.

Nick hesitated too long.

"No. Nick, seriously. She's not."

"Across the street. Relax, I doubt she's watching you through her spiffy new binoculars every night."

"She's not a stalker," I added. "Has she made any waves since the wedding?"

"Moving across the street from us is a wave!"

"Ankle high with no undertow," I said. "You'll survive having your fan club living across a fairly busy street."

"And a little hard work will make you forget about it," Nick said. "Pick up a shovel and start digging."

Kevin grunted but reached for the shovel, flicking the beer can at Nick. They both fell quiet, Kevin staring daggers at Nick until he looked away.

"What?" I asked.

"Beer, Nick?" Kevin grunted.

"Just one."

"You fucking moron."

"Kevin, it's one beer," I said, wondering about the sudden tension. "Don't tell me you've never had a beer before noon."

"I can handle a beer!" he snapped.

"So can I," Nick sighed.

Kevin tossed the shovel down. "You *swore* you would stop drinking and smoking."

"Smoking?" I asked, not expecting to be heard.

Nick got up, angrily facing his brother. I willed myself to stay put, though I was sure – judging from the dark look in Kevin's eyes – that I was going to have to get between them. If that happened, Nick would be wise to run; neither of us was a match for Kevin if he cut loose, and I wasn't sure Nick really knew that.

"I haven't smoked a damn thing since you and Paul cleared out the motor home. I've cut the drinking down to one or two beers a day. I *can* handle it."

"Does Katie know?"

Nick didn't answer. He stood there with his hands on his hips, scrambling for something that wouldn't upset Kevin any more than he already was.

"Does she know?" Kevin pressed.

Nick barely nodded.

"And?"

"What the hell do you want? You want me to admit my marriage is imploding around me? Fine. Katie knows. She's mad as hell and barely talks to me. She doesn't get it any more than you do."

"You're choosing *beer* over her."

"No."

"Fuck you! You made a freaking promise to her, Nicky. You can't just give up the grass and expect her to fall all over you. Give it *all* up."

"Grass?" At this I stood up, next to Kevin, staring at my oldest son. "You're smoking *grass*?"

"Your son the pothead," Kevin said hotly. "Are you still

growing it? If I go into the greenhouse, will I find more than tomatoes?"

"No."

"And I'm supposed to believe that."

Nick shrugged. "Believe whatever the hell you want, Kevin. I don't owe you any explanations."

Kevin pushed past him, throwing open the greenhouse door with a bang. He came out a minute later, still seething. "Dig up your own goddamn yard, asshat. I can't believe what a huge fucktard you are."

"And you've *never* smoked it," Nick seethed. "Quit being such a pretentious hypocrite."

"I tried it twice, and when I saw what it was doing to you I decided I could live without it. What the hell, anyway? In what world is it all right to pollute your marriage by making a promise and drinking it away with a royal Screw You?"

"My marriage," Nick said evenly, "is none of your business."

"You're smoking grass," I said when Kevin was gone, trying to not let myself be totally blown away by the revelations of Nick's behaviors.

"Not anymore."

"And you have a drinking problem."

He took a deep breath and nodded. "Apparently."

"Well," I sat down on one of the deck steps, "that explains why you're about to lose a significant body part. If I were Katie I wouldn't just let it shrivel up and fall off, I might rip it off."

"What?"

"Little ears, Nicholas. You need to watch what you tell your brother when she's around." I patted the step next to me, urging him to sit down. "Son, I don't care if you can handle a beer or two or ten—if Katie has a problem with it, then you need to quit. Period."

"I'm not a drunk, Dad."

"You don't have to be a drunk to be an alcoholic."

He didn't say anything.

"If it makes you feel any better, when you were a baby your mom took every ounce of liquor in the house and poured it out. I was drinking way too much and she had enough. I got the message, it was her or the booze."

"You drink," he said numbly.

"Now. But I had to respect what she wanted at the time, Nick. If Katie wants you to stop drinking, then stop. If you can't do it, then get some help."

"Katie doesn't know what she wants, Dad. I could become as sober as a fricking Mormon and she's still not going to be happy."

"Is she angry that you quit school?"

"Who knows? She was at first, but I don't think it really mattered to her. I don't think I can do anything that's going to be exactly what she wants."

"Not drinking is a start."

He shook his head.

"Then what?"

He sighed deeply. "It's all excuses, Dad. Be pissed off about school. Be ticked about me drinking. I asked her for some time to make sure it really wasn't a big problem for me, but until I do what she wants, she's keeping her distance. Son of a bitch, Debby moved out and suddenly I was sleeping in the guest room. It's emotional blackmail, and I don't want to be played like that. I don't care how pissed off Kevin or Paul or Eileen get. Hell, I don't care how pissed off *you* get. I won't just roll over."

"What does she want so badly?"

"Same thing as always. She wants a kid."

"And you don't."

"I have *things* I'm trying to figure out. And definitely not until I know one hundred per cent for sure that I won't start drinking like a fish if another shoe drops. And especially not until I know I've gone long enough without toking my little head off that I won't be damaging a baby."

I didn't buy it, but sighed, "Ask Doug."

"Too damned chicken. Dad, I wasn't just a casual weekend smoker. I was stoned out of my mind most of the time and she won't listen to that. She never really saw it, so in her mind it must not have been that bad. The only thing she sees is what she wants, and to hell with anything I'm trying to tell her."

I never saw it, either. I never would have suspected it, especially not from Nick. "Do you want kids?"

"Sure," he said. "Someday."

"And you want them with Katie?"

"Dad." He sighed again, shaking his head. "I can't believe you're asking that."

"Yeah, well, I never thought I'd feel like I had to. I just want to be sure you're clear on why you want to wait."

"I'm clear."

"Then talk to Doug. Get a physical, and find out if you've screwed yourself up. Then sit Katie down and tell her you love her, you want kids with her, and tell her how long Doug says to wait. Have you thought about what you'll do if Doug tells you don't have to wait at all?"

"Not really. But Christ, Dad, I feel like she's blackmailing me to get her way."

"Women do what they feel like they need to do. If I

know Katie, she's just using what she thinks will work to get you to take this seriously." I stood up. "I'll talk to her. But I expect you to talk to Doug today and be ready to face her when she gets home."

"Her class doesn't get out until three o'clock."

"So I'll interrupt. But Nick, I agree with Kevin. You made her a promise. If you so much as breathe on a beer can or anything else until she's sure you're fine, I'll kick your ass myself."

"Gee, thanks."

I stopped at the gate. "Nicholas, I'm serious. Pull it together, and do it now."

Terry

I heard Chip's car door from the back of the house, and his feet on the stairs, slow, deliberate steps up, shuffling around the bedroom, and slow, deliberate steps down. When I finished putting Nicole's laundry away I went looking for him, sticking my head in nearly every room.

He was out by the pool, his back to the door; I watched him for a minute or two, trying to decide if he was just lost in thought, or profoundly sad. He sat hunched over at the edge of the pool with his feet dangling in the water, elbows digging into his knees. I couldn't see his face, but he looked unhappy.

I kicked off my shoes and went outside to sit beside him, tapping his foot with mine when I plunged them into the cold water.

"Were we good parents?" he asked without looking up. "I mean, I know we made some major mistakes, but were we good parents for those kids?"

"I think so," I replied, wondering where he was going with that thought.

"They why do they all – except for maybe Eileen – make such bad decisions? One kid out of four I could see screwing up, but three? What did we do or not do along the way that made them think stupid things were good ideas?"

I waited.

"Paul … God, I loved Monica and I don't even want to think about life without Nicole, but he started making wrong turns when he was just fifteen. He began walking in circles then and never really has quit.

"Kevin can't make up his goddamned mind about anything. We finally put a foot down and tell him to go to school or get a job, so what does he do? He registers for gym class and buys the dojo."

"I thought you approved."

"I do." He approved of the dojo itself, but questioned his son's reasons for buying it. Chip wasn't sure if Kevin honestly wanted it, or just wanted to shut us up. "And I love Lydia like crazy and think he couldn't have picked a better partner, but…"

"But he had to get married awfully damned fast," I finished for him. "I honestly expected them to turn around after they said 'I do' to say 'she's due sometime this fall.'"

Chip nodded. "And he's so angry. It's just under the surface—I thought I was going to have to pull him off Nick today. Kevin went from laughing to looking damn near homicidal in less than five seconds. And he still bristles at just the idea of Debby."

"Go back a thought or two," I said. "Why was he so upset with Nick?"

"Same reason I am." He lifted a foot out of the water and picked at an imaginary hangnail. "Nick's been drinking a lot. Kevin knew about it, and evidently Nick had promised him and Paul and Katie he would quit."

"And he hasn't."

"You don't sound surprised." His foot splashed back into the water and he looked at me. "You knew?"

"No, but I'm not especially surprised. Our boys drink, Chip. They have since they were teenagers."

"Have they smoked pot since they were teenagers?"

If he hadn't looked so obviously pained, his surprise might have been amusing. "Don't most teens try it at some time or other?"

"Nick says he's been stoned most of the time, Terry. He swears he's stopped, but I never realized he'd started to begin with. At what point did we make them think that was acceptable?"

When we told them an occasional drink was fine, I thought, but kept it to myself. "It's one of those things that isn't up to us, Irish. We *did* raise them to make their own decisions. If that was one of his, there's not a whole lot we can do about it."

Chip thought that decision was probably why Nick dropped out of law school, and it was going to drive Katie away. If he would do something, anything, and quit drinking, she would be fine with his decision to quit school. Nick existed in the same kind of limbo Kevin had, too paralyzed to get past the thought of what comes next.

The comparison hadn't occurred to Chip until Katie made it, but he agreed with her. "And why," he wondered, "was Kevin so angry with Nick? It wasn't reasonable anger, Terry. It was over the top."

"Kevin's been angry for over a year."

"Still?"

"He came home angry and he stayed angry, Irish. I think Lydia is the only thing that kept him from exploding."

"Has he ever given you any idea why?"

"No. But I stopped obsessing about it when he started dating her. He seems more happy than anything else."

"Terry … you've got to recognize what feeling like that can do to him. Or what it could do to Lydia."

I knew. I'd dealt with Chip at his angriest, after his father died and he was completely lost inside himself. He was rude, spiteful, and determined to push me away. If Kevin suffered the same demon, he would risk losing everything if he didn't learn to deal with it.

"Of all the things he could have gotten from me, why did it have to be that?"

"If parents could control that, the world would be full of lifeless, personality drained clones, Irish. That temper is part of who you are. If Kevin can keep it under control, it's not such a terrible thing. He didn't clobber Nick after all, did he?"

Chip shook his head.

"But you wanted to."

"No. I wasn't completely ticked at Nick. Just extremely disappointed. And before you say it, I know you once had to issue the same ultimatums Katie has. I know I used to drink way too much."

"For about ten minutes, a long time ago."

"Was it a mistake to not try to get him and Katie to wait to get married?"

"They would have eloped," I reminded him.

He sighed hard again. "I'm over reacting to everything?"

"You," I told him, sliding my arm across his shoulders, planting a kiss on his cheek, "are just trying to be a good father. And you are, Chip. No matter what stupid things they've decided to do, you've always been a good father."

He kissed me back, his lips lingering just long enough to make me want more. "Katie is giving Nick until his birthday to decide what's more important, her or alcohol. And she wants him to at least have an idea about what to do with himself. Playing around online all day every day evidently isn't an option."

"He has a couple of weeks, then. He'll make the right decision."

"Yesterday I would have agreed with you."

"He will."

"How can you be so sure?"

"Because you did."

Twenty five years earlier, when faced with staying angry and drunk, or letting it go and staying with me, Chip made the right choice. Surely deep down, Nick had that much of his father in him.

21

Kevin

The Evil One—that's how I had begun to think of her—was invited to Nick's 25th birthday party, but declined to attend. She took presents to his house the night before, and then took him and Katie to dinner, but she didn't want to spend an afternoon with Nick's family.

He said he understood, and counted it as getting two parties for one birthday.

Nick, Mister Maturity, is a party whore. He likes parties, and he likes presents, and he's not ashamed to admit that that particular part of him is still around 8 years old. He's happiest when you get him lots of small, junky things; he prefers quantity over quality. The funnier, the better. Give him a choice between a $200 video game system and $50 of assorted junk from Spencer's Gifts, and he'll take the junk every time.

Debby came bearing gifts – half a dozen paperback books, each individually wrapped, a cake, and paid for food – and to Nick that counted as a party. His sister in law fed his need for annual attention.

The rest of us were relieved. While Debby was not exactly disliked, she wasn't trusted.

I thought I should feel bad about that, reasoning that just because I had issues with her didn't mean everyone had to have a problem with her, but Katie summed it up nicely.

"She's responsible for her own behavior, Kevin. If she's embarrassed it's her own fault."

The party was dry, not a drop of alcohol to be seen. Dad and Uncle Doug polished off the last of a six pack of beer earlier in the week, and anything else was locked in a cabinet in Mom and Dad's bedroom.

None of us believed Nick was an alcoholic, but none of us wanted to tempt him, either.

"He poured out the last of the beer himself," Katie reported when Nick was out of earshot. "I don't know what you said to him, but he listened."

"He's afraid of Kevin," Dad grunted.

I doubted it. Nick was afraid of disappointing Dad, but most of all, he recognized his last chance with Katie.

"They look happy," Dad observed later from the kitchen, watching Nick and Katie splash Nicole in the pool. "I don't think I've seen them so relaxed with each other in over a year."

"They got laid," Aunt Kris said dryly.

I wondered if Nick could feel the weight of the collective stare bearing down on him from the house. Everyone, except Eileen and Lydia, was in the dining room or kitchen, watching him play in the pool.

The absent two were pinging from room to room, whispering to each other, and giggling; it almost felt like junior high, the girls whispering and pointing at the boys they liked, too nervous to actually walk up and talk to them.

All right, I was also fully aware that in junior high I was one of the geeks too terrified to walk up to someone of the opposite sex and strike up a conversation. But I never giggled about it. Not that I'll admit to.

I was just about to get up and chase them down to find out what they were up to when Dad plopped down in the chair across the table from me.

"I'd watch out if I were you," he said, nodding in the general direction of the living room, where Eileen and Lydia had just vanished to. "Those two are up to something and I suspect it involves you."

Good. It wasn't just me being paranoid.

They were conspiring, and I didn't like it.

"I drove by the dojo this morning," he went on. "Looks like it's coming along."

I was still half distracted by my wife and sister. "You know, the builder wouldn't let me have a dungeon? He said it wasn't safe to dig that deep."

"Maybe if you'd asked for a basement instead."

I asked for a lot of things, and was damn near getting the dojo I had dreamed up when I was twelve and counting on being able to lock all the instructors up in the dungeon when they ticked me off. We would have air conditioning. A weight room. Locker rooms with real lockers and showers. Two separate workout floors, a place where students could work out on their own while another class was in session.

And we'd have the second story, Eileen's music school. When shown the plans, she let out a low whistle, muttering that it was five times the space she needed.

"Better too much than too little," Spider reasoned.

Eileen wasn't complaining, she was just surprised.

Dad wasn't finished, though. "I've been biting my tongue for a long time. Are you sure this is what you want, Kevin? Once the dojo is open, you're pretty much stuck. Those kids and the other instructors are depending on you."

I could hear what he wasn't saying. It was a whim, an idea I probably hadn't thought all the way through. He approved of it purely as an investment, but it was still a whim.

I started to give him the same speech I had given Lydia. With it I could help women learn to defend themselves. How I believed in empowerment.

"That's not what I asked," he interrupted. "Is this what you *want*?"

"This feels more right than anything else I've ever thought about doing."

"Answer the question, son."

"It's what I want."

"Why?"

I gave him my laundry list of reasons. Too many people become frozen with fear when attacked—they never see it coming, they don't know how to listen to that gut feeling. Women aren't encouraged to learn self defense, and they don't know where to turn to find it. There aren't enough instructors out there qualified to teach the disabled.

"You know as well as I do," I told him, "most people, especially women, haven't given themselves *permission* to fight back. If I can help even a few realize they have a *right* to fight back, if I can make them understand that they're *worth* it—"

"Stop and take a breath, Kevin."

Uncle Doug was laughing. "I don't think I've ever seen the boy so animated."

"It's important." I gestured to Nicole, who was drying off out by the pool. "Look at her. She's helpless. But if she starts learning self defense now, maybe when she's an adult the odds will be stacked in her favor."

Paul leaned over the breakfast bar. "She'd cry the first time someone hit her."

"So did Kevin," Dad pointed out.

"You've got to let her train, Paul. For her own good."

"If she wants to." When she opened the back door and came in, he asked her. "Kiddo, your Uncle Kevin wants to teach you karate."

"Self defense," I corrected.

She looked at Paul, and then at me. "Would I get to fight with boys?"

"You'd spar with boys sometimes."

"Good. Because I hate them." She stomped across the dining room, leaving a trail of wet footprints on the carpet.

"Victor Martinez," Paul explained. "She *loves* him, but he called her a retard in front of everyone in her Sunday School class, so now all boys are horrible and disgusting, and she wants them all to just go away."

"Good," Dad grunted. "I hope she still feels that way when she's thirty."

Paul started to agree.

"You two," Mom sighed. "In seven or eight years she's going to bring some boy home, and you'd better be nice."

"And she'll already have kissed him," Aunt Kris added. "Or if she's anything like her grandfather you only have about five years."

"Bite your tongue, old lady," Dad said.

"This," I said to Paul, "is why you want Nicole to learn to defend herself. Boys."

"Boys like you at fourteen," Mom said.

"Remember fourteen?" I asked. "Or worse, you at fifteen?"

He frowned. "All right. You can teach my daughter to protect herself from my fourteen year old self's clone. I'm lucky some irate father didn't come after me with a shotgun."

Monica's father might have, if Dad hadn't interfered.

Later, when Nick was blowing out the candles on his cake, Paul watched her with a new sense of who his daughter might become. I don't think he had considered the fact, not really, that she wasn't going to be frozen in time as a mostly happy pre-adolescent who only liked boys when they weren't calling her names.

He'd forgotten about the evil teen years.

"I can't imagine being as patient with her as Mom and Dad were with us," he said while he waited for her to get ready for bed.

We waited in her bedroom while she brushed her teeth; she wanted me to read her a story, something Paul said she'd given up months ago, but he wanted to tuck her in and kiss her goodnight.

"Dad was a hell raiser when he was a teenager," I said. "He knows he didn't get it as badly as he dished it out."

The reserves of patience our parents had, or why they had them, Paul wasn't sure he had. He didn't think he could handle a teenage Nicole if she turned out like him.

He listened to her bedtime prayers, kneeling beside her, gently prompting when she had trouble thinking of the words she wanted. When she finished he kissed the top of her head and tucked her in, stealing one last kiss on the cheek before leaving.

"That," I whispered to him before he left, "was just like Dad."

Nicole didn't want a bedtime story; she waited until she heard Paul's feet on the stairs, then threw the blankets back and started to get up.

"Will you go with me into Mommy's room?"

I didn't know what to say. I nodded and followed her;

no one had been in the room since the day after Monica died, when Mom pulled all of Paul's clothes out of the drawers and closet, leaving Monica's neatly in place. She closed the door behind her, and no one opened it again.

Nicole sat on the bed, looking around the room; I leaned against the door frame that led into her bedroom. "Why doesn't Daddy come in here anymore?" she asked after a while.

"It makes him sad, sweetheart."

"Because Mommy died in here?"

I nodded.

"He should come in. It might make him feel better."

"Does it make you feel better?"

"Maybe. I miss Mommy but I think she's okay where she is."

"I think so, too."

Then, out of nowhere, she said with complete seriousness, "Daddy needs a girlfriend."

"I don't think he's ready for that. Your mom hasn't been gone very long."

"I know. But she would want him to have fun."

That I agreed with. Monica wanted Paul to get on with life. He was trying, but dating was still a far off concept for him.

"Can I have your bedroom?" she asked suddenly.

"You don't like yours?"

"It's a baby room, Uncle Kevin. Yours is bigger, too."

And, she didn't add, it was right next to Eileen's old room, where Paul had taken up residence.

"I think that'll be all right," I told her. "But you have to ask your Daddy first."

"Do you think he'll say okay?"

"You're a big girl now, Nicole. You deserve a big girl's room."

She smiled.

"Angel, you also need to tell him that you want to be able to come into this room. He'll understand that it makes you feel close to your mom."

"I don't want to make Daddy more sad."

"It'll be all right," I promised.

After she was back in bed and I turned out the lights, I wondered if I should warn Paul. He was healing and his grief was fading to shadows, but knowing his daughter wanted to open the bedroom where Monica had died might knock him back a step or two.

I told Mom first.

"He'll be fine," she assured me. "Let Nicole bring it up. They need to talk about Monica without it turning them inside out."

In other words, quit worrying so much and mind my own business.

I started to tell her that worrying was just my nature, but I saw Eileen poke at Lydia, urging her to do something she wasn't sure she wanted to do. Without Dad in the room to sidetrack me, I went over to her—and as I made my way across the living room Eileen walked away.

Before I could ask, Lydia grabbed my hand and pulled me into the study.

"What is it with you two today?" I asked as she shut the door. "Neither of you could sit still."

"We were looking for your Dad's old Polaroid camera. And after that … you looked like you were deep into a conversation with your dad and I didn't want to interrupt. Plus with it being Nick's birthday, I didn't want…"

"Want what?" I prompted when she trailed off. "What were you taking pictures of?"

"Just one picture." She pulled it out of her back pocket, but held it away from me. "Promise you won't get mad if you don't like it?"

She was trying not to smile, otherwise I think a loud alarm would have been screaming through my brain. So, naturally, I went with the thing I hoped for instead of feared.

"Are you nekkid in this picture?"

"No," she snickered. "Come on, promise."

I nodded and reached for the picture. It was a white plastic stick, lying on the bathroom counter. "Oookay."

"Look at it, Rabbit."

"I'm looking. It's a stick."

"With?"

"With a little plus sign on it."

She waited for it to sink in.

"Holy crap." I looked up at her. "This is yours?"

She nodded, looking uncertain, not sure whether I was happy or not.

"Does anyone besides Eileen know?"

"I wouldn't tell anyone before you. Eileen only knows because the test was her idea. I mean, we were sitting there watching TV and making fun of this really stupid commercial with some woman jogging, and she's thinking, 'I can't seem to concentrate. Could I be—?'"

"Pregnant," I finished for her.

"I was rolling my eyes, and we were both laughing at how lame it was, and how since neither of us can concentrate worth a damn on any given day, we were probably both pregnant. So we took these tests—this is what I got."

"Eileen?"

Lydia shook her head.

"God, you know I want to start jumping up and down and squealing like a little girl right now."

"But?"

"But you said you didn't want this for a couple of years."

"I didn't think I did, but when I set that on the counter and waited … Rabbit, if that thing had been negative I think I would have cried."

"So I can start squealing?"

She put her arms around me. "You can kiss me. Quietly. I don't want the whole world to know just yet."

I kissed her. Quietly. And then asked why we couldn't tell the whole world just yet.

"It's Nick's birthday, and you know Katie wants a baby," she explained. "Besides, I kind of like the idea that this is just our secret for a while."

"Then we need to go home," I said. "Dammit, I want to squeal!"

Terry

Chip sat at the edge of the pool, flicking the water with his fingers, watching the water drip from his fingertips, and ripple the surface of the pool. He played with it the way Max played with water in the bathtub, completely fascinated and lost in thought.

For half a minute, as I walked from the house to the deck, I thought about sneaking up and pushing him in. Instead, I sat beside him, plunging my feet in next to his.

"You should be swimming in it, not playing with it," I said, leaning over to kiss his cheek.

"I thought about it, but that would require going all the way upstairs to get my swimsuit, and frankly, I'm feeling pretty lazy right now."

"You could just skinny dip," I pointed out.

He turned and looked up at the house. "Little eyes might be watching."

"That never bothered you when our kids were little." I stood up and began to peel my shirt off. "Nicole is asleep. Paul is watching TV. The other kids went home."

"Kids," he sniffed. "We'll be calling them kids until we're eighty."

"Probably."

He watched me undress, and when I kicked my shorts off onto the deck, said, "You keep that up and Nicole will be seeing a lot more than her Grandpa's naked ass zipping through the water."

"Grandma hopes so." I jumped in, and when I popped my head back up, Chip was tossing his clothes onto the deck.

He jumped in with a loud splash, and swam up against me, slipping his arms around me when he came up for air. "You get to explain to Paul if Nicole comes pestering him with questions about what nasty things Grandma was doing to Grandpa in the pool."

"You need to stop thinking about the kids, mister."

"I can't help it," he sighed. "I feel very old tonight. Nick can't be twenty five already."

"It doesn't seem like it should be that long, does it? I still remember threatening you with bodily harm if you ever so much as thought about touching me again when I was in labor with him. God, we really were young then, weren't we?"

"You're still my teenage witch," he said, tightening his arms around me. "I was thinking, maybe this year for our anniversary we could go somewhere. Just the two of us. Stay gone for twenty six days."

"A day for every year?"

"We can go anywhere you want."

"We could just get in the car and drive. Go to Disney Land and then Las Vegas. And then go peek at the Grand Canyon. Where ever we feel like heading."

"We could do that," he said, spinning me slowly through the water. "I just think we need to be by ourselves for a while. You realize we've spent over a year worrying about one kid or the other? First Paul and Monica splitting up, then Kevin coming home when he did. Then Nick and then Paul again. Eighteen months of solid worry."

"The kids are all right, Irish." I looped my arms around his neck and wrapped my legs around him as he spun us in slow circles. "Nick and Katie are back on track. And Paul isn't as numb as he was even two weeks ago."

"Paul is healing," he agreed. "Nick will be fine if he doesn't pop open another can of beer. Did he tell you, he's seriously considering going back to school for his doctorate. He wants to teach."

"What he wants is to teach college chemistry so he can show a bunch of eighteen year olds how to blow crap up."

"At least it's an aspiration." He smiled for the first time since jumping in the water. "Leading our youth into a more explosive future."

"It suits him better than law. I never could really picture him in a court room. I can see him with a bunch of kids, trying to get them excited about the Mole and Avagadro's number."

"Whatsahoozit's number?"

"Never took chemistry?"

"I dropped out when I was sixteen," he reminded me. "I did well in biology, though."

"I'll just bet you did. But"—I leaned in for a kiss—"I think we can stop worrying about the kids."

"There's still Kevin."

"He's fine. You heard him. He has a dozen reasons for running the dojo and they're all good ones."

"All very good reasons."

"I hear a but in there."

"But he was lying. He was lying and he doesn't even realize it."

22

Kevin

In the search for some real time with each other, Lydia and I started meeting for lunch every day. Otherwise, it felt like we were living separate lives; she was gone by the time I woke up most mornings, and fast asleep by the time I came crawling home after midnight. I'd creep in smelling of booze and stale pretzels, and she was never coherent enough to complain about it.

So, we decided to drop everything at noon every day. She either came home for lunch – which inevitably turned into a struggle to actually get food down her throat – or we met somewhere. It was either fast food or freebies at the Charybdis. Or, if the day was nice enough, we grabbed sandwiches or cold chicken and headed for a picnic in the park, where we could watch pre-schoolers overthrow the playground and pretend the high-pitched squealing wasn't annoying.

Parked on a blanket under a tree, July didn't feel too hot; I would have preferred to be lounging in my parents' pool instead of battling bugs in the park, but Lydia was convinced that if my mother saw her in a swim suit, she would *know*.

"My mom," I told her, "is not psychic and you're a long way off from showing."

Lydia was lying on the blanket, squinting up at the sky through the tree branches. "I put nothing past your mother, Rabbit. If I so much as off-handedly remark I'm feeling a touch queasy, she might suspect. Your folks are looking for signs in everyone, you know that. They want us all to start a little Irish breeding program."

As if the Irish were about to become extinct; she was right, though. The hints were stronger on all fronts, subtle poking at Eileen and I to stop pretending to be joyously childless and start procreating. Nick, they were just waiting for him to get his crap together, though he wasn't immune from the obvious hinting.

"Any idea when we'll tell everyone? We should do it before I explode. Or before Eileen lets it slip."

Her hands automatically went to her stomach. "I was thinking that three months would be a good time. Right around your birthday." She turned her head to look at me. "You could tell your parents that you're giving them a birthday present this year. Maybe even wrap up a baby blanket or something to give to them."

She'd given it a lot of thought; first, see if Eileen wanted to celebrate at the parents' house, invite everyone, and give them the wrapped box just after we blew out the candles on the cake.

"Presuming Eileen doesn't feel like doing it that way would intrude on her birthday," she added. "We have to clear it with her first."

I didn't think Eileen would mind. Not as long as she got her presents, and they were damn good ones.

"I kind of owe her for blowing off our last birthday," I said. "We should get her something really good this year."

"What was so important that you blew her off?"

"I was busy." I leaned over to kiss her; she tasted faintly of strawberries and yogurt. "She forgave me."

"Busy doing what?"

"Falling in love with this really hot chick," I reminded her. "Eileen approved, though she still thinks I'm an idiot for not trying to spend the night with you."

"I wish you had."

Another kiss. "You had to know what you were getting into. And who knows, we might not be here right now if I had."

"I think we'd still be making out in the park," she snickered. "It would be nice if we had more than an hour."

"It would."

She sat up, grabbing for empty food containers to shove into a plastic trash bag. "Your hours will be pretty much the same once the dojo is ready, won't they?"

"I won't come home quite as late, but for the most part, yes."

"Hire me," she sighed. "Anything. Receptionist, bookkeeper, toilet swabber, just something a couple hours a day so we can actually see each other once in a while."

"You can hang around the school all you want."

"It's not just that. I want to work, but I don't want to keep working at the bank, and I want to keep the baby with me, and I want to see more of you…"

"Slow down. You want to quit your job?"

With a heavy sigh, she nodded. Every day she hated it more, and she especially didn't want to stand there while she was eight months pregnant, trying to be nice to customers and not let hormones get to her around her boss, whom she decided "needs to be bitch-slapped back to nineteen fifty."

"Woman, you can not only have the job, I'll make my office as baby-friendly as possible, and I'll have it hard-wired for an intercom so you can hear the munchkin from the front desk while she naps."

"Or he," she said, smiling. "You're okay with this, then? I know I made a big deal about wanting to keep my job."

"Go in this afternoon and tell your boss to kiss your ass."

"How about if I put in two weeks' notice instead? The ass kissing might be taken as an invitation."

I stood up, holding out my hand to help her get up. As we folded the blanket, I asked her to have dinner with me at the restaurant to tell me how it went.

"You'll pull yourself away from those throngs of women that hang out at the bar for me?"

"Hey, I'm learning a lot from listening in on their conversations. Last night I learned that women have a favorite body part on men, and it's *not* what I assumed it would be."

"What is it?" she asked with a hint of a laugh.

"Abs." I admit, it surprised me. "They like six packs."

"No flashing yours at work," she warned.

On the way to the parking lot she slipped her arm around my waist and asked, "Do you think we'll get sick of each other after I quit? All that togetherness."

"I'll give you a break from me. I think I'm still going to take a class or two next semester. I don't know where I'm going with it, but I want to stick with the writing classes."

"Good." We stopped beside her truck; she stretched up on her toes and kissed the tip of my nose. "You have the talent, Rabbit. You just need some confidence in it."

"Maybe."

"Give me another kiss. I really am going to be late."

"So?" I kissed her, and then opened the truck door for her. "What are they going to do? Fire you?"

By the time the dinner crowd started shuffling in, I had wiped the bar down at least a dozen times and had tossed out three different batches of rapidly-turning-stale popcorn, looking for anything to consume the vast expanses of boredom that filled most afternoons.

Will had the TV on, glancing at it occasionally as he plowed through paperwork, but I had no idea who was whom on *General Hospital,* little interest in Rosie O'Donnell's guests, and only a passing curiosity about Oprah's topic of the day.

Well kept personal secret: I was in love with Oprah when I was around seven or eight years old. I confessed that particular crush only to my mother, who swore she would never tell a soul, not even, I think, my father. She became my enabler, dropping onto the sofa at 4 o'clock every afternoon to watch, and I sat on the floor in front of the TV, pretending to build skyscrapers with Legos, sometimes pretending to do homework.

I lost interest when Dad agree to take karate lessons with me, but I still stole glances at the TV when she was on, and half listened if the topic was remotely interesting.

Every Tuesday Will and I both made no pretentions about working. With the bar quiet we sat in a booth and watched Dr. Phil dispense his quick psychological wisdom, with Oprah interjecting, "Ohhhh, that was gooood!" every once in a while.

"I could have been Dr. Phil," Will occasionally grumbled. "I have the degree. I know all the keywords."

"Too ugly," I'd say. "And you lack all those Texas metaphors. You don't really know that the dog won't hunt if you stick a firecracker up its ass."

We mourned when Dr. Phil got his own show. Our Tuesday afternoons, we agreed, would never be the same.

"I'm not," Will declared, "getting up to watch him in the morning."

I didn't point out that he probably owned a VCR. Nor did I tell him I'd bought a TiVo. I wasn't missing Dr. Phil.

When the credits to Oprah were rolling past I tossed the wet rag I'd been using into the sink under the bar and turned my attention to the news. Will had the remote and kept changing the channel; I kept reaching up to the TV to change it back.

"You have a thing about channel three?"

"Yes, goddammit, now leave it alone!"

I turned at the sound of laughter. It wasn't Will, who was still over in the booth brandishing the remote; it was Topher Tedeski, who sat on a stool, half spinning it, absently picking at the popcorn.

"That Lois Hart does things for me, too," he laughed. "So how's your life going? I'm still waiting for my wedding invite."

I held up my hand to show him my wedding ring. "Sorry, dude. We ran off and got married less than two weeks after she said yes. But I definitely owe you my gratitude."

"I'll settle for a drink. Something too fruity to be manly. I'm feeling emasculated today."

Will finally changed the channel back and set the remote down; I made Topher a tall raspberry daiquiri and shoved a tiny umbrella into it, something to make him feel a little less macho.

"On the house," I said. "But if you're going to keep drinking, I want your car keys."

He waved it off. "I walked. I was supposed to meet someone here, but I think I've been stood up." He shrugged. "Story of my life. I spend more time waiting than I do dating."

I couldn't help but laugh. "It's all that amazing charm."

"One would think. Right now I'd settle for a one night stand."

I thought if he waited long enough, he could have his pick of any of a dozen or so women who had been frequenting the bar every night.

"So how's the lovely bride?" he asked, poking at his drink with the straw.

"I think she'd like to see you, and thank you herself. Dude, you really are the reason she finally said yes."

"I'm good at that. I've caused many women to run straight down the aisle with someone else. But I would like to see her again, if it's all right with you."

"I'm her husband, not her keeper."

"And I'm her ex, and absolutely would not interject myself where I might not be welcome."

"Lydia would like to keep you as a friend," I told him. "I don't have a problem with that. Hell, if you're that desperate, maybe she can fix you up with one of her friends."

"I am long past desperate," he groaned. "Well, maybe not enough to give tonight's unwilling participant in the Date Topher Game another shot. Dammit, she was going to teach me to golf."

"Golf."

He nodded. "I'm the only person in the office who doesn't play. I need suck up points with the boss, so I figured I'd learn. You play?"

"No, but I wouldn't mind giving it a try. It would be an excuse to buy clubs and other golf toys."

"There you go. It's all about the toys. Want to give it a

shot? There's a pretty good driving range down on Dover Avenue. The course looks to be nice, too."

And there it was. I had a play date with my wife's ex-boyfriend.

We picked a day the following week, agreed to meet in the parking lot, and decided we would learn to golf. Or, as ass backwards as I was liable to be, flog.

"I don't have to be any good at it," he went on. "Just good enough to lose to my boss without looking like a—" He broke off, distracted by the short blonde easing onto the stool next to him. His eyebrows rose and fell in studied appreciation.

She ignored him. "Kevin. Hi. How's things?"

"Hi yourself." I reached for a glass and ice, and poured her a diet soda. "Debby, this is Topher. He's an old friend of Lydia's. Toph, Debby Forrester."

She smiled at him. "I hope Kevin hasn't told you a thing about me."

"No." He looked at me uncertainly. "Why?"

She giggled and turned back to me. "Hey, I still owe you an apology about your wedding. I was upset, I admit it."

"Apology accepted." I was about to offer one of my own, but she jumped off the stool and grabbed Topher's hand.

"You're cute enough. Let's dance."

Topher shot me a look of complete astonishment, but I just smiled and watched as she led him away. That had to be one of the fastest pickups in the history of the Charybdis. I didn't doubt for a minute that whatever Debby wanted from him, she'd get.

I watched through the lattice work that separated the bar from the dining room and dance floor as Debby spun across the floor with him. She was fluid in motion, dancing as if part of the music. It was no wonder she'd been in such demand in Washington; the girl gliding across the dance floor had the ability to breathe life back into the old fogeys she complained so heavily about.

Topher looked completely bewildered when he came back to the bar for drinks. "Is it me," he breathed heavily, " or is the lady a few ants short of a picnic?"

"It's not you. But what the hell, she's an easy lay."

He perked up. "You don't say. There may be some hope for my evening after all." He started to pick the drinks up and head for the dining room, but stopped. "Don't tell me I'll be chasing after more of your leftovers."

"No. She's a pseudo-relative."

He trotted off happily, and I watched, off and on, for the next half hour as they talked to each other. Debby was paying close attention to him, frequently reaching across the table to touch his hand, laughing often. She pulled a lighter out of her purse and lit the candle at the table. Instant romance.

There was hope for Topher's night, all right.

Unless his date showed up.

I turned my attention to the customers who were beginning to drift in on their way home from work, and forgot about them, until I heard Debby call out my name as she bounded back into the bar.

"Christ, Debby, did you chase him off already?"

She hopped up onto a bar stool. "Don't be an ass. He went home to change. We're going bowling."

"Sure you want to let him out of your sight? What if he doesn't come back?"

"He'll be back." She smiled confidently. "Don't ask me how I know, I just know. Sixth sense or whatever. I'm rarely wrong."

I bit back my retort.

"I know what you're thinking. The dumb bitch missed a big one. Don't count me out yet. An apology for bad behavior doesn't constitute a peace treaty. Lydia may have you for now, but you never know what might happen."

"We're happy, Debby. Don't hold your breath."

"Not my style. There's no way I'm sitting at home every night waiting for you to get tired of playing house, but I still think that I have a chance on down the line. Instinct tells me it's not going to last."

I watched her take a slow sip of her drink, stared at the lipstick imprint she left on the rim of the glass.

"It'll last." When she lifted an eyebrow in response I asked, "Planning on hurrying the end along yourself?"

"Would I do anything like that? You forget, married men are not my forte. I left a lieutenant back in D.C. devastated because he wanted to leave his wife and kids and I didn't want him to. Breaking up marriages is not my thing."

"Yet you still think I'll turn my back on her for you."

"Are you kidding? You leave? Get real. You couldn't walk away any more than I can breathe under water. But your wife—she loves you now, but when the honeymoon is over and she's facing real life? Enjoy it while you can. I was serious before, I don't think a year from now you'll be talking about how wonderful your life is."

I thought I should be getting angry with her, but I couldn't. She didn't sound smug or mean; she sounded as if she believed everything she was saying. Hanging onto an imaginary thread of hope.

"She's not going to leave me, Debby. It won't always be perfect, but we'll be happy."

"Like Katie and Nick? Get real. The perfect marriage is

falling apart like an old cookie, only those two as so dumb they'll hang on until it kills them."

"That's the idea. Till death."

"Not if you're smart. Have fun and then get out before anyone gets seriously hurt."

"What about commitment?" I pressed. "Kids, a family. You can't have that if you're always waiting for things to fall apart. Don't you want that for yourself? Or are you strictly on a party-till-I-drop path?"

"I want it," she murmured. "With the right person. And don't look at me cross eyed. I never said for sure that you're him. I only want a chance to find out."

"But I *am* married. And I adhere to the principle of hanging in there until I'm six feet under."

"I could make your head spin…"

"I believe you, I really do. Poor Topher isn't going to know what hit him, and in the morning he's probably going to drop to his knees and start to worship you. Just don't get so hung up on something you can't have that you miss out on some real possibilities."

"Like Topher."

"He's a nice guy, Debby."

She frowned indignantly, eyes twinkling to suggest she didn't mean it. "And what's this about 'in the morning?' I didn't say I'd sleep with the guy."

A dozen sarcastic comments were screaming to get out, but I shrugged instead.

"Okay, so I might. He's cute and he can dance, and he's been nothing but polite and sweet to me. I don't doubt that he could talk me into it if he really wanted."

"He wants," I assured her. "I recognize the look. Determinedly horny."

"Your wife."

"What?"

She pointed across the room. "Your wife. She's over there with Will. Probably saw me here with you, but we both know what the odds are that she would lower herself to my level. You'd better go to her, don't you think?"

"She doesn't hate you."

"Well, she should." She looked up at me. "No, I don't actually hate her. She just has every right to not trust me. I accept the fact that for now, she has you. It'll do for the time being. But I'll win, Kevin. I swear, I'll win."

I left Debby sitting at the bar, spinning her lighter on the counter. I told Will I was taking a break, grabbed Lydia by the hand, and headed for the quiet of Paul's office.

We would not, I was determined, talk about Debby Forrester. What would be the point? I thought I could exist easily in a family that included her as long as she kept her horny hands to herself. We could be civil, even friendly, to each other. Yes, I could be a real live grown up with some effort.

When I closed the door Lydia dropped onto the sofa and grunted, "So, what did the little firebug want?"

"Debby?"

"Who else?"

I had to stop and think for a moment. "She wasn't lighting everything in sight. One candle. Otherwise she was just playing with the lighter."

She waved it off. "That's not what I meant. What did she want?"

"Nothing. She was just waiting for her date to get back." She perked up at the idea that Debby was seeing someone.

"You are never going to believe who she picked up in the bar tonight."

"I believe she's picking up strange men."

"Would you believe Topher?"

That look, eyes wide, could-have-been-a spit-take, was priceless. I don't think she quite believed me.

"He was here, she came in, she pounced ... she had him on the dance floor within two minutes."

"Rabbit, please tell me you warned him about her."

"He's a big boy," I said, leaning against Paul's desk. "He can handle her. He has high hopes of getting some to-night."

Lydia shook her head. "No, I mean *really* warn him about her. Topher doesn't deserve the kind of heartache he'll wind up with if she latches her hot little hands on him."

"He just wants to get laid!" I protested.

"Now. But Topher is a lot like you. I don't think he can do the one night stand thing. I know him, he will fall for her, and he'll get hurt."

"Who's to say she won't fall for him?"

I could see it. Debby finds someone else, someone who not only makes her laugh, but makes her feel like more than a punch board, and she falls in love. Hard. She forgets about me, and we all go on our happy, merry ways, family and sanity intact. Possibly even as friends.

"She's a goddamned freak," Lydia hissed.

I was thinking "so what?" but never got it out. Paul threw the door open and leaned in, looking at the both of us before saying, " Sorry, squirt, but Mom and Dad are here with some guy who wants to talk to you."

Lydia and I both sighed, and nodded, a quiet agreement that we could finish the argument later.

We could have had that argument once I got off work, but we didn't.

We could have done a whole lot of things, but I was in jail.

Lydia

Kevin took about five steps out of the office and stopped in his tracks. His jaw clenched, nostrils flared as his breathing started coming in deep, expansive draws, and I could hear him swallow hard.

I tried to reach for him, grab either his hand or his arm, but he shot forward, running to the bar, leaving Paul and I in the hallway.

"Who is he?" I asked Paul, heading for Kevin.

Paul was right beside me. "Some guy named Jake."

I could feel Kevin's world tilt and slip off its axis. The dread that was tingling in my fingertips had to be pounding through his head. The blood I felt rushing in my ears was surely screaming in his.

Kevin's hands were around Jake's throat, squeezing hard; Jake clutched frantically at Kevin's arms, his eyes red and bulging, head tilted back as if his neck was about to snap.

Chip was tugging at Kevin's arms, begging him to let go. Terry was shouting at him to stop. Customers in the dining room were standing and watching through the latticework wall.

I wanted him to hurt Jake Catero.

I wanted Jake dead.

Still, while Chip tugged frantically, trying to break Kevin's grasp, I set my hand on his other arm and said as calmly as I could, "Rabbit. No. He's not worth it."

Kevin's eyes flickered toward me, and then back at Jake.

"Let him go, Rabbit. For me."

With a shove that sent Jake into the counter, he let go, turned around and shoved his way past his parents and brother, and left.

Chip didn't know where to go—to help Jake or run after Kevin.

Terry started to help Jake up, she had her hand extended and he was reaching for it, when I said, "Leave him there. Let him choke on his own goddamned spit."

They both turned to me.

"This bastard," I spat, "this *pig*, is the reason Kevin left the seminary." I looked directly at Terry. "He doesn't deserve your help. He raped Kevin."

23

Paul

Finding Kevin might have been a problem if he hadn't taken off once before, or if looking for him had been left up to me. My first inclination was to drive up and down I-80, hoping he was cruising between Fairfield and Vacaville, blowing off steam before heading home.

Dad had other ideas. His hiding places, he said, had been the beach house or the park, depending on his mood and how alone he really wanted to be. When he felt completely lost as a kid, he'd take off for Bodega Bay to sit on the beach to stare out at the ocean. Later, after he'd married mom and they had Nick, he generally wanted to be found and would go to the park to sit on one end of a teeter-totter, watching the pond sparkle under moonlight, or watch the ducks play during the day.

When Kevin last ran off, he headed for the park. Dad was fairly sure that's where he would be.

"He wants to be found," Dad surmised. He spoke quietly, pain and fatigue pooling in his red tinged eyes.

Kevin was there, on a bench beside the pond. He looked like he was just lounging by the water, his legs stretched out and chin resting on his chest. Any other time and he could have been some odd guy taking a nap in the park. Any other time and I would have walked up behind him and yanked on his hair.

The police officer that pulled into the spot behind us kept his lights off, waiting for Dad to go to him first.

The perks of Kevin having been so popular in high school; the officer answering the 911 calls made by several customers had been a classmate, and was willing to cut him some slack. He let Dad talk to Kevin first, and promised he wouldn't come gunning up behind us with sirens blaring and lights flashing.

Kevin didn't move when Dad sat next to him, sliding his arm across Kevin's shoulders; he didn't flinch when Dad pressed a long kiss onto his head, just above his ear. They sat there like that for a long time, Dad with his head rested against Kevin's, until he put his other arm around Kevin and pulled him into a tight hug.

I stood off to the side, afraid that just by being there I was intruding. I could count on three or four fingers the number of times I'd seen my father cry, and most of those were tears of happiness. Seeing him cry now not only hurt, it made me feel like a voyeur.

He didn't ask any of the things I wanted to: Why hadn't he told us? Why wasn't Jake Catero in jail? How could someone as strong and as fast as Kevin be overpowered by such a little runt?

Instead, Dad sat there and held him as long as Kevin would allow. When Kevin pulled away, he sucked in a shaky breath and whispered, "I'm sorry."

Dad's hand was on Kevin's chest, still trying to hold on. "You don't owe anyone an apology."

Least of all to the worm who had been curled up in a tight ball on the Charybdis's floor, spit and blood dribbling out the corners of his mouth as he muttered a single word over and over.

Kevin turned at the sound of crunching gravel, and with a heavy sigh, stood up. Dad stood with him, sliding his hand from Kevin's chest to his shoulder.

"You have to go with him," Dad said. "I swear, you'll be out by morning."

"It's a formality," the officer told him. "I doubt you'll even be booked, but I have to take you in to satisfy a few complaints."

"Some of the customers—"

"It's all right, Dad."

"Kevin." Dad let out a small chuckle, and tried to smile. "If nothing else, I need you to go with him just to keep an eye on your mother."

Kevin's head turned sharply.

"She kicked the crap out of him, son. They took her in, too. But by God, she wailed on him so hard he *might* be able to stand up straight in a week or two."

Chip

After Lydia warned Terry off of helping Jake, after she told us what he'd done and why Kevin seemed to snap, my teenage witch's blue eyes went dark, and in less than a second her expression went from confused to homicidal.

Jake was sitting on the floor, his back against the bar, legs splayed open, and his hands massaging his bruised throat. He didn't see Terry's foot whipping toward his crotch until it was too late to react.

She nailed him between the legs twice before snapping

her foot against the side of his head, and was on her knees pummeling him with her fists by the time I was able to lift her – screaming and practically spitting – off of him.

Jake slumped onto the floor, blood dripping from his nose and mouth, his eyes glazed over and legs drawn up in pain. Through labored breathing he chanted "salvation" over and over, mouthing the word after Lydia warned him to shut up or she would pick up where Terry left off.

No one moved to help him until the police barged through the door, followed by paramedics.

Paul turned to the throng of employees watching from the kitchen entrance. "Get out there and apologize to the customers on our behalf," he ordered. "Give them whatever the hell they want, and tell them their meals are on the house. I'll comp your lost tips."

One of the waitresses nodded, then asked, "What do we tell them? You know every single person out there will want to know what happened."

"Tell them it was a personal matter, and we're letting the police handle it."

They scattered, and by the time Jake was on a gurney and headed out the door the dull roar settled into confused murmuring, with a spattering of nervous laughter.

My brain was already going into overdrive. Find Kevin. Protect Kevin. Bribe whomever I needed to in order to keep his name out of the newspaper. Find Kevin. Consol Lydia. Find Kevin.

I was on my tenth or fifteenth 'Find Kevin' when I realized the officer who had taken customer statements was headed for Terry.

Then Lydia stepped in.

"She was protecting her son," she began to protest, but

stopped and looked at him closer. "I know you. We went to high school together."

The cop turned from Terry, and smiled at Lydia. "I really doubted you'd have a clue who I am. Don Heywood."

Lydia held her hand out level to her waist. "Little Donny Heywood?"

"Late growth spurt."

I was about to interject – let's have this reunion another time – when Lydia set her hand on his arm.

"Don, you remember Kevin Davis?"

Little Donny Heywood not only remembered Kevin, but credited him with keeping half the football team from using him as a practice ball. He listened intently as Lydia gave him the short version, ending with, "We just got married, Donny. I know he thought he was past all of this."

Officer Donny was completely smitten by my daughter in law.

They had to, he explained, take Terry in to satisfy all the complaints. And they would have to find Kevin and take him in as well, but he would make sure they were both treated well and not thrown into a public holding cell.

"It will just be questioning," he said. "A formality in case the victim files a complaint."

Several customers were complaining, but he didn't think much would come of that.

Lydia went with Terry to the police station; Officer Donny followed Paul and me to the park, where I was sure we could find him.

The five minute drive from the park to the police station, following behind the police cruiser where my youngest son sat hunched over in the back seat, was intolerably long.

Later, sitting at a table next to his mother, with Officer

Donny, Lydia, and I standing behind them, Kevin told his story, numbly but with vivid detail, his eyes focused on the pen that was scratching out every word he said.

I couldn't touch him.

My son's heart was ripped open and bleeding onto a yellow legal pad, and I couldn't touch him.

"He had Will trying to help him sort through it," I told Terry. We were at the park, sitting on the same bench where I'd found Kevin the night before. "Of all the people—"

"He trusts Will."

Neither of us wanted to believe that he didn't trust us. We wanted to hold onto the idea that he only told Will because Lydia insisted he talk to someone.

"He wanted to protect you from it," she told me while we waited for them to be released. "He was afraid you'd never look at him the same way."

"Eileen knew," I told Terry. "And he told Monica just before she died."

"Don't ask him why he didn't tell us," Terry sniffed, wiping her eyes with the back of her hand. "He doesn't have to justify anything to us. He'll tell us if he wants."

I reminded her that was what brought us to the park on a hot July morning: we'd waited for him to tell us something, waited and left him to stew for over a year.

"I won't make him wait again," I said gently. "I will ask him, for no other reason than to have the chance to tell him that I love him no matter what his reasons were. I want him to know he *can* come to us."

"He knows that already. This was his choice, Irish."

I wasn't sure. If we had pressed, just a little once we understood that he was seriously depressed and not just going through a bad case of the blues, he may have told us. We could have gotten him real help.

"I can't get this picture out of my head," Terry sobbed. "Kevin with a shirt shoved halfway down his throat … I keep seeing his eyes, how bewildered he must have been."

I had the same image, only in my mind the bewilderment in his eyes was tinged with anger.

"Change the picture in your head." I pulled her closer to me. "Think instead about the look in his eyes the day he and Lydia got married. Overall, he's happy."

"Or was until we marched the devil right in front of him."

"We didn't know."

"I wanted to kill him, Chip. I'm not proud of it, but I wanted to twist his little putty-filled head right off. If you hadn't stopped me, I think I would have."

I thought she would have, too.

None of us would have blamed her.

Least of all, I thought, Kevin.

Will, given what he thinks is a good reason, whines. He grunted complaints on the treadmill, in the weight room, and was especially pissy sitting in the steam room, a towel pressed to his face to ward off the heat.

He was only there because his wife decided he was a cupcake away from dropping dead of a heart attack.

"I can't believe you two do this every day," he moaned through the towel. "It's almost a hundred degrees outside and we're sitting in a steam room?"

"It opens your pores," Doug told him. "Follow it up with a cold shower and you'll be beautiful the rest of the day."

"I'd rather stay ugly, thank you."

"Shouldn't be difficult."

If Will hadn't needed the towel to breath through, he would have snapped it at Doug. Forty minutes in the weight room and half an hour in the pool had sapped what little strength he had left.

"How's my youngest godson?" Doug asked while Will groped for a come back.

I wasn't sure how Kevin was. He was either fine or putting on a good show; I made him take a week off from work, thinking he would need time to regroup and to catch his breath, but by the time he'd been released from police custody he seemed mostly fine.

Two days later, when we got word that neither Jake Catero nor the D.A. were pressing charges against, he shrugged it off and said he wanted to get back to work, back to normal.

"I mostly understand why he never told us, I think," I said to them both, "but I'm still itching to ask him."

"Don't," Will advised. "He won't be able to give you a straightforward answer because his reasons are still changing every day. He doesn't really know why yet."

I could accept that.

I also wanted to know why Kevin walked away from the seminary without telling anyone.

"Don't assume that because he didn't report it they don't know," Will said quietly.

"You did?" Doug asked.

Will sighed hard. "Kevin didn't report it because he didn't want to be blamed for it. You have to understand the climate of the seminary—they need every warm, male body there they can get. On some level Kevin feared the worst that would happen to Jake would be a transfer to another seminary, and

Kevin would have been left there to face the scrutiny, and all the gossip that would have come with it."

"But you reported it," I murmured.

"I went to a friend," he admitted. "He promised to take care of it and not allow anything to be brushed off as the curiosity or regrets of a couple of curious young men. I don't know for sure, but I'm guessing Jake was kicked out."

"Can you find out?" Doug asked.

Will thought he might be able to.

"Answer me this, Padre," I said to Will. "How can Kevin be so emotionally charged that he'd try to kill the bastard one day, and relatively calm the next? What am I missing?"

"Chip, to you it just happened. To Kevin it's been over a year. He still has an incredible amount of anger, but he's dealing with it. He has other things in his life that mean more. He's making a concentrated effort to look on the bright side."

"The weight of being Kevin," Doug said. "God forbid he should let himself just hate the guy."

"But he does," Will said. "And I think it scares him."

24

Kevin

Being back in the bar was like standing behind a wall of glass; everything looked right, but I wasn't quite in touch with it. Every customer who looked my way knew. All the whispers and muffled laughter was because of me. Every sniff and sigh was misdirected sympathy.

I had enough sense to realize I was paranoid.

"Business didn't drop off," Paul replied when I asked. "A few people came back the next day, but free food will do that. It never made the newspaper so most of the regulars don't know that anything happened here."

The closest mention in the paper was an obscure reference to a bar fight somewhere on this block. No gory details, no mention of the restaurant, nothing about my mother going ballistic and her brush with attempted homicide.

"You should have seen her," Paul marveled. "She was going to bitch-slap the fear of God right back into him. Seriously, you would have been proud, stunned, and afraid all at once. I didn't know she had it in her."

"Remind me not to piss her off. I can't read them, Paul. I can't tell if they're angry or upset, or what."

He shoved empty popcorn bowls down the counter towards me. "Fill. They're upset. Not with you, just that it happened at all and because you carried it alone for so long. Mom feels wounded and Dad feels impotent. He can't fix this for you."

If I had told them, Dad would have visited an Irish wrath never seen this side of hell on the seminary. And while I blamed the church at first, I knew it wasn't the church or even the seminary.

It was one seriously screwed up kid. I wasn't up to the forgiveness part – if I saw Jake I'd probably try to kill him again – but I knew whom to blame.

"Are you really okay, squirt?" Paul finally asked. "That was one hell of a secret to hold on to."

"I didn't hold onto it. I told Lydia. Eventually Eileen."

"And then Monica," he said softly.

"Sooner or later I would have told everyone else, when I could be sure of the reaction I'd get."

Paul flinched.

"Come on. Can you honestly say the thought that I must be some kind of little puffball to let that happen hasn't crossed your mind?"

"No, it hasn't. Why would anyone think that?"

"Why *wouldn't* you? Come on, I spent over ten years learning to defend myself. How could I let it happen?"

"You didn't fucking let anything happen," he hissed. "You were drunk. Passed out. There's not a goddamned thing you could have done to stop him. I don't care how many black belts you have or how good you are in the ring. You couldn't stop him."

His own anger surprised him. Paul was breathing hard and talking through clenched teeth.

"If I had never gotten that drunk," I told him, "if I had maintained some sense of control, it wouldn't have happened. Pure and simple. It may not be my fault, but I helped create the situation that allowed it to go from bad to worse."

"That's bullshit, and you're not a wuss."

"Do you see now why I want Nicole to learn self defense? I don't plan on teaching those kids just how to physically fight. I intend to teach them how to avoid being in the wrong place at the wrong time. I don't want Nicole at fifteen to be impaired and at the mercy of some horny sixteen year old who doesn't understand boundaries."

Paul blinked hard, and then sighed. "I get it now. But everything you just told me, you need to tell Mom and Dad so they can see where you're coming from." He spun the barstool around and got up. "Nicole will be there the day the dojo opens. And she's not allowed to quit until she's thirty-eight."

I wanted to be there when she hit fifteen and decided she'd had enough.

"You can't make me."

"Want a driver's license next year?"

"That's not fair!"

I ducked behind the bar to clean the liquid traps, imagining an almost grown Nicole stomping her feet and sneering at a graying and balding Paul. I didn't think he remembered what being a teenager was like.

He never had much of a chance to be one. He went from fifteen to old married man in one giant blink.

"Something funny down there, dude?"

I looked over the edge of the bar. Topher was leaning over the counter, looking for me.

"Just laughing at the voices in my head," I said. "What can I get for you?"

"One of those fruity things. The frozen kind."

"Grow a pair and order Scotch sometime."

He grimaced. "I'll stick with the frou-frou stuff. Dude, you're a fricking liar. What was all the crap about Debby being a sure thing?"

"She's not?" I admit it, I was surprised. I was positive Topher's introduction to the Evil One would ending in a huffing sweatfest.

"Not anymore!" He waved it off. "Not a big deal. I got the four-one-one on her social life. I get her point. But damn."

Debby told Topher everything, how screwed up she was, all the sleeping around, how many people got hurt. She decided that she'd go slow from now on; if he could accept that, terrific, she'd like to go out with him again. If not—goodbye.

He didn't want to say goodbye.

He wanted to find out what made her tick.

"She's an odd bird, Davis. The girl can talk about anything from politics to finance, and I can babble on about my job and she doesn't get lost. She gets it. She knew what GAAP and FICO and LIFO were. Hell, she can quote Shakespeare and obscure poets, *and* she understands football."

"You're in luuuuuuv."

Topher pursed his lips thoughtfully. "Well, there's the thing. I think we've spent every minute together we could this week. We just clicked. I think it could go somewhere if we let it."

"Then where is she tonight?"

"Business trip. Don't you fricking laugh, but she'd been gone about ten minutes and I was already missing her. I've only known her for a week."

"Yeah, well, fish get hooked in less time. Enjoy the ride while you can."

Assuming he ever got to ride.

Topher wanted a nice, slow, steady trip and not a frantic speeding rush down the freeway. He was falling hard; that was a good thing, I decided. I was *not* going to tell him what Lydia thought.

She could pick my playmates.

Not Topher's.

"Still up for the driving range tomorrow?" he asked, now partially distracted by the TV and partially distracted by a redhead dancing by herself at the end of the bar.

"Quit looking at the babe," I said. "You're dating someone, remember? And yeah, I'd still like to whack the hell out of a bucket of balls."

"I borrowed some clubs," he said, trying not to sneak glances at her. "Whatever the hell she's drinking, I think I want some."

"Tequila," I told him. "Are you man enough for it?"

He stared into the glass I set on the bar, filled to the rim with strawberry daquiri and topped with a dollop of whipped cream. "I'm barely man enough for this. Crap."

Lydia

Pukefest 2002.

I thought I should have that silk-screened onto a t-shirt. Huge neon-yellow letters on a black cotton shirt. It might, I thought hopefully as I gargled Scope, make the whole day-long morning sickness a little more amusing.

Kevin was amused. He'd be trying to not grin stupidly while I heaved up breakfast or lunch, and it pissed me off. "I'm dying and you think it's funny."

"You're not dying. Another month and you'll feel much better."

He knew this because he was reading all the pamphlets I brought home, and books he bought at the mall when he thought no one was looking.

"Your second trimester," he informed me, "you'll glow. You'll have tons more energy and you'll feel beautiful…"

I told him to shut up.

He was still amused.

He was also enjoying his forced week off far more than I thought he should. "You're supposed to be curled up in a ball on the bed, refusing to get up or eat or shower," I said when I was feeling especially awful. "You're too damned chipper."

"My mom is the one probably curled up in a ball. I did all that last year."

We spent his week off playing, or at least when I wasn't trying to suck my toenails up from the inside and spew them forth into the nearest trashcan or toilet. Or when I wasn't too tired to do much more than blink.

I'd had more energy when I was working.

While I napped he sat at his computer and wrote. I could hear the gentle tap-tap-tap of the keyboard; he would type furiously for fifteen or twenty minutes, and then there would be stretches of silence when I imagined him leaning back in his chair, hands clasped behind his head as he read over what he'd just poured out onto virtual paper.

I peeked over the loft railing once and saw how he was filling the lull—he surfed the Internet, bouncing from one news site to the next.

Someone needed to show him how to find porn.

I was ready for him to go back to work. I needed to be able to hurl in peace. With the apartment quiet I could stretch out on the sofa and watch TV without being asked every fifteen minutes "Are you all right? Do you need anything? Do you want: ?" Insert a backrub, hot bath, ice cream, foot rub, or any of a dozen other things.

I appreciated his consideration, but I just wanted to watch TV. Or nap. Or read. Uninterrupted.

One especially annoying evening I pointed him to the computer, told him to go to Fark-dot-com, and play. Read all the news clips he could find. Laugh at the Photoshop contests. Peek at all the links marked "Boobies" and "Not Safe For Work."

He was quiet for over an hour, until he stumbled into a new website he had to share with me.

"Remember that kid from *Star Trek Next Generation*?"

"The smart one?" I lifted my head and looked over at him. "Wesley Crusher."

"Wil Wheaton. He's got a website. Like an online journal. You have to read this, Lydia. The guy can really write. He's got a wife, a couple of kids. Cripes, he's turning thirty in a couple of days."

"That skinny little kid is thirty?"

He considered it. "Well, that show ended a long time ago. We were pretty young when it started."

"Email him and rub it in," I said, settling back. " 'Dear Mr. Wheaton, I found your website and am amazingly impressed, but I was surprised to realize you're so old. Then it hit me, I was only like four years old when your show started, so of course you're old now. How's that feel, being so old?' "

"Very funny, woman." He tried to sound annoyed with me, but I could hear the hint of laughter in his voice. "He probably gets a thousand emails a day from gushing fans."

"So be one of them."

"I am not," he grumbled, though playfully, "a fanboy.

But you have to read his stuff. I swear, he writes very well, like he's talking to you. And he's damned funny."

I told him I would, just to appease him—well, to shut him up so I could go back to what I was watching—and he went back to immersing himself in the Wonderful World Of Wil Wheaton.

And while Kevin was suffering through his first night back at work, I remembered the half hearted promise to check it out.

Fanboy.

He'd made Wil Wheaton's website his browser's home page. And he was right, the guy was a gifted writer. I poked around for an hour, reading the archives, clicking on all the links.

I wondered how long it would be before Kevin discovered there was a message board on the website.

Out of curiosity I checked the browser's history files; even when presented with links clearly labeled "Boobies," Kevin still hadn't surfed for porn.

"Your daddy," I told my belly, "has a few hang-ups."

It was still too early to feel the baby move, but I rested my hand across my stomach, hoping and waiting.

Kevin and Eileen's birthday was only about a week away. My parents were coming home, timed, they swore, to celebrate with the entire family. Eileen was living with her teeth clenched, worried she would spill the surprise before then.

"You can tell Spider, you know," we told her.

She refused, swearing he was worse at keeping secrets than she was.

"You," I whispered to the baby, "are going to be so spoiled. Between your grandparents and uncles and aunt, you're going to feel like a princess."

Or prince.

Kevin was sure it was a girl. He reasoned that a boy would want to be around to see the misery he created. A girl would be practicing.

"Wait'll she starts kicking," he mused. "She's going to practice stomping her feet as hard as she can, so that when she's five she'll be ready to storm out of the room like a little drama queen."

I went back to the sofa and plopped down, rapidly changing channels with the remote, hoping to find some guilty pleasure to lose myself in.

By the time I settled on a *South Park* rerun my stomach was churning, doing little flip flops that had only one logical conclusion. I got to my feet, took a deep breath, and turned to head for the bathroom, when the doorbell rang.

Thinking it was Eileen coming over to check on me – it seemed like something Kevin would arrange – I went to the door instead. Eileen would understand if I yanked the door open, waved her in, and then ran off.

It wasn't Eileen.

The contents of my stomach, mostly toast and tea, surged forth and splattered all over the entry way, foul smelling droplets plinking off the tile and onto the door.

"Oh, crap."

Terry

Chip was lying on his stomach on the diving board, his hands folded under his chin, and his faced bathed by the shimmering lights under the water in the pool. He was staring into the water, and I don't think he even blinked from the time I stepped outside and closed the door until I was standing by the pool.

He didn't look up. "I was just trying to figure out the appeal," he said before I could ask. "I came out here to swim a few laps and then thought about all the times we used to find Kevin out here plastered onto the board … I wondered what he was always thinking about so hard. And I wondered if after he came home if he just wanted to fall in and never come up."

I knew what Chip was feeling, but I also knew that we had to have faith that Kevin never really wanted to die.

"If it had been Eileen," I asked, sitting at the edge of the pool, plunging my feet into the cool water, "would you wonder that?"

"Eileen wouldn't have kept it from us," he said mournfully.

"Telling us doesn't change how it felt to Kevin or how it would feel to Eileen," I pointed out. "He obviously had a crisis of faith at first—"

"He still does," Chip interrupted.

"—but I don't think he really ever wanted to die."

Chip finally sat up, turning on the diving board so he could face me. "Terry, I have so many things pounding through my head right now that I don't know what to think half the time. It kills me that *that* could happen to any of the kids. It bothers me that even though he seems all right he admits that he would try to kill the son of a bitch if he ever saw him again. And it really bothers me that it keeps crossing my mind that all I have to do is pick up the phone and say the right word to the right person, and the little freak would disappear from the face of the earth."

I reminded him that I would have ripped several essential body parts off the man, but he had stopped me. I wanted to kill him.

"Past tense?"

With a sigh, I nodded. "I realize that meeting out justice isn't my job—and it's not yours, or even Kevin's."

"Kevin should have some say."

"Irish, for whatever reason he made the choice to walk away from the seminary and to leave Jake there. If he wanted revenge, he would have done something then."

He wasn't so sure. He thought Kevin came home because he didn't feel safe, and he didn't trust the people around him.

"Will reported it, Terry. He thinks Catero was kicked out of the seminary, but with Kevin leaving without a word to anyone else, they couldn't really do anything. That made me think about calling someone in the agency to have the whole thing taken care of. I thought better of it when I realized that I would have been committing myself all over again. Or worse, Kevin."

"Is that how they deal with problems? Eliminate them?"

"Sometimes," he admitted.

"And when Nick was kidnapped, when you and Doug were chasing after Matt Rheule to get him back?"

He asked me not to press for any details, to just accept that he and Doug walked away from my former fiancé, leaving him very much alive.

"Is he still?" I asked.

Chip looked down at his feet.

I stared at the top of his head, angry at the silence I knew he wouldn't break, and finally I sighed, "Well, then."

"I'm sorry," he murmured.

"Do you know who killed Matt? And yes, it matters."

Chip looked up. "Ron."

Ron Gallery. The man Chip had believed, through the

first 24 years of his life, to be his father. Kris's first husband. The man responsible, one way or the other, for Chip being sucked into the agency machine.

"Does Kris know?" I asked.

"Doug told her. Angel, we *all* hoped you would never ask. I hated it, I never agreed with handling it that way, but no one asked me. They just ordered it done. I doubt Ron wanted to do it. Damn, he was probably operating on fumes by then and justified it as protecting his grandson."

"Chip—"

"I am sorry, Terry."

I nodded. I knew he was, and I knew it had happened a lifetime ago. Long enough for the pain of almost losing Nick to have healed over.

"Kevin will be just fine," I told Chip. "We just have to catch up to him."

Kevin

Topher sat in the bar and nursed a series of daquiris until the redhead left, when he was just drunk enough to declare her woefully inadequate for his tastes—"I think she's a bobblehead come to life. Watch. Dang, that head just pops up and down like a toy Chihuahua in the back window of someone's car!"—and to declare himself too tipsy to drive.

"God made sidewalks," he said emphatically, "so that I could get completely pissed without guilt. I will not run over kittens or puppies or redheads with floppy necks."

I figured the kittens and puppies of Fairfield would appreciate the gesture, promised his car would not be towed from our parking lot, and then watched him weave out the door.

"He's toasted," Paul said as he walked past Topher. "Did you call him a cab?"

"He's on foot," I replied, though Paul's attention was less on me than it was on Sherry Armstrong. She was wiping down tables at the other end of the bar, oblivious to the fact that she was being ogled.

"Ask her out already," I told him.

"Eh. Employee, Monica's best friend and all that crap. Haven't we gone over this before?"

"Yeah, but you're full of shit. She doesn't have to be the next great love of your life. Just go to a movie or dinner together. Or stay in and get naked."

"Christ, Kevin."

"You sputter now, but you're thinking about it. Why can't you two just help each other move on?"

"And we can do that by getting naked."

"It's worth a try."

"Clock out and go home," he sighed with a little bit of a laugh. "If you stay here you're going to corner her and tell her I said that's what I want. Go home."

He was right.

I had no problem telling Sherry that Paul wanted to jump her bones.

I clocked out and bolted through the door before he could change his mind. It was dark and had started to cool off, but I put the top down on the car anyway, and drove home with the wind rushing through my hair.

A block away I smelled the smoke, and heard sirens; when I turned the corner I saw the reflection of pulsating red bouncing off trees and buildings across the street.

Curious at first, it took a moment for it to register that there were three fire trucks lined up in the parking lot. It took another moment to notice all the people crowded on the sidewalk across the street, most wrapped in blankets, some barefoot and in pajamas or sweatpants.

I slammed on the brakes and swerved to park at the side of the road, gradually feeling panic bubble as the smell of smoke began to wrap around me. I looked from the crowd to the apartment building, looking at the jet streams of water pouring from the trucks onto the flames.

Flames that were reaching out the windows of my apartment.

25

Kevin

I raced to the crowd waiting and watching with fear across the street from the burning building, frantically searching faces; no one paid any attention to me, too mesmerized or frightened by the flames to notice. Spider and Eileen were standing in the middle, perched on the curb, staring numbly at their apartment, which was just beginning to ignite. Both were half dressed and Eileen was visibly shaking, though from cold or shock, I didn't know.

Her head turned sharply when I shouted her name; she touched Spider's arm to get his attention and nodded my way, signing "Kevin" when he looked up.

"Lydia," I sputtered. "Where is she?"

"No idea," Spider replied.

I turned with the intention of running across the street – if she wasn't on the sidewalk with them then she was surely there – but Spider grabbed my arm and yanked me back.

"Her truck is gone, Kevin," Eileen said. "I don't think she was home."

Spider nodded. "It was parked there earlier, but gone when they evacuated. She probably went to the store or something."

"How long ago?" I asked.

"We've only been out here for twenty minutes or so," Eileen replied.

If she ran to the grocery store, she'd be back in a few minutes. If she ran into someone and stopped to talk, she could be gone an hour. If she decided to call a friend and go to a movie, she might not be back for hours.

We sat on the curb and watched the building burn, until the apartment and the three to the left, including Eileen and Spider's, were gone. We sat there as the crowd slowly disbursed, grumbling of having to find someplace else to stay for the night. We sat there as a bus pulled up to take whomever needed one a ride to a local motel, courtesy of the Red Cross. We sat there and waited, and she never came home.

Eileen

"We waited all night, Dad. He refused to budge, in case she showed up. He was worried she'd think he'd been caught in the fire if she didn't see him there waiting."

Some time after everyone else left, Spider walked to Kevin's car for his cell phone, and then poked through the trunk for sweat pants and a sweatshirt. I took the shirt and the phone, called my father and Uncle Doug, but Kevin refused to move, and neither of us was willing to leave him sitting there alone.

Uncle Doug showed up at four in the morning, followed a few minutes later by Dad; Kevin barely looked at either of them, staring instead at the now smoldering apartment building. He watched the few remaining firemen douse hot spots, and watched police cars come and go, but he refused to look up at his own father.

When daylight finally broke, Dad gave him no choice.

He grabbed Kevin by the arm and forced him up and towards his car, promising him they would figure out where Lydia was.

Now he was sitting in the living room of our parents' house, staring out the window, waiting. Hoping.

Uncle Doug spent most of his time at the apartment quizzing firemen and police officers; no one could tell him one hundred percent for sure, but none of them believed anyone had been caught in the fire.

"She could be anywhere," Dad surmised, quietly so that Kevin wouldn't hear. "If she decided to spend the night with a friend and left him a note…"

"I think that's why he didn't want to leave. He's afraid she'll come home and freak out."

"She's not stupid," Spider said. "She'd call here before she completely freaked out."

"Kevin's just not thinking straight," Dad sighed. He glanced at the clock on the wall and then at the phone. "Start calling any of her friends you can think of at eight o'clock. Doug and I have an appointment with the fire chief in an hour."

Spider and I looked at him.

"We need to make sure they don't think Kevin is responsible."

"I was at work," Kevin said, finally turning from the window. "There were more than a dozen witnesses."

"I know."

Kevin went over to the sofa and dropped onto it, hard, leaning his head against the back cushions. "She would have called me at work if she planned to stay out all night," he said, tilting his head back to look at Dad. "She wouldn't have left a note."

"She would have if she'd only intended on staying out for a little while."

"She would have called me," Kevin insisted. "I've been thinking about it. She'd want to be sure I knew where she was and make sure I didn't have plans for when I got home."

Dad finally nodded his agreement. Lydia would have called him at work, or his cell phone, or even left a message with me if all else failed. She wouldn't have left him hanging, even if she intended on being home ten minutes after he was supposed to get off work.

When Paul came downstairs, already dressed and ready to do whatever he could, Kevin lifted his head to look at him.

"Do me a favor, Paul?"

"Anything."

"I'm supposed to meet Topher at the driving range on Dover in about fifteen minutes. Will you go get him and bring him back here?"

Paul was stuffing his wallet and keys into his pockets before Kevin's request was out. "How much do I tell him?"

"As much as you need to in order to get him over here."

Dad and Uncle Doug followed Paul out the door.

"No one will believe you're responsible," Spider said.

"A lot of people might," Kevin replied, hands moving slowly, belying his fatigue. "As long as Lydia is okay, I don't care. Let them think what they want."

Spider shook his head. "You don't want to let your reputation go up in those flames. When it's all over, you'll still want a life."

"I have enough money to buy another life," Kevin pointed out. "The perks of being Dad's offspring."

"You're going to want back the life you had," Spider insisted. "Then what people think *will* matter. You'll want the people teaching for you to trust you. And your students. Don't roll over and play dead on this one."

"Know what? I'm not going to worry about it, not right now. Right now the only thing I can even think about is where she might be."

Spider might have had more to say, but Kevin leaned back and closed his eyes, shutting him out. Spider started to poke him, but I shook my head and reminded him how often he shut out the world by turning a blind eye to it.

Kevin sat there like that, eyes closed, for half an hour. He acknowledged Mom when she tried to coax him into eating, and answered when any of us tried to talk to him, but he didn't move until Paul came home, dragging a confused Topher Tedeski with him.

Before Topher could ask what was going on, Kevin was on his feet, looking at him pleadingly.

"Dude, if you have any idea where Debby is, you have to tell me."

"Debby?" Topher looked at me, then at Paul, and back to Kevin. "Just some business trip, that's all I know."

"She never mentioned where, or how you could get hold of her?"

"She said she'd be home in a couple of days."

Kevin pointed to the chair near the fireplace and asked Topher to sit down. "Look," he sighed, dropping back onto the sofa, "Lydia wanted me to talk to you about Debby a week or so ago and I didn't. But you have to know."

A deep frown crossed Topher's brow, but he waited for Kevin to go on.

"Did she tell you why she moved back here?"

"Trying to start over," Topher said, sounding unsure.

Kevin nodded. "More or less. She and I were like pen

pals for a long time, since the summer I turned fifteen, I think. When I left the seminary and came home, she thought there was a chance…"

"With you," Topher prompted.

"Only she hadn't counted on there being Lydia. She was pissed, Toph, and she wasn't about to take no for an answer. She started playing the game hard—she'd come over here with Nick or Katie, and I'd find her sneaking up on me to cop a feel, or creeping around in my room. The last time she did that she was buck naked and trying to climb into bed with me. I ran screaming out of the room; Mom cornered her and read her the riot act. Later that afternoon my car went up in flames."

"Your dad—" Mom started, but Kevin was shaking his head.

"He was changing a part out. He disconnected the battery before he did anything. Dad didn't torch my car."

"You think Debby did," Topher said quietly.

"Not at first. It never crossed my mind."

"Then why?"

"When Lydia and I decided we wanted to get married as soon as we could, we invited the whole family to the beach with us. Nick and Katie brought Debby along, but never bothered to tell her why. She thought she was being included on a family vacation—she was beyond angry when she found out. Topher, I tried to talk to her but she was adamant, and said it would never last, and sooner or later she'd get her chance with me. She left the next morning."

Mom sat down next to Kevin. "And that night Will called to let you know the dojo had burned down."

Topher slumped in the chair, completely deflated.

"Even then," Kevin went on, "I didn't think about it.

But the night you met her – while you ran home to change – she pressed the point home again. She intended to win. Hell, Lydia even called her a firebug but it went right over my head until last night."

While Kevin talked, Paul moved across the room to the phone, quietly dialed, and the hung up without saying anything.

"Just trying Nick's house," he explained.

"Nick's at some seminar this week," Mom told him. "And Katie is at a church retreat."

Paul reached for the phone again. "At the parish?"

Mom nodded.

"Topher," Kevin said, almost gently, "I *am* sorry. But the thing is, if we find Debby, we find Lydia."

Chip

There was no one, the fire chief declared, found in the rubble of what was left of Kevin and Lydia's apartment. There were a few cases of smoke inhalation and a dead bird, but that was it. Every other known living being made it out relatively unscathed.

The building was a total loss.

"Did your daughter-in-law have a thing for candles?" he asked. "The inspector hasn't issued an official cause yet, but the apartment had candle wax all over it. If she lit several and then left…"

"Perhaps," I allowed. "One of our concerns is that we can't find her."

"And another is that Kevin not be considered suspect in any of the fires," Doug added.

"He probably should be," the chief said, "considering recent events. But as far as I know, the police have cleared him of any culpability. He was never near any of the fires he's been touched by and there's no motive. He never made a move to collect insurance on his car and he doesn't seem terribly upset about having to rebuild his school without reimbursement for the loss. It's a hell of a thing, three fires so close together, but we haven't connected them."

Not officially, I understood that.

We paid a visit to the police station and spoke with Officer Donny—"We'll have the entire precinct looking for her, I swear"—and followed that with a visit to Brad Colt, Terry's former boss and my sometimes-lawyer.

We could protect Kevin on every legal front, but in the hunt for my missing daughter-in-law, Doug and I both knew we were unprepared and out of practice. My gut was screaming at me: Lydia did not spend the night with a friend. She did not run an errand and forget to come home. Kevin knew her well enough to make that call.

"It could take the police days," Doug said, once we were out of Brad's office and in his car.

I agreed.

And then pointed him in the next direction I thought we should go.

"Are you sure you want to do this?" he asked once we were in the parking lot, staring at the nondescript building of the U.S. Defense Agency. "You know what the price will be."

I knew.

"A couple of decades ago you and I would have been able to take what little info we had, wave it in front of a data analyst, and we'd have her. But we need that analyst first, Doug."

"That won't be enough now, and you know it."

I did know. Any skills I had at the game evaporated as the years wore on. I would need help, and the people who could give it to me were on the third floor of that building.

We got out of the car and went inside, asked for someone I knew was still there, and waited for an invitation up the second elevator to the left.

I hoped Terry would understand.

Kevin

Everyone cleared the living room, leaving Topher and I alone. Mom declared that we would have breakfast, like it or not, and Spider took off with Paul to see if they could find Katie at Holy Spirit's annual Womens' Retreat.

I wasn't sure if Topher was angry or disappointedly surprised.

"It's too much to take in," he admitted. "I mean, not just Debby—"

"Yeah."

"I didn't clue in. A business trip? She's a goddamned file clerk, Davis."

"Yeah," I repeated.

"Still." He took a deep breath. "She wouldn't hurt Lydia. She might have her tucked away somewhere, but she wouldn't hurt her."

I nodded, but truthfully, I wasn't sure, and Topher hadn't known her long enough to know what she would do at any given time. I was sure he doubted she'd just wander up to someone and shove a hand in his crotch, yet that didn't change that she'd done it. I was certain he believed her when she said she didn't chase married men, yet she had a history of stepping between couples no matter how apologetic she was after the fact.

I intend to win.

"I just don't get this," he went on. "She was pretty up front about the sheer volume of men she dated and how much trouble she got into. Why didn't she tell me she had a thing for you?"

"Because I'm here and they're not?" I guessed. "I don't know that she has a firm grasp on the things she does. As far as I know, she had every intention of trying to work out a relationship with you, but there's that warped little part of her—"

"You think she's unbalanced?" he asked.

Unbalanced was not exactly how I would have put it, but it seemed as apt a description as anything else. Debby could be capable of compartmentalizing her wants. Or she could have been in need of some serious medication.

"If Lydia is all right," I said, "I'll let it go. Debby obviously needs help. I'm not even sure that what she really wants is me. Maybe she knows she wants something, but doesn't know exactly what."

"Or maybe she's just listening to the voices in her head."

"Toph…" I wasn't sure if he was joking or not.

"You know, I have the most screwed up luck with women. I seem to wind up with women who are hung up on someone else,"—he gestured to me—"on some political crusade that I don't fit into, or gay."

"Gay?"

"Twice," he groaned. "I swear they weren't gay before I went out with them. It was like 'Wow, Topher, you're such a wonder in the sack, I think I'd rather sleep with women instead.' Now Debby flakes out on me."

"She was flaky before. I figured that was part of the charm you went for."

Flaky, he thought, was fun. Dangerous or deranged changed the rules of the game. And he had no idea what he would do about her: stand by and hope she could get help, or run like hell.

Mom poked her head out of the kitchen and ordered us both to the table. Topher might not have been hungry, but he wasn't about to say so. As we sat down he sucked in a deep breath and said, "Man, that smells great."

"Yep. My mom can open a mean can of Pillsbury Cinnamon Rolls."

Nicole shuffled into the dining room, sleepy-eyed, suffering an extreme case of bed head. When she saw Topher sitting where her grandfather usually read the morning paper, she blushed and quickly looked away.

Before she sat down she put her arms around me and hugged hard. "I'm sorry your house burned down, Uncle Kevin. I think Aunt Lydia just forgot to call to tell you she'd be home late. I do that sometimes. I forget to call Grandma to tell her I'm still at Devin's."

"Maybe," I said, letting her go.

When she sat down, she worked up the nerve to look at Topher, and smiled brightly. "You're cute. Who are you?"

"Topher. You're cute, too. Who are you?"

"Nicole. I never heard the name Topher before. Is it made up?"

"It's short for Christopher," he explained. "My dad's name is also Christopher, and everyone calls him Chris, so they started calling me Topher. And then people like your uncle thought it would be funny to call me Gopher."

"Uncle Kevin is a butthead sometimes."

From behind me I heard Paul say, "What did you just call him?"

I turned to see if they'd brought Katie home. I expected a nice straight line of people: Paul, Spider, Katie.

I couldn't freaking believe it.

Debby.

Terry

In the dead silence that followed Paul's return home, the sound of keys in the front door lock was like the cracking of a whip. I heard Chip scrape his feet on the doormat, and the low grumbling of both his and Doug's voices. I headed for the door to get to Chip before he had to deal with Kevin, who was clearly agitated and reaching for the right thing to say.

Doug went into the kitchen; I pulled Chip into the study and filled him in on Kevin's theory, that Debby started all three fires and had probably done something with Lydia. Kevin hadn't seemed to consider any other possibilities, and after hearing his reasons, I thought he was right.

Yet Debby was now standing in the kitchen, surely wondering why Kevin and Topher were both staring at her, dumbfounded.

"My impulse was to hurdle over the breakfast bar and rip out her hair by those Barbie blonde roots," I admitted. "But if she's been with Katie all this time—"

Leaning back against the desk, Chip folded his arms, closing his eyes for a moment. "Who ever could have imagined we'd be going through this again?" he sighed.

Twenty five years before, it had been clear-cut. Unlike Lydia, there was no chance that nine month old Nick had wandered off to spend the night with friends, forgetting to let someone know. We'd put him to bed, and when I got up the next morning, he was gone.

"I did something that's going to piss you off in a major way," Chip said. "I didn't know what else to do."

"What?"

Carefully, he replied, "I went to see someone at the agency, Terry. My gut told me we'd need help finding her, and that seemed the most logical place to look for it."

He reminded me of Kevin at twelve; serious but uncertain. Wanting to say the right thing but fearing it would come out wrong and get him into more trouble.

"I hate what that means, but it's all right," I told him.

"I promised before, never again."

"That was before my baby's heart was at stake, Irish. I don't like the idea of wondering where you are for weeks at a time, but I'll adjust."

He shook his head. "That's the thing, you don't have to get used to it. They don't want me. They'll help, but they don't want me back."

Chip looked as surprised as I felt.

"At first my ego was a little wounded, but then I started to worry. They don't want me, but they'll want *someone*."

I wrapped my arms around him, resting my forehead on his chest. "Kevin."

He thought that was likely. Kevin was everything the agency coveted: smart, with an IQ almost off the scale, a trained fighter still in excellent shape. He had nothing to lose, either, Chip said. He was afraid that someone from the agency would be at the front door by noon, trying to cut a deal with Kevin. Find Lydia in exchange for a signed contract.

There was no way to keep Kevin from agreeing.

"I swear, if I'd thought that them wanting him was even a remote possibility, I wouldn't have gone. I was sure they would want me. I never considered my age."

"You're not that old," I assured him.

"By their standards, I'm ancient. If I had stayed with them, I'd probably be riding a desk by now."

If I had known that, I might not have been such a bitch about his residual ties to the agency.

Kevin was sitting with his head on the kitchen table when we finally went to join everyone else. Topher was quizzing Debby: why didn't she just say it wasn't a business trip? Why didn't she come right out and say it was a religious retreat? What was she hiding?

Debby's eyes flared with anger. "It was *personal* business, Topher, and I'm not under any obligation to share that with you yet. Son of a bitch, we've been dating for what, a week and a half? You haven't earned the right to get your shorts in a wad about the places I go."

"It was important," Kevin said, slowly lifting his head. "And it's my fault he thought anything other than that you were away on business."

"Why would you tell him any different?" she snapped. "It's none of *your* business, either!"

"Last night our apartment building burned down," he explained.

"And Lydia is missing," Topher added.

"You thought *I*—?" Debby's faced pinched, anger giving way to resignation in a matter of seconds. "Of course you did. I'm not an arsonist, Kevin. I wouldn't go that low to get you away from her. I wouldn't intentionally do anything to split you up."

"Yeah," Kevin sighed.

"I went to the retreat with Katie," she went on. "There are dozens of people who can verify that."

Softly, just realizing it himself, Kevin said, "I had hoped

it was you, Debby. At least then it would make some kind of warped sense and I'd have a shot at finding her."

"God, I'm sorry, Kevin." She continued, apologizing for every wrong she'd made with him, for making him uncomfortable and for being so far over the top that she turned herself into a suspect.

She also apologized to Topher. "I should have been upfront about how I'd felt about Kevin, and about the retreat, but I didn't know how." She went on the retreat, she added, because she was confused—all that energy spent on Kevin, waiting and hoping, and then all of the sudden there was Topher. Kevin didn't matter as much anymore. She wanted to go someplace quiet where she could figure out how it was possible to turn 180 degrees in one night, and where she could talk to other people about it. She wanted to know if what she felt for Topher was real; she wanted it to be real.

Kevin was only marginally interested in Debby's emotional revelations. He sighed and grunted, "Yeah, well."

Whatever else he thought was cut off by the phone ringing. Paul picked it up before the end of the first ring; his eyes went wide and he signed wildly, "Lydia."

He had the phone in Kevin's hand before Kevin could even turn around. Chip stopped him before he could say anything, signing, "Be quiet," to everyone, and to Kevin, "Let us listen in, son."

Kevin nodded, and Paul pushed the button on the speakerphone. Topher frowned in confusion; Debby held her finger to her lips, knowing he hadn't understood Chip.

After hearing her voice, Kevin asked, hopefully, "Where are you?"

Voice shaky, she replied, "It doesn't matter. It's not important."

Sounds scared, Chip signed to me.

"I've been doing a lot of thinking, Kevin, and you need to know—I'm not coming home."

Stunned, Kevin stammered, "What?"

"It was a mistake," she sniffed. "We didn't think this through, Kevin. It was just … a mistake."

Chip signed, *Go easy. She sounds terrified.*

"How?" Kevin asked, nodding to his father. "How is it a mistake?"

Chip leaned close to the phone. *Birds.*

"Remember how your brothers used to call you 'Father Kevin?' They were so proud that you wanted to be a priest. I keep thinking about that."

"I was just a kid, Lydia."

"I know. But I want you to be the father you were supposed to be all along. I want you to be Father Rabbit. You need to go back to the seminary."

Kevin frowned, puzzled. "Kind of late for that."

"But it's not! Think about it. Think about all the important people who need a Father Rabbit in their lives."

"But I don't want—"

"It's not a matter of want," she said. "It's about doing what's right."

She's talking awfully fast.

"The apartment burned down," Kevin said. "Did you know that?"

She took in a long, shaky breath and then said, "I'm sorry. That wasn't supposed to happen."

Paul signed *What the hell?* but Chip reminded him to be quiet.

"You have to promise me, Kevin," she said, pausing at the sound of a horn in the distance. "Promise me you'll do whatever you have to. Dance across the bay bridge if that's what it takes. Be Father Rabbit."

"Lydia."

"I'll call back tomorrow, Kevin."

With a click, the line went dead.

"What the hell?" Kevin muttered.

"All right," Chip said. "Everyone, tell me what you heard, beyond what she was saying."

"I don't know," Kevin groaned.

"Background noises. Anything."

"The birds were fairly loud," Paul mused. "She was calling from a phone booth."

"Some kind of whooshing sound," Katie added. "Traffic, maybe? And that horn—a truck stop?"

"Could be," Chip said. "It didn't sound like a semi, though."

I put my hands on Kevin's shoulders and kissed the top of his head. "Sweetheart, did you two have a fight recently? Something that might have made her think you regret leaving the seminary?"

"No, Mom. Nothing remotely close to a fight."

Suddenly, Debby clamped her hands over her mouth, and her eyes went wide. "Seagulls!" she finally blurted. "That whoosh was the ocean."

"And the horn?" Paul prompted.

"Tugboat. Coast Guard. I'm not sure, but it annoyed the hell out of me when we were at Bodega Bay."

"Dance across the bay bridge," Kevin whispered. "She's right."

Chip looked at Doug, who nodded. "We're heading out, then," he said to me. "If anyone from the agency shows up, tell them what little we know."

Kevin

I wanted it to be Debby. I wanted her to be the one who bit by bit tried to send my life up in flames. I wanted it to be her, so that Lydia would be right, I could eject Debby from my life, and so that I would have a clear shot at finding her.

She stayed in the dining room as everyone else filed out, looking at me sadly.

I wouldn't have blamed her for hating me.

I hoped she would forgive Topher his doubts.

"I got it," she said when we were the only two left. "I know what she was telling you."

For once, I listened.

"None of that was about becoming a priest. She doesn't want that."

"I wouldn't think so."

"It was that whole Father Rabbit thing. Nobody else called you that, right? Didn't they call you Father Kevin?"

I nodded.

"I think," she said uncertainly, "she was telling you that you *are* a father. I mean a real, flesh and blood father. As in a baby."

To be honest, I never thought Debby knew where the nail was, much less how it hit it on the head. She'd caught it; she heard what everyone else failed to.

"Don't tell anyone, please," I whispered. "We were planning on telling them on my birthday."

She allowed for a slight smile, and nodded.

"I don't get why she was driving that point home so hard, though. I *know* already."

"Because," Debby said, "she wanted you to hear what's important. If for no other reason, she wouldn't leave you right now *because* of the baby. She's in trouble, Kevin, and she needs you to get her out of it."

~

We entered the beach house from the street side; the front door opened to a short hallway next to the master bedroom, and from it the living room was in full view. Dad went in first, opening the door slowly as he sprayed the hinges with oil, and Uncle Doug followed him.

They let me in only after determining the house was empty.

"It doesn't smell stale enough to have been shut up since February," Dad said, sniffing.

Uncle Doug crept from room to room, frowning.

"Crumbs on the kitchen counter," he reported to Dad after he'd been in every room downstairs. "There's an empty toilet paper roll in the bathroom trash can. One pillow on the floor in the master bedroom. Flecks of dried toothpaste on the master bath mirror."

Lydia and I had been the last to leave the beach house, and we cleaned before we left.

"Terry made the bed before we took off," Dad said. "Did you two sleep in there after that?"

"We stayed upstairs."

"All right then." He walked around the perimeter of the living room, staying as close to the walls as he could, to get a better look out the bay window. "Don't turn on any lights and stay to the back of the house. If someone is watching, I don't want them to know we're in here."

That, I guessed, was why we parked a half a mile away.

"You don't think she's alone, do you?"

"Most likely not," Uncle Doug answered. He reached to the back of his jeans and pulled out a small gun, handing it to me. "Just in case."

I took it, turning it over in my hands, almost repulsed by the warm metal. "I've never fired one."

"It's for show," he said. "Your dad loaded it with blanks."

"Then what good is it?"

"The threat of it," Dad said. "You can't fight unless you can get close, and having it might buy you the few steps you need to get close enough to … whomever … to be able to defend Lydia. Doug and I will be there to back you up."

I didn't want it, but I nodded and slid it into the back waistband of my jeans, the way Doug had.

Damned uncomfortable.

"What do we do next?" I asked. "How do we look for her without being seen?"

For the moment, Dad said, we would stay put to see if Lydia came back to the house. She was there once, it was reasonable to think she'd come back. Uncle Doug wasn't as sure; he thought he should walk along the beach, up past the jetty, to see if he could spot her or her truck. He thought she was less likely to expect or to notice him, not the way she expected me or would recognize Dad in a quick blink.

"If she recognizes you, she gives you away," he said.

Dad and I waited at the table, far enough into the shadows that we couldn't be seen from the outside, but where we both had full view of the window.

There were few people on the beach, and most of them I recognized as year-round neighbors, or people who spent long weekends there. We watched as Uncle Doug made his way along the water's edge, hands stuffed into his pockets, trying to look as casual as the people who were there to play.

He knew what he was doing, I reminded myself.

"Just before we left you said something to Mom about the agency," I said, breaking a long silence. "How are they involved?"

He didn't take his eyes off the window. "I went to them for help. I had a hunch we might need it."

"But Mom—"

"She understands. She was all right with the idea that I would owe them a favor, but it turned out to be a moot point. They'll help if we need it, but they don't want me back."

"With no strings attached?"

"There are always strings. Surely they'll want something in return, someday."

"Or someone. Me," I guessed.

He was afraid of that. Paul they would never touch because of Nicole. No one could stop a field agent from having kids, but it was rare that recruitment extended to anyone with small children. Eileen was safe out of courtesy, because of Spider. Nick drank himself out of contention.

"And that leaves me."

"You're a third degree black belt and you're too goddamned smart for your own good. They'll want you, but that doesn't mean you have to accept."

"Yes, it does. If it means Lydia home safe, it does."

His eyes flicked away from the window. "We'll find her, Kevin."

Find her, maybe, but then what?

"They don't recruit people with small kids?" I asked, cutting through another stretch of silence.

"Not usually."

"All right then."

He glanced at me again. "What?"

"What we'll do is let them help if we need it, and I'll refuse to sign anything until she's home safe."

"And then what? Get her pregnant? You won't have that kind of time. Five minutes after they have her, you'll have a contract shoved under your nose."

"Yeah. Well."

He suddenly sat up straighter, turning away from the window. "Father Rabbit. Goddammit, I didn't catch that. She's pregnant already, isn't she?"

"Due in February."

While he groped with the news, something he normally would have been overjoyed about, Doug threw the door open.

"Her truck is up past the jetty, in the camper's parking lot. She's not alone."

Chip

He nearly knocked the table over in his rush to bolt out the door. Doug blocked his way, his hand hard against Kevin's chest.

"Don't," he warned, "turn cowboy on us. You rush up there in a panic and you'll get her hurt."

There were two people in the truck; Lydia sat behind the wheel, her head resting against the window as if she were asleep. Doug didn't get a good look at the person she was with, but presumed it was male.

"A woman," he reasoned when Kevin asked, "she wouldn't shy away from. She'd be looking for her first way out."

"Old boyfriend?" I guessed.

Doug shrugged. "Does it matter? The truck is parked facing the community bathroom on the other side of the jetty. We should probably approach it from both sides. I can go behind the parking lot to get to it from the passenger side."

"We'll lag behind thirty seconds and come in from her side."

Doug pointed at Kevin. "You *have* to stay calm. If we time this right, as I distract him you can rip the door open and get her out."

"What if the door is locked?" Kevin asked.

"The lock stem was up on her side."

"We have to time this perfectly, Doug," I said. "If we're even five seconds off from each other…"

"That's not an option."

He left first, jogging slowly up the sidewalk in front of the house, heading for the back side of the parking lot. Kevin and I followed, walking, our eyes peeled on Doug Stone's back.

"Look, what will happen is this: you and Doug will throw the doors open and the same time, and I'll lunge across Lydia. Doug and I both have to get a gun on him."

"What if he has a gun on *her*? She could be dead before she could blink, Dad. Just open the door and yank her out."

"If we do this before we have him secure," I told him, "she could be seriously injured. That baby brings an entire set of concerns to the table. If you just yank her out onto the pavement … we have to protect the baby, too."

He didn't answer.

"Kevin. God. If I'd ever had to choose between your mother's safety and an unborn baby, I would have chosen her every damned time, but we can protect them both. I need you to trust me on this. Doug and I can do this—and if we do it, the agency has nothing on any of us."

We were fifty feet from the parking lot when Doug turned back sharply, gesturing to the beach. The truck cab was empty, windows rolled halfway down. He pointed to the beach behind us, and signed for us to turn around.

Lydia was walking along the water, towards the house, twitching away from the shorter man beside her.

He felt familiar, hair and build from someone I knew, but as his face came to me, Kevin was already beginning to run.

I caught his arm before he could get far. "Look." I pointed to the thin space between them, the glint of metal held close to her side.

"That's not a problem," Kevin said calmly. "I just need to get up behind him. As soon as he goes down the knife is a moot point." He strained to look at the knife. "Worst thing she'll get is a nasty cut on the arm, and Doug can take care of that."

The possibilities I could imagine were far worse, but I nodded. We took off at a full run, Kevin a stride and a half ahead of me; I wanted to yell for him to slow down, but couldn't risk it. I suspected that Jake Catero was capable of great harm, and quickly, and my voice thundering behind them could have been the last thing Lydia heard.

We were less than twenty feet away when Jake spun around. Kevin stopped hard, nearly falling forward onto the sand, as Jake turned Lydia to face him. He made sure we saw the knife, flashing it as he poised it against her ribs.

His cheek was covered with bloodied scratches, red and inflamed.

"This would have been so much easier if you had just gone back to the seminary like she asked," Jake sighed melodramatically. "I wouldn't have hurt her."

"Like hell." Kevin was twitching, trying to inch closer.

"She's an innocent, really," Jake went on. "And she understands that you have to go back. It's for everyone's good."

"You're a dead man if you don't get the hell away from her."

Jake turned the knife over in his hand, keeping it close to Lydia's side. "I don't think so. You'll go back to keep her safe, and then she'll move on. Everything will be the way it's supposed to be."

Kevin took a tentative step forward; Jake nudged the knife, making her wince.

She stared at Kevin, eyes wild and red.

"I'm not going back. Jesus Christ, Catero, at this point they wouldn't even want me back."

"But they do. They know what I did to you. They tossed me out on my ass and said my only way back in is if I can get you to return. It's all about forgiveness. And I have to be a priest, Kevin. I *have* to be."

"Bullshit."

"You think you're the first person I've done that to? There's a long line of freaks and bullies ahead of you. I have to atone. I *have* get into the seminary." Almost lovingly, Jake added, "You're my salvation, you know that. You'll go back, I'll be forgiven, I'll be a priest, and everything will be all right."

Kevin shot a pleading look at me. *What do I do?* Doug had gone around the house, trying to get onto the beach behind them, but I wasn't sure Kevin knew that.

"Just listen to what he has to say," I told him.

Lydia nodded. "Rabbit…"

"Rabbit," Jake snorted. "Faaaaaather Rabbit. Hallowed by thy name. Thy kingdom come, thy will go up in flames. You stupid prick. You're going back, and you're going to tell them it wasn't my fault. *It wasn't my fault.* You made me do it, goddammit. You and all those other self righteous little freaks."

"I was wrong to treat you the way I did," Kevin said, trying to take a step forward, "but I'm not responsible for what you did. I can't get you forgiveness just by going back to the seminary."

"Yes, you can!"

Kevin shook his head. "I can forgive you, and the seminary might take you back, but that's not going to get you eternal salvation, Jake. You have to take it up with God. No one else can make it right or intervene on your behalf."

"How very Protestant of you."

"Jake, I love her." He nodded toward Lydia. "She's *my* salvation. God was waving her in front of me long before I even thought about the priesthood. She's what He chose for me, not the seminary. I'm not going back."

"You are!"

"Put the knife down, Jake."

He brought the knife up to Lydia's neck. "If she's not here, you'll go back."

"No." Kevin reached to his back waistband and pulled the gun out, holding it to his own head. "I won't live without her. Drop the knife or I'll end it right now."

"No." Jake raised the knife high, turning it over in his hand until the point was aimed at Lydia's head. "You won't."

"I will." Kevin cocked the gun.

"Rabbit, no," Lydia sobbed.

I felt like I was moving in slow motion, trying to reach my son as Lydia tried to twist away from Jake. Through frantic tears she begged Kevin to stop as she tugged at Jake's wrist. Doug was behind them, reaching for his own gun.

The shots came in rapid succession. One pop and Kevin fell sideways onto the sand; another and Jake Catero's head snapped back, blood exploding from his neck. The knife dropped with a dull thud as he crumbled onto the beach.

I looked up at Doug.

He hadn't had time to draw his gun; the shot came from behind me.

"Agency shadow," I whispered to myself, lunging for Kevin.

Blood trickled from his scalp and oozed from his ear. He moaned and tried to roll over, waving his hand as he groped for Lydia.

Doug hadn't moved. He stood there, staring past me.

I turned to look, curious now to whom I owed thanks.

As stunned as Doug, I sat down hard, blinking, praying I was seeing things.

It was Nick.

26

Doug

Lydia didn't scream, I'll give her that much. Jake Catero's head snapped back in a bloody explosion and she barely glanced at him. Instead, she lunged for Kevin at the same time Chip did, both of them reaching for him less than a second after he hit the ground.

I was rooted to the sand, numb, staring past Chip, wondering what kind of freakish joke this was. Nick stood there with his arms hanging limply at his sides, gun still in hand, his gaze fixed on Jake's still body.

Chip turned to see where the shot had come from, and fell back, landing on the sand with an audible thud, moaning, "No. God, no."

"Doug. Please."

Lydia was kneeling beside Kevin, trying to help him sit up. I shoved the gun back into my waistband and ran to them, trying to push Kevin back down, hoping to get him to lie still.

"Your dad is right," I told Kevin as he groaned and tried to reach for Lydia. "You are one special kind of stupid."

"Blanks," Kevin gasped.

I brushed the sand away from his face and pulled as

much hair away from his scalp as I could. "Flesh wound," I said to Lydia. "He'll have a bitch of a headache, but he'll be all right."

Kevin sat up, leaning against her.

"I thought you were supposed to be some kind of genius," I said. "Blanks or not, there was still a pack of wadding in that gun, propelled by one hell of a force of air. If you weren't such a lousy aim, you'd be dead. Or severely brain damaged."

"That would have been nice to know before, you know," he muttered.

"Yeah, well who would have thought you'd hold a gun to your own head?"

"Me," Nick offered. "What the hell were you thinking, Kevin?"

Chip snapped his cell phone shut—"Police will be here in two minutes"—and looked at Kevin to be sure he really was all right before turning to Nick.

Nick was looking at Lydia and Kevin, a concentrated effort to not have to face his father. "I waited to take the shot until I knew for sure she was in danger. I hoped one of you could nail him without—"

"Why the hell are you even here?" Chip erupted. "And armed?"

Neither of us wanted to hear his answer.

"I've been following you since you left the agency this morning," he answered, finally looking at Chip.

"You?" I sputtered. "The goddamned *agency*?"

He barely nodded.

"When?" Chip demanded.

"They approached me about a year ago. I signed just before my birthday."

Chip exploded. "Of all the things you could have done—goddammit, Nick, you could have been anything and it would have been all right. Teach. Drive a truck. Hell, become a goddamned porn star. Anything but *this*. You *knew* how we felt about it."

Sucking in a deep breath, Nick said, "I know."

"Then why?" Chip asked, suddenly deflated.

"Because things changed, Dad. The world changed."

"The world is always changing," Chip argued. "That's not reason enough."

Nick slipped his gun into the holster hanging from his belt. "The World Trade Center. The Pentagon. Pennsylvania. The people behind that are reason enough, but come on, Dad, you and I both know they're just the tip of a very ugly iceberg."

"Nicky…"

"It wasn't a whim," he said carefully, looking into Chip's eyes, which had turned red with tears he fought against. "It took me nine months to think about it. What I came to realize was that if I wasn't willing to take a risk to do something, how could I expect someone else to?"

"But not this," Chip pleaded.

Nick watched as Kevin struggled to his feet. His youngest brother slipped once and fell back, and had to be helped up. "You okay?" he asked Kevin.

"Brain dead, evidently. But that's nothing new."

"Dad. You knew someday it would be one of us."

We knew.

We just never believed it would ever really happen.

For the rest of the afternoon, as the police came and went, as Jake's body was covered and carted off, in the beach house where I fought with Kevin to get him to hold still long enough to clean the gash that ran from just above his ear to almost the top of his head, Chip watched Nick through red, bleary eyes.

In the over thirty years I'd known him, I'd only seen him that sad once.

And in over thirty years, I'd never seen him so proud.

27

Chip

The sense of déjà vu was curious. It had been almost eight years since we had crowded into the same waiting room, waiting for Nicole to make her grand entrance into the world.

Then, Kevin and Nick picked at each other until Nick's temper got the better of him. This time it was Nicole and Spider, fighting playfully for control of Spider's laptop computer.

As he had been then, Nick was absorbed in the weather channel. Back then he was simply trying to kill time and ignore his younger brother, and trying to kill the feeling of missing Katie, who had moved across the country. I knew better than to ask about his current fascination with world weather, though I did try to discern which area he seemed most interested in.

I knew better than to ask, but he was surely going somewhere.

I hadn't expected it to be Nick. I was sure that all the alcohol and marijuana would keep him out of it. I never would have guessed that he was drinking so much because he was groping with the agency's offer, trying to drown what he knew would be my disappointment if he accepted.

"Katie really was pressuring for a kid," he admitted on the drive home from the beach. "I wasn't sure I could do both. She's okay with the agency and everything it means, but she wants kids."

Nick did, too, and promised that when he was done with his initial training, he'd be all for it.

He had six more months to go.

I knew that in six months, if he wasn't careful, he could be dead.

"They want me for my brain, not my brawn," he said. "Data and intelligence analysis. Strictly a desk job."

"Mostly." I doubted he knew exactly what he was getting into.

And, he added, he'd extracted a deal of his own, a contractual point he demanded, and got. "They'll never go after Paul or Eileen or Kevin. I'm it, Dad."

I watched Nicole poke at keys on the computer and wondered if Nick realized that agreement would never extend to her, or his own children, or even the baby we were all waiting impatiently for.

"Doug," Kris was telling Lydia's parents, " knows the baby's gender and I couldn't get it out of him for anything."

"I'm not sure I trust that old man delivering my first grandbaby," Jim chuckled. "If he drops the child—"

"It's Kevin's kid. It'll have a hard head," Eileen said.

We waited almost fourteen hours, until Doug poked his head in and said, "Grandparents first. The rest of you will have to wait."

Eileen frowned. "At least tell me if I'm an aunt or an uncle."

Doug grinned and shrugged.

Lydia was propped up in the bed, her eyes radiating joy

past the fatigue that hovered like a fine mist. Kevin was in a chair near the bed, holding his first born close.

"His name," he said with deliberate slowness, "is Michael Ian Brennan, the fourth." He looked up, his eyes locked on mine. "We're taking back the family name, Dad. It's who we are. It's who *you* are. I wanted to name my son for my father."

I felt Terry's arms circle my waist, and her tight hug.

Jim touched a finger to the baby's chin and laughed, "I can see it now, he'll be the only Irish kid in town with an Afro."

I reached out for my grandson. "Since he's named after me, I get to hold him first," I reasoned, ignoring the amused tsks of my wife and Lydia's parents.

The newest Michael Brennan had jet black hair and his grandmother's brilliant blue eyes. His face was knotted into a scowl, lips pursed and fists drawn tightly to his chin. He looked like a tiny, angry old man who wanted nothing more than for someone to give him something warm to eat, and then a nice, long nap.

"When Nick was born," I said to Kevin, without taking my eyes off the baby, "I was positive that at that moment, I was as close to heaven as I'd ever get. Then came Paul, then you and Eileen—I felt like I was inching closer every time I held one of you for the first time."

Terry reached for the baby, kissing his forehead before handing him to Nan.

"After my father died, I swore I'd find a way to honor him, and I've been trying for twenty five years. I didn't think..." I stopped and inhaled deeply, fighting against a surge of emotion threatening to overwhelm me. "I didn't understand until now that raising you to be the man he wanted me to be, you and your brothers and sister, was what would have honored him most."

"Dad—"

"Come here." I held my arms out to my youngest son, who allowed me to grab on and hug tightly. "You're a good man, Kevin. A good son. Don't ever wonder … you honor *me* by being who you are."

He squeezed back before pulling away. "You're sleep deprived, old man."

"Could be."

Jim handed the baby to Lydia, gently placing him in her arms. "Now look at that," he chuckled. "My baby and my grandson. What could be better?"

"The mush factor could be scaled back a bit," she told him with a smile.

"We're entitled," Nan said, leaning over to kiss her daughter. "We only get this moment once."

We cleared the room to give Michael's uncles and aunt – and cousin – a chance to admire and fawn over him for a few minutes before leaving the new parents to get some rest. We returned to the waiting room, where Terry called her parents, and where Doug was waiting for us.

"Well, Grandpa," he grunted, sitting upright, "how's it feel? Your first grandson."

"I can't even begin…"

"Michael the fourth. You realize this means you have to start using your given name now. Kevin did go through a lot to quietly change his."

"Would take some getting used to," I mused. "When did he—?"

"Couple months ago. I'm quite proud of myself for not telling you."

"Kevin Joseph Brennan."

"With his confirmation name it's what?" he prodded.

I had to stop and think. "Kevin Joseph Michael."

Doug slapped his hands against his legs and pushed himself out of the chair. "Now, was that karma, or what?"

Nicole came running down the hallway, darting around Doug as he headed for Lydia's room. "Grandpa! He's tiny!"

"So were you," I told her, lifting her onto my lap. "Are you disappointed it's a boy?"

"No, not really. I like his name. Uncle Kevin says he won't be happy if you start calling him Mickey, though."

"Really? Well, you know what that means."

"You're gonna do it!" she giggled.

"I think I have to!"

"That's funny. And you know what else? Uncle Kevin said they're gonna live in the house across the street from us."

"Yep, they are."

After twenty five years, Terry agreed with me. It was time to close the street off; by the end of the month, the court would be locked behind walls and a gate, the protection I yearned for after Nick had been kidnapped. As leases expired on the houses dotting the street, people would move out, and the kids would move in.

"Our kids can grow up together this way," Kevin pointed out to his siblings on his birthday. "They'll be safe, and they can play outside without constant worry."

"It would be one less worry on my mind," Nick agreed. "Knowing Katie was close to you guys, and any future little rugrats."

"And it's not like we'd all be living together in the same house," Kevin pointed out.

Terry would have been happy with that. She settled for the idea that her children would be close by, close enough she could see her grandchildren at will.

Nicole rested her head against my shoulder and yawned. "I hope Daddy will let me stay home from school tomorrow. I'm tired."

I glanced at the clock on the wall. It was almost midnight.

"You can stay home," I promised.

"Good," she sighed. "Grandpa, is it true that your real name is Michael, too?"

I nodded.

"Daddy looked it up in a baby name book. He says it means 'like unto God.'"

"That's a lot to live up to."

Nicole slid off my lap when Paul came out of Lydia's room, and turned to leave with him. "Everyone needs goals, Grandpa."

28

Kevin's Journal
May 9, 2003

Nick left for We-Don't-Know-Where two days after the baby was born. That's how he put it—Dad asked where he was going, Nick answered, "Some place called We Don't Know Where." Dad sighed and shrugged, and said he'd been there dozens of times himself. In spite of Nick's assurances—it's just training, I'll be fine, there's nothing to worry about—Dad looked nauseous the entire time he was gone. Dad and Katie both kept thinking the worst, that Nick had been dropped somewhere in Afghanistan or Iraq … he came home a week later with a tan and tourist-type presents, and declared that We-Don't-Know-Where was a pretty awesome place. And that the rest of his training was going to be either local or in Washington, and he swears that he's going to be a desk jockey.

I think Dad's a little jealous.

I think he was also a little jealous when the dojo finally reopened right after New Year's Day. He walked in and mouthed "Wow," and ten minutes later was asking if he could train with one of the instructors to get his skills back—with the idea of being able to teach.

So, yeah, Dad is teaching classes of six and seven year old kids. I can hear shrieking laughter from the office, even with the door closed. I have to trust that he's actually teaching them and not just playing with them.

And sometimes in the afternoon, before classes start, if I sit quietly, I can hear Eileen upstairs, plunking out notes on a piano, the skeletons of the songs she's refusing to admit she's composing. And there are the odd days when I can hear 4 or 5 pianos at once, all out of synch, young kids trying to play scales with two left hands.

Most of them scramble down the stairs after being with her for forty minutes, run to the locker room, and then burst out onto the workout floor, ready for anything I can throw at them.

Nicole is there almost every day, ostensibly to learn to defend herself, but I'm seeing more and more of her true motive: she seems sure, that somewhere among the mothers of her fellow students, is Paul's next One True Love. She's positive that with a little work on her part he'll take one look at the woman of her choice and stumble into Happily Ever After.

It's been a year since Monica died, but he doesn't seem any closer to being ready to embrace a social life. His biggest commitment has been to tell Nicole that when they move out of Grandma and Grandpa's house in a few weeks, across the street and next to ours, that she can have a dog. She swears she'll take care of it, but I'm pretty sure Paul will be scooping up little doggy land mines for the next ten years.

I took Michael to visit Monica's grave, just to talk to her, to show her all the fingers and toes I was pretty sure she counted before we got the chance to. Out of everyone, I was sure she'd understand how having him felt; Michael is like the reward for getting through everything; he's a big gold star that spits up and poops like a maniac.

He's the Reason For Doing. He's the reason for taking school seriously. He's the reason for making sure the dojo is a success. He's the reason I need to tie up all the loose ends.

Which brings me to where I'm at right now. I'm sitting beside the seminary pond, on the cement bench Jake tied me to, scribbling down every stray thought that crosses my mind.

It's beautiful here. Bright and peaceful, in spite of how dark it was the last time I was here.

I thought I'd be overwhelmed by hate when I set my foot on the first step that leads from the path to the pond, but it was nothing like that. I felt curiosity. A sense of sadness. There was no sign that I had ever struggled to break free from those bonds, no scars on the bench, no marks in the dirt and gravel.

In two years dozens of people have been on this very bench, to reflect, or to read, or to pray. If there had been anything, it's been lost to time.

I wondered if I'd get here and suddenly think I should have stayed and gutted it out. But from where I'm sitting, I can look up and see Lydia on the other side of the pond, pushing Michael around in his stroller, walking slowly with Thomas. I know what they're talking about—she's telling him what I couldn't, why I left and why Jake suddenly disappeared—but it's okay. It doesn't have to be a secret. But I look up and my heart swells.

I miss the guys here. That doesn't mean I should *be* here.

Greg was right; there's no shame in starting out on the path to the priesthood and venturing off, no matter what the reason. I think it did make me a better person, a better man, and someone more ready to be a husband and father. I don't think I'd trade those three years for anything—not even the chance to be with Lydia three years earlier.

Before my 21st birthday, it wasn't time.

Do I think that Jake was some mysterious instrument of God, sent to push me in the direction I was supposed to go? Hell, no. I think Jake was just a screwed up person and I'm curious about what, or who, made him the way he was, but with him or without him, my gut tells me I would have made my way home.

I'd forgotten the sound of the bells ringing on the other side of the campus; it's not that jarring "wake up, you're late for church" clatter. It's music that drifts through the air. It's a soft, lyrical voice reminding the students that there's a reason why they're here. A reason to stay.

Or a reason to go home.

Thomas and Lydia are almost all the way around the pond; they're on the path near the cafeteria. If I get up now, I can meet them halfway, and head for the sound of the bells.

Mass starts in fifteen minutes.

About the Author

K.A. Thompson is a freelance writer and former editor of *Martial Artists Wired*. She currently resides in Ohio with her husband of over 20 years, a United States Air Force Nurse Anesthetist; they have an adult son.

To peek inside the author's head, visit her weblog, *Thumper Thinks Out Loud*, at http://kathompson.blogspot.com